DRAGONMASTER.

Suzanne stifled a gasp and checked her purse. Twin sparks of yellow fire flashed up at her. *Of all the goddam times to pull this, Silbakor, you sure pick the best.*

Solomon's ex-wife, Helen, stared into her drink as she told Suzanne the dream she'd had about her dead husband. "He was yelling your name. He said that you had to stop someone."

Dragonmaster. There is terror in Gryylth.

Suzanne felt sick. "Stop who? From doing what?" she asked Helen.

Helen shook her head.

Abruptly, a deep-throated howl went up from the front yard, and something thudded on the window. Suzanne heard a beating of great wings.

Dragonmaster, flee this house.

As the two women watched, the window glass took on a pale aqua glow, and suddenly, inconceivably, the entire wall began to buckle inward.

"Silbakor!" Suzanne called to her dragon.

"Flee, Dragonmaster. You are being attacked. . . ."

DRAGONSWORD

VOLUME 2: Duel of Dragons

Gael Baudino

A Byron Preiss Visual Publications, Inc. Book

A ROC BOOK

Special thanks to Cherry Weiner, Joe Mendola, Judith Stern, Leslie Skolnik, and Mary Higgins.

ROC
Published by the Penguin Group
Penguin Books USA Inc., 375 Hudson Street,
New York, New York 10014, U.S.A.
Penguin Books Ltd, 27 Wrights Lane,
London W8 5TZ, England
Penguin Books Australia Ltd, Ringwood,
Victoria, Australia
Penguin Books Canada Ltd, 10 Alcorn Avenue, Suite 300
Toronto, Ontario, Canada M4V 3B2
Penguin Books (N.Z.) Ltd, 182-190 Wairau Road,
Auckland 10, New Zealand

Penguin Books Ltd, Registered Offices:
Harmondsworth, Middlesex, England

Published by Roc, an imprint of New American Library, a division of
Penguin Books USA Inc.,

First Roc Printing, August, 1991
10 9 8 7 6 5 4 3 2 1

This book is dedicated to Angie Carder,
who was brutally and needlessly killed
in her society's ultimate act
of misogyny.

*History is a nightmare
from which I am trying to wake.*
—James Joyce

❖ CHAPTER 1 ❖

Though the Santa Ana winds that swept in from the east seemed bent on reducing the city to a gray desert, the cemetery remained green and lush, as if in defiance of the heat. The breezes rustled peacefully through the grass and pines, and the September sky was clear and blue.

Suzanne Helling pulled her VW through the wrought-iron gates and drove slowly up the winding streets. The road she chose swung north, then around, skirting the edges of a field called Summerland. When the landmarks looked familiar, she parked and shut off the engine.

The silence that flooded into the car unnerved her, for it reminded her too much of the aftermath of a battle. In Gryylth, the dead had stared up at the sky with sightless eyes, unmoving, uncaring. Here at least they were decently buried; but even with the passage of eight months and the acquisition of a new degree and a minor teaching position, the memory was too raw and glistening to be left comfortably in the past.

Taking a small spray of flowers and a sharp knife from the seat beside her, she left the car and started up the grassy slope toward a stand of birch trees. Her handbag swung rhythmically against her hip.

A voice thrummed softly. "Dragonmaster."

"Don't call me that," she said aloud. The title at times seemed a mockery.

"I am sorry, Suzanne," said Silbakor. "I did not mean to offend."

She continued up the slope. The sun was hot, and the gravestones danced in the light. The grass and trees trapped the humidity and sent trickles of sweat winding down her face.

"Suzanne."

"What is it, Silbakor?" The handle of the knife was slippery. She wiped her palm on her jeans and bettered her grip.

"Where are we?"

Suzanne stopped in the shade of the birches, dumbfounded. "We're in the cemetery. Can't you tell?"

"I . . ." Silbakor fell silent.

Solomon's stone was at her feet. The grass was trimmed around its borders, but there was no indication that anyone ever visited it. His family, she knew, had rejected him when he had divorced Helen, and Helen herself hated him too much to do anything save spit on his grave. Suzanne would not have been surprised had she made a practice of doing just that.

Suzanne had met her briefly at Solomon's funeral, and had wondered faintly why she had shown up. Perhaps to gloat. It was hard to believe that an ordinary, middle-aged woman could have been the key to the formation of Gryylth, but if worlds were created through rage and ire, there was more than enough of both in Helen Addams to furnish a solar system.

Once, Suzanne had directed the same depth of anger at Solomon. Up until his final hours as Guardian of Gryylth, she had hated him with a passion that had more than once made her wish to kill him. He had been abusive and manipulating, a perfect representative of the forces of money and entrenched power that she had always blamed for the murder of her classmates on a May morning in 1970. He had even gloried in that role.

She had hated him. But no more. She could not agree with him, could not find it in herself to admire him, but she recognized that, as was the case with everything—the Establishment, the Vietnam War, even the counterculture and the protests—Solomon had been a mixture of bad and good. And he had also been afraid, and deeply human.

That did not justify his actions, but it explained them; and perhaps he had done something toward redeeming himself in his final moments when, in a young body and in the armor of fifth-century Britain, he had sprung from the back of the Great Dragon and hurled himself against thirty-five tons of granite.

Maybe, in his own way, he had found a kind of balance. Maybe, in the end, he had found some intimation of the Grail that lurked in a nourishing, vivifying, and equilibrated glory behind the fabric of Gryylth and Corrin.

She sat down heavily beside the grave. Balance and the Grail. Her life contained neither. Placing her flowers on the headstone, she held the knife in her lap. "Hi, prof," she said softly. "It's been a while. I hope you're OK." She felt silly and ridiculous for talking to a dead man, and so she stopped.

Silbakor spoke from within her purse, within the paperweight. "Suzanne, I would advise you to leave this place."

"Dammit, Silbakor, let me sit for a while and bury him right without you bugging me."

A sound that was something like a high-pitched whine and something like a howl started up, ringing in her ears. She leaned back and stared up at the sunlight that filtered through the stand of birches. Something about the world seemed different today, ephemeral, as though it had begun to partake of the half-existence that had formerly characterized only Gryylth.

Memories, she thought. But she noticed that she felt different, too. A quick flash of fire had spread through her body, and she was suddenly afraid to look at herself for fear that she might find herself clad in leather and bronze, with a familiar sword at her side.

It's the heat, she thought. I've never done well with this kind of heat.

In spite of the disorientation, she picked up the knife in her lap and rested the keen blade against her left wrist. There were customs in Gryylth, and Solomon Braithwaite deserved to have them kept for him. This cemetery would do for a grave, but Suzanne Helling—or maybe Alouzon Dragonmaster—would have to attend to the rite.

Clumsily, she made a shallow cut in her wrist and watched as the red blood welled up. Extending her hand, she let the drops fall just below the headstone.

"Awake and live again someday," she said. It was no more than the respect tendered to any man of Gryylth—or woman—who had fallen in battle.

But rather than clearing her head, the sharp pain of the cut seemed to do nothing more than intensify the sense of unreality that grew about her like a clinging vine. What place was this? Whose wrist was bleeding in bright drops on the grassy earth? Suzanne Helling's? Or Alouzon Dragonmaster's?

"Suzanne."

Dizzy, she pulled the paperweight out of the purse and plunked it down in the grass beside her. The Dragon looked at her with its yellow eyes.

"Leave this place."

"Why?" She dithered. The whine grew in her ears, and she seemed to hear a distant baying, as of hounds. "Where's my sword . . . ?"

"Dragonmaster!"

She was not looking at the Dragon. Her attention had been caught by the sight of Solomon Braithwaite's headstone. Amid the rising humming and a shimmering of the landscape, the stone was moving, rising, the ground around it buckling as though thrust up from below.

The instincts of Gryylth were on her, and as she grabbed the paperweight and purse in one hand, she took the knife in the other and backed away from the grave, her eyes searching for an opponent. The air about her had turned misty, the heat replaced by a deadly cold.

Then, above the hum, cutting through the approaching howls like a razor, Solomon was suddenly screaming. It was not a cry of terror, or of pain: it was rather that of a man who, confronted with something he hated enough to rend with his bare hands, found himself totally impotent.

Suzanne! Stop him! Suzanne!

The words burned through her head in a shriek of fire. She dropped the paperweight and the knife and put her hands to her ears. The gravestone was moving, roiling as though it were a film on troubled water. Light shone from beneath it—dull, red, fevered light: the color of an inflamed wound.

Suzanne! Suzanne! Suzanne! Suzanne!

His screams cut off suddenly, and there was utter silence in the universe as the gravestone was blown noiselessly into dust. Lurid red light streamed up into a black sky, licking the air with tongues of blood. Suzanne saw hands reaching up from the grave, saw a face that, regardless of decay or desiccation, was still recognizable.

Solomon's eyes were pleading, his clenched mouth twisted in despair. He extended a hand to Suzanne, and she did not need words to understand. *Help me. Please.*

When she opened her eyes, the sun was bright in a blue sky, and the cemetery lay baking in the heat. She was propped up against one of the birches, and she felt a trickle of water running down her chin.

As she wiped it off, she managed to focus. A groundskeeper was looking into her face, his brown eyes concerned. He was fanning her with a large straw hat. "You OK? You want me call doctor?"

She glanced quickly at the grave. The stone lay quiescent and level, as though nothing had happened. Swallowing the rank fear in her throat, she took another sip of water from the cup he held out to her. "Nah," she said. "I think the heat just got to me."

* * *

Last winter, there had been no New Year Feast in
Gryylth. The cold season had been too long and hard,
the losses of the great war with Corrin too recent.
Food, also, had been scarce, for the burning of Corrin's crops had required that Gryylth share what it had,
and though not a soul had been lost to hunger, there
had been no excess, and meals had been spartan.

It was perhaps with those past privations in mind
that Cvinthil, the new king, ordered that the feast the
following year be marked with especial care and fes-
tivities. The war with Corrin was over, and both lands
were slowly healing themselves of the wounds of a
decade of conflict. Cvinthil wanted to show his people
that, in peace as well as in war, Gryylth could triumph, and that they had reason to look toward the
future with hope.

Cvinthil fetched the people of Kingsbury himself,
as Vorya had always done, walking the streets of the
town at dusk with a lighted lamp that seemed to burn
all the brighter for the frost in the air, knocking at
doors, and chanting the traditional summons in his
quiet tenor:

> *"The night is long and dark—*
> *Long and dark is the night:*
> *Come, my people,*
> *Come, my people,*
> *Come, my people, and feast with me!"*

And they came, filling the town square with faces
reddened with cold and with torchlight, a people who
had found peace, who were moving slowly into another age. To be sure, there had been complaints in
the past months about new customs and new ways,
about women who did not know their place, but tonight the grumbling was put aside.

Cvinthil toasted his people, and was toasted in return; after he had eaten he moved among them as an
equal, shaking their hands and returning the bows of

the women with bows of his own in accordance with the custom he had established. Santhe was at his side, and if there was a darker, more somber cast to the councilor's eyes since the war, his tongue and his wit were as quick as ever, and he made the townsfolk laugh.

From her place at the high table of the king, Marrget of Crownhark watched as Cvinthil and Santhe made their way through the crowd, spreading cheer and compliments. *I suppose that I should be with them. It is time the people knew me again.*

But even as she thought the words, she knew that these people would never really know her. When they thought of Marrget of Crownhark, they thought of the big man with the square jaw who had led the First Wartroop since Helkyying had died. They could never reconcile this slender woman with their memories.

"Marrget?" Santhe had returned to the table. He leaned down to her, his blond curls brushing her cheek. "Are you well, my friend?"

"I am well enough, Santhe."

He smiled, but his eyes were sad. "Your warriors: I do not see them here."

"They celebrate in their own way. We keep much to ourselves these days."

"I understand." He offered his hand, and she took it: two warriors, united by loss.

Yet Marrget knew that she was still essentially alone. Though her women could turn to one another in time of weakness or fear, she herself, their leader, was forced to ignore those emotions. She had broken under the strain only once, and none save Alouzon Dragonmaster knew of that time.

Sometimes she wondered if it would not be easier to leave Kingsbury, take a new name, and live as a different person in another part of the country rather than to endure the constant conflict between the past and the present. She had called herself Marrha once, and that was not an uncomely name. Maybe . . .

The idea sickened her. She was Marrget of Crown-hark. She could be nothing else.

When she came out of her thoughts, she realized that space had been cleared in the center of the square, and that a large man was standing there. Karthin. The big, blond Corrinian stood head and shoulders above even the tallest men of Gryylth, and his hair and mustache glowed in the torchlight.

"Karthin is going to sing," said Santhe.

Karthin's blue eyes were open and honest, his arms thick and strong. Marrget had ridden beside him for many miles during the autumn after the war, working tirelessly to bring the women of the land to the harvest; and later, when snow was falling, they had together supervised the just and even distribution of what sustenance there was to be had.

If she had admired him before as a warrior, her admiration had increased a hundredfold in time of peace, for he had remained in Kingsbury after the food crisis had passed, dedicating himself to helping the people who had fought against his own country. "He is a brave and honorable man," she said, smiling softly.

"I am infinitely sorry that we ever fought against Corrin," Santhe said with a sigh. "I do not know what madness was upon us." He looked at her as though he were trying to read a faint parchment. "I heard that he brought you flowers after the last battle."

Marrget shifted uneasily. "That is true, my friend."

"A brave man, indeed."

She would have replied, but Karthin was singing, his deep bass voice rolling across the square and the assembled people. Karthin knew as well as anyone that there were still hard feelings toward his country, and he appeared to be doing his best—as he always did—to demonstrate that Gryylth had no cause to fear or hate Corrin.

He sang of the seasons, and of work, and of the homely things that even two peoples who had warred bitterly for ten years could share. There was peace in the land at last, and through his music, Karthin sought to spread that peace wide, to soothe old prejudice and loss with this New Year carol.

He was eloquent, and something of a poet, and though his song was from Corrin, he had recast its chorus so as to include both countries. He smiled as he sang, his strong arms swinging wide with expression, and toward the end of the song, his eye fell on Marrget and stayed there. At the last chorus, he waved a hand for all the people of Kingsbury to join in, but Marrget realized that he was singing to her.

> *If then the land be wide and wild*
> *It matters not to me;*
> *For come the summer's sunny days*
> *Or come the winter's rain and snow,*
> *I travel free, I travel loved:*
> *I am of Gryylth and Corrin both—*
> *And peace be to you all!*

"And peace be to you all," she murmured. She passed a hand over her face.

The song was done, and the people of Kingsbury, from highest to lowest, from king to beggar, clapped and cheered as Karthin, blushing in the manner of a warrior who finds himself publicly honored, bowed.

Cvinthil rose, lifting his cup. "A toast," he called, and the people fell silent.

The king turned to the woman at his side. "Seena," he said quietly, and she smiled, rose, and joined her hand to his. "A toast," said the king, "to Gryylth and to Corrin, to those who were lost, and to those who lived. Peace, blessings, and the favor of the Gods upon you all, and may there never be a repetition of those dark days in which sword was lifted to sword and spear met shield." He smiled fondly at his wife. "Beloved?"

Seena was a queen, but the world outside her house was new to her. "I can only add my voice to that of my husband," she said. "But I would the Gods be merciful to the women of Gryylth in this time of great change, and grant them peace in their days, and wisdom in their lives.''

Marrget regarded herself, dressed in trews and a tunic that did nothing to disguise her feminine form. ''May it truly be so,'' she said, though her voice was drowned in the applause and cheers of the assembly.

She looked up. Karthin was smiling broadly, and he bowed to her with manly grace. Marrget felt something stir within her. Puzzled at finding herself staring at Karthin with such intensity, she gathered her wits and looked away.

''The men will do Cotswood Dancing now,'' said Santhe. ''And then all the people will dance as long as they will.''

''I will stay for the Cotswood, I think, but then I shall leave, Santhe.''

Santhe eyed her. ''Gods bless, my friend,'' he said, then bowed and went off to join the men who would dance.

As long as there had been New Year Feasts, there had been Cotswood Dancing for luck and a good year. With bells tied just below their knees, the men formed into a set of six, Cvinthil and Santhe in the first positions as befitted their status. The pipers and drummers started up a tune that bounced and jigged such that it was all that a listener could do to keep from joining in. Cvinthil called out *''This time!''* and the dance started.

Waving white scarves, their bells jingling merrily, the dancers processed up and down, crossed and recrossed within the set, wove through intricate patterns. Cvinthil bounded with kingly presence, Santhe's grin was magnified, and Karthin showed himself as able a dancer as he was a farmer, a singer, or a warrior. The other men, captains of Gryylth, were a match for their leaders, capering and leaping with easy grace.

After two dances, they laid aside their scarves and took up long sticks; and now the crack of wood against wood resounded across the square, echoing off the

stone houses and the stockade about Hall Kingsbury.
Advancing and retreating, the men clashed their staves
in mock battle, and all the while their bells kept up a
steady, joyous rhythm.

Marrget watched them sadly. Once, as a man, she
had danced the Cotswood. But that was over now.

When the last pair of sticks had clashed, and the last
scarf had been waved, and when the dancers had processed off into the torch-lit night, Marrget rose,
bowed, and slipped away. Her duties this night were
over.

She had almost reached the edge of the square when
Karthin's voice, close behind her, made her halt. "My
lady Marrget?"

She still winced a little at the title, though she knew
that, as a Corrinian, he tendered it out of respect.
" 'Tis I."

"Would it . . ." Karthin seemed unsure. He might
have been offering her flowers again, and cursing himself for being a rude bumpkin. "Would it please you
to dance, my friend?"

"I have no place in the people's dance, Karthin. I
cannot bear to be passed back and forth as the women
are, and I daresay that no man would want to take my
hand."

In the square, the musicians struck up a tune, and
the townsfolk were forming into lines: men—boys,
rather—on one side, women on the other. Smilingly,
as though amused that they bowed to striplings and
sons, the women stepped forward and gave the traditional bow of subservience, and the young men folded
their arms and, with an attempt at authority, nodded
in return.

Then the tune quickened, and up, down, the lines
took hands and turned into stars and weavings, part-
ners changing and ladies passing back and forth.

Karthin was flushed and sweating from the Cotswood. His bells jingled as he shuffled his feet. Marrget
felt his nearness and his strength, and found that her
mouth was suddenly dry.

He had brought her flowers once.

"I know of a man," he said, "who would be willing—more than willing—to take your hand for a dance."

She stared at him, wondering. "I do not know the woman's steps in these dances, Karthin," she said softly. "I am unwilling to learn. I will not bow to a man. You know that."

"I do know that. But we have different customs in Corrin, and perhaps you would be willing to learn one of our dances. Women in my land are equal to men, and the steps reflect that." He offered his hand. "You would do me great honor, my lady."

"Sir, I . . ." Her words faltered and stopped.

He smiled as though astonished by his own temerity. "At the battle of the Circle, Gryylthan, I swore that I would be your friend. Will you now be mine?"

And, without quite knowing why, save perhaps that she was lonely and that Karthin was a friend, she doffed her cloak and took his hand, and he led her to a clear space at the side of the mass dance.

The individual steps that he showed her were those that she knew already, but their sequence and their intent was different. Here there was no intimation of a social order that had for years relegated women to children and the home. Corrinian maids and matrons went about freely, conducted business in their own name, even bore weapons. The dances of their land told of nothing else. Here there were no bows, no aloof and tacit assumption of a woman's inferiority; only two dancers working together, giving and taking, cooperating as effectively as any pair of skilled warriors on the battlefield.

For a while, Marrget forgot the loneliness, and, like Karthin, she abandoned herself to the movements of the dance, conscious of her body only in that it responded to her wishes and touched his with a sensation that was akin to yearning. They had fought one another, Karthin and Marrget, and they had ridden together, and now they danced as friends.

And more than friends. For when the music ended, she found herself with her arms about him, and his about her. She discovered that it felt good to hold, and be held by, another, and she rested her head against his broad chest and closed her eyes with a sigh, trying to think of nothing save that, for a time, she was not lonely.

Karthin seemed unable to speak. He managed her name, that was all, and, ignoring the stares, ignoring everything save themselves, they swayed in their embrace while about them the dance resumed, the music bounced and leaped, and the stars spun in their courses across the sky.

But there were shouts suddenly, and the music faltered and ceased. Marrget heard the sound of horses galloping, and her instincts thrust her from Karthin as she groped for a sword that was not at her hip. She saw Relys and Wykla riding into the square, and with them, mounted on a horse that seemed about to drop with fatigue, was a thin man in black robes.

His face was smeared with soot and smoke, his dark robes stained with dark blood. When he reined in before Cvinthil, Relys put out a hand to hold him up.

"Senon of Bandon?" said Marrget. "What?" Her hand unconsciously found Karthin's as they ran toward the riders, the people of the town scattering to the edges of the square as though, with the appearance of this wounded man, all thoughts of a celebration of peace and plenty had fled.

Senon gasped, and Cvinthil, after regarding him somberly for a moment, put his own cup into his hands. With a swallow, Senon found his voice. "Bandon," he said. "Has been attacked."

Marrget felt the eyes of the assembly flick for an instant to Karthin. "By whom?" she said, her clear voice carrying over the murmur of suspicion and the snorting of the horses. "Did you see?"

"It came in the night," Senon managed. "And fire fell from the air. We saw no men or horses, just lights in the sky. There was a roaring as of great beasts, and other sounds that I cannot describe. The houses exploded, and the people in them died.'' He was trembling violently, and the cup slipped from his hands and fell ringing to the cobblestones.

Cvinthil's eyes had turned haunted. He bent his head for a moment. There had been peace in the land, but it had fled. ''And how fares it with Bandon now?''

Senon shook his head. ''Bandon is no more.''

❖ CHAPTER 2 ❖

Suzanne drove home with the windows down and the radio up, trying to put some distance between herself and the vision in the cemetery. But though fresh air, traffic, and rock and roll could dull the recollection, they could not banish it, and it remained a weight in the back of her mind, something that made her clench the wheel as tightly as she had ever held a sword.

"It wasn't the heat, was it?" she said without looking at the paperweight.

Silbakor did not reply for some time. The Santa Monica Mountains, gray and sunburned, rolled by. Los Angeles glittered across the hazy miles. Then: "No, Suzanne. It was not."

She took the offramp, pulled onto the quiet side streets of Westwood, and parked in the shade across from her apartment building. A mockingbird called loudly from the branches above her car and she flinched. "What was it, then?"

"I . . . am not sure."

As usual, the Dragon would not answer questions that were not asked. Its knowledge might well have been limitless, but it parted with information in a miserly fashion, in dribs and drabs, according to the wit of its interrogator.

Today, though, Silbakor seemed more reticent than usual, and Suzanne actually wondered whether it were hiding something from her. "Quit dicking around with me, Silbakor. Was that Sol Braithwaite I saw?"

"A part of him."

"Standing up in his grave and screaming? More than a part, I think."

"I am unacquainted with the afterlife of your species."

She blinked at the bald-faced equivocation. Of course Silbakor knew nothing of afterlives. But it knew about Gryylth; and as surely as she had seen Solomon's rotting corpse rising from the earth, its eyes pleading and its suppliant and decaying hands reaching out to her, she knew that the real question—the one that she had not asked, that she could not think of—was about the land she guarded and protected.

She was about to argue with the Dragon when another thought crossed her mind, one that, over the months, she had been doing her best to suppress. Gryylth was not alone anymore. There was Corrin, to be sure, but the war was over and the two lands might as well be considered together. But there was another place, too.

Vaylle. She had seen it once. Green, fertile, a broad plain backed up by high mountains, it had stretched out on the misty horizon where before there had been only empty space. If anything, it had a greater claim on her than Gryylth itself, for she had made it.

What would drag Solomon Braithwaite back from beyond death? What would he hate and fear so badly that his soul would twitch his corpse back into a semblance of life and make it plead for aid? Gryylth was at peace. Corrin too. And that left . . .

She dumped the paperweight into her purse and climbed out of the VW, a sickness roiling in the pit of her stomach. She knew the question that she wanted to ask, and now she was afraid to ask it.

At her door, she fumbled for her key, wondering if she had, once again, forgotten it. The strain of her dual existence was telling on her, and, increasingly, she had been forced to compensate for memory lapses

and momentary panics. Hiding spare keys in the rock
garden, ignoring personal horrors that thrust themselves on her while she lectured on fifth-century battles, putting her driver's license uppermost in her wallet
so she would know for certain what name she was to
be called—these, among others, were the small eva-
sions with which she fortified her life.

Before the Guardianship, she had been filled with a
dull resentment for the succession of child-men with
whom she had lived, worked, and shared her bed. They
had taken everything from her, had given her nothing,
and had left her unfulfilled and empty save for a single, aborted pregnancy.

But she had not wanted fulfillment, had, in fact,
kept herself as empty as was in her power, seeking
always an expiation for the vague and undefined guilt
that had eaten at her through the years that followed
the deaths of her classmates.

Now, though, her situation was worse. Now she held
an entire world in her hands, and her concerns
swarmed about her like a pack of rabid hounds, biting,
snapping, worrying at her mind and heart, filling her
with the sickly knowledge that this existence—dichot-
omous, fatiguing, harried—would never end.

Her dreams now were full of both M-1s and swords,
of student faces and warrior faces all painted over with
the still cast of death. She remembered too well the
slickness of blood on her arms, the cries of battle, the
clang of weapons. Solomon had been Guardian of
Gryylth also, but he had held that title in ignorance.
Suzanne knew her true status, and it was gradually
cutting through her stability like a swift river devour-
ing a sandbar.

There was an answer to the rising flood of madness
that lapped at her feet. It lay in Vaylle. But though
Suzanne had pledged herself to the Grail, she had
made no attempt to seek it out. Months had passed in
Gryylth and in Los Angeles, and still she hesitated,
fearful, shaking, afraid to dare the land that she had
created, terrified of what she might find there. Gryylth

had been Solomon Braithwaite's fantasy, his fulfillment, and his murderer. What would Vaylle be for
Suzanne Helling?

She found her key and entered her apartment, slamming the door behind her as though to shut out the
thoughts of vows unfulfilled, of duties left undone.

"I'm going to make a phone call, Silbakor," she
said. "And then we're going to take a little trip out to
Gryylth."

"Is that wise, Dragonmaster?"

She winced at the title. It seemed an unnecessary
reminder. "It's been a long time since we've been out
there. Aren't you worried about it?"

"I . . ." A flash of yellow eyes from the depths of
her purse. "I am. But for now I would advise against
it."

Again, a sense of dissemblance. "Why?"

"It is unwise."

"Dammit, you keep laying this Dragonmaster trip
on me. Treat me like one. Tell me why."

"It is . . . unwise. There have been occurrences."

"Like at the cemetery? Look, Silbakor, if there's
shit like that coming down in Gryylth, we both owe it
to those people to try to do something about it. I
thought you were worried about Gryylth."

"You are Gryylth."

She held the paperweight up before her eyes. "And
Vaylle, too. Right?"

Silbakor was avoiding her gaze. "That is true."

The phone started to ring, and she tossed the paperweight onto the sofa. Silbakor flapped its wings to
right itself as the glass ball bounced on the cushions.

The caller was Brian O'Hara. Solomon's unexpected
death had resulted in a period of frantic disorder in
the archaeology and history departments at UCLA.
Classes, lectures, grants, and fellowships had to be
hastily rerouted, and although Brian's opinion was that
history had not really started until gunpowder had entered the scene, he had wound up as Suzanne's supe-

rior and dissertation advisor. The arrangement was mutually unsatisfactory.

"How come you're not giving your lecture this morning?" he demanded. "You've got papers and tests that should have been graded."

"They're graded."

"Well? Don't you think you should pass them back to your students? They've been showing up at the office asking about you."

She rested her elbow on the kitchen counter and put her face in her hand. Reanimated corpses, intransigent Dragons, imperiled worlds . . . and Brian O'Hara was worried about her history classes. "I'll pass them back next class period. Given the grades I saw, at least half of those people should be grateful for the reprieve."

"You're five minutes from campus. You could bring them by the office."

"I was just going to call in. I'm sick."

He snorted. "I told you at the beginning of the semester that I accept no excuses other than death or dismemberment, traumatic amputation, or through-and-through wounds. I haven't changed my policy."

Brian had never served in the military, but he had an intense interest in the Vietnam War, and he thought his policy—culled from military reports of the damage inflicted by high velocity bullets and claymore mines—extraordinarily clever. Suzanne, having seen death firsthand, thought his affectations tasteless.

She held her temper. Here she was not Alouzon Dragonmaster. Here she was Suzanne Helling, a student of medieval archaeology with a brand-new master's degree, an already foundering dissertation, and a teaching position that was up for review at the end of November. "I'll bring them this afternoon."

"You bring them now, Suzanne."

The incongruity thrust itself at her, and she almost laughed. Suzanne. Quiet little Suzanne with the fading peace button and the long hair that belonged in a picture out of a late 1960s yearbook. It would be infinitely satisfying, she thought, if she could walk into his office as Alouzon, sword in hand, and see what he would do with thirty-three inches of magical steel leveled at his throat.

She shuddered. She was becoming as tasteless as Brian. "All right," she said. "I'll be over in an hour."

"But—"

The strain snapped the fine thread that held back her temper. "Take it or fucking leave it, simp."

Silence. Suzanne was as stunned as Brian. It was the tension, she reflected. It was getting to her. How long could she keep this up?

Brian found his voice after a minute. "Uh . . . OK," he said faintly.

She hung up feeling drained. "Silbakor."

"Dragonmaster."

"You said once that you'd help me."

"I did."

"Well then, do it. I wasn't cut out to be a damned God, not even a part-time one. We're going to Gryylth. Now. I care about those people."

The yellow eyes were unblinking. The phone rang again. Convinced that it was Brian with some puerile retort, Suzanne almost left it unanswered. But the ringing grated on her nerves and she snatched the receiver from the cradle and blurted out an angry hello.

But it was not Brian. "Is this Suzanne Helling?" The woman's voice was taut, choked, close to tears.

"Yeah, you got her."

"This is Helen Addams. I met you at Sol's funeral. I . . . uh . . . was his wife. I got your number out of the phone book."

"Yeah . . . OK." Suzanne glanced at the Dragon, surprised to see it stiff and attentive. A voice thrummed softly in her mind. *I am listening, Suzanne.*

Helen's tone veered abruptly toward hysteria. "I . . . I really don't know why I'm calling you, but you knew Sol toward the end, and after he was screaming and all . . ."

The cold fog at the cemetery might have invaded her apartment. "Screaming?"

"I . . . I heard him. I saw him. He was standing up in his grave—"

"When?"

"This morning. I was sleeping in—I lecture and write . . . so I can. And I was dreaming about him. And then I heard him screaming." Helen was nearly screaming herself. "And I saw him in his grave, and he was moving. You've got to believe me. *I heard him.* He was calling your name."

The Dragon was still. Its eyes appeared to be looking into other worlds. Helen was gasping, and if ever Suzanne wanted the surety—shallow though it was—of Alouzon, it was now.

"You probably think I'm crazy," said Helen.

"I . . . don't think you're crazy."

"You think something's going on with Sol? But he's dead. *He's dead!*" The hysteria in her voice was growing.

Suzanne tried to remember what she knew about Helen that might help calm her down, but in addition to Solomon, hate for Solomon, she could recall only a devotion to feminist politics that the former housewife had embraced with the fanaticism of a convert. "Calm down, sister," she said. "Are you going to let a man run your life for you?"

She might have struck the woman with a brick. Helen's gasping stopped. "I run my own life."

"Well, then act like it."

Helen controlled herself creditably. "What's going on with Sol?"

Suzanne bent her head. Yet another job for Alouzon Dragonmaster. "I'll . . . have to talk to you in person. How about tonight?"

"Yeah, fine." Helen might have been punching the words out of sheet steel, but she gave Suzanne her address and directions.

"Look, it's going to be all right," Suzanne said, trying to sound soothing. "Just take it easy. Sol can't hurt you anymore, and—"

"You better believe he can't hurt me, sister."

"Sure, OK. I'll see you tonight." Suzanne hung up. "Come on, Silbakor. Let's move."

There was no answer. The Dragon was gone.

Marrget, Karthin, and the First Wartroop rode to Bandon the next morning, starting out even before the weak sun of winter had risen. The darkness and cold made it a long, miserable ride, but the company was well bundled in cloaks, and the urgency of their mission made them put aside thoughts of warmth or comfort.

Their speed was such that they arrived well before dusk, cresting a small rise to the south of the town just as the afternoon light was beginning to fade. Marrget lifted a hand to signal a halt, for she was unwilling to let her warriors ride directly into such devastation.

Senon's words had been apt. Bandon was no more.

The town had been leveled, its walls broken into cobble-sized stones, its houses ruined, its once prosperous streets filled with wreckage. The blackness of soot and flame was everywhere, and Marrget wondered whether, had she examined the town inch by inch, she would have been able to find a single fragment of unburned wood.

The roads showed the same destruction, and long scorch marks streamed across fields that before had been patched only with snow. Outbuildings and steadings that had been scattered far and wide lay broken as though trodden on by a giant's foot. In the sluggish river, ruined docks and boats bobbed amid chunks of ice.

"O, you nameless Gods," she whispered.

Karthin was beside her. "Sorcery?"

Marrget's face was blank for a moment. Such outright and widespread destruction reminded her of nothing so much as the devastation unleashed by Tireas, the Corrinian sorcerer, when he had killed most of the army of Gryylth and had, simultaneously, transformed the best warriors of the land into—

"I do not know," she said abruptly. "But we have

little light left, and therefore we must move quickly. Relys, take the left column toward the mountains and search for survivors. Karthin and I will take the right and do likewise in the wood to the east. That done, we will if necessary examine the town itself.''

The wartroop fanned out. The winter dusk was coming on quickly, and the clouds that were building above the Camrann Mountains promised snow. Marrget kept her cloak wrapped tight and her sword loose in its sheath as she rode into the trees. Some fifteen yards off to her left, Wykla's horse snorted in the cold and was answered by a whinny from Timbrin's mount. Much closer was the sound of Karthin's breathing: the big man had, for his own reasons, elected to stay at her side.

His own reasons. She wondered if she, too, had reasons of her own for not ordering him to keep the same distance as the others. Since the night before, she had felt a need for his presence, a deep-seated hunger that she did not pretend to understand. He had ridden throughout the day by her side, and she had felt comforted by his nearness. And he, she knew without asking, had felt the same way.

Their search proved fruitless. Even the foxes and white-furred hares had fled the forest. And when Marrget rejoined Relys, she found that the lieutenant's search had been equally unsuccessful.

''The town, then,'' said Marrget.

''In the darkness, captain?'' said Relys. ''Is that wise?'' She alone of the wartroop wore her hair as close-cropped as a man's and disdained garments cut for a woman. Her tunic hung in folds on her slender frame, and her eyes had grown harder.

''We have little choice, Relys. A storm is coming.''

Relys grunted agreement and posted sentinels. The rest of the wartroop left their horses outside the town and made their way in on foot, swords in hand.

Bandon was a hell of still-smoking rubble, powdered and burned stone, and blackened timbers that had been strewn across the streets like handfuls of straw. A pungent odor as of tallow was thick in the back of Marrget's throat as she and Karthin, their hoods thrown back because of the lingering heat, picked a slow path down the main avenue that led to the town square.

Surrounded by this burned and shattered parody of Bandon, Marrget found herself thinking of the other times that she had trodden this street, when, manly and with a heavy step, she had swaggered through the town, the captain of the First Wartroop, a hero of Gryylth. Here she had been honored by the councilmen, and here also she had bought the slave girl who had thereafter kept her house—and sometimes her bed—until . . .

. . . until everything had changed.

Marrget stood for a moment amid the rubble, biting her lip, her eyes aching with suppressed tears. As a man, she had whored and boasted with the best, but now she had neither the body nor the heart for such empty actions. Too well she had come to understand her slave's humiliations, and when she had returned— a woman—to Kingsbury, she had freed the girl, sending her off with generous gifts and a grant of land from the king.

And there was another, too, who had been singled out by a combination of fate, perversity, and braggart lust. Years before, at the shore of the Long River, a slight, blond, Corrinian girl had struggled and screamed as her rapist had stripped her and pinned her to the ground, and Marrget could still feel the now incongruous sensation of penetration and violent release.

Senon's words would have been as apt for Marrget of Crownhark as they were for Bandon. The smoke made her cough, and she found that a tear was making its way down her cheek. She did not even know the girl's name. She wished that she could—

"Marrget?"

She wiped at the tear so that he would not notice. "It is the smoke, Karthin."

In the darkness, the fitful gleam of smoldering fires played with his expression. "Nay, friend. I would say that it is more."

"Am I so foolish, Karthin, that you can read me like a parchment?"

"You have ever worn your feelings openly, Marrget. For which I am grateful." His deep voice rumbled soothingly, took away what little sting might have been in his words. "I pray I am as open to you."

Relys's voice started up in the distance, hallooing loudly. "Captain, are you well?"

Marrget swallowed her emotion, loosened the knot in her throat. "Well enough, Relys," she called in return. "Have you anything to report?"

Relys, Wykla, and Timbrin forced their way through the wreckage, accompanied by the crunching and crackling of pulverized stone and charred wood. "Nothing, captain, save bones and burnt bodies. And the treasury." Relys smiled without mirth: Bandon had been her home, but she had always hated the town. "Cvinthil revoked the town's charter, but the merchants seem to have been doing well enough: there are sacks and piles of gold." She laughed, again without emotion. "There are a few hapless councilmen, too, who were less brave and more practical than Senon."

"None living?"

"None, friend or foe."

Marrget looked around. "Surely there are some survivors." Tilting her head back, she shouted loudly: "Ho! People of Bandon! Marrget of Crownhark calls!"

A stirring came from the remains of the town hall that lay a dozen yards ahead. Marrget bettered her grip on her sword and braced herself for an attack, but the stirring was suddenly replaced with a girl's tear-choked cry. "Marrget of Crownhark?"

"Who calls?"

"Gelyya, daughter of Holt."

"Speak to us. We will find you."

With Gelyya's voice guiding them, they scrambled forward and worked their way into the hall, Karthin lending his weight and strength as the women shoved timbers and stones out of the way. The wreckage made the ruins treacherous: walls collapsed around them more than once, and broken beams and posts threatened to fall.

Gelyya and three other girls were at the bottom of a deep cellar as black as a well. Perching on the edge and peering down, Marrget congratulated them silently for their luck: the cellar was deep and protected with thick stone walls, and the heat trapped by the stone had kept them alive.

"Shall I summon the wartroop?" asked Wykla.

"Nay. They may find others, and we five will suffice for this." Marrget looked further and discovered that the stairs had fallen in. "Karthin? Rope?"

The big man nodded and pulled a coil from his pack. Marrget took off her cloak and put it aside, then turned to Karthin. For a moment, she recalled how she had turned to him the night before, at the Feast. Then, they had danced together. Now, with a thin smile, she took the end of the rope, knotted it into a sling, and slipped it over her shoulders.

In a minute, Karthin and the women were lowering her into a darkness that was ripe with the unknown stench that seemed to pervade the entire town. Below, Marrget could make out pale faces.

She reached the floor, and the girls crowded about her. They seemed oddly quiet for being in sight of rescue, but the captain knew that they were probably still in shock. Quietly and professionally, with a calm assurance that she knew would do more than overt emotion, she asked names, ascertained injuries, and, one by one, sent them up to the surface via the rope.

Not until she and Gelyya were alone did the girl offer anything more than answers to Marrget's questions. "How . . . how did you find out about us?"

"Senon brought word to Kingsbury," said Marrget.

Gelyya nodded. "The townsfolk thought him a coward because he used to hide behind Kanol's skirts." She shuddered, sobbed weakly. "But he turned out to be braver than us all.'' Gelyya was the oldest of those in the cellar, and she had obviously taken on responsibility for the others. Now Marrget felt the girl's strength crumbling: she had sustained the others at her own expense.

And have I not done the same with the wartroop? She put an arm about the girl. ''You are very brave yourself,'' she said softly. ''As brave as any warrior of Gryylth. Was it you who brought the others here?''

''It was.'' Gelyya's voice was hoarse with suppressed tears. ''We were together when we met Alouzon Dragonmaster, and we thought ourselves a company.'' She clutched at Marrget's hand. Her fingers were icy. ''Did you . . . did you find my mother? My father? The fire trapped them in our house, and they told me to run.''

Karthin called down. ''The rope is coming.''

''We . . . .'' Marrget could see little of the girl's expression, but she could well imagine it. Someone was going to pay for this outrage. ''We have found no one else.''

Gelyya sagged, whimpering. The rope dangled down invisibly, and Marrget felt it brush across her arms. ''Be ready,'' she called up to the surface. ''We two will be coming together.''

''I am glad to hear it,'' Karthin replied. ''These stones seem unwilling to hold themselves up much longer. Fear not: there is strength in our arms for two.''

For a minute, she worked in darkness, reknotting the rope about its double load. Among such as Gelyya had she once walked, disdainful and arrogant. Now she was a woman too, holding the girl and willing strength into her like a mother. Silently she bent her head and kissed Gelyya's forehead, then shouted for her comrades to pull. If, somehow, her actions tonight could make up in part for what she had done on the shore of the Long River, she would consider herself well rewarded.

By the time Gelyya reached the surface, she was

near hysteria, and Marrget sat her down and held her. Tears, she knew, were streaking down her own sooty face, but it was some time before she realized that wider, stronger arms were wrapped about both herself and the girl of Bandon.

With a start, she looked up and found Karthin beside her, his embrace as gentle as a woman's, as fiercely protective as that of any warrior of Gryylth or Corrin.

❖ CHAPTER 3 ❖

Marrget and the rescue party spent two weeks combing through the wreckage of the town, working in a bitter cold that numbed their hands and made them long for a breath of something other than icy air. Slowly they unearthed other survivors, children who had found refuge in cellars and pits and cul-de-sacs that had been protected from the flames by collapsing buildings.

As the days went on, though, and the snow continued to fall, fewer and fewer were found alive, and Marrget finally called a halt to what had become fruitless and despairing work. In the spring, perhaps, what whole bodies there were could be buried. For now, the First Wartroop had boys and girls, injured and sound both, who deserved something more than the spartan accommodations of a winter camp.

The weather was breaking when the wartroop returned to Kingsbury, and its charges were made wards of the king and fostered out to relatives and friends and childless couples who would take the orphans. Some of the older girls, Gelyya among them, found work with the midwives of the town; but as she was the eldest of those who had survived the destruction, the red-haired girl was eventually called before the king and questioned.

Cvinthil's brown eyes were sad as he regarded her, for he had children of his own. "I regret paining you, Gelyya," he said softly. "Your wounds are still fresh."

"Fresh enough, my king." She sat before him, holding herself bravely. "But I will do my best."

"Senon told us as much as he could before he died, but he left the town early on, and therefore he did not see all. Pray, tell us what you can."

With Marrget at her side for reassurance, Gelyya recounted the story of the end of Bandon. At first there had been only sounds in the night, shrill roars and shrieks that had crossed from horizon to horizon in a matter of a few heartbeats. But the sounds had abruptly come closer, accompanied by bright, smoking torches that had drifted slowly through the air, shedding a wan parody of daylight on the doomed town.

The fire fell just before midnight, covering the southern wall in a sheet of billowing flame. More followed, ringing the town with an inferno. Moments later, buildings were exploding in showers of stone and splinters, and townsfolk who attempted to run for the blazing gates were cut down in mid-stride by something that left their bodies a mess of torn flesh and bloody rags.

Marrget's anger had already been kindled in the cellar of the town hall, but listening to Gelyya's shy voice recounting the horror that had befallen Bandon, she found that it was still growing. The attack had been swift, ruthless, and completely effective, and when Gelyya's tale was done, Marrget reported as much.

"It was an outrage," she finished. "Never have I seen a town so completely destroyed; yet we found nothing to indicate the presence of any army or band of warriors. In all my years of battle I have never seen the like."

One of the King's Guard, a new man who had entered the royal service only a month before, was staring at her. Marrget eyed him. Yes, it was strange to hear a woman speak of battle, but he, like many others, would have to get used to it. Irritated by his gaze, she folded her arms and examined him as though picking a place for a sword thrust. The man looked away quickly.

"I once saw something similar," said Santhe. "In the last days of the war with Corrin."

Karthin shifted uneasily at the words. He had been listening from his customary place near the edge of the king's dais, his eyes on the floor and the thumbs of his large hands hooked in his belt. Marrget knew that he was well aware that numerous people in the land were already blaming Corrin for the atrocity. She bristled. "Did you wish to make a formal accusation, councilor? I am sure . . ." She glared at the new guard, but he was keeping his gaze firmly fixed on the back of the room. ". . . that you are not alone in your suspicions."

Santhe started at her tone. "There are hasty folk in the land, I know, my friend. But I have no accusation to make. Forgive me if my words were ill-chosen."

As Gelyya's tale had unfolded, Cvinthil's eyes had turned from sad to murderous. He might have been envisioning his own children in the fire storm that had razed the town. "Sorcery. It must be sorcery."

"But whose?" said Marrget. "Mernyl and Tireas are both dead, and there is not another sorcerer in either Gryylth or Corrin."

Karthin himself spoke. "There is a sorcerer in Corrin."

Silence in Hall Kingsbury.

Cvinthil kept his tone carefully noncommittal. "I did not know that, friend Karthin."

Marrget suddenly felt bleak, and she looked away. There was doubt in the hall, and, more upsetting, in her heart too. Another sorcerer? Karthin had never said anything about this before.

"Truly, I cannot say that he is much of a sorcerer," said the big man. "His name is Helwych. He was apprentice to Tireas, but his studies, so I have heard, were neglected when his master turned his efforts toward the magic of the . . ."

He hesitated, flushed, and he looked at Marrget as though he wished that he had kept his mouth shut. But she forced her doubts aside and nodded at him. Kar-

thin was a friend. He had danced with her, had held
her in his arms, had done much to fill a private and
unspoken ache in her heart that, until the New Year
Feast, she had thought bottomless.

He smiled at her—fondly, she thought—and went
on. ". . . before he was overmastered by the Tree. He
commands some few small spells."

"Small spells?" Cvinthil blinked.

"How small, Karthin?" said Santhe.

The Corrinian ruminated. His thumbs worked in his
belt. "I suppose that, with effort, he could make a
spade look like a pitchfork."

His farmer origins were showing again, and even
Gelyya smiled. There was guile in the world, but there
was none in Karthin. The girl, though, spoke up.
"King Cvinthil," she said softly. "If it please you, I
saw the lights depart. They did not turn toward the
east."

All attention was suddenly on the red-haired girl.
Cvinthil spoke slowly. "Where did they go, child?"

Her answer was firm. "My king, they went west.
They crossed the mountains."

Marrget nearly shook with relief. Not Corrin, then. Def-
initely not Corrin. But on the other side of the mountains
was the coast, and then the sea, and then there was another
land.

"Our neighbors in Vaylle," she said, "do not love
us."

Cvinthil's hand was on his sword. "Nor do we love
them, captain. If this be their greeting to us, we shall
answer similarly. I heartily wish that Alouzon Dragonmaster were with us now, but since she is not, we must
settle matters ourselves." He thought for a moment,
then lifted his head. "Who will take a message to my
brother in Corrin? I would ask him for the loan of a
sorcerer, and for what men and arms he can spare."

The dawn was gray and cold, and Wykla shivered a
little as she saddled her horse in the shadow of Hall
Kingsbury. The town was silent, and she worked

quickly, wishing to be away before any folk were up and about.

Dogs barked. A cock crew. She tried to keep her mind on her hands as she fastened harness and tack and walked the horse out into the street, but she felt keenly the eyes of the men who stood at the gate in the palisade. Marrget was shielded from all but the most abject of fools by her status and her quick temper; but Wykla was neither captain nor councilor, and though her membership in the First Wartroop gave her some prestige, it did nothing to deflect the stares, the laughter, and the snide comments.

She had little trouble with the veterans of the battle at the Circle, for a camaraderie had grown up among those who had braved Corrin's assault of magic and men, a fellowship that persisted still. Within it, Wykla—or any other woman of the First Wartroop—commanded respect and admiration.

But there were others, men and boys who had come to Kingsbury from the distant corners of the land, who had been untouched by war or the experiences of the Circle and the Tree. To them, the decrees that set the women of the land on equal footing with their brothers seemed outlandish things, indications that the settlement with Corrin had actually been a capitulation.

And if the decrees seemed strange to them, then the sight of a maid who had once been a man was stranger still. Wykla could never determine whether they were amused or afraid, but regardless of their motives, their actions were unpleasant and painful.

The half-expected call drifted from the palisade as she prepared to mount. "Good morning, little girl. Where is your mother today?"

"No, Kerlsen, she is too old for her mother."

"Indeed! Your husband then. Does he allow you to go about like a whore?"

Sniggering. The shapes of the young men were faint in the early morning shadows. But their voices were loud enough.

Wykla tried to ignore them. She was a messenger.

She had work to do. "If you were within sword's reach," she murmured, "you would learn some courtesy." As though she had not heard, she continued with her work, checking the fastenings of the harness one last time, wartroop-style.

"Why is your hair not braided?"

The jibe stung, and she bent quickly, picked up a hand-sized cobble from the street, and flung it with skill. The crack of impact was a satisfying one, the cry of pain more satisfying still. She drew herself up, and her amber hair was bright as she pointed at the doubled-over form of her tormentor. "My hair is not braided because I am unmarried, bumpkin," she said, her voice clear and her tone sharp. "It is tied back because I am of the First Wartroop. And had you courage to match your foul mouth I would gladly show you what a real warrior can do with a sword."

She swung up into the saddle and rode down the street, trying to keep back her tears.

Having had eighteen months in which to get used to such incidents, she would have thought that she would be less affected by them. But such time appeared to be insufficient. She wondered if the rest of her life might be enough. She would, she supposed, find out.

There were guards at the town gate, too, but they were seasoned men, and they knew her from the war. They saluted her with the gruff manner of comrades and wished her a safe trip. "Gods bless, Wykla."

"Gods bless."

"Is it war with Vaylle, then?"

She stopped for a moment. "It could well be. Cvinthil is asking for aid from Corrin."

One of the men laughed. "It will be different fighting with the phalanxes rather than against them."

"I am not so sure," said the other. "Vaylle lies across the White Sea, and what would the folk there want with us?"

"What?" said the first. "You think that it is Corrin we should fight?"

He seemed bewildered. "I am of two minds. Karthin is a good man, and I look at him and I say to myself, *Shame on you, Dyylic, for thinking such thoughts.* But I do not know his countrymen, and so . . .'' He shrugged. ''What do you think, Wykla?''

She shook her head and tried to smile. ''I think that I have a long ride ahead of me, and . . .'' She looked back, listening to the cursing that was drifting from the Hall. ''. . . and I hope that the people of Gryylth will someday be as kind to me as Karthin of Corrin.''

''Well said.'' The first guard reached up, clasped her hand, and nodded toward the Hall. ''Dyylic and I will thrash the bumpkin tonight.'' He grinned. ''If you have left us anything to thrash.''

Wykla's smile turned thin. ''There are plenty of others like him if I did not, friend. Farewell.'' And she rode down the hill and into the growing morning.

Gryylth unfolded like a gray and white tapestry as she rode eastward, its hills and valleys thrown into highlights and shadows by the ever-rising sun, its trees and hedgerows transformed into pied apparitions of old snow and bare branches.

In this cold season she met few travelers, for there was little business save hers that would call for long journeys. She was glad of that. Better a long road and winter's loneliness than the deeper isolation carried by the inadvertent companions that summer would bring. The story of the First Wartroop was known across Gryylth, and there were those who stared and asked rude questions, and there were those who laughed . . .

Even her fellow warriors—the ones who spoke to her as to an equal—had uttered thoughtless words. *You are a woman now, Wykla. You understand these things.* Understand? Understand what? That she was now the sport of every dolt who believed that no woman, even one with the rank of warrior, was a match for a man? *What is it like to be a woman? What is it like to make love?*

She had no idea. She had gone to Kallye, the midwife, professing ignorance of herself, asking halting and embarrassing questions. But though the midwife

could teach her what any woman knew of her body—
of breasts and monthly flows, of strengths and weaknesses—Wykla was acutely conscious that she had yet
to grasp the connotations of her new identity. She was
a woman. What did that really mean? She could not
say. And as for making love . . .

A few weeks ago, one fool had tried to give her that
experience. Forcibly. He had died of a sword thrust.
Wykla still shuddered at the memory, still wondered
if she had done something wrong, something that had
falsely encouraged him.

Such events made for an uneasy and confusing life,
and she wished that Alouzon would return to Gryylth
soon, for the Dragonmaster had always been a source
of strength for her, someone she could look to as an
example. If Alouzon could be a woman, calm and sure
of herself, then Wykla of Burnwood could be a warrior, could eventually understand her own body and
her own loneliness, and perhaps could even hope that,
someday, there might be some love in her life.

Love. A hard thing to imagine. What man could she
ever accept? What woman would have her?

The sun crossed toward the west. Wykla made good
speed, eating while she rode and changing horses in
Amesbury and at the site of the old garrisons at the
southwestern end of the Great Dike. Afternoon was
well along when she crossed the border into Corrin,
but she expected to make Benardis by dusk, and the
idea that she could sleep that night in a town where
her dual status of woman and warrior was considered
nothing unusual was an attractive one.

The lands of Corrin looked much like those of
Gryylth. But there were differences. The few individ-
uals she saw working in the fields—forking out hay for
the cattle and horses, breaking holes in ice-covered
troughs so that the animals could drink— seemed to
be women as often as they were men. Regardless of
their sex, though, they waved to her and wished her a
good day with cheerful sincerity.

And later, when she was within sight of the capital,

a rider appeared on the road ahead, making haste for her. It was a young woman, her yellow hair ruddy in the streaming sunset and her way with her body easy and confident. She approached at full gallop, reined in at the last moment. "Hail and welcome to Corrin, woman of Gryylth," she said. Her smile was broad, and her hair, braided to one side, bounced jauntily over her shoulder. "Darham the king sends you greeting."

She was tanned and slim, and sat a head taller on her horse than Wykla. Her leathers were close-fitting and cut to flatter a woman's figure.

Now it was Wykla who stared. A woman, and a warrior, and proud . . . "I . . . I bring messages from King Cvinthil."

"We saw you coming, and I was sent to be your escort and guide. I am Manda of Dubris, of the King's Guard."

"Wykla of Burnwood. Of . . . of the First Wartroop."

Manda froze, stared at her, examined her face as though to memorize it. "Of the First Wartroop, you say?"

"Aye, lady." And to show Manda that she was not ashamed of her company or its fate, she tossed her cloak back over her shoulders to show her personal insignia and that of the wartroop.

Surprisingly, though, Manda did not seem so much curious as stricken. She examined the escutcheons earnestly, then shook her head and sighed as though with relief. "Come, Wykla," she said. "You are welcome in my land. Please forgive my discourtesy."

"It is well, Manda."

Still, the Corrinian maid seemed chagrined by her behavior. "Should your duties cause you to stay the night, my household would be honored to receive you."

But her look had been too searching, and Wykla still chafed at the morning's encounter. "I . . . I do not wish pity," she said softly.

"Will you . . ." Manda looked off toward Gryylth, pressed her lips together, bent her head. "Will you accept a friend, then?"

Wykla was puzzled. "Why should you be my friend?"

Manda smiled uncomfortably. "You look as though you could well use one, and it is a custom of Corrin to offer." She turned her horse. "Come, night is approaching." She set off at a brisk trot. Wykla looked after her for a moment, then followed.

Like the land of which it was the capital, Benardis was both familiar and foreign. Wykla saw the same houses of wattle and daub, stone and timber; she rode along the same dusty streets as were characteristic of any town of Gryylth. But here there were too many women out of doors, and they conducted themselves with too much freedom: their gestures broad and quick, their smiles and voices free.

Wykla felt her face color. *I am a woman, too. This should please me.*

But she had not always been a woman, and Gryylth was still inching toward this kind of freedom. She looked on enviously as Manda spoke familiarly to a young soldier in the street and sent him running ahead without apology or hesitation. Manda was in charge of her life, and she was comfortable with it.

She had also obviously given the lad a sense of urgency, for when they reached the king's lodge in the center of town, Darham himself was waiting for them. He was a tall, broad man, and what parts of his face were not covered by an immense golden beard were creased with lines of laughter. But Wykla, looking closer, noticed the streak of sadness in his otherwise bright blue eyes.

"Welcome, warrior of Gryylth," he said, standing up to greet his guest in the manner of the kings of Corrin. To either side of him, his personal guards, men and women, nodded formally. One, a young man with the faintest trace of a mustache, even grinned at her.

She felt suddenly cold, and fumbled with her words for a moment before she could speak. "Hail, King of Corrin," she said. To her own ears, her voice sounded pale and uncertain in comparison to Darham's. "Wykla of Burnwood brings you greetings from the King of Gryylth, who urgently desires your counsel and aid in the matter of Vaylle, the land across the White Sea."

She still felt cold, and would not have been at all surprised if her hands had been shaking, though she would not look. Darham noticed, though, and he turned to Manda. "Has this woman been offered refreshment after her long journey?"

"I requested it, my king," said Manda. "She asked that she see you without delay, and therefore I instructed the stewards to bring the food and drink here."

"That is good. Bring a chair for Wykla of Burnwood."

The young man with the mustache acted before the others, and nearly fell over himself as he dragged a cushioned chair forward. Wykla nodded to him, but she was thankful when her escort stepped up. "I shall attend to our guest myself," said Manda.

"As you wish." The guard sounded disappointed.

Bread, wine, and cheese were brought to Wykla, and though she protested at eating in front of a king, Darham insisted that she take something before she continued. "Time does not move so fast," he said, "that we must torment one another more than we already have. But if you feel you must speak, tell me something of my friend Karthin. Is he well?"

"He is, King Darham." Wykla nibbled at the food without real appetite, speaking between bites. She told of Karthin's work during the first, hard winter, of his continuing advice to Cvinthil. She even told of his friendship with Marrget of Crownhark, and was surprised that her words made it sound as though something more than friendship existed between the two captains. Marrget and Karthin? But—

"I am heartily glad to hear this news," said Darham. "Karthin and I pleaded the cause of peace before Tarwach in the final hours of the war, and though at that time my brother did not agree with us, it is pleasing to know that peace has brought so much to both our lands."

Wykla picked at the food without enthusiasm, wondering how Darham would react when he was told that Gryylth and Corrin were not through with war, that another seemed to be beginning. At length she could pretend hunger no more, and she pushed the platter aside.

Darham's eyes were on her. "And what news does Cvinthil have for me?"

Wykla would have stood, but Darham shook his head and motioned for her to remain seated. Feeling much as she supposed Gelyya had in Hall Kingsbury, and with Manda a blond presence at her shoulder, she recounted the story of the attack on Bandon, the experiences of the First Wartroop, and Gelyya's testimony.

At the mention of the wartroop, Darham seemed to start, and he looked at Wykla more closely, unconsciously covering his right forearm with his left hand. He said nothing, though, until she was finished.

"Helwych," he said.

"Here, my king," said a young man clad in a gray robe. Wykla had not noticed him before, and he now stepped out of the shadows as though enjoying the effect of his sudden, unexpected appearance.

"You heard?"

"Everything." Helwych regarded Wykla openly, rubbing his beardless chin. His face was neither narrow nor round, but seemed to hesitate between the two extremes, unwilling to commit itself to a position. His hair, the color of a brown mouse, hung lankly to his shoulders. His hands alone seemed definite: thin, finely detailed. They held his wizard's staff tightly, as though he were afraid that someone would attempt to snatch it from him.

Darham shifted on his simple stool. "What do you think?"

"Vaylle indeed seems to be the culprit." Helwych nodded with assurance. "I have . . . given some thought to that land these last days. I have studied my books and examined the upper spheres, and yet Vaylle is closed to me. Some working of magic, I think, shrouds the land."

"That does not sound good," said Darham.

"Needless to say," said the sorcerer, "it makes me suspicious."

Darham turned back to Wykla. "And King Cvinthil wishes aid from me? Arms?"

"Arms and soldiers, lord," she said, "and . . ." She nodded to Helwych. ". . . whoever else you might be willing to send. Bandon was thoroughly leveled. Such an action demands retribution."

Helwych spoke quickly. "I would be more than happy to go to Gryylth, my king. I am gratified that my small reputation seems to have spread so widely."

But the Corrinian king frowned, and the sad streak in his eyes broadened. "Gryylth was ever disinclined to leave a blow unrevenged," he murmured. He lifted his head and spoke more loudly. "Nor can I blame Cvinthil. My brother did not ignore the burning of our fields, and had I been king then, I would have made the same decisions as he."

But Darham's face softened into a faint smile. "But we all know where such decisions brought us. Our fields were burned, true. But Gryylth's were forced to do double duty, and her people worked long and hard to feed their former enemies. This, maybe, teaches us the value of circumspection."

Wykla stared at him. *Did I carry sword against this man?*

Helwych started to speak, but Darham held up a hand for silence. "Vaylle is an unknown," the king continued. "I am sure that my brother in Gryylth has given thought to the consequences of his actions, but I would he consider them further. Our two lands have but recently concluded their treaties, and I am unwilling to part so hastily with our new-found peace. Tireas—before madness took him—always insisted that, presented with two unsatisfactory choices, one should seek then another. That is what I shall do. To attack is but one choice. To ignore is a second. I will look for a third, Wykla of Burnwood.''

''Is this the message I shall take to Cvinthil?'' she said.

''Nay, I will give this matter further thought, and I will consult with Helwych.''

The sorcerer straightened up and nodded gravely.

Darham regarded him, smiled as though indulging a problem child, turned back to Wykla. ''If you would be willing to remain our guest for some five or six days, we would be honored.''

Manda spoke. ''I have offered my household, lord.''

''Good. Corrin will never be thought lax in its hospitality so long as Manda of Dubris lives.''

Darham rose, but he did not leave immediately. Pausing before Wykla, he regarded her kindly. ''The First Wartroop, you say, my lady?''

My lady. She felt the cold return. ''Aye, lord.''

Darham mused. ''I remember you.'' He looked at her directly. ''At the Circle. We called you The Amber One—for your hair.'' He lifted his right arm and turned it over, and Wykla saw that its underside was scarred from wrist to elbow. ''You fight well.''

She stared at the old wound. ''I . . . regret now that I struck that blow.''

''We all bear wounds from that time. Some more comely than others.''

Wykla flushed.

Darham stood over her. The great blue eyes of mirth and grief burned down. ''Do you have family?''

''I . . . do, my lord. In Burnwood.''

''You hesitate.''

''I . . . left them some years ago to join the wartroop.'' There was suddenly a lump in her throat, and she was annoyed at herself: by now, this wound should have been as scarred over as Darham's arm. But her voice was husky as she went on. ''After the war, I

returned, looking for comfort. They denied me . . .''
The room blurred to her eyes, and she gritted her teeth
and bent her head to hide the tears.

Darham considered for a moment and shook his head
sadly. "Daughters are not held in high esteem in
Gryylth.''

"That is true, my lord.''

"I also lost a family,'' he said gently. "And his
rejection was bitter enough. Perhaps the Gods will allow me to choose my own now.'' Lifting his scarred
arm, he placed his hand on Wykla's head. "This I will
say to you, Wykla of Burnwood, Amber One: should
you need someone to call *father*, call me. The wounds
of the past are deep: let us close them as we can.'' He
smiled wryly as he turned to the assembled guards
and attendants. "And I for one am proud to claim a
daughter who can best me in swordwork.''

He let his hand remain on her head for a moment,
then removed it, stooped, and kissed her brow. "It is
well. Manda, attend to Wykla. I shall send for you
both tomorrow.'' He bowed to his visitor and departed.

❖ CHAPTER 4 ❖

Hot coffee and a cold shower pulled Suzanne together enough to take the graded papers out to the archaeology department at the university. She had hoped that Brian would be gone when she arrived, but she found him in the office he shared with her, waiting.

Without comment, she set the two stacks down on the corner of her desk and turned to leave. Brian looked up. "You don't have to go running off."

"I'm not feeling well. I'm going back to bed."

"You look fine."

"I don't have any shrapnel wounds, if that's what you mean." Sure that her temper would be triggered by the sight of his face, she tried to avoid looking at him, but wound up staring at the poster above his desk: a life-sized photograph of the cockpit controls of an A-4 Skyhawk. Brian obviously thought of the warplane in terms of technology and armed might, but for Suzanne the poster brought only visions of napalmed and machine-gunned villages, incinerated Vietnamese peasants, and children left homeless or dead.

"You know," said Brian, "if you want your career to go anywhere, you're going to have to learn to conform."

"Maybe," she said, still avoiding his eyes. "And maybe I don't fucking want to."

He blinked. "How do you want me to take that?"

"Take it any way you want." Turning, she stalked

through the door and down the hall. There was a chance that she would not have a teaching position or a doctoral program in the morning, but she would always have Gryylth. And Vaylle, too. She supposed that she could call it job security.

In the hot parking lot, she paused beside her car and checked the paperweight for the twentieth time since Helen's phone call. No Silbakor. Cursing the Dragon under her breath, she drove back to her apartment, pulled the blinds in the bedroom shut, and crawled into bed.

In her dreams, she saw the grim closeness of fifth-century warfare juxtaposed with the disinterested slaughter of the twentieth. The towns of Gryylth were napalmed and bombed and riddled with twenty-millimeter bullets, the children of My Lai and Hanoi and Kingsbury were spitted on swords and spears, blasted by magic.

She awoke at sunset, trembling, soaked in sweat. The bedroom seemed a furnace, and when she threw open the window, the searing air of a Los Angeles heat wave offered no relief. Closing her eyes, she pillowed her head on the sill for a moment. "Oh, you Gods of Gryylth: please make sure that all stays a dream."

Another cold shower, a dinner eaten hastily and untasted, and she drove out to keep her appointment with Helen Addams.

Helen's directions took Suzanne up into the Santa Monica Mountains, deep into the sinuous rills and forested ridges of the Bel Air district. Filtered by lush leaves, the air was damp and cool, and the lights of the houses glowed from behind wrought iron fences and high hedges that spoke eloquently of wealth, leisure, and as much sylvan isolation as could be had within the confines of a sprawling city.

Suzanne parked across the street from the house. The windless night was as quiet as the cemetery had been that morning, the only movement that of the moths that hovered about the pale streetlamps, a

mocking reminder of her own fascinated obsession
with the elusive and ineffable Grail.

When she had first returned from Gryylth, she had
researched the legends of the Grail with the focused
intensity of a career scholar, but the information she
had found was thickly encrusted with successive layers
of belief and dogma, the legacy of small minds and
the theological bias of Pagan and Christian alike.
There was, though, one legend that had consistently
rung the bell of truth: that of Galahad. Pure and un-
stained by earthly concerns, he had looked into the
profound and inscrutable depths of the Holy Cup . . .
and had died.

*Some choice. I can give the whole thing up and go
crazy, or I can find the Grail and drop dead.*

She crossed the street and found a house set back
behind a dichondra lawn and a circular driveway. Plate-
glass windows glowed yellow from beneath red tile
roofs, and the front door was large and carved like
that of a mission. She rang the bell and glanced down
at the paperweight in the depths of her purse while she
waited. It was still empty.

Helen had changed little since Sol's funeral. She was
still a middle-aged woman who wore feminist theory
like a badge of honor. The gray in her tightly permed
hair matched the steel rims of her glasses, and the
loose, cotton blouse and trousers she wore hid her figure as defiantly as her lack of make-up bared her face.

She let Suzanne in without a word, bolted the door
behind her as though she were afraid of the long shadows in the front yard, and led her guest to a chair in
the living room.

"Drink?"

"No. Thanks."

Helen glanced at the sheer drapes that obscured the
big front windows. "Well, if you don't mind, I'll have
one myself."

The liquor cabinet seemed to be well stocked. As
Helen measured and poured, Suzanne examined the
room. Pale shag rug, chrome and glass furniture, real

mahogany paneling on the walls. It bore the unmistakable mark of both exquisite taste and money.

"Not bad for an ex-housewife who left her man with no marketable skills, eh?" said Helen from the bar.

"It's a nice place."

"I like it. The patriarchy doesn't make it easy for a woman on her own, but I turned that around." She spoke matter-of-factly, as though daring Suzanne to contradict her. "Sol used me the way men always use women, and I struck back just like any woman could. I write about it. I talk about it. I get paid well. You ever been to one of my seminars?"

"I'm a feminist, Helen. But I'm not political. I've got too many other things to worry about."

"If you don't worry about yourself, who will?" Helen settled herself on the sofa across the coffee table, legs spread mannishly. "You're probably a case in point," she said. "Most women are. They give everything, get nothing back, and wonder why they feel rotten about themselves."

Suzanne said nothing. Unwilling though she was to admit it, Helen had summed up her life.

"Tell me, honey . . ." Helen sipped at her drink. "What did you think of my prize?"

A branch scraped against the window. Suzanne looked up in time to see a flash, as of eyes, glowing bluely on the other side of the curtains and the glass. She looked again and saw nothing. "I . . . I'm not sure I understand."

Helen's back was to the window, and she had not noticed. "You almost look like you escaped in one piece."

"You're losing me."

"I think you understand better than you think." Helen's tone sharpened. "Sol couldn't love anything. He could own, but he couldn't love. He devoured me for twenty years. You got it for a lot less, but there's no way of dealing with a man like Sol without getting hurt." She examined her guest for a moment. "Did you sleep with him?"

Suzanne was genuinely angry. "What kind of question is that?"

Helen smiled. "Sore point?"

"Actually, most of the time, I hated his guts, just like you. Yeah, he was a manipulating son of a bitch, and he thought that all his male bullshit was just fine. But he had a few good qualities."

Helen was frowning. "You obviously didn't know him well enough. He had nothing but his prick and his ego. I got out because I realized that."

"So you tossed him. As hard as you could."

"He got what was coming to him."

The branch scraped the window again. Suzanne sensed that something was moving in the front yard. Something big. And her Dragonmaster instincts, awakening incongruously in her pudgy body, told her that it was not friendly.

"We have to learn to take care of ourselves," Helen continued. "If we don't, the men are going to keep screwing us over just like they always have." She leaned forward, stabbing a finger at Suzanne in time to her words. "I took everything that Sol did to me and threw it right back at him. He got his nose rubbed in it real good, honey, and he didn't like it one bit."

The presence outside the window was a palpable oppression. "Look," said Suzanne, by now both angry and frightened, "I agree with you about Sol. He hurt you. He hurt me a lot, too. But you called me this morning because he scared the shit out of you. Dammit, quit playing games. You want to hear him screaming again? Maybe you want to see his body come waltzing in through the front door?"

Fear flooded into Helen's face. "You know something, don't you?"

"What happened this morning?"

Helen fidgeted with her drink, her spines suddenly blunted. "I think I said everything when I talked to you. I keep my own hours, and when I work late, I sleep in. This morning I was dreaming of Sol. The usual. He used to grab me in the middle of the night and force me to have sex with him.'' She shook her head as though to drive the memory away. ''It was like being raped, night after night. It still is.'' She grimaced. ''Even after he's dead.''

''Go on. I don't want to hear about Sol. I want to hear about you.''

Helen appeared uncertain whether to be flattered or offended. ''I dreamed that there was a spear beside the bed, and I grabbed it and gave it to him right in the crotch. He started screaming, and then I was standing at his grave. Sol got up and started yelling your name. It wasn't any of this far-away stuff: it was like he was right there in the bedroom with me.''

Dragonmaster.

Suzanne stifled a gasp and checked her purse. Twin sparks of yellow fire flashed up at her. *Of all the goddam times to pull this shit, Silbakor, you sure pick the best.*

Helen was staring into her drink. ''He said that you had to stop someone.''

Dragonmaster. There is terror in Gryylth.

Suzanne felt sick. ''Stop who? From doing what?''

Helen shook her head.

A wind whined through the branches outside, and the branch creaked again on the window. Suzanne looked up into what were unmistakably eyes. They glowed through the curtains in shades of blue and violet.

''There was . . . one other thing that happened,'' said Helen. ''I heard Sol in my dreams a few months ago, too.''

The wind grew louder. *Dragonmaster.*

''I saw something that looked like Stonehenge. A bunch of women were trying to pull it down with ropes. That's when I heard him.''

''What . . .'' The eyes at the window had to be at least twelve inches apart and a good five feet from the ground. The wind had whipped into a fury, lashing at branches and leaves, battering against the house. ''What did he say?''

"He didn't say anything. He was crying."

Abruptly, a deep-throated howl went up from the front yard, and something thudded on the window. Suzanne heard a beating as of great wings.

Dragonmaster, flee this house.

Helen turned around, saw the eyes, screamed hoarsely. As the two women watched, the glass took on a pale aqua glow, and suddenly, inconceivably, the entire wall began to buckle inward.

"Silbakor!"

"Flee, Dragonmaster. You are being attacked."

A flash of fire went through her. Alouzon was awakening. Without hesitation, she picked up the paperweight, then grabbed Helen's arm and jerked her off the sofa as the window shattered.

Aqua phosphor poured into the room, gusted by a terrifying wind. "The back door," Suzanne shouted above the tumult. "Where's the back door?"

The phosphor was inching toward their feet. Suzanne looked up to see a glowing paw the size of a dinner plate step into the room, and the eyes were not far behind. And beyond that . . .

There was something else in the front yard, too. Something huge, white, with wings that drove the branches of the trees as though they were matchsticks.

"The back door, Helen. Go!" Suzanne shoved her in what she hoped was the right direction. Helen scrambled across the room, and Suzanne followed her down a hall and through the kitchen to a sliding glass door that opened onto a redwood deck. She heard the front door slam open and splinter against the wall, and then the wall itself gave way with a loud crack and a rattle of plaster and brick.

"Leave the house, Dragonmaster," said the Dragon, "and throw the paperweight behind you as you go."

She pushed Helen out onto the deck as the ceiling began to come down. The dark kitchen exploded into light, and something snarled in the hallway.

"Run!"

The Dragon itself sounded frightened, and Suzanne

plunged across the deck and down the stairs to the lawn, letting the paperweight fall behind her. Fire was spreading through her body, and she felt instincts and senses sharpening, felt a different body and a different flesh about her.

Alouzon was back.

When she caught up with Helen, the older woman looked at her and nearly screamed. *"Who are you?"*

Her cry sounded flat and lifeless. The house had vanished, as had the yard, the surrounding hills and the stars. The grass had been replaced by an endless floor of jet, and Silbakor waited a short distance away, wings unfurled, eyes burning.

"We must leave," it said.

Helen backed away and collapsed, huddled on the floor like a frightened child. Her eyes were wide, staring.

Alouzon glanced down at herself. She was wearing her leather armor, and the Dragonsword was at her hip. The tall, bronzed amazon had replaced the hapless earth-mother. No wonder Helen was terrified. "Dammit, Silbakor, why did you change me now?"

Howls. Drawing closer. In the blackness of the sky, Alouzon heard the beating of great wings.

"Mount," said the Dragon. "Quickly."

Helen stirred. "What . . . why . . ."

Alouzon knelt beside her. "It's OK. We're not going to hurt you. I'm still Suzanne. Really. Just believe me."

Helen remained where she was, knees drawn up, arms wrapped about her legs. The howls drew nearer. So did the wings.

Alouzon put a hand on her shoulder, shook her roughly. "Look, sister. You said a while back that you ran your own life. Well, start doing it. You haven't got a choice."

"Mount," said the Dragon.

Helen gasped, stirred, jerked her head upright. She looked younger of a sudden, her skin smooth and unlined, and she got to her feet with movements that had sleeked into feline grace. She stared at Alouzon out of dark eyes.

Alouzon stared back for a moment, but the howls and the wingbeats were drawing closer. Fighting alone in an impossible corner of the universe was not something she wanted to do, but her preferences had not mattered in a long time, and something large and faintly glowing was running at them.

Alouzon was already moving to defend. Without looking, she shoved Helen toward Silbakor, and she met open jaws and needle teeth with the edge of the Dragonsword. A howl of pain, and the beast sprang away.

Alouzon's blade was dripping phosphor, but the beast was closing again. Setting her feet, she leaned into her strike, and the sword bit deep, slicing the leprous thing nearly in two. It fell, twitching. Ichor spread in a steaming pool.

"Do something about Helen, Silbakor," she called over her shoulder. "Get her out of here."

A hand suddenly grasped Alouzon's arm, and she was pulled around to face a young woman. "I don't know what's going on," she said, her dark eyes glittering, "but I'm in charge of my own damn life. Don't forget it. And don't try to protect me."

Alouzon found her voice after a moment. "Just . . . save your ass and get on the Dragon, Helen."

Calmly, defiantly, the woman went to Silbakor and mounted in a swish of black hair and sable robes. More howls. Pallid forms flickered in the endless darkness. Faced with hopeless odds, Alouzon gave up and ran for the Dragon. Her booted foot found a toehold on one massive talon, and in a moment she was aboard.

The black wings spread, and they were lifted.

In the course of the next week, Darham questioned Wykla in ever-greater detail about the particulars of the destruction she had seen in Bandon, and Wykla sensed that he was searching her answers for the third choice that he wanted. He seemed well aware that

some action had to be taken, but in contrast to his
brother Tarwach's vengeful ire, Darham looked for
peace first.

"It makes no sense," he said one afternoon.

"Are you so sure, my king?" Helwych had been
listening with bright, eager eyes. "I think it is obvious. Bandon was destroyed by what can only be the
work of a master sorcerer. Vaylle cloaks itself in secrecy: again the hand of magic. What further proof do
we need?"

"You are hasty, Helwych." Darham did not see the
flash of annoyance that crossed the sorcerer's face, but
Wykla did.

At last, though, Darham gave Wykla his reply. No
arms or men would be forthcoming from Corrin, he
said, until some clearer idea of the identity and the
nature of the enemy was established. He suggested to
Cvinthil that a small party be formed to reconnoiter
the land of Vaylle in secret.

Wykla recognized the wisdom of his words, but she
could not help but wonder if his decision would have
been different had a town of Corrin been destroyed.
Nevertheless, she bowed deeply to the king and found
suitable words of thanks.

Her stay in Corrin had done much for her. Without
constant reminders of her former life, she had found
herself free to live as she was, and for the moment.
Here in Benardis, she was a free woman in a free land;
and as Manda had escorted her about the town, showing her the sights and introducing her to the people
simply as *Wykla, a warrior*, and as those same people
had nodded courteously and accepted her without
question, Wykla had found the old, frightened uncer-
tainties falling from her bit by bit, had found also that
she was often matching Manda's easy stride, imitating
her broad gestures, laughing as openly as the maid of
Corrin.

So, when she thanked the king, she held herself
straight, looked into the face of the man who had of-

fered his kinship in place of that which she had lost, and smiled.

But Darham was not finished. "I would not have Cvinthil think me a poor neighbor who sends excuses instead of bread. Therefore, Manda, you will go with Wykla to Kingsbury as my personal liaison. Tell Cvinthil that I commend you to him as one of Corrin's best, and that if he thinks well of my proposal, he could do no better than to include you in any expedition to Vaylle." He turned. "And, Helwych . . ."

The young sorcerer had been standing off by himself, his face clouded. He had advised a more militant action against Vaylle, and was plainly unhappy that his sentiments had been ignored. Now he looked up hopefully. "My lord?"

"You also will go to Kingsbury, and to Vaylle. Cvinthil will need advice in matters of magic. I will expect a full report from you upon your return."

"As you will, my lord." Helwych seemed caught between pride and fright. Wykla sensed that had he been sent to Vaylle under the protection of a large army, he would have been more enthusiastic.

She turned to Manda, though, and found that the blond maid's brow was furrowed, though not with fear. Wykla had noticed that Manda seemed prone to periodic bouts of depression: a deep shade would cross her face when, say, she examined the insignia on Wykla's armor, or when she watched the girls of the town carrying the week's washing down to the river. She would grow silent for some minutes, her forehead would crease, and her sight would seem to be elsewhere.

Such was the case now, but Manda made an effort, and the shadow passed. "I obey with pleasure, my king," she said. "I could not go to Kingsbury in war, but at least I will travel there in peace."

But something about her tone made Wykla wonder which of the two she actually expected to find in Gryylth.

* * *

Wykla, Manda, and Helwych, traveling together, made worse time than had Wykla alone. The garrisons and villages of Gryylth, while keeping mounts ready and waiting for the use of the king's messengers, did not have enough for three, even if two members of the party had not once been enemies of the country.

But Wykla doubted that they could have bettered their speed even with a constant supply of fresh horses, for Helwych, used to sedentary study, found the going difficult. He did not complain, but his temper sharpened as the leagues passed, and when dusk caught the group near the fallen stones of the Circle, it was plain to his companions that he was through for the day.

Manda looked at the tumbled remains of the great monoliths, then at the dark clouds that were massing along the western horizon. "Do you wish to camp here?"

"I do not," said Wykla. "I would rather sleep among barrows." But as they watched, the sky to the west became noticeably darker, and the sunset turned the color of old blood. The clouds bothered Wykla, for they raised painful memories of magic and transformation.

"We may have no choice," said the Corrinian maid. "The ground here is rolling and open. The stones will be the best shelter we can find for some distance." Helwych muttered under his breath, and she smiled. "I do not think that our sorcerer is of a mind to continue."

"This place is safe enough," said Helwych. "The magic was spent months ago: there is not enough resident potency here to fill up a field mouse."

A wind from the west started up, turned cold.

"Are you sure, Helwych?"

"Of course I am sure," he said peevishly. "I am a sorcerer."

In the fading light, Wykla saw Manda cast her eyes upward. But the wind freshened, and it carried the scent of frost. "It seems," said Wykla, quoting a Corrinian proverb, "that we must eat the meal before us whether we like the meat or not."

Manda grinned at her, and she grinned back. They had grown together in Benardis, and to Wykla there now seemed little that she could not face with Manda at her side.

They camped among a tumble of stones that lay at a little distance from what had been the center of the monument. Out of the wind, and with a fire and something to eat, Helwych's spirits improved greatly, and he even began to joke about spells and other subjects that the warriors found incomprehensible. But the day's journey had been fatiguing, and he soon nodded and dropped off to sleep in mid-sentence.

"Clever of him," said Manda, "to thus avoid taking a watch."

"We could wake him."

"Would you really trust his judgment, friend Wykla?"

When they had first met, Manda had offered friendship, and although Wykla had said neither yes nor no, Manda had always addressed her as though the offer had been accepted. And Wykla realized that it had. Shyly, she held out her hand and grasped Manda's. "Actually, my friend, I do not. Let us divide the night between us."

"First watch!" Manda claimed it with a laugh. "Go to bed, king's daughter."

Wykla rolled herself in her blankets and watched her tall friend for a minute. "Was Darham serious, Manda? When he offered . . . ?"

"He was indeed."

"Why?"

Manda folded her arms and stood amid the fallen stones as though daring any intruder to approach. "He is that kind of man," she said. "And he knows you for what you are: a brave woman who is worthy of honor."

Wykla felt warm at the words, and she started to reply, but she opened her eyes and found that the sky was overcast, and that Manda was waking her for the second watch. "Not a soul stirring," said the Corrinian. "The weather is cold, but there is no sign of snow."

"It is late in the season for snow."

"Aye, and late in the night for sleep." Manda yawned and reached for her blankets. "Gods bless."

The wind had died down, and in the quiet darkness Wykla heard Manda's breathing deepen. The light of the low fire played softly with the sleeping woman's face and hair, and she lay with her eyes closed and her hands drawn up to her chin, looking much as she had in her house in Benardis when Wykla, awakening one morning with the dawn, had spent the first few minutes of light watching Manda . . . and wondering about herself.

Had Wykla been a man still, Manda was the kind of woman she would have desired for a mate. That choice, however, being forever fled from her, she recognized Manda as the kind of woman that she wanted to be. There was pain in Manda's past, to be sure, but there was pain in her own, too, and that shared history of sorrow did nothing but strengthen Wykla's admiration for her new-found friend. Whatever her past, Manda of Dubris had, seemingly, transcended it. Wykla of Burnwood could do the same.

Gently, she knelt over Manda's still form and laid a soft hand on the rounding of her hip. If she had still been a man . . .

She sighed and rose.

Clouds had blotted out the stars, but the air was transparent with a cold clarity that made the faint lights of the distant towns dance like sparks. And as Wykla stood with folded arms, keeping the late watch, her eye was caught by something that glittered out among the tumbled stones that surrounded the center of the ruined Circle.

Drawing her sword, she approached carefully. Her boots made hard, brittle sounds on the tongue of fused sand that stretched off along the Avenue, but the glitter stayed where it was, twinkling like a star and, she fancied, beckoning.

She shivered. Out where the light burned, Mernyl and Tireas had died, their bodies incinerated in a blaze of power. And Dythragor too . . .

Cautiously, she eased closer, peered over the heaped and shattered monoliths. Before her, thrusting up out of the earth, was a pale staff that gleamed as though bewound with moonlight. She recognized it: Mernyl's staff.

Almost unwillingly, she went forward and bent over it. Two thirds of its length was hidden in the earth, and the sorcerer's initial flared with diamond brilliance inches above the ground. Wykla hesitated; but then, on an impulse that she did not understand, her hand went around the bright wood, and she pulled.

The staff resisted, but voices seemed to sing in her ears, encouraging her, and she closed her eyes, set her feet and shoulders, and brought the muscles of her back and legs into the work.

The wood seemed to conform to her grip, and when an icy cold arose and began traveling up her bones, she opened her eyes to find that the staff was no longer a staff. An arm now protruded from the earth at her feet, its hand as white and cold as the finest marble. But it was animate, and its fingers held her firmly in their clasp.

Panic added to her strength, but the hand had locked her in a silent battle in the darkness: human against other-than-human, flesh and blood against the spectral existence of the undead. Wykla could not speak, she could not even scream, and the only sound was that of her gasping breaths, hoarse and hollow in the frosty air.

Dropping her sword, she clasped her free hand about her captive wrist, closed her eyes again, strained until her joints cracked and her muscles turned white hot with pain. Head thrown back, mouth set in a grimace, she pulled.

The white hand gave a trifle.

She looked down again, and was almost unsurprised to find the face of Mernyl gleaming up at her from the weeds and grass. His wide, staring eyes appeared to see everything and yet nothing, their blankness both omniscient and blind.

"Mernyl," she whispered, finding her voice at last. "It is I: Wykla of Burnwood. Pray, do not hurt me."

The eyes in the pallid face did not change, but the lips struggled as if to speak.

"Mernyl . . . please. I am changed, but you know that. You must recognize me . . . you must . . ."

The face brightened for an instant, she saw the lips form her name, and the hand gave a barely perceptible squeeze as of encouragement. The voice of the dead sorcerer came to her ears suddenly: "Pull, Wykla! Pull!"

The cold racked her lungs, and her body ached such that she was sure she would cry out, but she heaved mightily against the grip of the dead sorcerer. The hand yielded again. Then more.

Release was a flash of white fire. She had a brief impression that she held, once again, a staff of wood, and then she fell into darkness.

❖ CHAPTER 5 ❖

The clouds that had gathered over the mountains to the west of Kingsbury formed a solid mass that blocked out the late afternoon sunlight, and, as night fell, they encroached upon the rest of the sky, eclipsing the stars, bringing a cold that reached into the town with hands of ice.

It was with a sense of unease that Marrget regarded them, for they reminded her too strongly of the darkness that once had gathered about the Tree and launched itself at the wartroops of Gryylth in a bolt of slaughter and transformation. Here there was no Tree, but the darkness was the same, and something . . . *something* had killed Bandon.

Night found her keeping watch at the door of her house as though she might thereby guard the slumbering town. Her sword was at hand, but swords, she knew, would be useless if Kingsbury had been targeted for the same kind of devastation that had overtaken Bandon. Her watch this night, therefore, was not so much for Kingsbury as for herself, a defiant shake of the fist at all the unknown powers that could level a town in an evening, destroy an army, or change a man into a woman.

These days, though, she was having increasing difficulty remembering that she had indeed been a man. She could recall old images, past thoughts, previous actions, but they all seemed to her to belong to another person: a Marrget of Crownhark who knew only war

and soldiering, who was content with the rough camaraderie of arms and men, who thought of little beyond honesty and orders.

More clear and immediate was her knowledge of the
woman who had taken his place, who had fought for
survival on a summer night, who had triumphed only
to find that the days of easy decisions and shallow con-
tentments were over. That she was a warrior in what
was still a man's land was a sufficient complication to
her existence, but her choice of life over death had
been concomitant with a deepening of emotion that
had turned each day into a puzzle to be solved.

And as she watched, sleepless, at the door of her
house, she turned the most recent piece of the puzzle
over in her mind. Since she had danced with Karthin
at the New Year Feast, and since he had wrapped his
large arms about her amid the ruins of Bandon, she
had found herself wondering how she might arrange
matters so that she could touch him again. Such rum-
inations were terrifying, but, unlike warriors, they
would not obey her orders to disperse. Nor did she
particularly wish them to. She tolerated their insub-
ordination because they brought into her cold existence a sense of warmth and belonging that she had
thought unattainable.

Were her thoughts and responses, she wondered,
those of a woman? Had she changed that much? Or
perhaps she had not changed, and the differences were
a result of her constant immersion in a new milieu,
seeing herself and being seen as female, living in a
body that possessed drives and desires that, moment
by moment, day by day, were awakening and growing.

Thunder cracked abruptly across the miles, and a
driving wind started up. Marrget reached for her
sword, but she could see nothing that might have responded to the threat of steel. Within minutes, though,
the wind had turned into a gale, and Kingsbury was
lost in the darkness and the storm. Marrget withdrew
into her house and shut the door. More thunder. More
wind.

She hung her sword on the wall and threw wood onto the fire. Old memories and new concerns banished sleep, but tears—silent, hidden, lonely—had been with her for a long time. As they were now.

That Karthin admired her, she knew well. He had treated her with courtesy since the first day they had met, apparently taking joy from the simple fact that she had consented to be his friend. But courtesy and friendship were not what she had come to want from him. They were a beginning, no more, and therefore she sat on a stool before the growing flames of the fire, put her face in her hands, and yielded to her confusion and her tears.

But there came a pounding on her door loud enough to be heard even over the wind and the thunder. "Marrget!"

Karthin. She started, not knowing whether to be glad or frightened. "I am here," she replied, but she knew that her voice would not carry over the storm. Rising, she unbarred the door, brought him inside, and shut out the battling elements.

He had obviously run all the way from the town, for he was breathing heavily, and cold sweat glistened on his forehead. He caught his breath for a moment and pushed his hair out of his face. "I saw firelight through your shutters."

"I could not sleep."

He looked much as he had when, after the battle at the Circle, he had stood before her, shy and uncertain, flowers in hand. "I know. I . . . I felt it."

"You did? Have I become so transparent now that you can read me a half league away?" He stood inches away from her. An excuse to touch him should have been easy to find, but she could think of none.

"Not transparent, Marrget. Just . . ." He did not seem to know what to do with his hands for a moment and finally hooked his thumbs in his belt. "You have been crying."

She dashed a sleeve across her eyes. "A passing thought, Karthin." Gazing at him so as to fathom both his appearance and his strange comments, she saw that his own eyes were red and swollen. "But so have you."

"I will not say it was the wind." He laughed sheepishly.

Facing one another, they fidgeted, groped for words. "You . . . you miss your people, perhaps?" Marrget shoved the question out to fill the aching silence. He was so close. But what, exactly, did she want of him? What did she want of herself? Her thoughts flashed ahead to the consequences of her desires, and her mouth went dry.

"I miss them sometimes."

"It must be hard to . . . live alone . . ." Her words trailed off, and she caught herself gazing at him as he was at her. With a gasp, she straightened. "I have become a poor host," she said, taking his arm and guiding him toward a seat by the fire. "Pray, forgive my discourtesy. I have not had much company in recent months."

Her hand was on his bare skin. Beneath her slender fingers, his farmer muscles were solid and strong. She felt dizzy.

"I would have gladly filled the lack," he said softly, covering her hand with his own, "had you asked."

He did not sit down. She did not let him. Her hand on his arm, she watched the fire as she had watched the gathering clouds: wondering what the night would bring. "What brings you to my door, friend?"

"Concern for you. I could see you from the town wall. You stood all afternoon, and when I tried to sleep, I knew you were still at your door. Cvinthil once called you Kingsbury's guardian, and perhaps he is right; but I worried when I saw that you did not rest . . . or even eat. And then when the wind and thunder came . . ." He smiled like a shy boy. "It must be hard to live alone."

"How else should I live?"

He swallowed uncomfortably. "I sometimes think . . . that . . ."

Marrget lifted her eyes to his face. His arm burned beneath her fingers. *Please speak, Karthin, else I shall surely bolt.*

He seemed to hear her thoughts. He seemed to hear everything. ''. . . that my being alone is a . . . passing thing.''

''Surely you will return home someday.''

''Someday . . .''

''But not soon,'' she said quickly.

''Nay. Not soon.'' His hand had tightened over hers. ''I would hope that I might find an end to my condition before I return to Corrin.''

Marrget could not think. She doubted that Karthin could either. They groped for one another's meanings like children in a game of blind-man's-buff. ''I wish you well,'' she managed.

''And I you.''

Silence again. The wind battered, the thunder roared. But the shutters and doors held. Karthin and Marrget were alone together, undisturbed.

''Why . . .'' Her jaw was trembling, adding a weakness to her voice that chagrined her. ''Why do you think it will end?''

He would not meet her eyes. ''There is a woman I know.''

''Oh.''

She let go of his arm and started to turn away, but he detained her with a hand on her shoulder, and then he was standing behind her, folding her in his arms, burying his face in her hair. ''Let me tell you of her,'' he said, stumbling through the words as though afraid that he would be struck dead for uttering them. ''She is as brave and bright as the noblest warrior of the land, and she wears her loneliness like a badge of honor: as indeed it is, for it was hard won. Sharp and deadly as a sword, she is nonetheless lovely, and . . .''

Marrget was rooted. *Is this how it happens? Oh you Gods of Gryylth, I have changed.*

''. . . and I believe—or at least I hope—that she feels for me as I do for her.''

The wind blew so that the house shook, and the brilliance of the lightning found its way in through the smallest cracks as Marrget grappled with thoughts that slid away from her like fish in a pond.

She could deny her feelings no longer, for to pretend to other emotions was a falsehood that she would not allow to stain her honor. Turning within his embrace, she filled her arms with him, clung to him as though by doing so she could slake a deadly thirst. Teeth clenched, eyes shut tight, she laid her face against his broad chest. "A fortunate woman indeed," she whispered hoarsely.

His lips were inches from her ear. "But I do not know if she will have me."

Lifting her head, she looked up at him. Her hands clutched at his arms, slid up to his throat, his face. *I do not know what to do. What is it that a woman does now?* "I . . ."

Had Karthin been a Gryylthan man, she would, she knew, have been bedded by now, dragged between the sheets regardless of her feelings. But Karthin was of Corrin, and his customs were different. In dance, in life, in love, women of his country made their own choices.

Perhaps, then, this strange territory through which she wandered was not so unknown after all. She straightened, swallowed, took a deep breath. Unaccountably, she found that she was smiling. "I will have you, friend Karthin. And, if you wish, I will . . ." Fright made her tremble, and she wondered that she had the strength to go on. But Karthin was smiling now also, and his strong arms seemed to uplift her in more than body. " . . . I will have you in my bed."

And, later, lying beside him, warm and spent and heedless of the storm, she discovered that she ached still. But now she ached with a fullness that made loneliness seem as distant as those days in which, swaggering, thoughtless . . . and unloved . . . she had lived another life, with another body, and, seemingly, another soul.

* * *

The clouds were wrong.

Alouzon knew that they were wrong, knew from flying cheaply and on standby into bad weather and early hours that, no matter how dark and threatening clouds were when seen from below, from above, lit by the moon, they were invariably the purest, ethereal, silver-white. They were not gray like these roiling gouts of darkness that seemed so opaque that the lightning they contained could manifest as no more than a lurid glow.

She leaned forward toward the Dragon's ear. "What's below us?"

"Gryylth."

"I mean the clouds. They're not regular clouds, are they?"

"I . . . do not know what they are, my lady."

Alouzon glared at the back of its iron-colored head. Silbakor knew, she was sure, and knew well. "How am I supposed to do anything in Gryylth if you won't tell me what the fuck's going on?"

"There is terror behind us, Dragonmaster. It is better for you to be Alouzon for now."

"For now? Until you decide to jerk us back to L.A.?"

Us. She stiffened and thought of the woman who sat behind her. Helen Addams was a part of Gryylth now, a part of everything.

From ahead and below came a flash of white light, and, in an area a mile in diameter, the gray clouds recoiled and dissipated as though from a concussion. As the Dragon swept over the clearing, Alouzon looked down and saw the remains of the Circle. Near the center blazed a flame like that of a newborn star.

Banking steeply, Silbakor dropped past the walls of gray confusion so fast that Alouzon's vision blurred. Not until the great wings flared and the adamantine talons reached for the grass did her sight return; and then she saw, in the bright, cold light, the body of a woman crumpled against a fallen monolith.

Wykla.

She turned around to meet the gaze of black eyes in a pale, aquiline face. "Helen," she said, wondering if the name still applied, "someone's in trouble. I may need you."

As though entranced, the woman nodded slowly. Alouzon leaped from the Dragon's back, broke her descent with a roll, and came up running.

Wykla lay like a discarded doll, and in her hand was a staff that burned with stellar radiance. It looked vaguely familiar, but Alouzon tossed it aside peremptorily, her attention fixed wholly on the still form of the girl. Pushing the amber hair away from the still face, she looked in vain for signs of life. "Wykla! Wykla!"

No response. No heartbeat. No breathing.

She looked up. The strange woman of sable and silver was watching her. "Do you know CPR?"

Helen's fists went to her temples and she dragged in a breath as though it were the first she had taken in an hour. "Yes," she said, her voice firm and young. "I do. I took a class at the Women's Building. Any broken bones? No? Then get her on her back."

In a moment, Wykla was stretched out, and Alouzon was leaning rhythmically on her chest, taking on the duties that the young woman's traumatized heart had temporarily abandoned. Helen was on her knees, bent over Wykla's head, supplying breath.

Silbakor was right: there was terror behind her. It had reached into Los Angeles and attempted to kill Suzanne Helling and Helen Addams, and now, Alouzon suspected, it had wrapped a slimy paw around Wykla of Burnwood. As she shoved blood through Wykla's veins, she berated herself for her long absence. Maybe, if she had not been so much of a coward, if she had returned to Gryylth sooner, if she had dared Vaylle, if she had looked for the Sacred Cup that promised everything, this would not have happened.

"Anything, Helen?"

"Nothing." Helen sucked in air and put it into Wykla. "Keep going."

If. If. If. Maybes. Might-have-beens. Alouzon was still living with them.

I'm not letting you go, Wykla. I couldn't live with myself.

"Push, dammit," Helen snapped.

Tears starting out, Alouzon bore down on Wykla's chest.

A voice, cold and angry, rang in the frosty air. "Who are you, and what are you doing to my friend?"

Alouzon looked up on a backswing. It was a woman of about Wykla's age, her hair yellow, her sword unsheathed. She wore the armor and insignia of Corrin.

Helen's voice was just as cold. "We're trying to save her life." Wykla's body twitched, and the black-haired woman took a moment to pry one of her eyelids open. "Pupils constricting. I think she may make it."

Wykla shuddered and then coughed: a sick, racking sound as though she had been touched with a cattle prod. Helen felt for a pulse and sighed. "Thank God."

"Gods," murmured Alouzon. She sat back on her heels, wiping sweat from her face, feeling her own heart throw itself against her ribs. Before her, Wykla gasped in labored, raw breaths. She might have been gagging on the air, but she was breathing, and she was alive.

Alouzon reached out and took one of the small, fine hands in her own. *I'm here, Wykla. It's going to be all right.* She looked up at the blond woman who stood over them, sword in hand. "I'm Alouzon Dragonmaster," she said, ignoring Helen's bewildered stare. "And you?"

"Manda. Of Dubris." Her eyes had widened.

"Don't worry, Manda. We're friends." Alouzon leaned over Wykla. "You're going to be all right, lady."

Helen was cradling Wykla's head. She nodded. "Her pulse is strong, but she's in shock. We'll need blankets."

Manda sheathed her sword. "I will fetch them."

Wykla became aware of Alouzon, and she reached up and wrapped her arms about the Dragonmaster's neck. Alouzon held her, rocking her as though she were a child who had awakened from a long nightmare.

"I found Mernyl's staff," Wykla said between gasps. "I tried to pull it out. It turned into a hand. Mernyl was there. He told me to pull."

Helen put a hand on her head. "Easy, honey. There's time to talk when you feel better." Her eyes met Alouzon's. "Dragonmaster? Alouzon?"

"They call me that here. Your ex was named Dythragor."

"Sol? What the hell does he have to do with this?"

Alouzon waved the question away with a shake of her head and was grateful that Manda returned just then with the blankets. Together they bundled Wykla up. "I can build a fire here," said Manda. "Though there is one a short distance away."

Alouzon was on her knees beside Wykla, holding her hand. "I don't think I want to move her."

The glowing staff lay a few feet away. Manda regarded it as though it were a serpent. "That bitch's whelp Helwych said that this place was safe. What does he know of sorcery?"

Helen was stroking Wykla's head. "Maybe little," she said. "Maybe nothing at all. But this place is safe: fear not."

Her voice possessed a caring warmth that was at odds with her usual cynicism. And her turn of phrase . . . "Helen?" said Alouzon.

Helen's tone hardened. "I said it was all right." She looked up and glanced about her at the tumbled stones and the burning staff. "What kind of place is this, anyway?"

Despite Wykla's story, there was now no sign of Mernyl, but Manda had positioned herself between Wykla and the staff, and her manner indicated that further visitants would approach only over her corpse.

She looked up at Helen's question. "Is the lady Kyria a stranger to Gryylth, then?"

Helen looked blank. "Kyria?"

"So the Dragon called you when I gathered the blankets."

Garb, speech, and now her name. Helen Addams was being thoroughly replaced. Alouzon could not guess for what purpose. "Relax," she said. "Everyone gets a new name here."

Helen looked at them both, her brow furrowed, then down at herself. She scrutinized her palms, shoved back her flowing sleeves and examined her arms. Plainly frightened, she touched her unfamiliar face and plucked at her black hair that hung to her waist. "Anybody . . . anybody got a mirror?" She was shaking.

"Manda," said Alouzon, "take care of Wykla." She moved to Helen and took her by the shoulders. "It's all right. You're OK."

Helen's eyes were angry and frightened both. "But I'm not me. Who the hell am I?"

"You're . . ." Alouzon let go of her arms and shrugged. She hoped that the Dragon would have some explanations. "You're the lady Kyria."

"Wonderful." There was ice in Helen's tone. "What is this place?"

"Gryylth."

"Nice name. What did Sol have to do with it?"

Again the question. Alouzon met it head on. "He made it."

Helen sagged as though struck, but she held herself up. She had weathered a marriage to Solomon Braithwaite, the preternatural destruction of her house, and changes of appearance and name. One more insanity would trouble her little. "You want to elaborate a little, honey?"

"You didn't know Sol as well as you thought. When you left him, he tried to kill himself."

The black eyes flickered.

"He didn't make it, but his mind took off and made Gryylth."

Helen laughed abruptly, a violent, derisive expression of contempt. "Sol Braithwaite," she said. "God of Gryylth. Sure."

"Look, *honey*," Alouzon snapped, "just believe it. I've put a lot of blood, sweat, and tears into this place. I know it's real."

Helen blinked at the outburst, looked at herself again, and touched one hand with another as though to confirm that what she saw and felt was indeed herself. "Yes . . . yes, I guess you do," she said slowly. "And when Sol died, you got stuck with this, right?"

"You got it."

"Why was I dragged in?"

"I don't know. The Dragon has its reasons."

Helen gestured. "The Dragon's gone."

Alouzon looked. It was true. The field was empty. She passed a hand over her face and cursed Silbakor silently. "It figures."

The silver borders of Helen's robes glittered in the light of the glowing staff. "Crazy," she said, plucking at her hair again. "I'm not sure I want a mirror."

But Alouzon had bent over the staff, squinting into the light that still poured from the wood. Wykla had called it Mernyl's staff, and it did indeed look like it. In fact . . .

Gritting her teeth, she reached down and picked it up. It burned with a cold heat, and it seemed to writhe in her grip like a living thing, but her attention was taken by the letter—Mernyl's initial—that glittered like starlight a third of the way from the top.

Slowly, so slowly that she rubbed her eyes to see whether she were imagining it, the letter was changing. It blurred, flowed, established new lines. When it solidified, the initial was no longer Mernyl's.

K

She looked over at Helen, who was gently touching her face. She had been given robes of black and silver. She looked like a sorceress. But she had no staff.

"Kyria," said Alouzon quickly.

"Yes?"

Off to the west, lightning flashed, and a dull boom
of thunder followed a few seconds later. Cradling the
staff in both hands, Alouzon approached Helen, offering it. Helen stared at it with black eyes. "What are
you giving it to me for?"

"It's got your initial on it."

"I . . ." Helen laughed nervously, backed away. "I
don't think I want to get involved in this. Thanks just
the same."

"You're already involved. Take it."

Helen's anger had been temporarily masked by
shock, but now it flared once more. "I'm not letting
Sol control my life."

"Take it."

"Nor you either."

"Take it. You haven't been in control since you
heard Sol screaming. This might be your only hope of
controlling anything for a while."

Lighting. Thunder.

The light from the staff flickered over Helen's face,
touching it with a softness that seemed to quell the
anger in her eyes. She stared at it, wondering, fascinated, a child faced with a magical toy on grandmoth-
er's knickknack shelf . . .

Decisively, she reached, grasped it with both hands
and swung it into a vertical position. Awe, reluctance,
and willingness flitted over her face as though she were
a woman faced with a new lover, and when its light
flared, dimmed, and at last faded, she brought it down
and grounded the butt in the earth, her hand wrapped
gracefully about the pale wood.

Kyria closed her eyes and sighed. "OK. It's mine."

Out to the west, the clouds were agitated. They
swirled and roiled and then, suddenly lowering, they
rushed eastward as though impelled by colossal detonations. A cold wind gusted across the rolling land,
and Alouzon sensed that there was nothing natural
about the storm.

She was reluctant to move Wykla, who was still
shocky and disoriented, but the approaching weather

left her no choice. Together with Manda, she carried the girl back to the camp and nestled her in the shelter of the fallen monoliths. Cradling her staff, Kyria followed as though in a dream.

Manda glared at Helwych. The sorcerer was still curled up by the fire, asleep. "A fine wizard," she said. "With all the magic in the world raging about him, he lies there like a poisoned sheep."

"Where did he come from?" said Alouzon.

"Corrin. He was Tireas's apprentice. Matters in Gryylth caused Cvinthil to request his aid."

"What kind of matters?"

"Vaylle."

Alouzon felt sick. It was as she had feared. Dragonmaster: what a farce. She was afraid to ask what had happened. She would find out soon enough.

The land tonight seemed poised, tense. The clouds had covered the sky like the lid of a coffin. The wind blew into a gale, then abruptly died.

Two lights flared in the west and drew closer, the clouds rushing after them in splayed fingers of darkness. The lights drew nearer, took on shape and form.

Alouzon cried out.

The first light was Silbakor, its black body and wings limned in flaming red, its eyes blazing yellow. The second, though, was something else. Although shaped like the Great Dragon, it was white, snow white, and it glowed faintly with a nimbus of blue. Its eyes were blue, also—black-blue—shading into the violet and ultraviolet so as to be more felt than seen.

And, mouth open, teeth bared in an unheard scream, it was closing on Silbakor.

Silbakor turned suddenly and drove for the heart of its antithesis, talons reaching, eyes flaming with expressionless passion. Folding its wings, it stooped on the pale horror that pursued it and struck with an incandescence that split the darkness and knocked Alouzon and her companions flat.

Half blinded by the light and concussion, she called: "Wykla! Someone protect Wykla!"

"She is well," she heard Manda say.

Helwych started up with a yawp. "My staff: where is my staff?"

"Where you dropped it, fool," Manda growled.

Above, the Dragon and the White Worm were circling, looking for openings. White-blue, black-red, they wound through the air, talons ready, tails thrashing, teeth eager.

Light, suddenly, from the ground.

Kyria was on her feet, the staff burning fiercely in her hands. A shimmer grew about her as she swung it up and aimed it at the Worm.

Silbakor's opponent noticed, turned, and dived for the Circle, eyes glaring invisibly. Adamantine claws reached for Kyria, and the worm bore down on her like a piece of falling sky. Desperately, Silbakor pursued.

But Kyria was faster.

Violet erupted from the staff, flashing out in a shaft of brilliance that struck the Worm squarely in the face and smashed it back into Silbakor's waiting claws. For an instant, they tumbled in free fall as they ripped and tore at one another, each seeking a lethal advantage.

Silbakor's talons tightened about the Worm's throat. A sound as of far-off screaming stretched through the air like a taut wire.

Kyria was ready with her staff. "Back off and give me another shot, Silbakor!"

The Worm drove a wing into Silbakor's eyes and managed to free itself, but Kyria's bolt seared the air about it as it struggled to regain altitude. Spun around by the violet impact, it gave up the attack and turned back toward the west with heavy wingbeats.

Alouzon saw the Dragon start to follow. "Let it go, Silbakor!"

The voice that thrummed in her head was possessed of an unearthly calm, as though whatever passion it contained was beyond the comprehension of mortals. *I cannot, my lady. I must destroy it. I have no choice.*

"Silbakor!"

The White Worm was speeding westward, back into the clouds and the lightning, and Silbakor was following quickly. They turned into indistinct patches of light, faded with distance, and finally vanished.

and rippled it to himself. The wind blew it away, he said.

"And none d now that you fell asleep. Ted on the woods are a dell will

❖ CHAPTER 6 ❖

The clouds dissipated quickly, withdrawing toward the west in the wake of the Dragons. The sky was clear and cold; the stars shone quietly.

Alouzon stood, shaking, wanting nothing so much as to go off to some isolated corner and be sick. Since she had assumed the Guardianship, Silbakor had been a constant in her life, something that, like the air she breathed or the ground under her feet, was an axiom of existence, a balance to the land that Solomon Braithwaite had created.

Silbakor was Gryylth. The White Worm, though . . .

Her knees buckled under her, but she had to face it. She had not gone to Vaylle, and therefore Vaylle had come to her.

All right. I'll do it. I took Gryylth. So I'll take the rest, too. And I'm gonna find that fucking Grail, no matter what.

Lifting her head as though to offer her vow to the nameless Gods of the land, she found herself looking at a lank-haired young man who was searching the grass in the light of the dying fire. He tripped over a piece of firewood and cursed under his breath, but his voice was choked and husky.

"Behind you, Helwych," said Manda. She was still with Wykla—had, in fact, shielded her with her own body.

Helwych turned, cried out, picked up a black staff

and clutched it to himself. "The wind blew it away," he said.

"You dropped it when you fell asleep."

"It was the wind." His voice was sharp, edged with hysteria.

Alouzon struggled to her feet. "Manda? Wykla?"

"We are both well," said the Corrinian maid.

"Hang on. I'll be there in a minute." With steps that dragged through the grass, she plodded over to Kyria. The sorceress was sitting on the ground, staring at the gleaming staff that rested across her knees.

"My God," she said, "I don't know how that happened. It just came over me . . . I swear . . ."

Alouzon squatted beside her. "It happens here, Kyria. Try to go with it. Back home, I cut myself on butter knives. Here, I do fairly well with a sword." She winced at her own words. The student agitators had done fairly well with slogans and speeches; the National Guard had done fairly well with M-1s; and Alouzon Dragonmaster did fairly well with a sword. So casual she was about it now!

"Am I . . . am I supposed to be some kind of magician?"

Sickness was still clawing at Alouzon's belly. "That staff used to belong to a man named Mernyl. That was what he was: a magician. A sorcerer. He died trying to save the land. I guess he wanted you to have it."

"To do what? Blow Dragons away?"

If the White Worm were anything like Silbakor, even the full energy of the Tree would not have affected it. But Kyria's blast had wounded it. The potencies that the sorceress controlled, therefore, had to be commensurate with the very forces that created and sustained Gryylth. She could indeed blow Dragons away. She could possibly do much more.

Alouzon shifted uneasily. "Yeah," she said, trying to sound noncommittal. "And with that Worm running around, I'm kind of glad you can."

Kyria remained bent over the staff, absently stroking

the pale wood. She did not speak for some time. Then: "Silbakor's the only way back, right?"

"As far as I know."

"So we're stuck here with the White Worm."

"Yeah."

"Did Sol make that, too?"

"Kyria, tonight's the first I've seen of it." *Listen to this double-talk. I'm getting as bad as Silbakor.*

The sorceress continued to caress the staff, and Alouzon could feel her anger as though she stood next to a hot stove. "I want out of this," said Kyria. "I want out of this so bad that I'd be willing to dig up Sol's body and put a stake through his heart just so I could be sure that he'd never bother me again." She gripped the staff hard, and the wood responded with a flare of rainbow hues. "He took my life, took my body; and now he wants to take everything else by making me a part of his little fairy tale."

"Kyria—"

Kyria stared at the staff and dropped it back into her lap. Its light faded. "I'm sorry you got involved, Alouzon."

The Dragonmaster looked away. She could not find the courage to tell Kyria about her own part in this world. "Don't mention it," she said, the evasion rank on her tongue. "It's part of my job."

"What do I have to do to get back? Find the Dragon?"

"That'd be a good start, I guess." The glittering, black eyes held her in their gaze, demanded elaboration. "There's a land across the sea. It's called Vaylle. I think we'll find Silbakor there. And the White Worm." She thought of the hound-like thing that had leaped at her throat. "And God knows what else."

Kyria did not flinch. "I'll be ready."

The simple piece of wood on Kyria's lap had channeled the energy that made and unmade worlds. Alouzon shuddered. "Yeah. I guess you will."

In the silence, she heard footsteps in the grass behind her. Helwych stood there, black staff in hand. He had apparently mastered his terror. "I . . . would not be thought discourteous," he said, his gaze flickering involuntarily to the staff on Kyria's lap. "I am Helwych, sorcerer to the King of Corrin."

Alouzon eyed him up and down. Darham, she thought, was obviously hard up for magic. Aloud, she said: "Pleased to meet you. I'm Alouzon Dragonmaster." She laughed, softly and ironically, and glanced up at the sky. "Welcome to Gryylth."

"Indeed, I had not thought my arrival would be the cause of so much commotion." He was still looking at Kyria's staff.

In the distance, Manda called out: "Do not smite him, Dragonmaster. He thinks overmuch of himself at times. It is a failing . . . like scabies."

Helwych whirled. "One more word out of you, woman, and—"

"And what?" Kyria's soft voice cut the night air like an obsidian blade. She rose, her hand easy on her staff, her long hair rustling across her robes. "Let me introduce myself, sonny boy. My name is Kyria. I don't like to hear women addressed in that tone of voice."

Helwych froze. He had seen what Kyria could do. "My . . . my apologies, lady."

Her glance was level, even, unforgiving. "All right."

"And mine also, mistress sorceress," said Manda. "My words were cruel and unjustified."

"Don't mention it." Kyria looked at Alouzon. "It looks like I get some respect around here. Amazing. How did Sol ever let *that* get by?"

"Sol's dead, Kyria."

"I don't believe that any more. Where do *you* think little tin gods go when they die?" With a swish of robes, she crossed the camp to Manda and Wykla. "How is the patient?"

Alouzon blinked. Kyria's tone had abruptly softened. Her voice held nothing but nurture and comfort.

"Weak, my lady," said Wykla. "I fear you think ill of me."

"Peace, child," said Kyria. "I do not think ill of you."

Alouzon approached as the sorceress knelt and rested her hand on Wykla's forehead. A quiet amber light glowed at the meeting of flesh and flesh. Kyria's eyes were closed in concentration, but her face looked relaxed, as though, at the end of a day of hard work, she had slipped into a soft bed.

In a minute, she stood up. Her black eyes were clear, untroubled. "Be changed," she said to Wykla. "Be healed. Rise when you wish."

Alouzon was staring, but Kyria regarded her calmly. "Did you think that I hated everyone?"

Alouzon had the feeling that she was suddenly facing a different person. "Uh . . . no . . ."

"Good." A flash, as of pain, crossed Kyria's face, and she lifted a hand to her forehead. "I . . ." Her voice hardened. "I wanted kids. Sol took that away, too."

"Kyria?"

She shook her head violently. "Don't bother me. Just leave me alone. We'll go to Vaylle tomorrow, right?"

"We'll stop at Kingsbury first. That's the capital. Cvinthil is the king."

"Sol put the men in charge, as usual." Kyria dropped her hand, looked at Manda and Wykla, then back to Alouzon. "I'm surprised he didn't stick the women at home . . . in chains." She started to walk away.

Alouzon reached down a hand. Wykla took it, her grip as firm as ever. "Almost," murmured the Dragonmaster. "But not quite."

Kyria did not seem to hear. She went off by herself, sat down on the ground, and bent over her staff again. Alouzon could not be sure whether she meditated or wept, but suspected that she did both.

They set off for Kingsbury before dawn, the women doubling up on horses, Helwych riding alone. Tireas's

apprentice grumbled quietly about the early hours, but
Kyria, mounted behind Manda, silenced him with a
look.

He seemed as pathetically friendly towards the sorceress as he was afraid of her. Alternately trying to
make conversation with Manda and Kyria and retreating off by himself when he met with nothing but monosyllables and brusque comments, he seemed almost
appeasing in his conduct.

"He's a big, overgrown puppy," Alouzon said to
herself. If he had possessed a tail, she was sure that
he would have been wagging it at the sorceress.

"My lady?" said Wykla, sitting behind her. Kyria's
healing abilities were as great as her destructive powers. Wykla was well and strong, and her blue eyes gave
no sign of her near encounter with death.

"Helwych. Look at him."

Wykla watched him for a few minutes, then stifled
a giggle. "Indeed. He seems such."

For a minute, Alouzon let Vaylle and the White
Worm fade into the future. Time for them later. For
now, she was with Wykla. And ahead were Marrget
and Cvinthil and Santhe, the women of the wartroop
. . . Friends. The only friends she truly had.

"So how are you these days, Wykla?"

"By the favor of the Gods, lady, I am well."

"Happy?"

She felt Wykla rest her head against her back. "I
cannot say, lady. I am often confused."

Alouzon had committed herself to the Grail. She
would not willingly leave this world without finding it.
And though that inner promise should have left her
queasy with the thought of the terrors and hardships
and, yes, killings that lay ahead, still, she felt hopeful.
The Grail glowed warm in the back of her mind, beckoning, echoing her own words back to her in golden
tones: *It's going to be all right.*

"Yeah," she said softly to the winter landscape.
"Yeah. Maybe it is."

"My lady?"

"One of these days, Wykla, I think you're going to be happy. And maybe someday you'll be glad you're a woman."

She glanced behind. Wykla's blue eyes were thoughtful. "I hope for the best," she said. "And sometimes . . ." She looked over at Manda, who sat before Kyria as though riding with a porcupine. "And sometimes, Dragonmaster, I think I might have reason to hope."

"Call me Alouzon, Wykla. You've earned it."

Wykla grinned and hugged her.

Darham had been generous with provisions, and there was plenty for five when they stopped for food and rest. Alouzon chatted with Wykla and Manda and did her best to be polite to Helwych—though the young man's quirky mix of bravado and uncertainty set her nerves on edge—but Kyria kept her distance, wandering off alone, treading the dead, winter grass with a measured pace, her hood up and her head bent as though in thought.

The party arrived in Kingsbury amid the early shadows of a winter dusk. Unlike Dythragor, Alouzon eschewed pomp and display, and hardly any one noticed or recognized them save for the guards at the edge of town.

But halfway up the street to the Hall, a dark-haired woman stood waiting, her bright blue mantle a pleasing contrast to the shades of gray and brown about her. In her arms she held a sleeping infant, well bundled against the cold. At her side was a thin warrior.

"Greetings, Dragonmaster," said Seena. "Welcome home."

Home. The word raised a lump in Alouzon's throat. She wished that she had a home. "Hello, Seena. You look well."

In truth, she did. No longer bound to her house, Cvinthil's wife had blossomed. She stood taller than Alouzon remembered, and her smile was open, her eyes frank. "I saw you coming," she said. "Cvinthil knows also, and is waiting for you, but I am afraid that business will leave scant time for proper welcomes. So I thought to greet you properly, so as to make up for . . ." Her smile turned a little sad, and she freed a hand and produced a spray of dried flowers from beneath her cloak. " . . . for the first time we met."

She offered the flowers to Alouzon. "Gods bless, Dragonmaster." She nodded to the other riders. "Gods bless, all of you."

Alouzon took the flowers. "Gods bless, Seena. Thanks." She had thought that the slender warrior who accompanied the queen was a young man, but she suddenly realized that Seena's attendant was Relys. "Relys," she said, reaching down, "how are you?"

Relys shook hands, her face harsh in spite of its beauty. "Well enough, and cold enough, Dragonmaster. Let me add my welcome to my queen's."

Alouzon understood: Seena now had a bodyguard. "There's been trouble, then."

"Some of our people have had difficulty accepting Cvinthil's decrees regarding the womenfolk." Alouzon saw Kyria lift her head as Relys continued. "There have been . . . incidents."

"Like?"

Wykla spoke up. "A man tried to rape me, Alouzon. He failed. Other women have not been so fortunate."

Manda muttered an oath. Her eyes had narrowed. "Did you kill him?"

Wykla hesitated. Then: "I did, Manda."

"Good."

There was an odd savor in Manda's voice, and Relys eyed her for a moment. "There is resentment toward the new ways," said the lieutenant. "And, after Bandon was destroyed . . ."

Alouzon froze. Bandon.

". . . the king decided to take precautions."

She steeled herself. "Bandon? Destroyed?"

"Aye. Wiped out in the space of an hour, it seems. Wykla, did you not tell the Dragonmaster the news?"

Alouzon shook her head. "I didn't ask, Relys."

"We do not know what happened," said Wykla. "From the report, it sounded as though sorcery was involved. Cvinthil sent me to Darham for aid."

Helwych sat straighter on his horse, and he glanced sidelong at Kyria. The sorceress, though, had left her hood up, and her face was no more than a pale blur in the failing light. Only her eyes were distinct: they were focused on Seena and her child with an expression of longing that made Helwych's envies seem puerile.

Alouzon swallowed both her nausea and her wonder. "OK. It looks like you're in good hands, Seena."

Seena put an arm about Relys's waist. It was a womanly gesture, and Relys looked uncomfortable. "I know that well, Dragonmaster. These times are hard, and fearful, but the women of my land must see that it is nonetheless good to walk abroad, to meet their brothers as equals, to know that they are respected. I am myself timid, but I am their queen, and therefore I must be an example to them. Relys allows me to continue to do that." She smiled at her bodyguard. "And she is also, in turn, an example to me."

Relys tried to keep the harshness in her face as Seena turned back to Alouzon. "If you will stay in our house while you are in Kingsbury," said the queen, "you will honor my husband and myself. Ayya wishes to see you again, and . . ." She smiled tenderly at the infant she held. "I am sure that Vill will be delighted, too."

Home, and babies, and all the common things that went into a lifetime, whether in Gryylth or America. Alouzon felt the lump rise again. Here she was loved. Here she was accepted. If she had any kind of a home, she supposed, it was in Gryylth. "I'll be there. Thanks."

Seena bowed. A slight nod of the head, a smile: the acknowledgment of an equal. Alouzon was flattered, and in spite of the news of Bandon, she watched Seena leave with a feeling of warmth and affection. The land she guarded was changing. And at least some of the changes were good.

Kyria spoke suddenly. "What decrees was she talking about, Alouzon?"

Wykla answered. "My lady Kyria, the women of Gryylth have only recently been given freedom. Until a year and a half ago, they were ruled by their husbands and confined to their houses."

Kyria looked about herself as though she had suddenly walked into a trap. "What kind of . . ." Abruptly, she turned, puzzled. "But you don't act like you were ever housebound, Wykla."

Wykla was silent for a moment. "My lady," she said simply, "I was not always a woman."

Kyria looked blank, but Alouzon gave her horse a light kick and continued up the street to the Hall, noting, as she rode through the gate, that one of the guards glanced fearfully at Wykla and then quickly looked away. He sported a black eye and a vicious cut on his cheek.

Some of the changes were good. But most were difficult.

Cvinthil was indeed waiting for them, and Santhe was with him. They came forward to embrace Alouzon. "My friend, you come in time of need," said the king.

"Yeah . . . I got that impression."

"You bring others."

"Just one. Wykla brought the rest. This is Kyria, a . . ." She looked at her companion. Appraisingly, coolly, Kyria was examining the Hall and the people in it.

Kyria returned her glance. "Go ahead."

"She's a sorceress," said Alouzon. "Mernyl passed his staff to her."

Cvinthil did not comprehend at first. "Mernyl has been dead these eighteen months."

"Yeah. That's what we all thought."

Santhe's eyes twinkled. "It seems that, for sorcerers, such difficulties are not insurmountable." He bowed to Kyria. "Welcome to Hall Kingsbury, lady. I trust you will not find us as tedious as the Dragonmaster did when first she arrived."

Kyria almost smiled, and with an uncharacteristic attempt at civility, she nodded to him. "Thank you."

Wykla introduced Manda and Helwych. Manda was polite but distant. Up until a short time ago, these people had been her enemies; and judging from the expressions of some of the newer men of the King's Guard, many Gryylthans shared her recollections and her caution. Helwych, on the other hand, drew himself up and tried to look confident, but compared with Kyria's easy grace and Manda's assurance, he seemed foolish.

Alouzon looked for Marrget, but the captain was not in the Hall. "Fear not, Dragonmaster," Santhe explained, "she is coming." He smiled conspiratorially. "She is, I believe, in bed."

"This early?"

His smile broadened.

Cvinthil formally welcomed all his guests, making special acknowledgment of Manda and Helwych. "I am glad," he said to them, "that the people of Corrin feel free now to visit their neighbor."

Alouzon could wait no longer. "What happened to Bandon?"

Cvinthil told her, and Wykla added firsthand details about the ruined town. Alouzon listened with growing alarm, and a look at Kyria confirmed that she was not alone in drawing certain nightmarish parallels and conclusions.

Alouzon did not speak when they were done. Kyria did, though. "It sounds like an air attack," she said. "Missiles, guns, napalm, the whole works." She turned to Alouzon. "What kind of place is this, honey?"

What kind of place? Unfinished. Fragmented. Warped. A world at the mercy of its creators' inmost

terrors. Alouzon passed a hand over her face and stared
into Seena's flowers as though to reassure herself that
there was still wholeness and sanity in the world. The
words she had spoken over Bandon came back to her:
*You ought to be burned down. And the ground sown
with salt. And if I ever get those kids out* . . .

"Any survivors?" she choked.

"Some of the children, Dragonmaster," replied
Santhe. He kept his voice low.

Alouzon felt the tears welling up. She heard Kyria
asking: "Are the kids all right? Are they being taken
care of?" Cvinthil explained his provisions for the orphans, and the sorceress swung back to Alouzon. "So
what the hell's going on?" she demanded. "Who's going around napalming kids?"

Alouzon shook her head. She had to lie again. "I
don't know, Kyria."

"You don't know much."

A murmur went through the hall at Kyria's words.
The sorceress looked up, her expression icy. "Pardon
me for living, boys."

Cvinthil regarded her with uncertainty. "Dythragor
Dragonmaster introduced us to strange companions. I
see that the tradition is being upheld."

"I didn't ask to get sucked into this," said Kyria.
"I got dragged in. I'd just as soon leave, but I'm going
to have to get to Vaylle first."

At the name, Cvinthil's mouth tightened. "You will
have company, then, mistress sorceress, for it is to
Vaylle that I also wish to go. With sword and spear."
He turned to Wykla. "What news from Darham?"

Wykla gave an account of her interview with the
king of Corrin. She seemed more confident than Alouzon recalled—her voice and manner firm and definite—and she looked Cvinthil in the eye and repeated
Darham's message without a shred of apology or hesitation.

And Darham's idea did indeed sound good to Alouzon. The story of the attack on Bandon had shoved
her face into the lethal potentials of the land she had

created. In light of airborne weaponry and the diseased creations that she had already encountered, an open invasion of Vaylle seemed idiotic.

She felt unclean. Napalm, machine guns, missiles: what kind of sicko would unleash such things on Gryylth? She stole a glance at Kyria, and found herself suddenly glad of the sorceress's powers.

Wykla was still talking when Marrget entered. The captain was wearing a soft, warm robe with a pattern of flowers embroidered at the collar. Her hair was rumpled, as though she had indeed come from bed. She nodded to Cvinthil and took her place at his side in silence.

Karthin had come in, too, and he stood beside her—closer than was really necessary. Marrget did not seem to mind, but when she smiled a greeting to Alouzon, she did so with an almost childlike embarrassment, as though she had been caught pilfering apples from a neighbor's tree.

"And then Darham said," Wykla finished, "that he would indeed be willing to send arms and men, but only after it is established that such a course of action is warranted. He desires a clearer idea of the nature of Vaylle."

Manda touched her gently on the shoulder. "He said more, Wykla."

Wykla colored. "It would be unseemly to mention it, friend."

Cvinthil was thoughtful. "Darham is a cautious man. Maybe he is wiser than the King of Gryylth."

Santhe shook his head. "There are many kinds of wisdom, my king."

"I think Darham's idea is pretty good," said Alouzon. "I'll go. I'll lead the party."

"As cowardly as the people of Vaylle have shown themselves, Alouzon, they are unworthy opponents for such as you."

"No, we don't know that." She wondered why she was growing so heated. Was it because she was afraid of what Vaylle might offer? Or was Cvinthil's blanket condemnation cutting too close to her heart? "A couple years ago, you were saying the same damn thing about the Corrinians, and you found out you were wrong. I say we take Darham's advice."

Marrget spoke. The steel had returned to her eyes. "But we all know that only a vicious and cowardly people would do such a thing as destroy a town without warning."

"Yeah, and you all knew that the Dremords were murdering bastards." Marrget and Karthin exchanged glances. Something that was not quite guilt, but close to it, passed between them. Alouzon stared, then found her voice again. "There are two sides to everything. Why don't we find out what's really going on?"

Marrget moved to rest her hand on her sword hilt, found that she was not armed, shrugged and folded her arms. "I am sometimes hasty, Alouzon. You know that. I fear that the fate of a small band in Vaylle might be cruel and quick, but I am willing to be swayed by your better judgment. If you wish to explore Vaylle in secret, I will go with you."

"And I," Karthin put in quickly.

Marrget lifted her eyes to his face, smiled. "I would not go without you, my friend."

Cvinthil seemed chagrined. He was a king for peace, not for war, and not only was he clumsy in the role of belligerent, he obviously knew himself to be so. "Who else wishes to go to Vaylle with Alouzon Dragonmaster?"

Wykla raised her hand, followed immediately by Santhe, who added with a laugh: "I am certain that I can find two men of the Second Wartroop foolhardy enough to join us."

"I am under orders from the King of Corrin," said Manda. "Unless there is serious objection, I must accompany Alouzon Dragonmaster."

Helwych was silent, uncertain. Manda prodded him. "I . . ." He glanced around, flushed. "Is the lady Kyria going also?"

Kyria did not look at him. "I said that I was."

Helwych squared his shoulders. "Then I shall go, too."

Santhe had been counting on his fingers. "Nine," he said. "Alouzon? Will nine . . ." He looked at Helwych and smiled wryly. " . . . nine stalwart companions please you?"

She nodded and turned to the king. "Cvinthil, it's up to you."

The king was sad, his doe eyes deep and serious. "I wish at times that Vorya were alive," he said softly. "He knew war, and he knew peace, too." He lifted his head. "But he is dead. So be it. I will provision you, and you will leave as soon as you will. But I will say this also: should you not return within two months, then my suspicions regarding Vaylle will be confirmed, and, with or without Corrin, I will bring an army across the White Sea."

Kyria folded her arms, her pale hand gripping her staff as though, had Solomon Braithwaite stepped into the room, she would have struck him dead without hesitation. Already raw from her own thoughts, Alouzon looked away.

Her eyes fell on Marrget. Shrewd, calculating, the captain seemed already to be planning the exploration of Vaylle, mulling over questions of strategy and tactics. But there was a depth to her expression that said that she was considering much more than mere soldiery, and Alouzon noticed that her hand was held—gently, firmly—in the large, strong hand of Karthin.

❖ CHAPTER 7 ❖

Eyes clenched, hands gripping his staff as though it were a python, Helwych grunted and strained his way out of his body. There were easier ways to do this, he knew, but Tireas's monomaniacal pursuit of the Tree had left his apprentice with only the most basic of techniques and spells.

As much as he resented the neglect, he resented even more the tacit condescension he received because of it. He read it in the eyes of others, heard it in their voices: *Ah, well. We all know about Helwych. Poor lad, he could not change hay into straw to save his life, but that is no fault of his own.*

The patronizing smiles had even followed him to Gryylth. Stalwart companions, indeed! Before the task was finished, he would wager, most of the stalwarts would find themselves as hopelessly unprepared as the sorcerer they so mocked.

With a wrench that made his mind spin, his spirit rolled off the couch he had been given in Hall Kingsbury, and he scrambled amid the astral currents, keeping his eyes firmly away from the inert heap of flesh and blood that he normally inhabited.

Cautiously, he moved through the Hall. About him, ignorant of his presence, guards watched and slept, spoke in low mutters. The sorcerer overheard a familiar name and drew near to two.

". . . and so what does Darham do but send us a woman." The speaker was hardly older than Helwych,

but he bore a black eye and a cut on his cheek as though
he had been brawling. "I am tired of woman games."

"I cannot blame you," said his companion with a
smile. "Woman games seem to have done your face no
good."

The first man flinched as though struck. "Damn
you, Dryyim. If I could once get that girl alone for the
space it takes to tell a hundred—"

"Most likely she would thrash you soundly, Kerlsen.
She can take care of herself. And you are drunk."

Kerlsen snorted sullenly. "And now Darham has
sent us another."

"The Corrinian maid looks able enough."

A laugh. "She would look better out of that armor
and in my bed."

If Helwych's spirit had possessed blood, he would
have colored. Manda's tart words had more than once
driven him to consider a suitable fate for her. That
proud head should be bent now and again for its own
good. He was not sure that he agreed completely with
Kerlsen's methodology, but the lad had the right idea.

Helwych fumbled his way into the street. Nothing
moved. With a sense of confidence, he brought to his
mind an image of a black-eyed woman whose hair fell
to her waist in a torrent of jet. His vision blurred, and
then he was standing in the king's house, beside Kyria's bed.

The sorceress lay, eyes closed in sleep, and Helwych
regarded her almost fearfully. Was there anything that
she could teach him? Probably much. Would she,
though? A difficult question. He had, he admitted, already erred several times in his dealings with her; had,
in fact, thoroughly antagonized her. He would have to
move carefully about Kyria, and he had resolved to
take a few minutes this night to learn how best he
might win her approval.

On the other side of the fire, the Dragonmaster
stirred, rolled over, and murmured to herself. She was
not asleep, but that did not matter. A simple warrior
would never detect the delicate workings of sorcery.

Settling himself on the rush-covered flagstones, Helwych rested his staff across his knees as Tireas had taught him. In a moment he was mentally feeling out toward the sorceress, seeking to read as much of her inner thoughts as his inadequate training would allow.

But as he groped his way toward her unconscious, he found his own thoughts seized suddenly, and he was pulled away into a realm in which ebony skies weighed down on a floor of jet. Before him, Kyria was locked in battle with a wiry, gray-haired harpy who quite obviously wanted to kill her.

Kyria, though, held the taloned hands away from her throat and spoke gently to her opponent. She did not even raise her voice. "You have to give it up sometime, Helen. You cannot live like this."

The hag snarled, incapable of words. Her teeth snapped at Kyria's face.

Kyria seemed unperturbed. "Please, Helen. Try to love. It is better that way. You know that." But her opponent got a hand loose and struck her. Kyria fell to the floor.

In an instant, Helen was on her, shaking her as a dog might shake a rat. Kyria's face remained calm, but though she fought to regain her feet, she seemed reluctant to strike a blow.

The sides involved in the conflict seemed obvious, and Helwych was delighted that he could be of service to the sorceress. Striding forward, he swung his staff at the hag, and she went down with a snarl. But she was up again almost immediately, her hands reaching for Helwych's robe.

Kyria had regained her feet, and she seized his arm and put him behind her. "Fly," she said softly. "You have no power here."

The words might have stung, but her voice was such that he had to accept fact as fact. "Remember that I tried to help."

As Helen closed in, Kyria smiled sadly, as though she had a long night ahead of her. "I will," she said. "Peace to you. May the Goddess protect you."

He goggled, but she thrust him away and turned to meet Helen with arms open as though to embrace her. Helwych fell back, felt the floor give way beneath him, and then was sprawled on the floor of the king's house, astral mouth choked with astral rushes, staff turned slippery as snail slime.

Spitting out rushes, but unsure of what he had seen, Helwych wandered out through the closed door, passed the ever-vigilant guards, and made his way up the street toward the Hall. He was too disoriented to think himself back to his body, but once he found it, he knew, it was a simple matter to re-enter it. Tireas had taken the time to teach him that. So nice of the old bastard.

He had found out nothing that was of any help, and he had been thoroughly shaken by visions that he could neither control nor understand. Who was the woman that Kyria fought? And how was it that Kyria—normally so vicious and harsh—could be the embodiment of such well-nigh divine gentleness?

The realms of spirit were disturbed, confused. Buildings warped and twisted in his sight, and eyes gleamed out of the shadows. He was within sight of the Hall when he looked into a dark place to find his gaze met by something that glowed with corpse-light, that opened its mouth to reveal a maw of phosphorescence set about with glistening fangs.

With a faint scream, he turned and ran, feeling the beast rise and follow. He had only gone a few steps when he was knocked flat and rolled face up to stare up the muzzle of a massive, grinning parody of a hound. The jaws opened, the teeth flashed, and his sight was suddenly blanketed by the roiling incandescence of a spectral throat.

When he came to himself, he was back in his chamber, his ears ringing with the sounds of shouts and alarms. Men called to one another, and he heard the clank of weapons. Eyes unclosed, he lay in the darkness for a moment, feeling drained and empty, as though the life had been sucked out of his body, leaving only a hollow shell.

* * *

Marrget was dreaming.

She dreamed of war, of a young Corrinian girl who had been stripped and raped amid a pile of dirty laundry by the shore of the Long River. The sky was clear, the water went by like oil. The girl's face was pained, her blue eyes outraged, but even as she was violated, she had stared her rapist in the face as though to impress on her memory every nuance of his being. She would find him someday, and she would kill him.

Marrget started awake to find herself in her own bed, beside Karthin, her head pillowed on his shoulder and a warmth in her belly that even a nightmare had been unable to extinguish.

"Oh . . . Gods . . ." She sat up, covered her face.

Karthin stirred. "Marrha?"

He called her that frequently, though he was ignorant of the associations that the name had for her. It was, apparently, a Corrinian diminutive, and she had not thought to complain. "Here, Karthin."

He touched her arm. "Are you troubled?"

"A dream. No more."

"About . . . before?"

She had never told him of the rape. She would not tell him now. "Aye."

He sat up beside her, put his hands to her smooth shoulders, and kneaded out the knots of tension. "And have I brought confusion to your already difficult life, beloved?"

"If it was brought," she said, "we brought it together: each holding one side of the bucket." She reached back, touched his face. "But I cannot say that I mind."

Under his hands, the stiffness left her, though the memory of the dream remained. Someday, she decided, she would find that girl and make reparation. She was not sure what she could do that might help, but when, inwardly, she had made the vow, swearing it before the Gods whose names she did not know, she felt better. Curling up in Karthin's arms, she rested her head on his shoulder while he stroked her.

"Do you want to sleep again?" he said.

For the girl left bleeding and bruised by the river, there had been no love, only violence, and Marrget burrowed further into Karthin's embrace as though to hide from her thoughts. "I would sooner remain like this."

The room was cold. Karthin gathered up the furs and covered them both. "I noticed that you did not stay to speak with the Dragonmaster at the Hall. I know you are friends. I hope that I have not . . ." Marrget felt him shrug.

"You did nothing, O man. I have changed since Alouzon was last in Gryylth, and now I hardly know how to present myself to her. If I spoke with her, I would have to tell her of myself and of my life. I . . . do not know if I am ready to do that."

"Santhe has guessed, I think."

She laughed softly. A woman's laugh, she realized. "Santhe guesses everything. We know one another too well for me to care. Alouzon, though . . ." She squirmed uncomfortably. "Alouzon is like a God. I am not certain how I might be judged. I am not certain how to judge myself."

He hugged her closely, nuzzled at the hollow of her shoulder. "Strange customs indeed you have in Gryylth. Is it unlawful for a woman to take a man to her bed?"

She made a small, impatient sound. "I was not always a woman."

"You are now." He ran a hand down her spine, and she stiffened, eyes shut, mouth half open. She wanted . . .

She found her voice. "It is easy to say that. It is difficult to live it."

His hand stayed at the small of her back. "You were once my enemy. You broke my ribs. But I love you, and I will help. In any way possible."

The fire was burning in her again, and she had learned at last that she had no reason to deny it. She turned and pushed him gently back onto the bed. "You do help,

my love. You have helped me greatly." She pressed
herself against him, sought his lips. "Help me now."

Suzanne Helling had grown up in the shadow of
Vietnam, and her earliest memories were of slick magazine pages emblazoned with four-color icons of death.
Beneath her chubby, pre-adolescent fingers and her
wondering eyes, the images in *Life* and *Time* and
Newsweek had revealed themselves, a burned village
that smoked in the tropical sun changing with the brush
of a hand into a child who screamed as she ran down
a dusty road with legs tattered by shrapnel, her place
taken then (another wave of the hand, another startled
glance) by a man, disheveled and sullen, who grimaced with one eye half shut as the shock wave of an
impacting bullet swept through his skull.

War seemed to be everywhere, bringing with it its
cartloads of bodies and its morning-edition casualty
statistics; and when Suzanne, filled with the horror of
a too-early acquaintance with death, had taken her
sentiments to the streets, shouting and screaming that
something had to be done to stop the endless slaughter, she had found war waiting for her there, too,
brought to life in the concrete verities of tear gas,
nightsticks, and, yes, high-velocity bullets.

If an uneasy and distrustful truce could be called an
end, then Vietnam had ended. But Suzanne knew—
and Alouzon had come to know even better—that wars
had no end, not really. To be sure, pieces of paper had
been signed, hands had been shaken, and perhaps even
a few backs had been slapped. But in America and
Vietnam and Laos and Cambodia, there were graves,
vacant chairs at countless dinner tables, fading photographs on a million walls. There were lives as empty
as an amputee's sleeve, as shattered as the stump left
by a claymore mine.

And, elsewhere, there were other artifacts.

Alouzon asked to see Gelyya after the evening meal.
The Gryylthans were confronted by unknowns; but the
Dragonmaster and Kyria knew what questions to ask,

and Gelyya's answers, guileless and direct, did nothing but bolster their theory that Bandon had been destroyed by modern weapons.

The apprentice midwife told her tale, and Alouzon, staring into the fire, saw again the magazine photographs of death: ruined village, screaming child, dying man. Snuffling and howling, the war that had soiled her childhood had tracked her across the universe to another world, for she recognized now that Vaylle was as much a remnant of Vietnam as the wasted and defoliated ridges of the Annamese Cordillera.

"That bastard," Kyria said after Cvinthil and his family had retired upstairs.

"Sol?"

"Yes. He couldn't hack this place, so now he's going to blow it up."

It would have been convenient to blame Solomon for Bandon and for such diseased creations as the White Worm and the leprous hound, but Alouzon knew that the responsibility lay with her own unconscious. "He died trying to save the land, Kyria. Why should he try to destroy it?"

"Because he couldn't have his fun anymore." Kyria's voice was an edged blade that cut with the accents of Helen Addams. "Sol was like that. You didn't know him."

"I knew him well enough."

"Sure. Come on, honey. He made this place to prove his manhood, but it got the better of him. Ever hear how an enraged husband kills both his wife and his wife's lover? He can't give it to her with his penis anymore, so he does it with a bullet. Same damn thing."

"I don't . . ." Alouzon could not admit the truth. "I don't think it's Sol."

"Well then, who the hell is it? Or do you get napalm storms out here like the Midwest gets tornadoes?"

Alouzon was silent.

Kyria cursed under her breath and rolled herself in her furs. "I'm going to sleep. Wake me if the world ends, and I'll try to do something about it." She hefted her staff and tucked it under her arm.

Alouzon lay back on her couch, listening to the muffled crackles and snaps of the banked fire, feeling her tacit lie chew slowly at her heart. Kyria wanted to find Solomon so that she could kill him. Cvinthil wanted vengeance on Vaylle. But neither Solomon nor Vaylle was the problem.

The fire crackled, and an ember glowed momentarily, illuminating the stone walls of the room, the timbered ceiling, the shutters closed tightly against the cold. Ayya's toy-sized broom leaned against the doorframe, and Vill's infant playthings were scattered in the rushes near the hearth. Outside, the men who stood watch at the king's door spoke in low voices and stamped their feet to keep warm. A few feet away, Kyria whimpered softly, the prisoner of some evil dream.

The Grail. She had to find the Grail. Somehow, a woman who had dragged herself through the blood and pain of two worlds had to grasp something that fled from the slightest taint of impurity, and she had to survive the experience so as to bring healing not only to herself, but to the land and the people she loved.

I'll do it. Oh, you Gods of Gryylth, somehow, I'll do it.

Kyria whimpered again, louder. Alouzon recalled her first night in Gryylth, and her second and third, and her fourth. Unless Kyria also had some intimation of the Grail's ineffable and nurturing presence, her dreams must be dark indeed.

The sorceress writhed for a moment, drew her knees up to her chin, cried out softly. Her hands felt her strange, new face. Alouzon slipped out of her blankets and went to her.

"Kyria."

"Who am I?"

"Wake up, Kyria. It's just a dream."

Kyria shuddered, jerked, sat upright. Her long hair was twined in her fists. "Oh God . . . no . . ."

"It was a dream."

The sorceress broke into tears. "No . . . no it's not. I'm not me. He took that, too. Who the hell am I? I want my home . . . I want . . . I want my babies . . ."

"Easy." Alouzon held her, felt the cool brush of Kyria's staff against her shoulder. "Easy. It's going to be all right." She tried to find words, failed, and contented herself with holding the weeping woman. Much as she disliked Kyria, she could not bear to allow her to suffer. There was enough horror in Gryylth these days, and probably more in Vaylle. She would not add to it.

Kyria was pulling herself out of her sleepy hysteria. "It's not right," she said. "How can you say it's right? We don't have our own bodies, towns are getting blown up, women are getting raped, and those kids . . ." She buried her face in her hands for a moment. "How old is Wykla? Manda?"

"I don't know. Eighteen, maybe nineteen."

"They're just kids. They're just goddam kids. They should be off having fun or something. How come they're carting swords around?"

Alouzon shrugged helplessly. "That's the way it is here."

That's the way it is here. Later, when Kyria had fallen back into an uneasy sleep, Alouzon was thinking, planning, wondering how she could give the lie to those words.

Guardian of Gryylth. What kind of a Guardian was she? Dythragor, for all his crotch-hitch and swagger, had at least kept the warfare comprehensible. It was Alouzon who had created weapons against which her people had no defense. What was next? Nuclear bombs?

The thought drove her out of bed and into her clothes. Wrapping a warm cloak about herself, she opened the door and greeted the guards. "Cold, huh?"

"Bitterly, Dragonmaster," said one whom she recognized as a veteran of the Circle. "But it is often this

way before the season warms toward spring. Next
week will bring fine weather.''

"Hope so. We've got a ride ahead of us."

"So I heard. Gods bless you, Dragonmaster."

"You too. I'm going to take a walk. That OK?"

The man smiled. "The Dragonmaster persists in
asking permission for those things which she could
well order."

"Yeah . . . well . . ." She shrugged and went off
down the street.

The moonlight was a rain of silver, the shadows like
pitch. Her boots made hard, brittle sounds on the fro-
zen streets. Unlike modern cities, Kingsbury slept
during the dark hours, and the only inhabitants who
were awake were those who guarded the king, those
who guarded the Hall and the fortifications of the hill,
and those who, like Alouzon, guarded the entire land.

Guardian of Gryylth. And what else? Guardian of
Vaylle? She wanted desperately to talk to Silbakor, to
pry some further information out of its recalcitrant
mouth, but even if the Dragon had been willing to
speak, it was far away from her, locked in an elemen-
tal battle of existence with its equal and opposite.

She found herself staring up at the cold, hard stars,
worried as much about the Dragon as she was about
the possible appearance of warplanes.

Her steps took her to the edge of the hill, and there
she spoke briefly with the guards. One, again, was a
veteran. The other, though, was a green lad who was
barely showing his first sprouts of beard. He stared at
Alouzon with a mixture of fear and unease, and she
read his thoughts. A woman. And a Dragonmaster,
too. What was the world coming to?

With a nod, she turned back into the town. Oh, she
had done such a good job with Gryylth! The whole
country was confused and threatened because of her
neglect. But what, really, could she do? At times, her
people seemed to consider her some kind of deific being, forgetting that the object of their near-worship
was as human as they. Alouzon's responsibilities were

crushing, but her powers were limited. *Dammit, if I'm supposed to be some kind of God, I sure could use some of the perks.*

As she rounded a turning midway to the Hall, she stopped and squinted ahead, her interior complaint interrupted by a flash of motion. Something had slipped into the shadows between two houses. Even in the clean-edged moonlight, it seemed to glow as with some inner radiance. Like phosphor.

She glanced up at the sky. No lights. No Dragons. No jets. Nothing. Just the stars. It was hard to conceive of anything so still as the sky of Gryylth. Not even a satellite marred the changelessness.

With her hand on her sword, she advanced toward the alleyway, straining her ears. At first she was surrounded only by the frosty silence of a fifth-century night, but then, growing louder as she closed on the alley, she heard a soft slavering interspersed with a slow, wet sound, as though a lion were feasting on a kill.

She stopped just outside the alley, dropped her cloak, and flattened herself against the wall of the house. Muttering, smacking, immersed in its feed, the thing around the corner did not seem to notice her. Or maybe it did. Maybe it was just waiting to add fresh Dragonmaster *du jour* to the evening's menu.

Alouzon eased the Dragonsword from its sheath and, moving slowly, slipped into the alley. Ahead, faintly glowing, its back to her, was a duplicate of the hound that she had slain in the spaces between the worlds. Its massive head was bent down, and its great jaws were worrying at a mess of blood and rags that lay in the cold dust.

She slipped closer. The Dragonsword had killed one of these things. It could kill another. But she nearly cried out when, in the faint glow that dripped from the hound's needle teeth, she saw Helwych's face, the scalp stripped back to expose a bloody skull, the flesh sucked away from one cheek. His clothing was in shreds, and there was little left of his body save a ruin of viscera that smoked in the frigid air.

Before she could strike, though, an arm encircled her throat and she was jerked back. "Were you looking for me, little girl?"

Her cry was choked off, and she toppled back into the man's arms. The hound raised its head.

"I will be scarred to my grave from that stone you threw, girl," said her assailant, his young voice thick with wine. "You will learn a few things tonight. You will learn to be silent when a man speaks."

You dumb shit, that thing's gonna eat us alive!

He was now reaching for her sword, trying to disarm her, but she had no more time to waste. Driving her elbows back, she felt the crunch of breaking ribs. His grip loosened, and she spun and backhanded him. He grunted, reeled, and crashed out into the street, staring up at the full moon with glazed eyes.

The hound was almost on her, but she met it with her blade, and its howl of pain was deafening after the utter silence of the town. "King's Guard! King's Guard!" In the rank stench of the beast's breath, her words came out in nauseated heaves. "Move your butts!"

Pivoting, the hound tumbled her back toward the rear of the alley. She fell to the ground, looked instinctively for Helwych's body, but saw nothing. While she stared, dumbfounded, the beast charged, and she barely had time to get to her knees before it thudded into her and toppled her again.

She rolled. The Dragonsword was bright, gleaming as though it had sucked in the radiance of the stars, and it cut deep. Phosphor poured from the rent in the hound's side, and the stench grew.

The hound backed up, and Alouzon scrambled to her feet. Putting aside thoughts of the sorcerer for the moment, she stalked after the hound. "Come on, guy. You started this. I'm gonna finish it."

The hound, wounded, retreated to the street.

Alouzon's anger was burning, and the Dragonsword

took her rage, amplified it, channeled it into her reflexes and her strength. "Here, doggy. Nice fucking boy."

Torchlight. Voices. Her call to the Guard had been heard. Beside her, a shutter flew open, and a householder stuck his head out. "What—?"

"Get your ass inside or you'll get eaten," she snapped.

He looked at her, then at the hound. He slammed the shutter closed.

In the street, the man who had attacked her was struggling to his hands and knees. He coughed, hacking up a spittle of blood that streaked down his chin. Alouzon recognized him as the guard who had looked so fearfully at Wykla, and realized that, in the bright but uncertain light of the moon, he had mistaken one armed woman for another.

It had been a fatal blunder. As Alouzon closed in on the hound, it turned instead on the man. With a smooth dip of its head, it rolled him onto his back and tore out his throat.

Blood sprayed its grinning face, and it wheeled to face the guards who were just then rounding the corner. With a howl that shivered the air, it bounded straight at them, knocked several to the ground, tore at the fallen for a moment, and then vanished up the street.

"Let it go," said Alouzon, her voice suddenly weak. The dead man's throat burbled and plashed. "You can't catch it." Cvinthil was hurrying up, wrapped in a robe and carrying a sword. "Everyone in your house OK?" Alouzon asked him.

"We are well. How is it with you?"

"I'm fine, but this guy bought it. And Helwych—"

She froze, looked past the king. Coming down the street from the Hall, staff in hand and sound as ever, was the Corrinian sorcerer.

She went back into the alley. It was empty. Helwych's body was gone. Not a trace of it remained, not even a bloodstain or a scrap of tattered cloth.

❖ CHAPTER 8 ❖

Much as Alouzon wanted to start for Vaylle the next day, it was unfeasible. A long and difficult journey lay ahead of her company, and she spent the morning with Marrget, making arrangements for equipment and discussing personnel and travel.

Despite the captain's hurried departure from the Hall the night before, this morning she seemed to be, for the most part, very much her old self; but again and again, Alouzon detected the presence of something new about her friend, a strange sense of diffidence that colored her usual bluff exterior.

Time flowed oddly between the worlds, and eight months in Los Angeles had, in Gryylth, expanded to eighteen: a long absence on Alouzon's part. Marrget might merely have become more private and retiring as the weeks had passed and she had learned to deal with her new life, but Alouzon worried that the captain might actually be annoyed with her. Faced with the problems of a land recovering from a long and devastating conflict and a wartroop fighting for its place in Gryylthan society, Marrget might well have decided that she had little time to give to such intermittent friendship and support.

Alouzon could not blame her. She could only try to make amends by facing the present situation squarely, without apology, without hesitation. Stripping off the petty concerns of a graduate student, she donned once again the tasks of a Dragonmaster. There was much to do before the company could depart.

"Do you have any ideas about how to get horses across the White Sea?" she said while they checked the available mounts at the stables.

Marrget was examining her own horse. The beast had never been unsure of her identity, even though, to human eyes, she had changed beyond recognition. "I would advise that we make first for Quay," she said. "It is a large town that trades along the coast. It has boats sufficient to transport ourselves and the horses." She gave her horse another pat, and he nickered softly and nuzzled her. "The man who taught me the ways of the sword lives there now. His name is Hahle, and, if I am not mistaken, he has become head of the council." An expression more of puzzlement than sadness crossed her face. "We will see if my old teacher is as quick to know me as my horse."

Alouzon linked arms with her as they went back out into the street. "Has it been that bad for you, then? I'd kind of hoped that . . . well . . . maybe you'd get used to it."

Marrget did not reply. She was biting nervously at her lip. About them, Kingsbury bustled through its day. Tradesmen with bundles on their backs shouldered their way past carts and knots of people. In the distance, a smith beat steadily on a piece of hot metal. Two women passed by, chatting animatedly about children. They paused to stare at Marrget and Alouzon, then gave them a *Gods bless* and went on their way.

"Ah . . . nay, Dragonmaster," said Marrget at last. She would not look at Alouzon. "I cannot say truthfully that it has been bad at all."

Her acute embarrassment was painful to hear. Alouzon wondered suddenly whether annoyance were actually the cause of it at all. "Is there something I can do?" she said gently. The captain paled, and looked away. "Hey, we've been friends for a while."

"I . . ." Marrget seemed close to tears.

A voice rang out. "Marrha! Dragonmaster! The king

asks that the company meet with him over the midday meal.''

Marrget started guiltily. Ahead, Karthin had come into view. His voice was cheerful, his blue eyes bright, and he was waving a large hand.

Alouzon stared. ''Marrha?''

''It . . . it is a name he calls me sometimes,'' Marrget said stiffly. ''As one . . . ah . . . friend to another.'' She glanced uneasily at Alouzon. ''I hope . . . I hope you do not think ill of me.''

No, it was not annoyance at all. Mentally kicking herself for not realizing sooner what was going on, Alouzon hugged her friend. ''I don't think ill of you, Marrget,'' she said. ''I think it's great.''

Marrget still looked worried. ''You do not find me diminished? Or dishonored?''

''For taking a lover? Why the hell should you be diminished? Particularly when it's a guy like Karthin. You've got good taste.''

Marrget passed a hand over her face, shaking with relief. ''I am myself still uncertain how to accept this.''

''Don't worry about it. It happens.'' Taking her hand, Alouzon led her toward Karthin. Perhaps the irrational hope she had felt the previous day was not unfounded after all. ''Let's go get your man and have some lunch.''

Marrget smiled, and to Alouzon's relief it was the easy, bluff smile that had always been so characteristic of her. Karthin, when he met them, bowed in the manner of his people, but he took Marrget's hand for a moment and looked warmly at her.

Marrget blushed, then laughed nervously. ''You see, Dragonmaster, to what end has come the proud, scornful warrior.''

''Dammit, lady. I envy you.''

Alouzon's words held an edge. In the world she knew, she had become a loner. Once, she had shared her body and her bed, even though her heart had long before turned in upon itself, but now she shared nothing. She lived alone, she worked alone. Only in Gryylth did she have companionship, but her responsibilities precluded intimacy.

Karthin's blue eyes were on her as though he guessed her thoughts. "I heard of your battle last night, Dragonmaster," he said. "Marrha and I—"

Marrget held up a hand. "Karthin . . . please . . ."

He colored. "Ach . . . I will strangle on my wayward tongue someday! Would you show us the place, Dragonmaster?"

Alouzon shrugged. "Sure." She led them up the street.

In the daylight, the alley was simply a shabby, rubbish-filled cul-de-sac no different from any other in Kingsbury. Near the back, though, where the refuse was piled up in a heap almost as tall as Karthin, dark stains gleamed iridescently on the cold dirt. It was as though a man-sized snail had crawled across the ground.

Marrget touched a stain gingerly and sniffed her fingers. Wrinkling her nose, she wiped her hand on her plain tunic. "I have never seen the like."

"Nor I," said Karthin.

"It was a big thing," said Alouzon, "and it glowed; but it couldn't have been entirely magical, because I wounded it."

Marrget eyed her. "With the Dragonsword."

"Well . . . yeah."

"Hmmm." Karthin took Marrget's hand suddenly. The slime was blackening her fingers. "You had better wash that, beloved."

"Aye," she said. "Who knows what this might change me into, eh?" She broke the crust of ice on a rain barrel with the pommel of her sword and scrubbed the stains off in the cold water. "Thank you, Karthin. It was dissolving the skin."

"Oh, great." Alouzon looked at the slime. "A bad out-take from *Alien*."

Marrget blinked. "I do not understand."

Alouzon shook her head. "Let me tell you some-

thing that *I* don't understand.'' She indicated a vacant
spot at the base of the rubbish pile. ''Right there, I
saw Helwych's body last night. The hound was eating
it.''

''But Helwych is—''

''Yeah, I know. He's fine today. Karthin, did you
happen to see him at the Hall this morning?''

The big man nodded. ''I did. The lad was quiet and
thoughtful, and Manda said that that was unusual, but
. . .'' He grinned. ''. . . but welcome. She does not
like him.''

''There's not much to like. But he's OK, right? No
wounds, no blood?''

''None, Dragonmaster.''

Alouzon gestured at the ground again. ''I saw it,
though.''

''I do not doubt you, friend.'' Marrget was on her
knees, examining the ground. ''I see no sign of a killing here. Perhaps a magician could say more.'' She
looked up at Alouzon. ''What of the lady Kyria? Would
she be of help?''

The sorceress was off by herself today, wandering
the town as though she were a tourist, her scowls turning aside questions and stares like armor plate. She
had not even thanked Alouzon for comforting her last
night, and, in fact, the incident had only intensified
her foul mood.

Alouzon threw up her hands. ''I'm almost afraid to
ask.''

Marrget rose, checked her hands for traces of slime.
''She does not love Gryylth?''

''I don't think she loves anything, Marrget.''

''A grievous fate,'' Marrget replied, unconsciously
laying a hand on Karthin's arm. ''Can we trust her?''

''In Vaylle?''

''At all.''

Alouzon shrugged. She never seemed to have any
choices anymore. ''I think she'll be fine as long as
we want what she wants. So far, that's the way it
is.''

Marrget's eyes, though warmed by love, were as
steely and unforgiving as ever when it came to her
people and her land. "And if that changes?"

Kyria wanted Solomon. Alouzon wanted the Grail.
She could not help but think that the two quests were
related. But how long could she keep the sorceress
ignorant of Vaylle's true nature? "Then we're in trouble. But I think we'll be all right for a while."

The captain picked up a stick and prodded at the
slime. The wood smoked at its touch. "I pray you are
right, Dragonmaster."

Parl and Birk were the men whom Santhe had
brought to fill out the expedition. As quiet and solemn
as Santhe was bright and cheerful, they nonetheless
shared with their commander the dark, interior seri-
ousness that had marked those of the Second Wartroop
who had witnessed the terrible slaughter of Vorya's
army in the last days of the war with Corrin.

They sat together at the end of the king's table and
listened without comment to the plans that were discussed over lunch. Now and again they nodded in
agreement or pursed their lips in thought, but their
eyes—Parl's gray, Birk's brown—changed expression
not at all. To Alouzon, they appeared to be men who
had seen enough killing that questions of life and death
had grown paltry: they would tend the wounded or slit
throats with equal dispassion.

She found that comforting and disquieting at the
same time. Her company would be traveling into hos-
tile territory, far from supplies and friends and home.
Santhe's men did not seem to be worried, but the ruthless efficiency their manner implied reminded Alouzon of the search-and-destroy patrols that had, in
Vietnam, turned killing into a calm, emotionless art:
the hunting of men instead of beasts.

Manda, Alouzon noticed, shared something of their
focused indifference, for though she was quite capable
of bright smiles and effortless laughter, she also sat
silently at the table today, her blue eyes quietly obser-

vant but filled with a sense of incipient violence. But neither Santhe's men nor Darham's representative concerned her as much as Helwych. Abstract, almost absent, he looked at nothing, seemed to be aware of everything; and there was an intensity about him that had not existed the day before. Only his habitual sullenness seemed at all normal.

Seena's words upon meeting Alouzon had been prophetic: there was indeed no time for proper welcomes. Dinner last night had been hasty and serious. Lunch today was no different. Talk occupied the participants more than food, and the gravity of the discussion rendered the meal tasteless in any case.

But it was difficult for the company to construct a plan of action in any kind of detail, for aside from certain facts that Alouzon would not reveal, Vaylle was an unknown. There had been no communications from that land, no emissaries, no visitors, not even an exploratory vessel.

In fact, Alouzon found it strange that Cvinthil and his people knew that there was any such thing as Vaylle at all. The land was far enough from Gryylth that she had only been able to see it from Silbakor's back at cruising altitude, and even then the Dragon had been some distance from the coast. Since there had been no contact, there should have been no knowledge, and yet everyone in Gryylth—and in Corrin, too—was aware of a land that had only existed for the last eighteen months.

Alouzon felt queasy at the thought that her mind, in creating Vaylle, had at the same time reached into the collective memory of Gryylth and Corrin and, much as a computer programmer might add lines to an extant file, had brazenly typed in the necessary information. This was something that no human being ought to be allowed to do. Gods, maybe. Alouzon, no.

But she had done it nonetheless.

Guardian of Gryylth: the title had staggering implications. In Los Angeles, she had become worn and frayed even from a simplistic conception of her relationship with her world. But faced now with the plexed intricacies and depth of her role, she wondered that she stayed sane.

It had to be the Grail. Silbakor was a balance to the land, but the Grail was nurturer and dynamo. The intelligence resident within the Sacred Cup would, by necessity, be as passionately committed to the preservation of the world as the Dragon. Perhaps more so. By its nature, though, it would be constrained in its manifestation: mere mortals were unfit to experience its limitless purity and life, and therefore it had to remain a hazy glory at the borders of consciousness. But it had revealed itself, and therefore, paradoxically, the Grail was willing, even eager, to be possessed, and so had directed a fragment of its harrowing but loving sustenance at the frail creature that sought it . . . so as to further the seeking.

At the end of the meeting, Marrget stood. "I believe that all our preparations will have been made by nightfall. If Alouzon wishes, we can depart tomorrow morning."

Alouzon nodded, swimming up from her thoughts as though from the bottom of a shimmering sea. "Yeah. Sounds good."

"There is one question, though." Marrget examined her plain tunic. It was streaked where the slime had eaten through the fabric. "The beast that Alouzon battled last night seemed to be other than natural. My experiences in the Blasted Heath lead me to believe that, in many cases, mundane weapons do not affect magical beasts. Does the lady Kyria have—" She broke off. Helwych was staring at her, his dark eyes suddenly alive with resentment. Gracefully, she corrected herself. "Do our magicians have anything to say about this?"

Helwych launched immediately into an involved explanation of magical and mundane weapons. He seemed to know what he was talking about, but his meanings were obscured by the technical language he employed. His conclusions, however, were clear: mundane weapons would not serve magical ends, and magical weapons took time and energy to make.

"What of the beast itself, Helwych?" said Karthin offhandedly. "Do you know anything of it?"

"Nothing."

Karthin's voice did not change. "Are you certain?"

In an instant, Helwych was on his feet, shouting. "Damn your eyes, nothing! Do you have to keep pressing me? In the name of the Gods, you are my fellow countryman!"

In the silence left behind his outburst, Manda's voice was tight, careful, low. "Sit down, please, Helwych, else you will disgrace our country even more than you have already."

"I—"

Kyria rose, staff in hand. "She said: *sit down*."

Helwych glanced between Kyria and Manda. With a mutter, he took his seat again.

Parl and Birk settled back onto their stools. Alouzon realized that, smoothly, without anyone noticing, they had half risen and drawn knives at Helwych's outburst. Now they replaced them and resumed their silent, unmoving watch.

"Lady Kyria?" Marrget nodded to her respectfully.

The sorceress took her seat and shrugged. "If we need something done with the weapons, I can do it. It'll take a few minutes."

Helwych stared, eyes wide. "But—"

Kyria fixed him with a pointed finger. "I play by different rules, sonny boy. You want me to ask you what you were doing in my dreams last night?"

He opened his mouth, considered, and shut it.

"Next time, you'll get burned real damn good. Stay out of my way." She looked around at the assembly. "Actually, that goes for the rest of you, too. Alouzon and I can handle this whole trip by ourselves. Anything else is just stupid heroics, and will probably just get everyone hurt. This doesn't concern you, anyway."

Alouzon saw the insult register on the assembly. "Is that your personal opinion, Kyria? Or professional?"

The sorceress lost patience. "What do you want to do, Suzy? Swagger around like a man and swing your sword and be macho? Come on, you're playing games. What's worse—you're playing Sol's games." She turned to the others. "You're all playing Sol's games. How long are you going to let this little fairy tale go—"

Alouzon moved. Kicking back her stool, she leaped for the sorceress, clapped a hand over her mouth, and dragged her toward the door. "Excuse us, please," she said through clenched teeth. "Kyria and I have to have a little talk."

She had moved too fast for the sorceress to react, but by the time she had dragged her out into the court-yard, the staff was a coruscating shaft of fire. "Hear me out, Kyria," she said. "You going to hear me out?"

"I'm going to fucking kill you, bitch!" Kyria's words were muffled by Alouzon's strong hand, but her tone made her meaning clear enough.

"Lemme put it to you this way: you can blast me, and probably do yourself in, too; or you can listen for a second."

Glaring at the Dragonmaster, Kyria stopped struggling. The staff quieted, and Alouzon cautiously released her. "OK," said Kyria, settling her robe grimly. "Talk. This better be good."

"Look," said Alouzon, "I know you hate Sol. I know you want to kill him. But these people don't know about him."

It took a moment for her words to sink in. Kyria's eyes turned wide. "They don't know about this place?"

"Nope."

For a moment, Kyria stared as though she had been clubbed. Then: "O Christ . . . that's horrible." She grounded the staff as though daring the solidity of the world to justify itself. "Sol Braithwaite: little tin god."

She peered at the ground, at the wooden palisade that enclosed the courtyard, at the cold sky. "They really don't know?"

Alouzon shook her head.

Kyria sighed. "All right. I'm a bitch. But I'm not so much of a bitch that I'm going to take it out on the others. They're macho, and they're ridiculous, but you've got some nice kids in that bunch." She stood, shaking her head. "God. What a thing to do. He ought to have been shot."

The morning was cold, and the thin layer of clouds that had moved in during the night was now dropping sleet and rain. About the hill that held Kingsbury, the land was cloaked in gray and silver mist.

Alouzon mounted Jia, leaned forward, and laid her head against the horse's neck. "You ready to go through the ringer again, fella? Boy, you don't learn any faster than I do."

Jia whinnied as if to confirm her statement. Alouzon looked at the guard who stood at the gate to the road. "I thought you said the weather was going to get better."

"Next week, Dragonmaster. Mark me."

She laughed, but she heard her tension even if no one else did. "I will."

Behind her, the members of her company were checking supplies and equipment. Manda was already on her sturdy Corrinian mount, and Helwych had wrapped himself in sullen thought, his dark eyes examining the day from within the shadows of his hood.

Kyria eyed her horse warily. The beast seemed resigned to a cold ride and a colder rider; but with a curiously tender hand, Kyria stroked her muzzle, then whispered to her for a moment. The horse perked up, and Kyria swung into the saddle with a swish of black robes.

Cvinthil strode toward them. His bright blue cloak was embroidered with the crest of the kings of Gryylth, but the colors were muted on this gray day. "Every-

124   **Gael Baudino**

thing is ready,'' he said. ''By the terms of their charter, the councilmen of Quay will give you what you
need.''

Alouzon looked at him and smiled sadly. ''I've heard
that one before.''

Cvinthil reached up and clasped her hand. ''I have
no doubts.'' He put his ring on her finger. ''And this
will remove theirs.''

''OK.'' Alouzon examined the heavy circle of gold.
''I'll buy it.''

The king turned serious. ''I meant what I said at our
first council. If you do not return within two months,
I will contact Darham and raise an army. We have few
who can bear arms compared to the days before the
Circle, but Vaylle will feel our vengeance nonetheless.''

''I don't think that'll be necessary, Cvinthil.''

''I pray not.'' He held to Alouzon's hand, his eyes
watering. Alouzon leaned down and embraced him.
''I heartily wish that I were going with you,'' he said
into her ear. ''I will beseech the Gods for your safety.''

''Thanks, friend.''

''Be careful, Alouzon.'' His voice was a fervent
whisper.

She kissed his forehead. She would have to be careful, for if she were killed, Gryylth, Corrin, Vaylle . . .
the whole world—good and bad, nightmare and fantasy—would dissolve. And yet if she did not endanger
herself, the Grail would never be hers, and the world
would slowly tear itself to shreds.

*This is probably the last thing Silbakor wants me to
do. But* . . . She smiled inwardly, wryly. When had
she last been given any real choice?

Marrget appeared, armed and in armor. The leath-
erworkers of Kingsbury were skilled, even at novel
tasks, and her cuirass fitted her woman's form trimly.
Her escutcheons glinted in the dull light.

With a nod to Karthin, she rode up to join Alouzon
and the king. ''I believe we are ready.''

Alouzon sighed as she straightened up in her saddle. "Everyone's ready except me."

"Alouzon?"

"I feel like sh—" She caught herself. She was Alouzon Dragonmaster. Despair was something she could not afford. "I feel like I'd like to go to bed and sleep for a week."

Marrget laughed softly. "A soldier's dream."

"Yeah. Let's go." She took Cvinthil's hand once again. "Give Seena my love."

"She would have come," he said, "but Vill is being fierce this morning."

She shrugged, smiled wanly. "It happens."

And with that, she led her company down the hill and out across the countryside.

The weather was an impediment. The sleet chilled them despite thick cloaks and deep hoods, and the rain turned the surface of the roads into slippery mud. "I sure pick the good days, don't I?" Alouzon remarked to Marrget.

"Some matters do not wait for fair weather," the captain replied. She grinned at Alouzon. But for her form, she might have been the same sturdy commander with whom Alouzon had traveled toward the Blasted Heath. Her eyes, though, betrayed a new life, for there was a softness and depth within them that had not been present a year and a half before.

Alouzon was infinitely grateful for her presence. This journey made the exploration of the Heath seem tame, and was complicated by half-hidden motivations and half-expressed hostilities within the company.

At least, she thought, Karthin and Marrget had no problems, nor did Wykla and Manda. The Corrinian maiden was prone to bouts of depression, true, but she seemed a sturdy and able warrior. In all, she was a blessed counterbalance to the strange young sorcerer that she had brought with her.

As they rode, the weather lifted. A cold sun shone down, drying the roads and adding a bit of cheer to what had been a bleak day. The company stopped for rest and food, and Manda started a fire so that they could dry their cloaks and warm themselves.

Helwych stayed within his shell. Kyria came out of hers. The sorceress's instinct to protect those she thought of as children had temporarily overridden her resentments, and she went so far as to smile at some of her companions and thank them when the scant meal was passed around. "Tell me, honey," she said to Wykla as the girl handed her a cup of hot broth. "What did you mean the other day when you said that you weren't always a woman? I never figured that out."

Wykla stiffened. "My lady Kyria, I did not know that you had not heard of the fate of the First Wartroop."

Kyria sipped at her broth. "So tell me."

Wykla did not seem quite sure how to begin, and she looked to Marrget, who had overheard the exchange.

The captain's eyes were frank, proud, unashamed. "Lady, some time ago, we were men," she said. "But in the war that set Corrin against Gryylth, tempers ran high, and a sorcerer struck us with a great working of magic. Now we are women."

Kyria dropped her cup. The broth smoked on the cold ground.

"Thank you, my captain," said Wykla.

"Carry on, lieutenant."

Nearby, Manda whistled and shook her head. "First, a king's daughter," she said, though Wykla blushed and moved to shush her, "and now a lieutenant. I have fallen in with a very fortunate friend. I hope—"

Her sentence might have been cut off with an axe. Even Parl and Birk looked up at the sudden, brutal termination.

She was staring at Marrget, her eyes—wide but focused, startled but seething with a passion that might have riven mountains—transfixed by the insignia of the First Wartroop . . . and of Marrget of Crownhark.

❖ CHAPTER 9 ❖

"**W**hat's with Manda?"
    At Kyria's question, Alouzon looked up from her thoughts. "I've been wondering."

Manda was riding by herself, hanging back from the rest of the party in self-imposed isolation. Since she had broken off in mid-sentence, she had not uttered another word, and now, after hours and miles, the oppression that hung about her had become impenetrable. If moods had colors, Manda's was certainly the deepest shade of black imaginable.

"She just clammed up," said Kyria. "Right after Marrget dropped that . . . that bombshell . . ." She fell silent, her mouth pursed up in a little frown that reminded Alouzon strongly of the disdain she had once seen on the faces of proper establishment ladies confronted with the hippie riff-raff.

Alouzon sighed. She was bungling this journey from the start. Even the time of year was wrong. Fifth-century culture waited for warm, clement weather in which to fight wars and battles. And here was Alouzon Dragonmaster going off into the tail end of winter with half her company at one another's throats.

Marrget cantered up. "Night is falling, Alouzon. Perhaps we had best consider where we shall camp for the night."

Kyria shied away from the captain and pulled her hood close about her face. Marrget noticed and frowned briefly.

Alouzon noticed, too. "How far are we from Bandon?" she asked Marrget. "I'm not recognizing landmarks."

"Two, perhaps three leagues."

"Shit." They had made worse time than she had thought. There was not even a town nearby. "OK, let's go on a little more, and then we'll call it quits for the day."

"It is well. I believe there is shelter ahead." With another look at Kyria, Marrget nodded to Alouzon and dropped back beside Karthin and Santhe.

Kyria sat with her head bowed, letting her horse find her own way. "I suppose that I could ask you the same question," said Alouzon.

"What question?" Kyria's voice was tight.

"What's with *you*?"

With the sun hidden behind the Camrann Mountains, the meager colors of the land had faded. They were gray riders on a gray road, traveling through a gray country. Even the sky was colorless, featureless. But Kyria's eyes were gleaming points, as though they drew their light from inner sources. "I take it that Marrget wasn't speaking figuratively."

"No. She wasn't."

"They were . . . I mean . . . the whole wartroop?"

"Yeah."

Kyria turned around and looked pointedly at Marrget, then at Wykla, as though trying to find, beneath their womanhood, some vestige of maleness. But Marrget was riding beside Karthin, her features soft and lovely but nonetheless prideful; and Wykla still looked for all the world like a college coed.

Kyria turned back quickly. "They're . . . they're freaks . . ."

Alouzon drew a breath and let it out slowly. "I'll remind you that they're my friends."

"But you just can't go around changing your sex like that!"

Alouzon allowed an edge to creep into her voice. "I

don't think they had much choice in the matter. You got a problem?''

Kyria was muttering angrily. "You're damned right I have a problem. I went along with this idiocy because I thought I was dealing with women. I thought that maybe there was some saving grace to this place. But now I find out that I'm riding around with a bunch of transsexuals.''

"They're women, dammit. They fought good and hard to survive.''

"Once a man, always a man.''

"Yeah, sure. And the System isn't the solution; it's the problem. I know slogans too.''

"Listen, honey, aren't you the least bit worried about them?''

"Worried about what?''

"Well . . . they're men. They don't think like we do.''

Alouzon resisted the temptation to backhand her. "Where the fuck do you get this stuff?''

Kyria regarded her evenly. "Experience.'' Alouzon snorted with derision and made as if to put distance between them, but Kyria went on. "I got my start in writing doing columns for one of the local women's papers. *Big Mama Rag*, or something like that. It was a strictly volunteer thing, and it showed it, but it gave us a space where we didn't have to deal with men. Not in the paper, not in the offices. One day, though, this sex-change showed up.''

Alouzon bristled. Kyria was no longer trying to keep her voice down.

"He thought he could pass as a woman and get his two cents into our paper. He ran around, trying to tell everyone what to do: typical male bullshit. Well, I told him right where he could get off. It was women-only space in the editorial offices, and it was going to stay women-only space. Bobbi—I think that's the name he was using—went off crying, but . . .''

She faltered for a moment, a genuine hesitation, but her face steeled again. "My God, Alouzon! Surely you don't expect that we're just supposed to welcome people like that with open arms?''

People like that. The same words had been used to describe her classmates at Kent State. Sandy had been a quiet Jewish girl, more interested in marriage and a future career in speech and hearing therapy than in politics. Bill had been in ROTC. Jeff had been a boy who was trying to answer some questions about life. Allison had been in love with a man and with humanities.

No matter. With their deaths, they became simply *people like that*, and drugs, lice, dirt, casual sex, communism—anything at odds with the prevailing dispensation suddenly characterized them. Martyred once by bullets, they were murdered again by rumor.

"If that's the way you operate," Alouzon said quietly, "I think that your experience isn't worth shit."

Kyria snorted. "You sound just like Sol. Go on, play with the boys. You'll learn."

Alouzon left the sorceress to ride alone and fell in beside Marrget. "Is that shelter anywhere nearby?"

"Ahead, Alouzon. And very close."

"I . . ." Alouzon groped for words and found none.

"I heard, friend. I have heard worse." Marrget brooded for a moment, then glanced up at Karthin. He smiled. She smiled, too. "And better."

But she glanced back at Manda uneasily. The Corrinian girl had known of the fate of the wartroop all along, and she had nonetheless befriended Wykla. Something deeper than mere prejudice, therefore, was the cause of her dark mood.

Marrget led the company toward the mountains and brought it at last to a slope covered with tumbled boulders, the remnants of an eroded cliff face. The house-sized stones would provide enough shelter to trap the heat of a fire and keep everyone tolerably warm through the night.

Kyria, a prisoner of her politics, did not even deign to speak to Marrget or Wykla. As a result, though, she found herself generally ostracized, and even Santhe—who took it upon himself to make sure that she had food and a place to sleep—said no more to her than what was absolutely necessary.

Karthin questioned him later, after most of the others had gone to sleep. "Are you not afraid that she will snap at you like a rabid dog?"

Santhe seemed immersed in some memory. "I feel heartily sorry for her, Karthin. And even rabid dogs must eat."

Manda had drawn first watch, and she stood just outside the range of the firelight. "I suppose they must," she said. It was the first she had spoken since the noon meal, and there was a well of bitterness in her voice that made Karthin glance at Marrget protectively. Marrget, though, was already asleep, her face quiet, her breathing even.

Alouzon listened to Manda's tone with dismay. Unlike Kyria, Manda had not withdrawn from the company. She had taken on her share of the chores and had even taken the first watch upon herself so as to spare those who had been exhausted by the day's ride. But her silence. And then, when she had spoken, her tone . . .

Could I leave one of these problems in Quay? It would be a hard decision. Manda, for all her roiling and unspecified anger, had turned into Wykla's confidante, and Wykla had fairly blossomed as a result. Kyria was the hinge of the entire expedition, and could no more be left behind than the Dragonsword.

And though Helwych was an unknown quantity, he had done nothing that she could call negative or evil. He was merely immature, and resentful.

But that hound in Kingsbury had been eating *something*.

Dithering in her blankets, she fell asleep. The moon and stars had moved when she was next aware, and Manda was shaking her. "Dragonmaster, you are needed."

Her voice was expressionless. Behind her, Alouzon could make out Karthin, and Santhe and his men. Marrget appeared next, wearing the armor that she had not taken off, not even to sleep.

I'll bet that's hard on Karthin . . . But she pulled her thoughts into order quickly, for a long, mournful howl drifted out of the dark plains to the east.

"Would you wake Kyria, Dragonmaster?" said Santhe. He smiled thinly at Karthin. "I have been told that I have already risked my fingers this night."

Alouzon crossed the camp and bent over her, but the sorceress was already awake. "Dogs, right?"

"It sounds like it."

Her staff was already glowing, but she switched it off with a word. "I was out looking around and ran into one," she said.

"Out?"

"On the astral. Or dreamland. Or whatever they call it here." Kyria tried to sound offhand, but Alouzon could sense that she was disturbed about her abilities. Just another adaptation that made her fit in more perfectly with what she saw as her ex-husband's fantasy.

"Is that what Helwych was doing in your dreams?"

Kyria shook her head violently. "Leave it. Just leave it."

When they rejoined the group, everyone was awake except for Helwych. No one had been able to rouse him.

"I have heard that he makes a practice of this," said Santhe, keeping his voice low. Plainly audible now, the howls were drawing closer.

"What if we need him?" said Karthin.

"Need him?" Kyria had turned surly. "I can handle it."

Santhe kept his smile gentle. "I do not doubt that, lady. But I daresay you cannot be all places at all times. Pray, do not deprive us of some crumbs of glory."

The sorceress looked him full in the face, found his smile unnerving, and gave up and turned away. "Crazy . . . just crazy . . ."

They spread out, forming a perimeter around the camp. From the sound of the howls, Alouzon estimated that there were at least a half dozen of the beasts. She suddenly recalled that Kyria had not taken the time to enchant the mundane weapons.

"Kyria—"

"I said I'll handle it." Kyria had climbed to the top of a boulder and was peering into the night. Off in the distance, distinct in the moonlight, shapes were moving.

With a glance back at Helwych, Alouzon drew sword. Kyria was murmuring to herself, and her staff had taken on an odd sheen, as though it were glowing in spectra imperceptible to human eyes.

The howling stopped. Fifty yards away, the hounds milled about on the grass.

"Can we cut them with regular blades?" whispered Alouzon.

"Shut up, will you? I'm busy."

The shapes milled a little more. Then, with a chorus of sharp yelps, they headed directly for the camp. "Arms, warriors," came Marrget's voice.

But with a sharp crack, Kyria's staff spewed out a shaft of brilliance as blindingly invisible as a burst of gamma rays. The beasts' howls turned to piteous whines as the meadow about them pulsed at the edge of sight, and their shadowy forms seethed into shapeless blobs. An odor as of fetid pools hung in the air.

Alouzon stared. "Damn . . ." Maybe Kyria could indeed handle it all alone.

The night was silent. Kyria sighed. "That wasn't easy. I . . ." She sat down on the rock, hands to her face. "I could use a break."

A soft sniff behind Alouzon made her turn, and she caught her breath at the sight of the single hound that was nuzzling at Helwych's motionless body. She thought fast, recalled the positions of the company. Manda was closest.

"Manda! Helwych!"

The maid leaped lightly down behind the beast, her sword ready. The hound paid no attention. But rather than attacking Helwych, it seemed to be entreating the young sorcerer to follow it. Grinning and growling softly, it seized the hem of his robe and tugged, then retreated a few paces and crouched, whining plaintively. The sorcerer was now wide awake, but petrified with fear.

Manda put an end to the game. Bravely, she advanced and cut the hound's hind legs out from under it with a single swing. With a roar, it turned on her. Her return stroke caught it in the chops, but as the beast fell back, phosphor from the wound sprayed her in the face.

She screamed and clawed at her eyes. "I cannot see!"

Santhe and Birk were closing quickly. With the precision of warriors who had fought long in one another's company, they separated so as to confront the enemy from two sides. Dragging the stumps of its legs behind it, its muzzle a seething mass of phosphor, the hound turned first toward one, then toward the other, hesitating.

Helwych got to his feet. His face said that he was terrified, but his staff was burning yellow. Wykla was pulling Manda away. Parl had taken her place. Alouzon backed up Helwych. Karthin and Marrget closed off the only exit from the camp. Unless the hound could add flight to its list of abilities, it was trapped.

As though to prove himself, Helwych jumped in and swung with his staff. The magical wood sank deep into the beast and crushed its ribs, but though it yelped in pain, it refused to attack him. Instead it made for Parl, who was armed only with a black knife.

He stood his ground until it was almost upon him, then ducked to the side, evading its spring, and simultaneously struck with the razor-sharp blade, allowing the hound's own momentum to open its side. Phosphor was suddenly everywhere, but Parl threw himself clear.

"Back off!" Kyria's voice was sharp, but there was a tremor in it.

The beast was wheeling again. Parl did not hesitate. With a lithe grace, he dived behind a boulder just as a flash of incandescence struck the hound, turned it white, then transparent, then invisible . . . and left nothing behind save a charred patch in the dead grass.

Marrget's voice was cool and efficient. "Wykla, stay

with Manda. Karthin, Santhe, Birk: circle the camp and look for further hounds. Alouzon, please throw me the water skin."

Manda's face and throat were black and smoking, and Alouzon doubted that water was going to be of much help, but she tossed the empty bag to Marrget, who caught it and ran off in the direction of a stream.

"Kyria?" said Alouzon. "Can you help Manda?"

The sorceress was tottering, and her hand was pressed to her forehead as though her brain was attempting to batter its way out. "I . . . I may be able to . . . I know not . . . I am . . . weak . . ."

Again, her tone was different. As she made her way blindly toward Manda, she fell into Alouzon's arms, and her eyes stared up at the sky. Their angry glint was gone. What Alouzon saw was relaxed, tranquil.

"I . . ." She seemed to strain inwardly, then gave up. "I am not myself, Alouzon."

Boy, I'll say. "What can I do?"

Kyria considered. "Forgive me."

While Alouzon stared at the stranger in her arms, Marrget returned with a full skin and bathed Manda's face. The maid held herself stoically, wincing but not crying out when the stream of water struck her wounds; but what was left by the slime was a ruin of raw tissue and bare bone.

"Oh . . . Manda . . ." Wykla bent over her friend, but Manda was hardly recognizable. Only patches of her golden hair remained, and she did not have enough left of her lips to form words.

Helwych spread his hands helplessly. Kyria shuddered. "I cannot wait." She wrenched herself out of Alouzon's grasp and, crawling, started toward Manda, but Alouzon and Santhe took her by the arms and half dragged, half carried her the rest of the way.

"Child," said the sorceress as she touched Manda's face lightly, "I would heal you."

The maid's sightless eyes registered nothing but pain, but Kyria did not wait for a reply. Gripping her staff with a pale hand, she laid her head against Manda's and whispered softly, singsonging the syllables of what seemed a children's lullaby. The words hung in the air like a shimmering veil, and Alouzon had a sudden vision of Manda as she had been before the phosphor had ruined her: her face sound and whole, her hair bright, her eyes deep blue.

Then Kyria was lifting her head, and Alouzon saw that the vision had been made real. Manda was healed.

Weeping, Wykla hugged her friend. Manda straightened up and passed her hands over her face as though unbelieving. Her hair hung down in damp ringlets, as though she were a little girl fresh out of her bath. "Mistress sorceress," she said. "My thanks . . ."

"It is nothing." Kyria got to her feet slowly, her eyes still full of that curious peace. She turned to Marrget. "I hope that you will forgive me also . . ."

The captain stood beside Karthin, her arm about his waist and her head resting wearily against his chest. "Forgive you?"

"For my words. I will say them again, I am sure. But I ask pardon while I can."

And while Marrget puzzled, Kyria smiled softly and collapsed. Santhe, who had been hovering nearby, caught her, led her to her blankets, and made her lie down near the fire, away from the smoldering phosphor that stained the ground like the sins of an impure heart.

Kyria was still dazed and quiet the next morning, but she insisted that the party push on. Santhe took it upon himself to care for her, and the warrior and the sorceress rode side by side. Kyria's eyes were clenched with something that seemed to partake equally of both pain and pleasure. Santhe was watchful, as though afraid that his charge might suddenly waver and pitch headlong off her horse.

They reached Bandon by late morning, and when Alouzon entered and examined the blackened ruins, she found her fears confirmed. The evidence glared at her from every bullet-riddled wall, spoke from every bomb crater, revealed itself in the smudged and blackened crisscrossings of multiple napalm strikes. But for a few peculiarities of architectural style, Bandon could well have been a burned-out village in the central highlands of Vietnam. Or a city along the coast. Quang Tri had looked like this—powdered stone mixed with charred timbers, muddy water pooling in the craters that dimpled the ground like a smallpox infection—and so had parts of Hanoi.

Kyria had stayed with the party. Addled still, and touched with uncharacteristic gentleness, she poked through the ruins, nodding absently at a line of bullet holes, weeping over the burned corpse of a little girl who had died in the flames halfway up the main street.

Kneeling in the ashes and rubble, she held the small body to herself, and though she bent her head down to the withered and charred remnants of a face as though she thought to heal, the time for healing was long past, the gesture one of hopelessness. Alouzon recalled her hysterical cries in the night: *Where are my babies?*

They were not here. There was nothing here. Kyria shook her head slowly, sadly, placed the remains of the child on the ground and turned away. "Is there . . . is there any chance that there are more survivors?" she said, laying a hand on Marrget's shoulder.

The captain shook her head. "We found who we could," she said softly, meeting both Kyria's distress and courtesy with cautious acceptance. "The rest . . ."

"You found the children, didn't you?"

"Some, lady. Gelyya, and others."

"But not all."

"Nay. For many it was too late."

The afternoon sky was cold and gray. Kyria passed a hand over her face. "Why is it always the kids? The adults do it to themselves, but the kids . . ."

Manda, who had remained within her icy detachment, turned away suddenly. Wykla put an arm about her shoulders, but she might as well have embraced a stone.

". . . but the kids . . . the kids never do anything."

Kyria's voice was hardening again. "They just suffer. War, incest, abuse, rape . . . the damned adults drag them into everything. And then they grow up . . . if they have a chance . . ." She turned to Alouzon, and the anger was back in her eyes. "Now you see why I hate him?"

Alouzon turned away, fighting back tears. Solomon Braithwaite had nothing to do with Bandon. The city—children and adults both—had perished because of Suzanne Helling.

Marrget was speaking. "I agree with you, lady Kyria." She seemed to look elsewhere for a moment. "Indeed, there are actions of my own that I would gladly undo."

Manda stiffened, fists clenched. Wykla took her hands. "Manda, Manda . . ." she said softly. "The war is over."

"Which one?" Alouzon muttered bitterly.

They left Bandon in the early afternoon. Marrget guided them west through a pass in the Camrann Mountains that led to the coast and to Quay. The high ground was dry, and the roads were good, but night caught them on the downhill side of the pass, with no shelter except that of scrub oak and scrawny pine.

Alouzon and Marrget set watches, but Kyria shook her head. "We won't be bothered tonight."

"I'm not going to sleep without watches," said Alouzon.

Kyria shrugged. "Suit yourself." She ate quickly, ignoring the camaraderie that the others had offered since she had healed Manda; and afterward she wrapped herself in her cloak at some distance from the fire. Her dark garments made her effectively invisible: she wanted to be left alone.

But Alouzon sought her out. "Look, I hate to bother you about this, but I think we're going to need those weapons enchanted. And soon."

Kyria did not look up. "Why? The standard issue stuff seems to work all right."

"You saw what that phosphor did to Manda. I don't

want that happening again. I didn't have that problem with the Dragonsword.''

Kyria held her staff across her knees, but in the faint light of the rising moon, Alouzon saw her regarding it dubiously. ''I don't like this thing,'' she said abruptly. ''It runs me just like Sol did.''

''What does that have to do with the weapons?''

''Lots. It's just like you said: out in L.A., you cut yourself on butter knives. Here you can handle a sword. Well, here I do pretty good with a staff, but it costs me.'' She gestured at the Dragonsword. ''You don't like what that does to you, do you?'' She did not wait for an answer. ''The staff is the same way. You saw what happened last night.''

It was an improvement, Alouzon wanted to say, but she bit back the words.

''I'm not sure how much help I'm going to be to you anymore,'' Kyria continued, ''because I don't like the side effects.''

''Dammit, Kyria, we could get killed!''

''Yeah, and I could lose my mind.''

''So what happens if Manda takes another faceful of phosphor?'' A thought struck Alouzon. ''And what happens if it's Marrget or Wykla?''

Kyria's mouth was pursed up like a miser's pouch. ''I don't know. I'll have to decide then.''

''You told me once that you cared about the kids. You said you'd protect them.''

Kyria's eyes flickered uneasily, but her voice was defiant. ''I care about myself. I make my own choices.''

Alouzon stood over her, wishing again that she could be rid of the sorceress. But then the party would be protected only by the dubious talents of Helwych, and with everything from jet fighters to hell-hounds running loose in Gryylth—not to mention what was waiting in Vaylle—that was certain suicide.

But if Kyria simply refused to help anyway . . . ''Then you'd better tell me about Helwych, if that's who we're going to have to count on.''

Silence. Then: "My dreams I keep to myself."

"I'm not asking about that. You saw that hound last night. It wouldn't attack even when he wounded it."

Kyria shrugged. "Sol's cagey. He likes to play. This is probably his idea of a good laugh. He laughed about that kid who got shot at Berkeley. Some things don't change."

"Come on, Kyria." The sorceress's hard-boiled persona was patently artificial, a melange of feminist politics, bull-dyke bravado, and moneyed cynicism. Alouzon was losing patience. "I saw Helwych getting eaten in Kingsbury."

Kyria started. "You didn't tell me about that."

"How the hell am I supposed to tell you anything? When I found that hound in the alleyway, it had its teeth buried in his chest. When it took off, the kid was gone. But a few minutes later he showed up looking like he always does. You got any ideas?"

Kyria glanced at Helwych. The young man was preparing for sleep, and he moved with some assurance, as though the blow he had struck against the hound had validated his membership in the company. "He doesn't seem hurt."

"I know," said Alouzon. "What's going on?"

Kyria shrugged impatiently. "I don't know." She held the staff as though it were a stiff—but very alive—rattlesnake. "I've lost enough of myself in the last day and a half. I'm not going to lose any more just because of your curiosity. If he gets in the way—my way—I'll handle him. But I'm not using this thing without a good reason." She stared off at the rising moon, her pale face set. "Sol would be a real good reason. I can't think of too many others."

❖ CHAPTER 10 ❖

Quay was a large cluster of white houses and buildings that wrapped round the tip of a wide arm of the sea as though pale hands cupped the cold, gray water. It was a peaceful sight, one that wanted only the skimming sails of fishing and trading boats to complete the picture, but as Alouzon's party descended the slopes down to the foothills, they began to notice disturbing details. There were no people in the streets: only the smoke of kitchen fires indicated that the town had not been deserted. Large blocks of houses and shops had been burnt black. And ringing the main body of dwellings was a deep ditch backed by defenses of timber and earth. Quay might have been under siege.

Kyria touched Alouzon's arm and pointed to the northern edge of the town. Where the houses gave way to small steadings and patches of farmland, two fresh craters marred the landscape.

In the late morning, they approached the ditch and the earthworks. "This is new," said Marrget. "Unlike Bandon, Quay was never a walled town. It had the goodwill of its neighbors and a good remove from the war."

"Well, it's walled now," said Alouzon.

The drawbridge was raised, and the road terminated in a twelve-foot drop to the bottom of the ditch. But before Marrget could call out, a man stood up from behind the defenses. He was strong and stocky, and his skin had been browned by the sun and weathered by the sea. He held a great bow in his hands. The tip of the arrow gleamed with the brightness of steel.

"Who comes?" His voice was flat, uncompromising.

"Hahle?" said Marrget.

"Who comes?" The arrow was nocked, and Alouzon did not doubt that he could draw the bow and send it off within seconds.

The captain hesitated. Hahle had once been her teacher, and she had already expressed doubt about this meeting. Karthin made as if to join her, but she waved him back. "Marrget of Crownhark," she said to Hahle. "With my companions Alouzon Dragonmaster, Santhe of Kingsbury, Karthin of Rutupia, and others. We bear the king's signet, and ask aid."

At her name, Hahle had lowered the bow. "Marrget?"

She smiled thinly, and nodded. "The same, master."

"Then the story was true."

"Aye. You have a woman among your students now. I . . ." She lowered her head, shook it slightly, and sighed.

But Hahle was motioning to others who were hidden behind the earthworks, and the drawbridge swung down. "If you are Marrget," he said, "then that is enough, even without the king's ring."

"I thank you, master."

The bridge thumped into place, and Hahle advanced across it with an outstretched hand. "Now I know you are Marrget. You still call me master even though you have bested me a hundred times in sword practice. Always the polite lad—"

He stopped, coloring under his tan, but Marrget pretended not to hear the reference. She took his hand. "I am pleased to see you again, my teacher. I regret that we seem to have come in time of loss."

"Aye . . . Marrget. Loss it was." Hahle peered at her, searching for the gray-eyed boy he had known.

He gave up. "Come in, all of you. Let us do you what honor we can."

There were at least fifty men behind the earthworks, armed and ready to repulse an attack. Many of them bore scars, as of acid burns, on their arms and faces. Several joined Hahle to lead the travelers up the street as Marrget performed introductions.

Hahle bowed deeply to Alouzon. "I have heard of your valor, lady," he said. "You saved our land."

Alouzon wondered. Saved it? Or had she merely prolonged its existence so as to subject it to a slow, torturous death? She did not know, could not say anything about it. "I had lots of help, Hahle."

Marrget hesitated when she came to Manda, for the maid's seemingly unprovoked anger had, if anything, increased over time. She would not even look at Marrget, and she acknowledged the introduction with a curt nod.

And when she reached Kyria, Marrget hesitated again. Kyria had virtually withdrawn from the company, and presenting her as a sorceress would only arouse vain hopes.

Hahle looked at Kyria, eyebrow lifted. She glared back with hostility.

"She is a noble lady of wisdom who travels with us," said Marrget.

Even Kyria blinked. Given the sentiments she had expressed about the First Wartroop, the description was over-generous.

"I bid you all welcome," said Hahle. "Since yesterday, food is scarce, as are lodgings, but you may stay in my own house until the council can provide for your comfort and aid."

His eyebrow lifted again, inquiring as to the aid they sought, but Marrget had a question of her own. "What happened, master? It looks as though we should be the ones bestowing aid."

"The last weeks have been difficult." Hahle's voice was as blunt as the rest of him, and he told his story without frills or ornament.

Up until Midwinter, the town's existence had been relatively uneventful. But with the turning of the year had come nocturnal visits from things that had snuffled about the houses at night, bayed in the darkness, and left behind puddles of corrosive slime. There had been no direct assaults on either people or property, but a man who had gone out to see what so disturbed the town had been found the next morning without a face.

Quay had slowly turned into a town under siege from unknown entities, but yesterday had brought an indescribable attack in broad daylight. There had been explosions and fire, and houses had collapsed, burying their occupants in stone and burning timber.

"There was roaring in the sky, and things that flew like birds, but which were not birds," Hahle said. "Those within doors died in the falling rubble; those without were covered with fire and torn to pieces by weapons that I do not understand. Perhaps a sorcerer might have knowledge of such things." He looked at Helwych, but the lad could only put on a grave face and appear thoughtful.

Kyria shifted uneasily.

They passed a burned-out section, and Hahle indicated the shattered ruins. "This was the house of Nallren, the leatherworker, and his family. Seven children, four of them sons. His daughters were strong and brave." He nodded to Marrget. "The king would have liked that. But they are all dead. I tried to rescue them, but though I could hear them screaming, the flames were too thick."

"Kids . . ." Kyria looked bleak.

Again, Alouzon wanted to crawl away and be sick, but she knew that no simple physical release could cleanse her.

"We buried the dead yesterday," Hahle continued. "Today was spent in council and in tending the wounded."

"You . . ." Kyria was staring fixedly, struggling with herself. "You have wounded?"

"Aye, lady."

"Children?"

"Many."

Despair crossed the sorceress's face. She spoke quickly, as though afraid that the words would flee if she did not utter them. "I can heal," she said. "Take me to them."

Alouzon touched her arm. "Kyria."

"Leave me alone, dammit. I'm screwed up enough by all of this. I don't need two of you meddling now."

Alouzon did not understand. Two?

"You do us honor, lady," said one of the guards.

"Just take me to them."

Hahle motioned to the man who had spoken. "Show her the way, Myylen."

Kyria dismounted and handed the bridle of her horse to Hahle. "Her name is Grayflank," she said simply. Myylen set off, and she followed, but she paused at a corner. "Kids," she said to them. "Kids again." She went off after her guide, then turned once more. *"Why is it always the goddam kids?"* Her voice was half strangled, and her hand was white on the pale wood of her staff as she followed Myylen around the corner.

Hahle's house was large and relatively undamaged. Nonetheless, a section of wall that faced away from the street was pocked with bullet holes, and the west front showed signs of a desperate struggle to stem a fire.

"I regret that my home is so comfortless," he said, showing them in. "My wife is tending the wounded, and life in general has turned hard."

"We can fend for ourselves, master," said Marrget. "I lived here when I apprenticed with you. I know where everything is."

"Aye . . . aye . . ." Hahle stared at her again. "You slept up in the loft. Such a strong lad you were."

"A strong woman, now, master."

He seemed sad. "Aye."

Despite the long journey, Manda and Wykla insisted that they be allowed to help at the infirmaries, and Hahle—obviously chagrined that guests should consider themselves forced into even voluntary labor—sent them off with a guide.

Helwych insisted that he go also. Alouzon was reluctant to let him out of her sight, but Karthin gave her a wink and accompanied him. Santhe and his men left to examine the damage that had been done to the town, and Marrget went to see to the horses.

Alouzon was sitting on a low stool before the fireless hearth, her face in her hands. She heard her host approach. "We have a guest room, Dragonmaster. I respectfully offer it to you."

She looked up from thoughts of napalm and twenty-millimeter bullets. "Thanks, Hahle. I appreciate it."

"There is no food for the time. May I offer you drink?"

"Uh . . . yeah. Cyanide, if you've got any."

"My lady, there is beer."

She shook her head. "That's OK, Hahle. Thanks just the same."

He watched her for a few moments, as though trying to decipher both her language and her mood, then bowed slightly and departed.

Wearily, she unfastened her armor and dropped it to the floor, leaned her sword against the wall. It was a relief not to feel the weight of either, and she wished that she could put off her guilts as easily.

A step at the door. Marrget entered. "The horses are provided for, Alouzon."

Hahle's words and Manda's manner had both told on Marrget. There was an uneasy look in her eye, and she glanced about the house as though afraid that, here on the coast, in a conservative town that held itself aloof from Cvinthil's reforms, the former lot of Gryylthan women might somehow overtake her.

"How are you doing, Marrget?"

"I am well." She noticed Alouzon's armor leaning against the wall. "Did you wish to rest, friend?"

"Nah. I wanted to talk to you."

Marrget's brow furrowed. "Of what matter?"

"You and Manda. She's got something against you. What?"

Marrget shook her head, genuinely puzzled. "In truth, Alouzon, I do not know."

"Manda just wouldn't have made something up, Marrget." Alouzon rummaged in the kitchen, found a barrel of beer, and poured two cups. She handed one to the captain. "Let me put it to you this way. I've got my hands full with this group. Kyria is bad enough, but Helwych gives me cramps, and this thing with Manda is one more problem I don't want. If you can think of anything that might explain her, tell me."

Marrget sat down with her beer and pondered the hearth as though contemplating nonexistent flames. "I can think of nothing."

"Where is Dubris, anyway?"

"It is a town near Whitewood, in Corrin. It lies hard by the Long River."

"You ever been there?"

"Nay. It lay always far away from the battles." A thought struck her. "Once, Dythragor and I rode deep into that part of Corrinian territory, but we did not enter the—"

She broke off suddenly. As suddenly as had Manda. Alouzon turned around in time to see her puzzlement change into horror.

"You Gods of Gryylth . . ."

"Marrget?"

Marrget rose and covered her face. She seemed on the verge of running from the room, but Alouzon took her arm. "Marrget . . ."

"O Alouzon . . . do not press me . . ."

"Marrget, I've got to know. This whole expedition is already falling apart, and you and Manda will be the last straw. You'd better level with me."

Marrget's pain was a white-hot lance. "I had thought to look for her," she murmured, "and now she has come to me."

Loath as she was to further torment her friend, Alouzon pressed. "Talk."

Marrget sat down heavily, dropped her hands. Her eyes, though closed, were full of tears. ''Dragonmaster, I . . .''

Alouzon knelt beside her. ''Marrget, cut the Dragonmaster bullshit. We're friends. You can talk to me. You've got to. We're going to be taking those kids through hell, and we've got to resolve this thing.''

Marrget wept silently. The room was still, the street quiet. ''Do you remember the night in Vorya's tent when Dythragor denied me?''

''Yeah. I remember.''

''I proved my identity by recounting two events. One took place in the Blasted Heath. The other had occurred some years earlier.

''Dythragor and I had ridden far into Corrin. It was a mannish game of foolish bravery, but we did it.'' Her eyes were still closed, as though she wished in vain for the privacy of a confessional. ''We passed near Dubris, and, at the shore of the Long River, we found two girls doing their wash.''

A horrified leanness had returned to her face, as though the recounting of the past had thrust her back into her first struggles with her new status. Her hands clutched at her bare knees.

''We . . . '' The word caught in her throat. ''We raped them. The one I chose . . . was Manda.''

She covered her face again. Alouzon stood helplessly, unable to form a coherent thought.

''O Gods, I have changed . . .''

A soft voice spoke from behind them. ''Indeed you have, captain. Were it not for your escutcheons, I would never have known you.'' Manda stood in the doorway, her sword drawn, her face pale.

Alouzon reached to her hip, realized that her sword was leaning against the wall. Damning herself for thinking so readily of weapons—nice little pacifist!— she searched for words. ''You heard, huh?''

''Everything.'' Manda walked into the room, still holding the sword.

Marrget lifted her head. Horror was etched deeply

in her face, but pride was there, too. "What would you have of me, Manda of Dubris? If you wish my life, I would have you know that I will fight."

For some time, Manda did not speak. She looked from Alouzon to Marrget with an expression of frustrated anger, of well-nourished despair. "Six years ago," she said, "I was the daughter of a farmer, and I carried the wash down to the river with my beloved friend, Kasi. I had never done you injury, Marrget of Crownhark. I did not even bear you malice, for in my innocence, I thought that perhaps the war would end someday. And yet . . ." She struggled with the words as she had struggled beneath her rapist: impotent, mastered. "And yet you took me."

She looked down at the sword in her hand. "When I came here, I intended to kill you. But now . . ." Her voice broke under the weight of her rage. "I . . . I find I cannot." She flung her sword to the floor, and it rang shrilly on the flagstones. "It seems that the man I sought is already dead."

Alouzon watched a tear trace a path down Marrget's cheek. O Gods, she had changed.

At last, Marrget found her voice. "Is there—"

"No, captain, there is nothing you can do. Is it within your power to unmake the past?"

Marrget's lips barely moved. "Nay."

Manda advanced until she stood directly before Marrget, her hands balled into fists. "I . . . cannot . . . forgive you."

Marrget bent her head.

"I will obey your orders, captain, as well as any warrior you could command. But I cannot but wish that, someday, you might know what I felt that afternoon. Perhaps I can only wait for that justice."

Marrget did not look up. "I understand, Manda."

Manda picked up her sword and sheathed it. With a slight bow to Alouzon, she left the room.

Alouzon felt as though the space behind her eyes had been blasted out with hot sand. "Marrget."

"Dragonmaster."

The title hurt. "No. No Dragonmaster. I'm still your friend, Marrget."

"What shall I do, Alouzon?" Marrget's voice was barely audible. "Shall I say to Manda *I am sorry*, and expect that to be the end of it? I am a woman now, and I understand her. I have lain with Karthin in love, and now I wonder how I have ever been allowed that intimacy when I myself have . . . have . . . "

As she had once seized hold of her emotions and, by dint of sheer will, forced herself to accept her womanhood, Marrget now caught her grief and stifled it with a wrench that Alouzon found painful. Rising, the captain turned desolate eyes on her friend. "I will survive," she said, but it seemed that this survival, unlike that which she had found on a midsummer night, did not allow for the smallest shred of happiness or joy, but was only a prolongation of a deep and indelible sorrow.

Out beyond the breakers and the foam, sea gulls stitched through the sea, flapping and crying mournfully in the cold air. The water was gray, and fish, it appeared, were scarce, for the gulls had a frustrated, dissatisfied look about them.

Manda walked along the shore, head bent, sword sheathed at her side, arms folded across her chest. She felt like a fool. Somehow, despite her knowledge of the fate of the First Wartroop, she had always thought that she would eventually find the man who had raped her (if he were still alive), and kill him. The bitter vows that she had made had not allowed for any other outcome.

But Tireas the sorcerer, in working magic that he had thought would both demoralize Gryylth and avenge a friend, had provided a third option. Marrget of Crownhark was dead . . . and yet alive. Or perhaps neither. Marrget was as much a different person as it was possible to be without an intervening death and rebirth.

Manda admitted that she should have been satisfied.

Marrget had been violated by Tireas's spell beyond any conceivable justice—raped, and raped again. And yet, it had not been Manda's own hand that had exacted the retribution, and so she was left empty and hollow. When she had faced Marrget, she had felt no exultant flush of long-awaited vengeance. Instead, everything upon which she had built her life had, abruptly, crumbled like towers of dust.

Warrior? Was she indeed a warrior? Or had she trained and practiced and hardened her body so as to prepare for the one single action that was now forever beyond her reach?

A breaker approached, toppled, licked up along the sand and tugged at her boots. She looked out at the ocean. "Where is my comfort, O Gods?"

"Manda! Manda!"

Wykla was running after her, amber hair streaming. Watching her, Manda smiled suddenly. She was surprised: she had thought that her smiles were gone forever.

Wykla fell into step beside her. "I missed you," she said. "I looked up from my work, and you were gone."

"I had finished what I could do at the infirmary. So I left."

Wykla looked disturbed. "I would you had told me."

"Why?"

"Because . . ." Wykla seemed puzzled. "Because I . . . I am your friend . . ."

Friend. The word had an odd sound, as though it did not quite fit.

". . . and friends care for one another. You have been unhappy, and I would help if I could, if only by my company."

Manda reached out a hand, and Wykla took it. They continued along the shore. "Your company is welcome."

"I would do more, if I could." Wykla smiled softly, and the breeze from the sea fluffed her hair into curls and tendrils that had—Manda knew, though Wykla did not—caught the hearts of quite a number of the men of Gryylth and Corrin.

The thought made Manda suddenly jealous, and she clung to Wykla's hand. "You are kind and generous, Wykla of Burnwood. When I offered my friendship on the road to Benardis, I had no idea that I would be so handsomely repaid."

"I could say the same, Manda. But I do not wish to speak in terms of payment."

"Nor do I." Manda stopped, awash suddenly with emotion.

"You are troubled," said Wykla.

She had never told Wykla of the rape, and she was now terrified that she would indeed tell. What would the girl think? "I have memories that I would be very willing to forget."

"Would sharing them with another be of help?"

"I . . . I do not know."

Wykla pulled gently on her hand, and they started off again. "Perhaps you should try, Manda. I am no midwife, skilled in counsel and advice. But . . . but I love you."

Manda stiffened. In what sense did Wykla use that word? "Share with me something first, friend," she said. "Tell me of the time when Tireas . . ." She did not finish the question. She was surprised that she had even begun it.

Wykla understood. "I wanted to die," she said. "Everything that I had worked for was suddenly gone. I had grown up being thought of as womanish and weak, and I desired to join the First Wartroop so as to prove otherwise. And then to find myself . . . " Her voice caught.

"Forgive me, Wykla. Do not go on."

Wykla licked her lips, swallowed. "Nay, friend. I will speak. I remember sitting by the fire with the other women, thinking that I might will myself to die if I strove mightily enough. But Alouzon came to me, and I found the strength to endure. And then I met you . . ."

She bent her head quickly, embarrassed at her words, blushing in spite of cold wind.

"I met you, Manda," she continued. "And I learned to do more than endure. I think now that perhaps someday I may be proud to be a woman, if I can be a woman like you."

Raped? And angry? And hating Marrget with all the passion of a blazing star? "You do not know me, Wykla."

"I could know you better."

"Very well, then. You shall judge." Without emotion, Manda told of the rape. She did not name Marrget or Dythragor: the violations were anonymous, impersonal, as they should have remained.

When she finished, Wykla was silent for some time, and Manda fought a sudden urge to run. But Wykla looked up at last and slipped an arm about her waist. "I grieve with you, Manda. You are strong: stronger than I. I do indeed hope someday to be a woman like you."

"Have you . . ." It was obscene to ask. But Manda asked. She had to know. "Have you ever lain with a man, Wykla?"

The girl did not meet her eyes. "Nay. Nor with . . ." Her mouth worked for a moment. "Nor with a woman. Before or after."

"Nor I," said Manda. "Before . . . or after."

Wykla pulled her to a stop and stood facing her. "The night at the Circle, Manda, when I took the watch . . ." She flushed with the admission. "I touched you."

"I felt it."

"If I gave offense, I am sorry."

"You gave no offense. I was flattered."

Wykla's eyes were troubled. "Do you mean that?"

"I do. I . . . I had wished that perhaps you would have remained for a minute more . . . or longer . . ."

"Is it . . ." Wykla bit at her lip. "Is it seemly for a woman to do that?"

Manda touched her cheek, her hand shaking. She had

loved Kasi, and fate had parted them forever. Now
Wykla . . . "I care little whether it is seemly or not."

They held one another then, and Manda had to bend
only a little to bring her lips down to Wykla's. But the
kiss was merely confirmation: it was enough to embrace, to know that the world was not empty.

Their arms full for the first time, they found that they
could not bring themselves to let go, and they stood for
many minutes on the beach—amber hair and gold hair
woven together by the wind—trying to reassure themselves that, should they find the strength to open their
arms, they would not be swept apart.

Manda saw it first. High above and far out across the
sea, drawing closer with a rapidity that was fearful in
itself, something approached that was like and yet unlike a bird.

It screamed as it came, and it was suddenly very
close, banking and diving on them, spitting flashes of
light with a sound as of cloth being torn in two. A
hundred yards away, sand and foam erupted in a line
of destruction that swept toward them like a scythe.

The women reacted instinctively and shoved each
other away just as the ground between them exploded,
scouring their arms and legs with hot sand. Blinded by
grit, deafened by noise, they fell, groping frantically
for one another, and when their vision cleared, they saw
that the thing had finished with them.

But it was now diving toward Quay.

...

... to ...
... ...
...

... ...
... ...
... ...
...

❖ CHAPTER 11 ❖

The first explosion threw Alouzon into Marrget, and the two women tumbled to the floor as the front wall of Hahle's house crashed down in a shower of stone, wood and thatch. Alouzon clawed her way to her feet more by instinct than by intent, terrified at the thought of lying inert and helpless in the face of such an attack.

She pulled Marrget up beside her, grabbed the Dragonsword, and then they were climbing over the rubble, splinters and fragments of stone lacerating their hands. When they gained the top of the pile, they saw that, on the other side of the narrow street, the buildings and houses had been leveled. Red flames were already springing up in the heaps of thatch that had slid from fallen roofs, and the dust of stone and mortar hung in the air like a shroud.

Alouzon buckled her sword over her linen tunic, wishing that she had not doffed her armor, but a screaming came across the sky, and she knew then that leather would be no more protection than cloth, for she recognized the unmistakable sound of a turbojet engine.

They gained the street, and Alouzon saw, high up and off to the north, the flicker of white wings as a McDonnell Douglas Skyhawk banked around for another run at the town. Afternoon sunlight flashed on the cockpit canopy, and dark beneath the fuselage were the bulges of napalm pods and bombs.

She grabbed Marrget's hand. "You lived here. Where are the infirmaries?"

The captain seemed fascinated by the sight of the jet, but with the discipline of a seasoned warrior, she turned to the task at hand. "I believe the Council Hall would be the likely choice. It has large rooms, and is at the center of town."

The Skyhawk was diving again. Sprinting across open ground, the women threw themselves into the shelter of a thick stone wall just as the plane strafed the length of the street, churning the bare earth into the consistency of a plowed field.

In the wake of the shriek of the turbojet came screams and cries. People were trapped in houses, buried under rubble, dying slowly or quickly. The jet circled again.

My fault. This is all my fault. Damn the war. Damn all of it. Aloud, Alouzon said: "It's going to be napalm next, I bet."

"Napalm?"

"Fire."

Marrget sheathed her sword. "We need Kyria."

Alouzon was already running toward the center of the town, moving as fast as she could along the rubble-choked street, trying to ignore the frantic whimpers and cries of the wounded. Behind her, Marrget kept pace, calling out directions with what breath she could spare. The sound of the jet picked up, Doppler shifting in a rising whine as it accelerated toward the town once more. It streaked overhead and flashed into the distance, and Alouzon heard the *crump* of impacting napalm pods. Thick orange flames erupted off to her left. The westering sun was suddenly obscured by black smoke.

They found Kyria standing in the middle of the town square. The wizard's staff was burning in her hand, but she looked vacant. She stared at them, then at herself, then at her staff, then at the flitting image of the Skyhawk that screamed through the sky.

"Kyria! Do something!"

Helwych was standing beside her, his eyes wide and his face gaunt with fear. He shook his head. "She has been like this since the last healing, Dragonmaster." He could scarcely get the words out. "She is not herself."

"Helwych, you got any tricks up your sleeve?"

The lad was striving valiantly to master himself. "I know little, Dragonmaster." He looked ready to cry. "I was taught nothing."

"Find something, big guy." Alouzon gave him a gentle shove in the direction of the circling plane. "Anything. Leave Kyria to me."

Marrget had plunged toward the Council Hall, calling Karthin's name. Alouzon seized Kyria by the shoulders. "Helen! Kyria! Dammit, come out of it!"

Kyria looked blank. "Alouzon? Is that you?"

"We need help!"

"Who am I?"

Perplexed, and damning herself for being so, Alouzon tried to decide on the best answer. How deeply had the identity of Kyria rooted itself into Solomon's angry ex-wife? How deeply did she resent it?

Regardless, Helen Addams had only words and spite at her command. It was Kyria who had the power that Quay needed. Alouzon shook her. "Kyria! You're Kyria!"

Her words were nearly drowned out by the roar of a Pratt and Whitney turbine. Bullets riddled the Council Hall, and part of the roof fell in. The heat of napalm fires flickered at her back, and dust and smoke added a twilight cast to the scene.

Stifling her fears, Alouzon kept at Kyria. "You're a sorceress. Do something. People are getting killed."

"I've . . . I've got to make my own choices."

Another explosion. Alouzon grabbed Kyria and shielded her from the hail of dirt and gravel propelled by the concussion. Her back stung, and a baseball-sized stone sent blood trickling through her hair. "You haven't got any more choice than I do," she said. "You want those kids to get killed?"

Kyria looked hopelessly at her staff. "Kids again . . ."

Nearby, a flash of blue fire sprang up. Helwych was conjuring, sending trails of light toward the speeding jet. The colors snaked through the sky, but the Sky-hawk flew through them unharmed and began another run.

The mention of children, though, had galvanized the sorceress. Sucking in a breath, she struck the butt of her staff on the ground, and blue-white light leapt along its length. "All right, Sol," she cried. "You want to play? Come and get me!"

Her staff blazing like a star, she ran out into the square and took aim at the Skyhawk. The plane banked sharply, dropped another pod of napalm, and came directly for her, twin cannon twinkling with death.

"Come on . . ."

The tracers streaked whitely through the smoke, but Kyria's staff eclipsed them with stellar brilliance. Blue-white shaded now into blue-violet, as though, with the urgency of her need, Kyria was tapping deeper and deeper into the fundamental powers of the universe.

The bullets were almost on her when she let the charge go. Instantly, the Skyhawk was enveloped in a lethal cloud of seething glory. The cannon cut off as though a switch had been thrown, and, a moment later, the jet exploded in a massive fireball studded with bits of metal and plastic. A wing pinwheeled off to the side. The tail section tumbled through the air. Burning, trailing smoke and flame, the wreckage arced over the town and crashed to the earth some distance outside the fortifications.

Kyria fell to her knees, sobbing. "Leave me alone. Just leave me alone. I can't do this . . ."

Alouzon tried to raise her to her feet, but the sorceress was hysterical now, her eyes unseeing, her cries obviously directed not at Solomon, nor at the Sky-hawk, but at something else.

"Go away! I don't want you anymore!" She beat her hands on the cobblestones and seemed ready to batter her head in a like manner, but Alouzon held her, pinning her arms to her sides. Kyria wept and screamed. "Stop it!" But again, Alouzon knew that she was addressing someone—or something—else.

"Kyria . . . please . . . it's going to be all right." How easily the words came to her lips now! Bandon was dead, Quay was dying, and the corpses of her friends and companions might well be scattered throughout the city, their eyes as sightless as those of the dead men left behind by the wrath of the Tree; yet still she insisted that all would be well.

What prompted such foolish optimism? The Grail? Was she now offering the promise of the Sacred Cup to one who would doubtless spit at it?

Kyria wept. "Kids . . . always the kids . . . and me too now . . ."

Would she spit, though? Alouzon found herself echoing Kyria's question: who was she? Certainly not Helen Addams. And yet she was Helen Addams indeed.

"We are well, Alouzon," came Marrget's clear voice, seconded by Karthin's basso.

Still struggling with Kyria, Alouzon offered thanks to whatever Gods heard prayers from Gryylth. "What about the others?"

Karthin answered. "Of our own company, we do not know, Dragonmaster. But those whom Kyria healed are now in need of healing again."

"Kyria . . ." The sorceress was sobbing weakly now, exhausted with healing, killing, and struggle against herself. "Kyria, we need you again."

"Can't . . . can't do it . . . I don't even know who I am . . ."

"You're Kyria. You've got the power. You have to use it."

"It uses me."

"I know. We're all being used. Come on: one more push."

Kyria sobbed again and slumped in her arms. "I can't. I can't. I can't."

Abruptly, in spite of her words, she rallied. Straightening, she opened eyes that were suddenly clear and dashed a sleeve across her face to wipe away her tears. "I will heal," she said, her voice touched with strange inflections. "But I am weak, Alouzon. Pray, take me where I am needed."

"Kyria?"

"It is I."

Alouzon hesitated. "Who are you?"

"One who is needed at present. Please, Alouzon. Quickly."

Amid the pungent odor of high explosive, the smoke of burning napalm, and the crackling of burning thatch and timber, Alouzon took her toward the Hall as townsfolk—stunned, wounded, bloody—began trickling into the square. Santhe, Parl, and Birk showed up a moment later in the company of Hahle and the men from the defenses; and after assuring himself that his wife was safe, Hahle began organizing those who had not been hurt into firefighting and rescue teams, sending the injured to gather before the doors of the Hall.

The Hall itself had been damaged, how heavily no one knew, but Marrget and Karthin plunged back into the building. With Helwych helping as best he could, they brought out the survivors and laid them in the square. Newly-healed limbs had been shattered once again, and wounds that sorcery had closed minutes before now gaped wide and red.

In the fields to the north of the town, the jet burned fiercely, streaking the sky with smoke.

"And what if there's another?" Alouzon murmured.

"There will be no others . . . for a while," said Kyria.

"You sure?"

"I am. But we must be away by tomorrow morning, for we are but one step ahead of those powers that seek to destroy us."

The sorceress's black eyes were serious, and their brightness told of a depth that might have contained worlds. Alouzon nodded, wondering at what she saw. "Yeah. I got that impression."

In the smoke-darkened sunlight, Kyria's staff shown pale yellow as she went to work, and she moved quickly from person to person, pausing to touch, to chant, to lay her head against that of a terrified girl or boy as the magic did its work. Chest wounds vanished, bullet holes healed in moments, arms and legs that had been mutilated beyond recognition were made whole and reattached.

Marrget and Karthin brought forth the sick, and Kyria healed them. It seemed natural to her: a simple, loving gesture of one human being to another, with no conditions, no judgment, no anger or hate or vengeance. Boy and girl, woman and man, she left them all alive and wondering at the health that was now theirs.

And when she was done with those from the Hall, she, with Alouzon and Marrget supporting her, moved into the town. Quay was a ruin of smoking buildings and tumbled stones, and some sections were still burning fiercely, but those of its inhabitants who had not been killed outright in the attack were, by sunset, unharmed.

But the effort sapped her. Whether from the flow of power or from the interior struggle against herself, Kyria grew visibly paler with each working, and though her smile and her comfort remained undiminished, her eyes were glassy with strain by the time the last healing was done.

She stood up from smoothing Wykla's sandblasted legs and touched the girl lightly on the head. "I seem to heal you often, child."

Wykla was speechless. She also had heard Kyria's words the day before.

"Fear not," said Kyria. "Be well. Be . . ." She glanced knowingly at Manda. "Be happy."

Then, with a lurch, she gasped for breath and fell full-length on the ground.

* * *

Helen Addams lurked in the crawling shadows of the world, waiting for a chance to move. Kyria was hard at work, her white hands lying lightly on the wounds of child and adult alike, bringing healing and comfort; but soon the healing would be done and the battle would begin again.

Weak, silly little thing! If Kyria was so powerful, why then did she not destroy the woman who was waiting for an opportunity to strike a killing blow? Why did she insist upon merely pinning her in place?

An enemy left alive was an enemy who could rise up and attack. Solomon had found that out. The stupid fool should have gotten out of the marriage while he could. As it was . . . well, his stupidity had cost him, and if he had come back, it would cost him again.

Again, Helen tested the invisible walls, reaching out taloned hands to feel the flavor of the energies that washed against her hide. She was growing increasingly desperate, and she cursed the half-existence she was forced to endure while Kyria moved with graceful ease in the physical world, admired, even loved, by the very people that Helen had come to hate.

Kyria finished her work and the walls crumbled. The sorceress had been taxed by her efforts, but as her assailant leaped at her, she turned, smiling softly, her arms open. "Come," she said. "I will not hurt you. We must do this together."

Helen tried to curse her aloud, but inarticulate screams were all that she could manage as she bore the sorceress to the ground and slid her hands about her throat.

Immediately she smelled the sea: salt, the fresh clear air of a New England morning. The Atlantic was quiet today, and the hills were as green as the sky was blue.

No . . . no, not this . . .

It was her eighteenth birthday, and arrayed in her youth, her womanhood still a new thing that offered questions and wonder with each day, she had gone from her father's house and descended to the shore. Solomon had left for Korea the day before, and though his absence was a hollowness in her heart, she felt paradoxically full, as though the very fact that she would be here, at home, waiting for him to return, could supply both of them with the strength that they needed to endure the hardships and separation brought by the distant war.

That was, it seemed, her duty: to wait, to support, to nurture through the days and weeks the love that they had come to share. Solomon had the outer world of battle and male camaraderie; she herself had a quieter universe of more tender emotions. And both, she divined on this rarest of mornings, were good, and necessary. Through Solomon she could be complete, and thus could he be made whole.

Kyria stared up at Helen with gentle eyes, but Helen's hands tightened on her throat. Damn her for these recollections! In reaching into her mind and pulling them forth, the sorceress was violating her just as surely as had Solomon when, in the predawn darkness of their bedroom, he had grabbed her—fatigued, sore, and frightened though she was—and forced her to take his penis.

Raped, and raped again: morning after morning, year after year.

"Come," said Kyria. "This is both of us. We must work together."

With a howl, Helen struck her in the face. Kyria wept, but more memories came, and, indeed, the sorceress's tears seemed to be more of sorrow than pain.

We must work together . . .

There was no light in the bedroom, and Helen was huddled into the dark corner between the bed and the wall, wanting nothing so much as to make it darker, to pull the bedspread and blankets off the bed and cover herself, as though there were any refuge black and silent enough to hold the hell of her.

Mercifully, it had been quick: a trip to the parking lot of a grocery store on the other side of town, an automobile slipping up in the night, an open door. All quick. And then another trip with a blindfold over her

eyes, the car turning and vibrating and turning again
while, up front, the woman in the passenger seat
counted out the sheaf of hundred-dollar bills, quickly,
the numbers murmuring off her tongue in a practiced
monotone.

Sol's money. It was fitting that it be Sol's money.
After all, it was his lust and his wad of sperm that had
started it all. That had been quick, too: a harsh breath
as he penetrated her, and fast, rhythmic gasps as he
worked himself to climax. He might have been stabbing her, thrusting a blade into her body again and
again, whimpering in a killing frenzy that now ended
in the obligatory death.

Quick. Up the back stairs of the warehouse, her
blind feet stumbling on the metal steps. Quick again.
Out of her clothes and into the frayed hospital gown.
Quicker still. On her back in the dingy room, her feet
in the stirrups, the doctor's voice (she hoped that he
was a doctor) muffled as he asked the nurse for imple-
ments with names so arcane they might have denoted
the tools of sorcery.

Quick. Quicker. And then she was home, cramping,
bleeding, the house dark and the corner of the bedroom darker. Maybe in the blackness of this Berkeley
evening—just maybe—she could hear the cries of her
lost child, cries that, unuttered, rang nonetheless in
her imagination and mixed with the sound of her own
voice as she screamed incoherently into the muffling
presence of the down pillow.

Stop. Stop it. Damn you!

And then Sol coming home at last, stumping up the
stairs, dropping his briefcase on the bedroom floor.

"Where's dinner?" he said.

But Helen was crying, wrapped in the blackness of
the corners of the universe, Kyria's arms about her
with the warm comfort of infinite nurture. "Helen . . .
Helen," said Kyria. "It is ours. You are not alone. I
love you."

Helen could not speak, but words were meaningless. They could convey neither the depth of her loss

nor the violation perpetrated upon her by intimate flesh and impersonal stainless steel. She wept and she wailed, asking in her incoherence for the return of her children, the return of her body, the return of her soul. She could not demand, she could only ask.

Please don't do that to me . . .

"I will not do that again," said Kyria, rocking her back and forth like a child. "I will not. Please do not try to kill me, though. Believe me—please believe me—when I say to you that I love you. And let me help."

And what frightened Helen beyond the loss of her voice, beyond the strangeness of the state to which she had come, beyond even the memories with which the sorceress defended herself with passionate and yet gentle violence, was the fact that she now could not say for sure who was speaking, for Kyria's voice was ripe with the repletion of a summer morning in New England, dark with the sorrow of a winter night in Berkeley, and touched with the words, thoughts and tones of Helen Addams.

"Come, child. Come to me. I can help."

Exhausted, Alouzon dozed at Kyria's bedside. The sorceress had not moved since she had collapsed from her labors, and, in fact, she hardly seemed to be breathing. But Marrget had examined her and pronounced her living, and Helwych had verified the captain's judgment magically, though he had seemed afraid to do even that; and so Kyria had been brought to one of the few undamaged houses in Quay to rest in safety.

Alouzon's thoughts drove on relentlessly in spite of her fatigue. *We are but one step ahead of those powers that seek to destroy us,* Kyria had said, and those powers had materialized fully now, reified not in the half-material presence of spectral hounds, but in the prosaic anachronism of a jet fighter that might have rolled off an assembly line in Long Beach, California.

Half asleep, yet watching for any sign that might

indicate that Kyria was returning to consciousness, Alouzon shuddered with the recollection of the explosions, the screams, the white faces of the people of Quay as they struggled to understand the reason for the terror that had been unleashed upon them.

But there was no reason. Or, if there were, it was buried deep within her own unconscious. How, she wondered, was she supposed to stop the violence when the violence was coming out of her own mind? How could she end it when she did not even understand its origins?

The Grail remained in the background: as ephemeral as a dream, as real as the bullets that had swept through the town that afternoon. Somehow, the Grail was the answer. And as that Sacred Cup had chosen to dwell within the shadowy unknowns of the land called Vaylle, she would find it there.

Vaylle might well be a hell, but the only way to the Grail was through the flames.

"But I don't want this," she murmured. "I don't want any of this. I want to go home."

Kyria stirred. "Home . . ."

Alouzon came awake. "Kyria?"

"I want to go home." The sorceress echoed Alouzon's sentiments. "I want my house. I want my babies . . ."

Helen Addams had borne no children, but Kyria's grief was real. Alouzon began to suspect that there were events buried in the history of Helen and Solomon that, unearthed, would reek as corrosively as the blood of the hounds of Vaylle.

"Easy, Kyria," said Alouzon, taking her hand gently.

Kyria's eyes flicked open, and widened at the sight of the dark, beamed ceiling and the lap of firelight on stone walls . . .

And then she was huddling into a trembling ball, pulling the covers over her head and burying her face in the pillow as she screamed in a grief so deep that it made Alouzon's sorrows seem petty.

Across the room, Santhe lifted his head. "Dragon-master?"

"I'll handle it, Santhe," she said. The councilor did not look convinced, but Alouzon turned back to the sorceress. "Kyria, come on. It's me: Alouzon. You're having a nightmare."

"I want my babies. He took my babies."

"Kyria." Alouzon knelt beside the couch and wrapped her arms about the sorceress. "Come on, we're all friends here. We all care about you."

"Leave me alone, Kyria . . ."

Alouzon wondered at her words, but held her none-theless. "Wake up, Kyria. Come on . . ."

The sorceress stopped thrashing, though she was shaking uncontrollably. "What's . . . what's going on?"

Alouzon licked dry lips. "You healed a bunch of people, and then you blacked out."

"How long?"

Alouzon shrugged. "I don't have my watch. I'd say about twelve hours. It's almost dawn."

Kyria sat up, clutching the pillow to her stomach. "I hurt," she whispered. "I want to go home."

Alouzon's face was against her long, black hair. Kyria had said it perfectly. *I want to go home.* Cars, and soda pop, and her own bed: all the little comforts that could be summed up in a single word. Right now she wanted to hear rock and roll so badly that the desire was a physical need. But this was Gryylth, and Los Angeles was far away, and even if, by some chance, Silbakor returned this instant and swept her back to the city, there would still be Vaylle, and hounds, and McDonnell Douglas Skyhawks . . .

. . . and people would still be dying.

"I'm sorry, Kyria," she said softly. "I want to go home, too. But we can't. The only way out of this is through it. And we can't go home until we're done."

"That bastard . . . I haven't even got myself any-more. And he's killing everyone." Fists clenching suddenly, she closed her eyes and shrieked. *"I want out!"*

Santhe rose quietly and came to kneel at her bedside. There was no laughter in him tonight. "Honored lady," he said softly, "I believe that we all do. But as you healed the children of Quay this afternoon, so you may now be able to heal an entire land by coming to Vaylle with us. And I most earnestly ask that you do."

Kyria listened, her eyes owlish. "You're a pretty decent guy, Santhe," she said, her voice hoarse. "You've been good to me. How come you're in such a screwed-up world?"

"My lady," he said gently, "the Gods do not burden us with more than we can endure. I do not know their reasons, but reasons there must be."

Alouzon looked away.

"I know one reason," Kyria said. "And I'm going to Vaylle to find him, Santhe. And you can bet that I'm going to stop all this shit."

Her outburst had calmed her, but a new note had crept into her tone and manner as though she were storing up her anger, allowing it to accumulate drop by drop, memory by memory, event by event, holding it in check until it was needed.

"Alouzon," she said. "When do we leave for Vaylle?"

"Hahle has a boat for us. We can leave as soon as we're ready."

"Tomorrow."

"Kyria, it's a long crossing. We'll have to get everything together, and you've been unconscious."

"Tomorrow." Kyria found her staff and clutched it tightly. The wood flared. "We're going tomorrow."

❖ CHAPTER 12 ❖

Dindrane awoke with her heart pounding and her hand reaching for her healer's staff. She was often pulled out of sleep this way, the screams of dying and mutilated townsfolk ringing in her ears on the physical plane and, upon the subtler fabric of the spiritual world, the wails of souls that had found themselves suddenly—terribly—bereft of life cutting her psyche like shards of hot glass.

But no: from the next room came the scrape of wire on wood, and she realized that one of the bronze strings of Baares's harp must have broken, startling her out of sleep. Even now, Dindrane could hear her husband fumbling through his work-box, measuring and cutting the right length of wire, winding the lower end about a toggle. He worked methodically and silently, but he cursed passionately under his breath when the new string slipped from his fingers and rang against the others.

Sitting up, she covered her face and willed her heart to cease pounding, but she winced at her husband's temper. Despite frayed nerves and broken sleep, this was no time for emotions that could only add to the sorrow.

"You are awake, Dindrane?" Baares's voice was soft—chagrined and sorrowful both. "Forgive my outburst."

"Fear not," she called back. "I was awake already."

He pushed back the curtain and entered the bedroom. "You should sleep, my flower."

"I slept a little." She tried to sound reassuring, but
rest had been in short supply these last few months.
With each night bringing new terrors, the healers of
Vaylle were frequently summoned from their beds to
restore limbs, close wounds, ease pain. Too often,
though, they could be no more than a comfort to the
dying: an embodiment of the Goddess, a feminine
touch to help the soul along the path of the Sacrificed
God.

But tonight there was peace, and Dindrane stretched
out a hand and brought her husband to bed. For a
while, they lay together, arms wrapped about one another, and then Baares rose, fetched his harp, and sat
by the bed, weaving a sleeping spell about her.

Her eyes growing heavy, she watched him as he
played, his head bent in concentration, the fingers of
his big hands striking and muting strings, making music and magic that befitted the skill of the king's
harper.

*And he is angry, and sometimes violent . . . and so,
to our shame, are we all. But we can hold to other
ways. And—O my Goddess!—he is mine and I love
him.*

She drifted off then, and when she awoke, it was
morning. "Time to rise, my flower," said Baares.

He must have spent the night playing, wandering in
a world of melody, deriving renewal from the music
he drew from the harpstrings. She wrapped her arms
about his neck and pulled his face down to hers.
"What time, husband?"

"The second hour past dawn. You are due to make
your magistrate's report to King Pellam."

Her smile turned pained. "A happier tale I wish that
I could tell."

"He wishes to hear it, nonetheless. He is a wise and
holy king."

"Hard it is to speak of death when one is a healer.
And too much death there is these days."

Baares sat down beside the bed, holding her hand while he stroked his great mustache thoughtfully, deliberately. "Sometimes I am wondering, though . . ." He paused, seemingly unwilling to continue.

Dindrane tugged at his hand. "Better spoken than not."

The harper shrugged uncomfortably. "There are dissonances within the harp," he continued. " 'Twas last night I was thinking of them. Among the concord are pairs of strings that yield only pain. I sometimes wonder if they bear a lesson for us."

Dindrane stroked his hand.

" 'Tis angry I am," he said softly. "Angry we all are, I think. Our people are killed, our children are dragged out of their beds and savaged . . ." His eyes were full of tears. "I am too violent for this place. But the Goddess and the God made the harp so that it can cut the ear, and so I wonder sometimes whether we might be forgiven the cutting of our enemies."

Dindrane said nothing. They had discussed this question before. Many times. The answer was the same.

"I know I am wrong," he admitted. " 'Tis the grace of the Goddess I am wanting. She perhaps can give me peace: no one else."

"I cannot?"

He bent his head to hers, smiling shyly. "This I will tell you, my flower: should it ever be my fortune in life to meet the Goddess face to face, I do not doubt that Her ways would be as yours: Her voice, your voice. Indeed, I think that at night I hold Her in my arms already."

Dindrane felt her face grow warm. "You have a glib tongue, O harper."

"I have a truthful tongue, O Great Lady."

She shushed him. "Do not give me Her title."

He shrugged. "The Goddess knows that it is well bestowed, even if Priestess Dindrane does not."

Still blushing furiously at his sacrilege, she arose and dressed, and she and Baares broke their fast on

the terrace of their house after first offering thanks to
the rising sun, Dindrane holding the cup of wine while
Baares conjoined his knife with it, an emblem and re-
enactment of the rite that sustained and nourished the
world.

Breakfast was good: dark bread, hot porridge, dried
fruit, and the sacred wine of the Great Rite. Below,
Lachrae was awakening, and somewhere nearby a
woman and her man were singing a soft duet as they
went about their morning tasks, her voice riding lightly
upon his supporting bass: woman and man together,
complementing one another, fulfilling their sacred
roles.

A lump rose in Dindrane's throat at the thought that
such wholeness still endured in the face of the continuous attacks from the land across the Cordillera. Any
night could bring another visitation from the howling,
ravening dogs, or from the brutal Grayfaces. And just
two days ago, in broad daylight—daylight!—one of the
flying things had streaked across the sky, ignoring the
city and the kelp fishermen, making instead for
Gryylth.

And what havoc had it raised in that distant land?
She did not know. But it had not returned, and that
fact made her uneasy. Was Gryylth in league with the
dark land? Or had the people there actually found it
within their will and their power to . . .

Dindrane paled and set down the cup. The thought
was a grievous one. The dogs took life. The Grayfaces
took life. The flying things brought fire and explosion.
But what besides such unnatural horrors could wan-
tonly and willfully kill?

The thoughts were still with her as she made her
way toward the King's House along the broad, white
streets of Lachrae, her torque of office about her neck
and her long cloak wrapped tight against the morning
cold. Townsfolk greeted her and exchanged hugs and
news, but there was a sense of desperation and fear in
their manner that was the product of nightly killings.

Dindrane tried to smile reassuringly so as to give

them hope and strength, for as she was chief priestess, she could not but give of herself to sustain the people that were in her care. Her duty—indeed, the duty of all the women of Vaylle—was to provide that link with Divine Nurture that preserved both the people and the land.

But though she bade the townsfolk *Goddess bless* and *good day*, folding those she greeted in her arms in token of the Arms that, invisibly and constantly, held them all, her manner was somber, and she felt a despondent chill that could not be alleviated even by the sight of the children playing in the gardens or the sense of warm life that surrounded passing mothers-to-be. How long could Vaylle survive? For how many more mornings would that young woman and man, flushed with young love, consummate the Great Rite and blend their voices together in sweet song?

As though he shared Dindrane's feelings, King Pellam was slumped in his throne when she entered the vaulted hall of the King's House. His white head was bowed, his old fingers pressed to his forehead. He looked up as she approached. "Ah, Dindrane. 'Tis well you look today."

She curtsied before him, her full skirts rustling gracefully across the polished marble floor. "It is Wednesday, my king. I am here to make my report on Lachrae and Vaylle."

"More tidings than yours we have of Vaylle today." Pellam gestured to a dark man who was dressed in the rough garments of a herdsman. "This is Orlen, a man of Armaeg. He arrived in the night. Orlen, I present Dindrane, chief priestess of Vaylle and magistrate of Lachrae."

"The Goddess bless you," said Dindrane.

"And the God, you," said Orlen. He had kept himself well wrapped in his cloak, but when he approached to take Dindrane's hand, she saw why: his right arm was badly scarred and burned, as though by teeth and acid.

" 'Tis bad in Armaeg then?" Dindrane kept her

voice low, trying to instill into it the essence of comfort. But her heart was as cold as the morning.

Orlen shrugged and covered up his arm. " 'Tis bad everywhere. We live as we can." There was a quiet despair in his voice that, coupled with his maimed arm, lent him an air of one who continued to live only because his body refused to die. Dindrane was shaken when she looked into his dark eyes and saw nothing save bitter resignation.

We are all dying, she thought. Whether by the hounds and the Grayfaces, or by our own broken hearts, we are dying.

Pellam spoke politely. "I would first hear of Lachrae, and then of Armaeg. Dindrane?" He gestured for an attendant to bring her a chair, but she shook her head and gave her report standing.

Still shaken, she began with mundane affairs: commerce, the conduct of the marketplace, the decisions of the clan chiefs regarding disputes and agreements. Children had been born and fostered, strangers who had arrived from distant parts of the country had been adopted by local clans, peasant farmers had applied for landholder status.

Life went on in Lachrae. But there was another part of her report, one which, less happy and more grave, had grown steadily over the weeks and months.

"Last night brought no new damage," she said, "and that is a blessed relief."

"Could it be that our tormentors have wearied of their sport?" said Pellam.

" 'Tis doubtful, my king." She went on to describe the attacks of the previous week. A household in the western part of the city had been breached in the night, the family dragged from their beds. Their bodies had been found the next morning, their skulls shattered by the weapons of the Grayfaces. The women of the family had been raped repeatedly.

The night before, hounds had broken through the shuttered and bolted window of the magistrate of the north precincts. Her husband had been killed, her children wounded. Her mother, though untouched, had retreated into a state of numb shock from which even Dindrane had been unable to rouse her.

And on and on. Dindrane had to fight to keep her voice from breaking as she recounted the tolls. Pellam slumped further in his throne, and several of his attendants turned away in an effort to compose themselves. Even Orlen, who seemed resigned to everything, seemed affected.

"This cannot continue," said Pellam when she had finished. "Therefore I have given orders that earthworks and palisades be erected, encircling the city from north coast to south."

Orlen spoke. "My king," he said dully, "Armaeg did that thing months ago, to no avail."

"Speak, then, sir," said Pellam. "The hounds and Grayfaces have made news of the distant parts of my land hard to come by. I am shamed by my ignorance of what passes in my realm." But he set his face as though preparing for a tale worse than that which had gone before.

Orlen's voice was a monotone. Faced with ditches and fences, he explained, those who besieged Armaeg had taken to the air. Burnings and explosions were now a common occurrence each night, and the last state of Armaeg was far worse than the first.

"Only the hardiest now look for the bodies of the slain," said the dark man, "for they are a terrible sight. Some of the women the Grayfaces take for sport, and they cry out through the night. Our magistrate and healer are ill from overwork, but there is little that they can do. I have come to ask for aid, if there is any aid that can be given, but I perceive that those of the great cities are as helpless as . . ." He broke off, despair overwhelming him.

Helpless. Surely, thought Dindrane, Orlen spoke accurately. Bit by bit, Vaylle was being devoured by an implacable enemy who knew nothing of reason or mercy. And even if the people of Vaylle could bring themselves to strike a blow in return, what good would it do? At present, death would at least bring the Goddess and the God, and rest in the Far Lands, and rebirth. Killing would end even that, and the forces of Broceliande, the land beyond the Cordillera, would triumph in a wasteland that would be at once physical and spiritual.

Footsteps in the outer court: light, quick. A young girl wearing the tunic and trews of a boy ran into the hall, her blond braids dancing. "Father! Father! A kelp fisher from Daelin is here! He says that there is a boat coming from Gryylth!"

Hard behind her was the man: tall, lanky, his hair bleached almost white by the sun. At the sight of the king and the great hall, he stopped, pulled his cap from his head, and found himself speechless.

"This is so?" Pellam said to him.

The man bowed deeply and bobbed his head.

Dindrane's heart caught. From Gryylth. And the flying thing had not returned. Evil news either way.

The girl ran to Pellam and leaped into his lap. "He told me all about it, father. The boat is still some leagues offshore, but there is a strong wind, and it will arrive by afternoon."

"And what of the sailors in this boat, sir?" said Pellam to the fisher. "Come they in peace?"

The man found his voice at last. "My king . . . I saw swords . . . and armor . . .''

Dindrane went to him and embraced him solemnly. "Our thanks for this news, friend." But when she turned back, her face was as drawn as that of the man of Armaeg. "My king," she said, "I know my duty. I will go with Baares and meet these people, be they good or ill."

Pellam shook his head, his arms wrapped about his daughter as though to shield her. "They might kill you both."

"Then the blood is on their hands, not ours," she said. "Should they come to attack Vaylle, though, they can do no better than to kill me first, for I am Vaylle. Should they desire to break our spirits, why then they

should start with Baares, for he is the soul of my flesh,
and the spirit of the land. Should they come as friends,
well . . .''

She shrugged. Swords. And armor. What kind of
friends could they be?

''Take with you also the wise, the learned, and the
skilled,'' said Pellam. ''I would have the Gryylthans
see us as we are. They might slaughter us, true, but
they will know who it is that they slaughter, and perhaps by our deaths we might bring to them some
knowledge of the sanctity of life. So the God teaches
us: so we will, in return, teach others.''

''My king is wise,'' said Dindrane softly. ''It shall
be done.'' She turned to the fisherman. ''The Goddess
bless you, sir. Will you take now the role of the God
and guide us into the dark lands?''

The fisherman nodded and set off as though glad to
be away from such frightful grandeur as that of the
King's House. Clutching her staff, Dindrane followed.

The vessel that Hahle provided was more a barge
than a boat, and though it was capable of holding ten
people and their horses, it was not designed for sea
travel. Nonetheless, Kyria was now as driven by the
prospect of finding Solomon as Alouzon was by the
Grail, and she insisted upon an immediate departure.

It was a long crossing. Up the coast first, skirting
the rocky shores of western Gryylth, and then out
across the open ocean. The weather was fair—Kyria
saw to that—and Helwych knew enough magic to keep
a fresh breeze in the sails; but darkness found the party
floating midway between land and land, and in this
indeterminate condition they spent the night, holding
a course to the northwest and soothing the nervous
horses in shifts.

Kyria kept to herself, using just enough magic to
keep the sea calm and the sky clear. Still, her spines
had been somewhat blunted over the last few days, and
she spoke civilly to Marrget and Wykla, and even

found it in herself to thank them for their help and efforts in the aftermath of the attack on Quay.

Marrget, though, had no such luck with Manda. Indeed, the Corrinian hardly spoke to her. Alouzon had to admit that Manda's rage, though futile, was justified, and even Marrget seemed to agree, for the captain had withdrawn into contemplative solitude, eschewing at times even Karthin's company.

On the second day, Vaylle was a winter-pale presence lying across the western horizon. The party members saw farmland and the faint tracks of stone walls and roads. Farther inland were mountains that looked as though they surely must touch the sky—elfin pinnacles and craggy peaks and cliffs—but on the coast were towns and cities and the obvious handiwork of men and women.

"It doesn't *look* that bad," said Alouzon.

Kyria grimaced. "Sol didn't *look* that bad."

The barge drove onward, forging through the waves. Swift sails appeared in the distance, tacked for a better view, then fled back toward the coast. "So much for secrecy," said Alouzon.

"I can handle it," said Kyria bluntly. "They try anything, I'll blast them like I did that jet."

His strong hand on the rudder, Parl tipped his head back and checked the position of the sun. "It will be afternoon before we land," he said simply.

"They've seen us, Parl."

"True," he said quietly, "and we have seen them." With his free hand, he pulled his long knife and checked its edge.

Alouzon would have preferred an isolated landing, but towns and villages spotted the Vayllen coast. Parl and Birk piloted the barge some distance northward, but they found nothing better than a short stretch of beach that lay within the lee of a rocky promontory. "If we continue, night will find us still on the water," observed Santhe. "And the wind may push us ashore."

Alouzon cocked a thumb over her shoulder. "How are the horses?"

Santhe grinned. "As nervous as their riders, Dragonmaster."

She nodded. "Then let's go for it. Battle stations, everyone. Parl, Birk: take us in."

As they approached, Alouzon was again struck by Vaylle's apparent innocence. White sand gave way to thick grass, and then trees and bushes rose up, sparkling with the buds of early spring. Crocuses and optimistic hyacinths and daffodils unfurled at the base of gray and brown trunks, and the sea breeze fluttered blossoms in a shimmer of color and movement.

This was Vaylle, her own land. Regardless of the horrors that might lurk in its depths, Alouzon found herself responding instinctively to the beauty and tranquillity of what she had created. Perhaps, then, she had not done such a bad job after all. Perhaps there was hope.

Within the promontory the bay was quiet, the waves rolling in smooth as oil. Parl and Birk heaved on the rudder together, asking for changes of sail in monosyllables. The barge turned clumsily toward the shore, picked up speed, and then crunched to a stop on the gently shelving beach.

Santhe nodded, and his men let go of the rudder and hit the sand with swords unsheathed and ready. In moments, they had vanished into the tree line, and there came the sound of a shrill whistle.

Santhe lifted his head. The whistle was repeated. "That is Birk," said the councilor. "There are people coming."

Staff in hand, Kyria dropped off the bow of the boat and, holding her skirts up, waded to shore. Manda and Wykla were not far behind. Escorted by the warriors, the sorceress crossed the beach, her staff a shaft of violet. If violence were offered, Kyria would strike the first—and final—blow.

Marrget, Karthin, and Helwych were struggling with

the horses and packs, and Santhe and Alouzon ran to help them. "Can we depend on Kyria?" said Santhe.

Alouzon grabbed Jia's halter and led him down the ramp. "She's scared of that staff. But I think she means business."

Her land: her people. What would they be like? Alouzon suddenly felt fiercely protective toward beings she had never met, and the thought of battle was an icy hand on her heart.

She brought Grayflank off the boat. There was no sign of the warriors or the sorceress. "How long do we have?"

Another whistle, shriller than before, repeated more quickly. "Long enough to saddle the horses, I think," said Santhe. His eyes were bright, but his humor was edging slowly toward calculation. Alouzon had seen it before: for all his laughter, Santhe was a deadly presence in a fight.

Alouzon was reaching out to Jia and Grayflank soothingly, reassuring the beasts that dry land was once again beneath their hooves, but the thought of the hair-trigger lethality of her companions made her queasy. "Santhe," she said quickly. "We won't attack unless it's necessary. It's got to be that way."

The councilor looked mildly shocked. "My lady Alouzon, we are warriors. We do not act without reason."

"Just wait for a little better reason than usual, OK?"

Santhe furrowed his brow. "As you wish, Dragonmaster."

Manda, Wykla, and Kyria appeared then, running back to the barge. "About fifty," called Wykla. "On horses."

Marrget gestured for Wykla to saddle her horse and handed Manda her harness without comment. "Armed?"

"I did not see arms, my captain. But a woman among them carries a staff."

To Wykla, Alouzon realized, a staff could be anything from a dry stick to an M-16 automatic rifle. "Kyria?"

The sorceress shrugged. "It *looked* like a staff. I'm not taking any chances, though. If the bitch moves, she's dead."

"Kyria, please be careful."

"Honey, I intend to survive this welcoming committee."

Her stomach twisting, Alouzon mounted Jia, waited for the others to ready themselves, and then gave the signal to move out.

They did not have far to go. Despite the deserted appearance that the area presented from shore, there was a road just on the other side of the line of trees, and a short distance away, whitewashed huts and houses gleamed in the afternoon sun. The village folk were keeping indoors, though, and the only people to be seen were those in the party that had been sighted by Santhe's men.

The Vayllens advanced cautiously down the road. Most were blond and fair, but there was a sprinkling of redheads and brunettes, and the party was made up equally of men and women arrayed in silks and linens of many colors, their clothing and persons ornamented with jewelry that Alouzon recognized as being of fifth-century Celtic design. The woman who held a staff was riding in the lead, her head uncovered and her hair shining in the sun. She was small, pretty, even winsome; but she carried herself with an air of authority, and there was a torque of gold about her neck.

No one looked particularly threatening. The large man beside the staff-bearer, in fact, carried a harp.

Alouzon and Kyria brought their horses to a stop and waited side by side. Loath as she was to contemplate violence, Alouzon moved her hand to cover the Dragonsword. Kyria's staff was a lethal, violet glow.

Marrget trotted forward with Karthin and positioned herself next to Alouzon. Her gray eyes were narrowed. She examined the Vayllen party with suspicion.

"What do you make of it, Marrget?" said Alouzon.

"No arms, no armor," Marrget mused. "And harpers and—I would guess—poets, and learned men and wise women. Cvinthil might greet Darham in such a fashion, but to meet strangers whose purpose is unknown without any display of strength seems to me to be the action of a fool."

"Blondie there has a staff," said Kyria.

"Aye. I do not understand this."

"It's a trap," said the sorceress. She let her staff tip forward until it was leveled at the Vayllens.

"No, Kyria," said Alouzon, quickly. "Don't. It's too easy. Any place with jet fighters doesn't have to worry about traps."

The sorceress did not look convinced. Her staff shaded into the ultraviolet sheen that Alouzon had seen before. "Just try it, bitch," she muttered.

"Dammit, Kyria . . ."

"Alouzon," said Marrget softly, "we do not know them, and Gryylth has suffered mightily."

The blond woman gestured for her party to halt, then rode forward alone. Twenty feet from Alouzon, she reined in and, drawing herself up, nodded gracefully to the Gryylthans. "In the name of King Pellam," she said, her voice high and clear, "I greet you. I am Dindrane, magistrate of Lachrae and chief priestess of Vaylle. Come you in friendship, or in enmity?"

Alouzon looked at Kyria. "Will you quit playing Dirty Harry with that staff? She's a woman, a magistrate, and a priestess to boot. What more do you want?"

Kyria tightened her grip. "I got fooled before. I want to see what she really is."

Dindrane was waiting patiently. The man with the harp rode up to join her, but Dindrane shook her head. "Do not, Baares," she said softly. "Flesh feels the blow first." He nodded unwillingly and remained a half-length behind her. She met Alouzon's gaze. " 'Tis the favor of a reply I would beg of you. Are you friends, or enemies?"

"That . . . uh . . . depends. . . ." Alouzon was

taken aback. These were not monsters or savages: they were people. Her own people. In fact, regardless of her caution, she felt her loyalties shifting rapidly toward them.

Dindrane waited patiently. Her staff was of white wood, but it did not glow like Kyria's. It might have been a symbol of rank and no more. Alouzon hoped that that was indeed the case: Kyria was a frightened child with an atomic bomb.

Marrget spoke. "It depends upon your intentions toward us, my lady. Should you offer us welcome, you will find us the fastest of friends. But if you attempt to harm us, you will fall to our swords."

The captain's words were no more and no less than the greeting of a cautious emissary, but Dindrane paled and glanced to the sky. "O Great Lady," she said. "That friendship and swords should be presented as one." With an effort, she forced herself to nod to Marrget. "We mean you no harm, lady." She suddenly looked more carefully at the captain and seemed faintly horrified. "Forgive me, mother," she stammered. "The Goddess . . . the Goddess bless your time."

Marrget looked puzzled. Alouzon put a hand on Kyria's shoulder. "I think they're OK."

"You're nuts. When do the jets get here?"

"I don't think these people have anything to do with the jets."

"Whose goddam side are you on, anyway?" The staff's light shifted further into invisibility as its power grew.

"Our side," Alouzon said urgently. She nudged Jia forward. "I'm Alouzon Dragonmaster, the leader of this expedition. I believe you."

Dindrane examined her for a moment. "I wish that I could be reassured by your words, my lady," she said. "But your weapons speak as loudly as you."

"We're from Gryylth. Things are different there. I have to say I'm surprised that . . ." Alouzon swept the Vayllens with her eyes. Not a sword, not a spear, hardly a knife was in evidence. ". . . that you're un-armed."

Dindrane looked stricken. "What kind of people are you?"

Much as she instinctively loved these people, Alouzon found impatience creeping into her voice. "Dindrane, Gryylth has been attacked. The signs point to Vaylle. What do you expect from us?"

Dindrane met her gaze with blue eyes that did not flinch or falter. "Something other than death, Dragonmaster. But so be it." Proudly, almost disdainfully, she lifted her staff. "In the name of the Goddess and—"

Alouzon heard Kyria's voice behind her. It hissed like a knife sliding from a sheath. "Nice try, little girl."

Energy crackled suddenly, and Alouzon whirled to see the staff's discharge leaping along its length, driving straight for Dindrane and her company. Desperate to protect, heedless of the consequences of the action, Alouzon threw up an arm and caught the tip of the staff, flinging it skyward just as the bolt of energy roared out in a torrent of death.

For an instant, Alouzon saw nothing but violet and darkness, the reified incandescence of the forces that made and unmade worlds. Her arm seemed immersed in a pool of molten steel that tipped suddenly and inundated her with white fire.

"Alouzon!" Marrget threw herself at Alouzon so as to pull her away from the blast, but Alouzon was hardly aware of it. She felt herself falling, and she was only mildly surprised when the ground opened up and swallowed her in a darkness so profound that it did not allow for such meaningless questions as those of identity . . . or of consciousness.

❖ CHAPTER 13 ❖

Stars. The chime of harpstrings played by an expert hand. Cool wind.

Alouzon turned away from all three and trudged slowly back into the safer realms of darkness into which she had fallen. Here in the shadows, the battles were all finished. Here there was peace—and a freedom that had eluded her in the course of a life of forced decisions.

"Alouzon Dragonmaster." The voice of a woman: soft, gentle, an embodiment of all that was feminine. Alouzon did not recognize it, and in any case, it called to her from the lands of life. She did not want life anymore. Much better to follow this path on down into the shadows. There was rest ahead.

Alouzon turned away from the voice and continued. Ahead, a glimmer of light manifested and grew.

"Alouzon."

"Leave me alone."

The light expanded, shining in green and gold. Alouzon found herself dressed in Levi's and a peasant blouse. Her sneakers trod the sunlit grass at the side of Taylor Hall, and above, on the terrace, Vorya and Mernyl leaned on the balustrade, nodding thoughtfully.

Everyone was waiting for her. The Guardsmen stood near the pagoda at the southwest corner of the hall, rifles ready, shuffling their feet in the manner of young men who are ill-at-ease and impatient. The photographer readied his camera. Off in the parking lot, Allison's jacket flapped in the breeze as she waved. Sandy began walking toward her classroom. Bill was pondering. Jeff glowed in what he thought was a triumph of students over militia.

Alouzon took her position near the metal sculpture. It would be but a small matter now: a few inches, a minor correction of history, a willing sacrifice of a not-particularly-spotless victim who had lived too long on time that rightfully belonged to someone else. The Guardsmen brought up their weapons, and the one who had haunted her dreams leveled his rifle at her head for the last time, squinted carefully along his sights, and squeezed off a round in the prescribed manner.

Other bullets sped off toward the parking lot. Alouzon, though, was only concerned about the one that approached her, that swam out of the barrel of the M-1, phase shifting like a ball bearing rolling down a sewer pipe. The photographer behind her snapped a picture and threw himself to the ground.

Alouzon waited for the bullet. Only a few inches . . .

Harpstrings. And soft hands. And a staff that glowed with the purity of moonlight. Again the strange voice: "Alouzon."

"Leave me alone."

"You have friends here who will grieve."

She stopped. The bullet drifted closer. Yes, friends. And, for that matter, a whole world.

She was creator and guardian. The ending of her life would end the lives of many others: friends and enemies and people who had never met her, who did not even know that she existed. Her choices had been forced, true, but that fact did not alter her commitments.

The bullet, promising freedom, passed by. Alouzon sat down on the grass and wept, regretting all the love she had ever been offered, the love that tied her to life.

Dindrane's face was a study in the soft light of early evening when Alouzon opened her eyes. Nearby, someone was still playing a harp, the sound of the

metal strings at once antique and timeless. "Do you
hear my voice, child?" said the priestess.

Child. After years of responsibility and burden, the
word had a refreshing sound. But she could no more
be a child than a God. "Yeah. I hear. Thanks." It was
paltry gratitude, but it was all she could manage.

She sat up. There was a fire burning nearby, but
most of her companions were gathered about her, their
faces mirroring concern. Wykla was weeping with relief, Manda's strong arms wrapped about her, and at
Alouzon's first word, Marrget had sagged against Karthin, who himself looked worn and frayed.

With an instinct born of battle, Alouzon knew who
was missing. "Santhe?" she said. "Parl? Birk?"

"Fear not: they are well," said Dindrane. "They
keep watch over your companion, the one you call
Kyria." The harp fell silent. "You saved our lives."

"Our thanks," came a deep voice, and Alouzon
looked over her shoulder. The harper was a big man,
almost the size of Karthin. In the firelight, his eyes
gleamed like the bronze strings of his instrument.
"Though your manner is strange, we perceive that you
are indeed a friend."

"Alouzon," said Dindrane, "this is Baares, the
king's harper and my husband. I add my thanks to
his."

"What was I supposed to do? Let you fry?"

"I might have thought that you would do that
thing," said Dindrane. She shook back her blond hair.
She was as feminine as her voice; and her gestures,
her language, even the set of her shoulders were soft
and yielding. "You are very much unlike us, Alouzon
Dragonmaster. You, a woman, bear arms, and you
think of violence and death. And yet you would sacrifice yourself for us in a manner worthy of the God."

"It's part of the job," Alouzon mumbled. She
passed her hands over her face, surprised that she still
had a right arm. The last she remembered, it felt as
though it had been incinerated. She examined it in the
firelight. There was not a mark on it.

"She healed you, Dragonmaster," said Helwych, keeping his distance. "I have never seen the like before. She . . ."

Dindrane examined the lad curiously. " 'Tis a healer I am. All priestesses are. With the power of a man's spirit behind me, I can sometimes reform flesh and blood."

Alouzon flexed her fingers. "Where's Kyria?"

Santhe's voice came to her from a short distance away. "She is here by the fire, Dragonmaster. Unconscious."

"She is unharmed," said Dindrane. "She merely sleeps. She seems to bear us ill will, and therefore I thought it best not to disturb her."

Marrget spoke, her voice angry and flat. "Dindrane and Baares returned good for ill, and yet Kyria would have slaughtered them without hesitation. I would she did somewhat other than sleep." Wykla murmured assent, as did Manda and the others.

"Enough, mother," said Dindrane. "You offered us violence, we offer you peace. 'Tis not as a friend that I hold Kyria, but I will not have her death contemplated here." Her mouth tightened. "There is enough death in this land already."

Alouzon understood. "The dogs, the jets: you don't have anything to do with them, do you?"

"Nothing. We suffer from them ourselves."

"Where do they come from?"

"They come from across the Cordillera, from the land we call Broceliande."

Alouzon almost laughed, but she stopped herself: it would have been too bitter a sound. Broceliande. In the Grail legends, it was a forest of nightmare and dream, where knights found guidance, adventure, and a spiritual fire that cleansed and harrowed their souls, readying them for the ultimate secret: the Grail itself. Here, the name might have been a signpost pointing her along her journey with an implacable finger.

"We need to go there, Dindrane," she said. "We've got things to do."

The priestess looked disturbed, and she exchanged glances with her husband. Alouzon rose and went to her companions.

Wykla clung to her. "Alouzon . . . your arm was gone . . . it was . . . gone . . ."

"I'm OK, Wykla. Dindrane fixed it. I think we've got some good people here in Vaylle." She pulled Manda in beside Wykla, put her arms about them both, and felt the depth of the bond that had grown between the maid of Corrin and the girl of Gryylth. "I'm glad you two found each other."

"Indeed, Dragonmaster," said Manda, her steel facade cracking for a moment. "Wykla is a great help to me. But . . ." Her eyes, hard and sorrowful both, met Alouzon's, and she shook her head.

Marrget came last, and she embraced Alouzon formally. "There is another matter we must settle now, friend." She indicated the still form of the unconscious sorceress. "I do not trust this woman."

"No one trusts her," said Karthin. He wrapped a protective arm about Marrget. "The blast threatened you, Alouzon, and might have killed my beloved, also."

His outspoken declaration of his relationship to Marrget made Manda blink and turn away, her fantasies of revenge suddenly complicated even more than they already were. Dindrane spoke softly. "An action doubly grievous for the life she bears within her."

A sudden thought struck Marrget, and her hand moved as though to rest on her belly. Catching herself, she instead grasped the hilt of her sword. "What is to be done, then, Alouzon?"

"I wish to hell I knew, Marrget." Alouzon looked around. "Where are the rest of your people, Dindrane?"

"Baares thought it best to send them home, and I yielded to his wisdom. Keeping them here would have needlessly exposed them to the nocturnal evils that stalk the land."

Kyria was stirring, a prisoner once again of the

dreams that followed hard upon her expenditures of power. "Where . . ."

Alouzon stood over her. "Parl, Birk," she said without looking up, "secure the area." The two men drew knives and moved out among the trees, but Santhe seemed reluctant to leave Kyria's side. "I'll handle this, councilor."

"I will tend to her, Dragonmaster," he offered.

"She'd just as likely take your hand off."

Chagrined, he turned to Karthin. "It seems, my friend, that others share your view of her."

"Can you blame them, Santhe?" said the big Corrinian.

"Nay. But sick dogs might be cured. And perhaps friendship is the physic that Kyria needs."

Karthin's eyebrows lifted. "Be careful, Santhe. I spoke in a similar fashion once, but I harvested love. I do not know what might lie amid your wheat."

The councilor shrugged, unsheathed his sword, and vanished after his men.

Kyria was struggling in the grass, whimpering. Her staff lay on the ground several feet away. Eyes steely, Marrget planted herself before it.

"Wake up, Kyria." Alouzon stood over her. "Don't give me any more gas." The thought that Dindrane and her company might have been reduced to so much slag had kindled her anger, and she was not gentle as she prodded Kyria with a foot.

Kyria came up screaming. *"Leave me alone, Kyria! My God . . ."* Her voice cut off suddenly. She regarded those about her like a trapped fox. "What the hell's going on?"

"Think about it," said Alouzon. "You might remember."

Kyria looked at Dindrane. The priestess folded her arms gracefully, but Kyria did not back down. "You can never be sure. If Sol taught me anything, he taught me that."

Alouzon wanted to strike her. "You nearly killed my people, bitch."

Dindrane spoke, her voice gentle and conciliatory. "Do not violate yourself by denigrating her womanhood. I—" A look from Alouzon made her fall silent, seemingly surprised at her own acquiescence.

Kyria caught sight of her staff and, still too unsteady to walk, crawled toward it, her long hair trailing in the dirt. "Get out of my way," she said to Marrget.

Marrget did not answer. Her sword rang as she drew it.

Kyria stared. Then, her anger taking control, she came on. "Get out of my way, little boy."

Marrget paled, but the gleam in her eye turned murderous.

Alouzon caught hold of Kyria's arm, dragged her to her feet, shook her like a puppy. "Look, little girl, you listen now, and you listen good. You nearly killed a bunch of people because you were scared shitless. Why don't you just admit it? Dammit, do you want to get out of here?"

"You know what I want." Kyria's voice was a hiss.

"So what are you going to do? Kill everyone you meet until you find Sol? Nice fucking job. How many kids are you going to knock off in the meantime?"

Alouzon might as well have struck Kyria, for the sorceress went white. "How dare you—"

"Don't give me that nose-in-the-air New England crap. We're all in this together, you don't know jack shit about this place, and if you want to get anywhere, you're going to have to play ball."

"You act just like a goddam man!"

"If you're the alternative, then I thank the Gods!"

Alouzon and Kyria had been shouting, faces inches from one another. Now each struggled for words to convey the anger she felt, but in the silence came another sound, one as strange and yet familiar as that of jet turbines.

. . . *pok-pok-pok-pok* . . .

Everyone looked skyward. "Chopper," said Alouzon.

A shrill whistle came from one of the sentries. "People are coming," said Karthin.

Dindrane put a hand to her mouth. "Grayfaces."

"Who?"

Baares spoke. "They come in the night, and they kill." His eyes had turned troubled, and he looked at the Gryylthans' weapons with something that seemed very like envy.

The rotors of the helicopter changed pitch as the craft slowed, turned, and began to approach. "I'll bet it's looking for us," said Alouzon. "The chopper will call in an airstrike, unless it's got rockets of its own."

Karthin did not understand the terminology, but he was already smothering the fire. With a strained look at Dindrane, Baares moved to help, scooping earth with his large hands. The flames sputtered and smoked and refused to go out easily. If the helicopter had infrared detectors, Alouzon knew, even the residual heat would be enough to draw its attention.

If? Vaylle was her land. She had created it. The very fact that she thought of infrared detectors at all practically guaranteed that the helicopter possessed them.

Helwych ran to the protesting fire and lifted his staff. "Allow me." The flames died instantly, and all traces of heat vanished.

With a roar, the helicopter sped directly over the camp, a dark shape that sent a fleeting moon shadow across the bare branches of the trees. The fire had been extinguished just in time, but another whistle from Santhe and his men told of the proximity of the intruders.

Alouzon had no idea what the Grayfaces were, did not want to find out, was going to anyway. "Kyria, will you help?"

"Will you give me my staff?"

Alouzon was stuck. Helwych's spells were severely restricted, and armor and swords were as nothing against the weapons of the twentieth century. She needed magic. "Damn."

To her surprise, Kyria did not gloat. "Just give me

the goddam staff and let me screw myself over again,''
she said resignedly. "I promise I won't blow anyone
up unless I absolutely have to."

"I am not reassured," said Marrget. She picked up
the staff and offered it to Kyria. "Here, mistress sorceress. I pray you: use it well."

Dindrane spoke up. "I pray you: do not kill." Even
in the face of multiple threats to her life she main-
tained her quiet dignity and surety of purpose.

The helicopter made another pass. Once in Kyria's
hands, the staff sprang into lambent life. "Look,
honey," she said, "I don't particularly want to die out
here."

"Nor do I," returned the priestess. "But if I am to
be led into the Far Lands, I would prefer to meet my
God with clean hands."

The helicopter closed on them. Perhaps it could pick
up body heat. Cursing herself for the thought, Alouzon considered having the party spread out, then recalled the Grayfaces. "Kyria, we're fucked."

The sorceress was scanning the sky. "Creaming the
chopper won't do anything, will it?"

"It might bring in the B-52s."

"That's what I thought."

A series of shrill whistles, the sudden crack of a
rifle. In the distance, wood splintered with the impact
of a small-caliber, high-velocity bullet. Kyria reacted
by striking her staff on the ground. In the darkness, a
deeper darkness began to gather. "This should make
you happy, Dindrane," she said. Then, lifting her
voice, she cried: "Santhe! Parl! Birk! Get in here!
Bring the horses!"

She had just advertised the location of the party to
every being within earshot, but she seemed confident
of her powers. Given the demise of the Skyhawk and
the battering of the White Worm, Alouzon reflected,
perhaps she had reason to be.

Branches crashed as Santhe and his men plunged
back toward the camp, each leading several horses.
"Where's Jia?" said Alouzon.

Santhe looked over his shoulder and counted noses. "O Gods."

Alouzon did not wait: she gestured for Santhe to go on and herself made for the stand of trees where the mounts had been tethered, pausing only long enough to shove Baares toward Kyria's gathering darkness. The Vayllen man had been staring at the weapons about him, but he shook himself out of his thoughts and followed his wife into the gloom.

About Kyria's staff had grown up an impenetrable blackness, and in a moment, sorcerers, warriors, and Vayllens had vanished as though a curtain of night had been drawn over them. "Get in here, Allie," shouted Kyria.

Alouzon winced at the diminutive, but did not reply. She heard the sound of Jia's breathing a short distance ahead, and heard also, to her left, the faint crunch of boots on grass and dry moss. Grayfaces.

The footsteps were suddenly almost on her, and she plastered herself against the trunk of a great oak, willing her heart to beat silently, holding her breath. A figure passed in the night, so close that she might have reached out and touched it, and faintly—very faintly— she saw the moonlight gleam dully on a rifle barrel.

M-16. Fascinated in spite of the danger, she stared as the man, for it was indeed a man, moved slowly by, his hands ready and easy on his camouflaged rifle. His head swung carefully from one side to another, searching, listening. Alouzon caught a glimpse of goggling lenses where his eyes should have been, and was very nearly sick before she realized that the travesty of a face she was seeing was, in reality, a gas mask.

He seemed of no particular nationality and no obvious allegiance, for his uniform seemed to partake equally of all times and places, and the mask hid his features. He could have been anyone, of any race, and might have come from any modern battlefield . . . or from Kent State.

The universal soldier. She was shaking so badly that she thought he must surely hear. *My universal soldier.*

Another passed, then another, their garb and masks identically nondescript. One carried a machine gun—an M-60—on his back; the rest were armed like the first. Picking their way along the path, they glided almost silently through the trees, their weapons ready.

Then they were gone, moving away, the sounds of their passage fading into the background chatter of the helicopter. Jia was on the other side of the path they had traced, and had held himself in utter silence. Alouzon hoped that he would stay that way: she did not want to have to fight.

Easing away from the tree, she stepped carefully across the track and slid through a dry thicket without a sound. Barely ten feet behind her, she knew, were her friends; but they might as well have been on another planet for all the help they could offer.

She found Jia more by touch than by sight or sound, for the thicket hid the moon, and the helicopter was returning, moving slowly over the tree tops, rhythmically gusting the branches. "Come on, guy," she whispered. "You've gotten me out of some bad shit, and now I'm gonna do you."

A flare blossomed suddenly above her head, and she heard the squawk of a radio. *"Delta-nine, this is two actual. I have movement in the trees twenty yards to the southwest . . ."*

She was already swinging up onto Jia's back. "C'mon boy, let's move. Find that road."

A bullet made a sucking noise through the branches above her head, followed immediately by the crack of the discharge. Jia needed no more urging. He leaped a fallen log and detoured around to the right. When his hooves hit the road, he was in full gallop.

Within seconds, though, Alouzon saw lights burning ahead. Darkness and fright had thoroughly muddled her, and she was leading the Grayface patrol straight toward the defenseless village she had seen when her party had first encountered the Vayllens. "Jia, no!" She had no bridle, but she tugged at his mane and forced him to slow, stop, and reverse direction.

The helicopter wheeled, dropped another flare, and turned to follow the fleeing rider.

What next? Grenades? Mortars? . . .

Tracers—orange, blurring with speed—punched holes in the forest and whipped by her head. The Grayfaces were closing on the road, moving to cut off her escape. She sent Jia into the tree line and wove among the trunks. Once again she was playing a lethal game of hide and seek.

What kind of place had she created that could include such disparate entities as pacifist healers and search-and-destroy patrols? Vaylle was a study in nightmare contradictions, and as she rode Jia through the dark, bullet-haunted forest—blundering into low hanging branches, starting in fear at puddles of moonlight (uncertain and fitful guides in this blackness!)—she knew that it could only have arisen from the melange of violence and victimization, frantic hope and fierce hate, that had characterized her life.

I did it to them. I'm going to have to fix it.

The moon rose toward the zenith, laving the forest in silver. Alouzon saw motion ahead, but a moment before she turned Jia away into the deeper parts of the forest, it took on shape and form and turned into Marrget and Karthin.

They beckoned urgently. Alouzon rode straight for them, the helicopter almost directly behind her, the downwash from its rotors shredding branches and buds. "Come on, Jia. Another flare, and it's gonna be curtains."

The ground was clear, almost a meadow. Marrget and Karthin pointed to a blackness that lay behind them, and Alouzon sent Jia leaping into it.

She could see nothing. She might have been blind. Jia stopped short and whinnied frantically, but Kyria spoke nearby. "Easy, boy. Easy. You're safe here."

The white hand of the sorceress gleamed in the enveloping pitch and descended on the forehead of the beast. Jia calmed.

Alouzon was still straining her eyes. "Where am I?"

"At the camp. Keep it down, will you? I'm not sure how good the aural shields are."

The sound of the helicopter was muffled, distant. It drew nearer, then faded. Panting, sweating in spite of the cold, Alouzon bent her head down to Jia's neck and sobbed. She had finally realized how terrified she was. "Dindrane?" she choked.

"I am here, Dragonmaster."

"This is . . . ." She instinctively looked for the priestess, but Kyria's shields were impenetrable. "This is what you've been living with?"

"For the last six months. Surely."

Tears were streaking her face. *I'm gonna do it. Not for me. For them.* "How the hell do you manage?"

"We live and we die," said the priestess. Her voice was proud and unshaken. "We move from one border of the Far Lands to the other, leaving and returning. We are not afraid of death."

Marrget and Karthin had entered the camp immediately after Alouzon. "Do you not defend yourselves?" said the big man.

"Defend? What a curious way you have of using that word. To take up arms and kill seems to me to be more an attack than a defense."

Marrget was shocked. "You do *nothing*?"

As though in response came the muffled sound of gunfire and explosions. Dindrane sighed, and Alouzon guessed that she had hung her head. "That is Daelin being destroyed. The Grayfaces turn on the less fortunate."

"Then," said Marrget, "let us go and offer what assistance we can, even if we must die fighting."

"Surely not!" Baares's cry was one of shock and horror. "Of all those who should not take life, you should be foremost among them."

"You will let go of my arm, O man." Marrget's voice was cold.

"Baares!" Dindrane said sharply. "Do not touch her so. She bears life."

"Aye," said Marrget, "and death too. Alouzon? Karthin? Santhe? Kyria? Will you come with me?"

Alouzon could have felt the Vayllens' shock through a brick wall. "Dindrane," said Baares, "can we not stop them?"

The priestess was already groping through the murk. "Marrget, child, do not do this to yourself. That you bear arms is evil enough, but to kill others when your soul is so inextricably bound up with creation is an obscenity."

Another explosion. Faint screams. The automatic fire of the machine gun was a sound as of the distant tearing of paper. Daelin was obviously being leveled, but though Alouzon sympathized with Marrget's sentiments, she wondered what help fifth-century weapons could offer.

"My lady," Marrget was saying, "do not speak to me of obscenities. To stand idle while your people are killed is the basest kind of cowardice. For what reason should I stay my hand?"

Dindrane's reply was framed by two colossal detonations that seemed absurdly out of proportion with the size of the tiny village. "For the sake of the Goddess and the God, woman! Are you so unfeeling that you do not know?"

"Know?" Alouzon heard a frightened suspicion dawning in Marrget's voice. "Know what?"

"Child," said Dindrane, "you are pregnant."

❖ CHAPTER 14 ❖

Marrget's innate courage had sustained her through the weeks and months of her womanhood, and it did not desert her now. She allowed Karthin to fold her in his arms, but even in the darkness it was obvious that the captain was holding herself as straight as ever, her proud head unbent.

"Marrha," Karthin was saying softly, "Marrha. I love you. I am here."

"So are we all here," said Santhe as he groped his way toward Marrget. "Dear friend, give me your hand."

Marrget did not speak for a moment. Then: "You have it, Santhe," she said, her voice husky. "But I am afraid that this is a far cry from Vorya's tent. I know not whether to weep or laugh."

"A woman would know, perhaps. I confess I do not."

Marrget chuckled. "Well, I suppose that I shall tell you when I find out." There was effort in her voice, and she changed subjects with an almost physical jerk. "But we have obligations. Bandon has yet to be avenged. Quay, also. Our common enemies are destroying another town. What say you? Shall we show them in what currency Gryylth repays its debts?"

"Child," said Dindrane, "I implore you: give up this madness."

Daelin continued to die in a distant melange of blood

and detonation. Marrget drew her sword. "I know not what you mean by madness, Magistrate Dindrane. To do otherwise than follow the dictates of my conscience seems to me to be true madness." She snorted. "Or would you have me bent over the cooking fire, or scrubbing pots?"

" 'Tis among the honored of any people that you should find your place," said the priestess. "Bearing children is a holy thing."

"I have only to give up my sword and my freedom," said Marrget ironically. "Am I correct?"

"You . . ." Dindrane floundered in incomprehension. "You cannot take life and bear it too."

Santhe and Karthin muttered angrily.

"I can, and I will, lady," said Marrget. "I will do what I must. I have done so before, in spite of affliction."

Alouzon slid from Jia's back and stumbled through the murk. "Marrget? Can I help?"

Marrget drew a deep breath. "I said before that I would live. I know who I am, and I will not disgrace myself, whether in battle or in childbirth." She squeezed Alouzon's hand. "You will not need to beat me this time, friend."

The gunfire and explosions died suddenly, the helicopter made a final pass, the radio squawked one last time. Daelin was gone. Alouzon's senses, sharpened by danger and the Dragonsword, told her that the Grayfaces had faded back into the forest. At her word, Kyria dismissed the darkness.

Moonlight flooded the clearing. Leaning heavily on her staff, the sorceress nodded to Marrget. "Don't let them give you any shit, girl. You just do what you have to." She slumped suddenly. Tears were streaking her face. "Just don't ask me for anything more right now," she choked. "I'm through. Santhe? Put me to bed, will you? I'm making an ass of myself."

The councilor embraced Marrget, then went to Kyria and silently led her to her blankets. She leaned on him, her head heavy against his chest. His arm was about her shoulders.

Manda was standing off by herself, shaking, eyes downcast. If Marrget's pregnancy had further entangled the snare of emotions in which she was caught, she said nothing of it. Solemnly, she approached Marrget and saluted her in the manner of a common soldier. Marrget examined her from within Karthin's arms—face drawn, eyes uneasy—as though she expected a sudden attack.

"In my land," said Manda, "women are honored as maids and mothers both. Therefore I wish you well. May . . ." She fought with her tongue. "May your time be easy." Her mouth tightened, and she turned to Wykla. "Friend and beloved, will you stand watch with me?"

Wykla had been watching, and there was a faint suspicion in her eyes that she thrust away of a sudden as though it were a serpent. "I will," she said, and she kissed Manda. Dindrane and Baares exchanged looks, but appeared resigned to whatever further horrors Alouzon's company could offer.

The forest was silent and the air was still. From the sea came the odor of salt; from Daelin, the pungent scent of high explosive and burning wood. Santhe and his men made a cautious foray into the village so as to look for survivors, and Dindrane and Baares insisted upon accompanying them. But the five returned quickly, and Alouzon saw from the quiet sadness of Santhe's eyes that no inhabitant of Daelin remained alive.

"There is hardly anything left that I would call a town," said the councilor. "I have never seen the like . . . save at Bandon."

"It is always this way," said Dindrane. Her voice was firm, but her face was pasty white. Closing her eyes, she murmured to herself, apparently in prayer.

Baares muttered under his breath. His dark eyes were angry, and he clutched at his harp as though he

would have liked to use it as a club. Dindrane put a
hand on his shoulder, but he turned away from her
and sat off by himself, softly plucking the strings of
his instrument, his music discordant. He did not
sleep that night.

When the sun rose over the ocean, Dindrane and
Baares led the party toward Lachrae through a heather-
colored land that was just beginning to show the onset
of spring. Early crocuses lined the broad, straight
roads, and the dense forest—wide oaks and sheltering
beeches and slender birches—seemed to beckon the
observer into solemn and druidic mysteries. Colors
were pastel, the air transparent.

They rode on throughout the morning. The way was
easy, and along the coast there were many small villages, clusters of whitewashed houses and cottages as
neat as Daelin had been. But Alouzon noticed that
Dindrane was careful to take turnings that did not lead
through any of them. The expedition might well have
been under a polite, unobtrusive, but very effective
quarantine.

"Are we that bad?" she said to Dindrane.

The priestess blinked. "Bad?"

"Come on, Dindrane, 'fess up. You're keeping us
away from the villages, right?"

Dindrane kept her eyes on the road. " 'Tis obser-
vant you are, Dragonmaster."

"So what's the problem? Afraid we'll give everyone
cooties?"

Dindrane was small and soft, almost girlish, but her
eyes were clear and blue and penetrating. "My land
is deeply troubled," she said. "The hounds come and
kill. The Grayfaces come and kill. The flying things
come and kill." She glanced levelly at Alouzon. "And
now you and your people also come . . . and kill."

Alouzon met her gaze. "We haven't killed anyone."

"Not yet. But had you not risked your life, Dragonmaster, there would have been death aplenty. I know

your sympathies now, and some of your customs. Truly, I wish I did not. But my people already grieve at the depredations of Broceliande. Some spend their days in sorrow, others live in numb shock. Shall I allow you to add to this?''

Alouzon felt as though she had been slapped by her own child. ''I think you judge us pretty harshly,'' she managed.

''How am I to judge you, then?'' Dindrane's voice was sharp. ''Armed and armored, you come to my land, questioning our motives, denying life.'' She fought for words for a moment. ''Your women deny their own bodies, risk the unborn in combat, take . . . take one another in love—''

Kyria had been brooding, but she lifted her head. ''Hang on there, honey,'' she said, a catch in her voice. ''I'm sorry I screwed up. You can go ahead and be pissed at me, but don't give us guff about our women.'' The strident tones were missing from her voice: she spoke angrily, but with evenness. ''Marrget's got herself in a hell of a fix because she hasn't even figured out the ground rules yet and now she's going to have a kid. And as for Manda and Wykla: if that man of yours is as good for you as they are for each other, you're doing pretty damned well.''

Dindrane paled. ''Mother Goddess . . .'' She dropped her eyes. ''You do not understand, do you?''

''No, I don't.'' Kyria's voice had turned ugly. ''And I don't think you understand, either. So quit judging us. If you're so big on men, how come Baares isn't saying anything?''

Baares spoke without looking up. ''Dindrane is the land, and I am the spirit behind her. My time is not yet come.''

''And do you have a time to kill, too?'' Kyria snapped. ''I saw you drooling over our swords.''

Mouth clenched, Baares looked away as though caught in some pernicious and solitary vice.

''That's enough, Kyria,'' said Alouzon.

The sorceress had become enraged. "I'm trying to
help! Whose side are you on?"

"Ours." Alouzon found that she was regarding the
sorceress almost affectionately. She reached out and
patted her shoulder. "Simmer down. We need all the
friends we can get."

"Some friends." But Kyria fell silent and went back
to her brooding.

Alouzon wondered again at Kyria's question. *Whose
side are you on?* A week ago, she would have answered without hesitation: Gryylth's. But her allegiance had shifted. Vaylle was her land, her people,
her unconscious. She did not like much of what she
had found in it, but she loved it nonetheless, and it
seemed to her now that, if she had to choose a side,
then she had to be on everyone's side, whether they
were Gryylthan, Corrinian, Vayllen . . .

Kyria was muttering under her breath. Alouzon
touched her shoulder again. "Hey, thanks."

"Thanks for what?"

"For sticking up for Marrget."

"What the hell am I supposed to do? Hate her?"

"That's what it sounded like a couple days ago."

"So I was wrong. Shut up and leave me alone."

. . . or Californian. Alouzon felt a stab of guilt when
she considered that, since the sorceress had come to
this world, she had been fed only a steady diet of lies
and deceptions.

She shifted uneasily on her horse. "I think, Dindrane," she said, "that we might surprise you."

The priestess looked sad. "You have surprised me
already."

The road took them over a hill and into a valley.
There, beside a large bay of the sea, Lachrae glittered
in the sunlight as though sculpted of alabaster.

This was no reconstruction of a fifth-century town,
with muddy streets snaking through a collection of
rude huts that seemed not so much planned as cobbled
hastily together. The capital of Vaylle was ordered and

purposeful, its stone buildings flanking broad tho-
roughfares that radiated from a central plaza like sun-
beams. The King's House was a grand presence of
sloping roofs and curving eaves, and next to it were
the precincts of the temple: gardens and wide lawns
in which stood a ring of standing stones that rivaled
the Circle in beauty and strength.

Alouzon stared, wondering. In creating Vaylle, she
had, it seemed, not merely slavishly continued Solomon Braithwaite's theme of ancient Britain, but had
instead reached even further into the realms of fancy
to erect shining cities of glory and peace.

Her companions were moved by the sight, and in
silence they rode toward the eastern gate. It was no
more than an archway over the road, and was large
and white and constructed of fine marble that had been
thickly carved with Celtic motifs and meanders.

Dindrane signaled a halt and faced the company. "I
will take you to King Pellam," she said, "but I beg
you: leave your swords in their sheaths, your knives in
their scabbards, and let your staves of magic be idle.
These days, Lachrae is a place of sorrow. Do not add
to our woes by showing weapons."

"We are guests," said Marrget. "To do other than
the will of our hosts would be a grave discourtesy."

Dindrane looked at her. "I will never understand
you," she said softly. "Noble and barbaric both, you
shame yourself with your actions, and yet you shame
us with your words."

Shaking her head, she led them into the city. Baares
rode on her right, Alouzon on her left, and Santhe and
Parl and Birk followed after, their swords sheathed but
their hands nonetheless close to the hilts. Behind them
came Kyria and Helwych, the one with lowered head
and suspicious eyes, the other erect and eager to make
a good appearance.

Marrget and Karthin rode hand in hand, Marrget's
face at once contemplative and tender, fearful and
defiant. She might have entered this city as she en-

tered her own sense of womanhood, passing an imponderable door that led into both mystery and glory, gripping the hand of one who was a friend and a lover.

Under the guise of providing a rear guard, Manda had stayed far behind the column. Wykla was with her, and the two women were open with their affection. But though Wykla's eyes shone with wonder at the marvels that opened before her, Manda's were shadowed and grim.

Lachrae was lovely. The streets were paved with stone, and the white buildings might have been freshly scrubbed that morning. Banners hung from poles and spires, and fountains bloomed in the squares and commons, filling the air with the sound of water. Though the people of the city looked at Alouzon and her party with amazement and perhaps a little fear, they greeted the strangers with bows and polite words; and children ran up to stare and then followed after, laughing.

All was peace and friendship in Lachrae, and Alouzon felt unclean for intruding into such a place with weapons of war and thoughts of violence. But, looking carefully, she saw that the Vayllens' tranquillity was muted. If the townspeople looked fearfully at their weapons, it was because they had come to the knowledge of what weapons could do. And though Dindrane took a course through the city that bypassed the worst signs of destruction, Alouzon caught glimpses of damaged and shuttered houses, and of doors hung with black garlands of mourning.

And they won't fight . . .

It was perfect pacifism, the idealism of the 1960s brought to life, the jeans and t-shirts gilded with a more dignified and ancient raiment, the storefronts and cheap student apartments clad in marble, chalcedony, and bronze. Peace, it had once been believed, would triumph; but that sentiment had flowered in the summer of love, borne bitter fruit in the Days of Rage, and rotted on a May morning at Kent State.

Give peace a chance. Suzanne Helling had said that herself. But peace was a fragile thing, easily crushed by the threat of enslavement on a summer night in Bandon, rent by bullets, or corroded by tear gas. And even a Gandhi would meet defeat at the hands of an enemy who did not blench at mass slaughter.

King Pellam had no need of guards, but his state demanded attendants, and when Dindrane led Alouzon's party into the courtyard before the King's House, they were met by several men and women who were dressed in a rich livery of white and gold, with the king's emblem on their tunics.

Alouzon stared as she dismounted, not only because Dindrane and Baares embraced each of the attendants as though they were family, but because the insignia they bore depicted a cup and a knife, conjoined, surrounded by thorns of red and black. The correspondence to the symbolism of the Grail legends was too close to be a coincidence, and she suddenly wondered if, impossibly, the Holy Cup were actually here, in Lachrae.

The horses were led away, and Dindrane and Baares stood before the tall bronze door of the House and turned to the members of the expedition. "Enter in," said the king's harper. "Here we have left the land, and come to another place. Therefore, as spirit of the realm, I greet you and ask you to put aside your weapons."

Kyria's eyes narrowed. "Thanks, but no thanks."

"We'd like to go along with your wishes, Baares," said Alouzon, "but I'm afraid that we can't. We agreed to keep the swords sheathed. We're not putting them aside."

"You may not enter this sacred ground armed."

"Come on, Baares. You know we won't hurt you or your king. We've been nice up until now. Please don't strain our courtesy."

Baares stood firm. "This is the heart of Vaylle. To enter in with arms is a violation."

But Alouzon sensed that his words were hollow. He

had looked on the swords with envy, and had scowled at the destruction of Daelin as if he would, with sufficient provocation, renounce his vows of peace and lash out with whatever weapon was closest to hand.

But though his eyes were uneasy, Baares was shaking his head. "I cannot let you pass."

Dindrane stood beside him. "I will add my voice to my husband's."

Alouzon was half of a mind to call up the fading hippie within her and sit down on the floor of the courtyard until the Vayllens saw reason. But the hippie would never have protested Baares's demand, and in any case her place had long ago been taken by someone who knew the value of a sword, who knew that there was a time for battle as well as for peace, who had gained the profound and uneasy knowledge brought by deliberate homicide.

Several minutes went by. Kyria was raging, though to her credit she was saying nothing. The warriors seemed inclined to trust Alouzon with the matter, but Helwych seemed acutely embarrassed.

But then, noiselessly, the thick bronze door cracked open, and a young girl stuck her head out. Fair haired and blue eyed, she was dressed like a boy, and her hands were dirty, as though she had been playing in the street. "My father says that you should come in," she said gravely.

"They bear weapons," said Baares.

Halting footsteps approached the half-open door. "So do the Grayfaces," said another voice, "and the hounds have teeth, and the flying things bring their own death."

The door swung open to reveal King Pellam, white-haired and solemn. He examined the expedition fearlessly. "Come," he said after a moment. "Come into my house, all of you. Bring what you will: if what is Vaylle is so tender that it will not withstand the tread of a booted foot, then we are all lost indeed."

For his looks and his voice, he might have been

Vorya come back again in different robes, and for a moment Alouzon wondered if that were not the case. But Pellam was lame, and she again recalled the legends of the Grail. No, this was not a simulacrum dredged up out of recent memory. This man came from deeper sources. This was Pellam, the Fisher King, who kept the Holy Cup, who waited for the asking of a single question so that both his body and his land could be healed.

Broceliande, and now Pellam himself, surrounded by attendants whose livery bore the conjoined cup and knife. How close was the Grail?

Leaning on the arm of his hoydenish daughter, Pellam led the party into the hall. Vaulting soared up in peaks and ribs, and stained-glass windows rose from floor to ceiling, spilling their colors across the inlaid floor, drenching the room in their multicolored hues. Here was blue. And red the color of blood. Here was a springtime green, a sun-struck yellow, a pain-filled indigo as deep as the evening sky.

Pellam laboriously climbed the three steps to his throne and sat down. He smiled at his daughter. She smiled back and scampered away to a side door.

Though large, the hall was all but deserted; but the aura of sanctity and authority that hung about the King's House was not dependent upon large numbers of people or the ostentatious display of wealth or arms. It was, instead, a presence in itself, one that would have remained even if the building had been leveled; and Alouzon wondered from what depths of her soul had come something so holy and peaceful.

It's the Grail. It wants me. Maybe I'm doing something right after all.

Baares and Dindrane presented each member of the company by name, and Pellam fixed them one by one with his old, gray eyes, as though he were examining a palimpsest. "My magistrate and my harper went to Daelin to find you," he said at last, his voice dry and tired. "And you came to Vaylle, I think, to find us. Here we are. What do you wish?"

Slowly, respectfully, Alouzon told him of Bandon, and of the hounds that prowled in the night. She recounted the decisions of the council held at Kingsbury and described the purpose of her expedition.

Pellam listened, unmoving, his eyes flickering slowly in the changing colors from the windows. "You are called Dragonmaster, Alouzon," he said. "Why is this?"

"I . . . uh . . ." Where was the Dragon? In what part of the universe was it locked in perfect and unresolvable conflict with its antithesis? She had no idea. She had not even attempted to summon it for fear that she would distract it and so give the White Worm a momentary and lethal advantage.

"Lord king," said Marrget, "upon occasion, Alouzon rides on the Great Dragon called Silbakor."

Dindrane and Baares exchanged glances: worried, silent.

"And where is this beast?"

"We do not know, King Pellam."

" 'Tis yet another quest you have before you, it seems," said Pellam. He looked at Marrget carefully, nodding his white head. "Honor to you, mother."

Marrget flushed. She acknowledged his words with a stiff bow.

"You have met us, Alouzon," said Pellam. "Are you satisfied that the troubles that afflict your lands also afflict ours?"

"If I had any doubts," she said, "Daelin got rid of them."

"Daelin?" The king looked grave.

Dindrane spoke. "My king, the Grayfaces destroyed Daelin last night."

Pellam bent his head. "May the God take them into the lands of the Goddess," he said softly. "May they find peace in Her arms." For a minute, he was silent. Finally: "The horrors that you seek come from Broceliande. What will you do now, Alouzon? What do you want?"

It was tempting to believe that the answer to Pellam's question lay among the bright cities of Vaylle, or sheltered in its deep forests, or enshrined among its sweet meadows. And it was true that, in the legends, Pellam himself guarded the Cup. But legends were one thing, and freshly created worlds and search-and-destroy patrols were another: the Grail could never be an aggressor but, constrained by its own divine being, neither could it could ever be so passive as to allow its ineffable presence to be so often violated.

The answer and the Grail lay farther on. Beyond the Cordillera. In Broceliande.

Knowing that they would understand her unspoken question, Alouzon looked to her companions. Marrget and Karthin nodded, as did Santhe; and Parl and Birk merely looked ready for whatever was asked of them. Kyria was as defiant as ever: she would follow her ex-husband's footsteps over the edge of the world for a chance at revenge. The loyalty of Manda and Wykla was perfect.

Helwych alone seemed distressed at the prospect. His fear might have been painted on his face. "Dragonmaster," he said, "we have fulfilled our task. The enemy is not Vaylle. We should return before . . ." He searched for a plausible reason. ". . . before we bring more harm to this place."

"What harm have we brought?" said Marrget suddenly. "We have responsibilities. To turn back now would mean . . ." She faltered for a moment, regarding her body as though it had suddenly turned into an alien presence. "It would mean . . . weakness." Her eyes turned hollow, and Karthin and Santhe put their arms about her shoulders.

"Helwych," said Alouzon, "you can stay here if you want—if the Vayllens will have you—but we're going on to Broceliande." Helwych looked angry and indignant both, but Alouzon bowed to Pellam. "If the king will permit us."

Pellam considered. "You are armed. Your customs

are strange. But the Goddess and the God teach us that we are all perfectly suited for our purposes in life, being given neither too much nor too little for the accomplishment of our tasks." His gaze turned to Dindrane, piercing and level. "Is that not true, priestess?"

" 'Tis true, my king." Her voice was a whisper in the stillness of the hall.

Pellam nodded slowly. "Flesh knows what spirit knows. But its knowledge is instinctual. That of the spirit is conscious."

Baares spoke. "Are we therefore reprimanded, lord?"

"You are not. Wisdom is a slow growth." The king's eyes were deep. "We live for peace, but even so, 'tis only imperfectly that we understand that ideal." He lifted a hand, and a sunbeam conspired with the stained glass to turn it the color of blood. "Peace may well be of as many hues as these windows. Even the Goddess bears a sword."

He turned to Alouzon. "I perceive, Dragonmaster . . ." And when he spoke the title, his eyes searched her face as though reading, line by line, the almost-effaced history of the war-protesting hippie. ". . . that your accouterments may indeed be in perfect harmony with what might lie across the Cordillera. Therefore I give you these permissions: to come and go as you please, to have the help and succor of all who dwell within my realm, and to defend your lives as may be necessary." He stood up and raised his hand in the manner of a priest bestowing a benediction. "All this do I grant in the name of the God who is called Solomon, and the Goddess who is known as Suzanne."

The names struck Alouzon like a club, and she was still reeling when Pellam bowed to them and departed, limping, his hand bracing his weak thigh and his white head flickering through the rain of colors that flooded the great hall with living light.

Dindrane approached Alouzon, her face concerned. "Are you not well, Dragonmaster?"

"I'm . . . I'm just tired," she managed.

She should have realized it before, felt like a fool because she had not. Guardian she was. Guardian . . . . . . and *God*.

❖ CHAPTER 15 ❖

When the interview with Pellam was over, the attendants reappeared and led the members of the expedition to the guest rooms of the King's House. There they found hot water for baths, and soft beds; and though the food offered was entirely meatless—the Vayllens adhering to their principles of nonviolence even in matters of diet—everything was provided with smiles and courteous speech.

For Marrget, though, the Vayllens reserved their kindest words. They addressed her as *mother*, wished her health and an easy birth, but seemed uncomprehending when Marrget, first gently, and then with a rising sense of urgency, requested that they call her *captain*.

Since she had first picked up a sword, her life had been a life of action and of deeds. She could be proud of her behavior in battle. She could count the number of enemies that she had slain. But the Vayllens cared nothing for her battles or the lives she had taken. Concerned only with her capacity for bringing forth life, they honored her not for something that she did, but for something that she was. A woman. A mother.

Shock finally flooded into her like a spring tide; and that night she slumped before the hearth in the room that she shared with Karthin. The fire crackled and snapped, and Karthin rocked her like a child, humming a Corrinian harvest song under his breath.

"Are you frightened, Marrha?" he said at last.

"There is a great silence within me, my love. And a storm, too."

"In me also." Putting his hand beneath her chin, he lifted her head until he could look into her eyes. "When I told you of my love, I had not intended to burden you."

"When I took you to my bed, I had not intended to burden myself." She forced a smile. "Save with you. But . . ." Lifting her hands, she touched her body. Soon, very soon, it would be unfamiliar once more.

"Do you wish you were a man again?" he said softly.

Marrget flushed. "Had you asked me the first day or the first year, I would have said yes. Now . . ." Her mouth worked. "Now I cannot say that. It seems you have made a woman of me." Her voice broke. "And a mother." She refused to weep. Tears were a weakness.

Karthin cradled her. "The Vayllens think highly of that."

"I do not know what to think."

"In my land, as Manda said, women are honored both as maids and as mothers. We do not chain them to the cooking pots."

"Then . . ." There was her fear: ripe with the odor of female musk, slick with a woman's melt, loud with the cries of children. Regardless of her deeds, regardless of her valor, her very being pointed toward a future of subservience as unmistakably as her breasts (were they growing tender now?) filled the front of her tunic. "Then we must live in Corrin forever," she said. "For I will not submit."

"I do not ask you to."

"Manda's revenge seems—" She caught herself and stared. Her tongue had tripped her.

"Marrha?"

"I . . ." Oh, Gods, he had given her love and respect, had held her as she had learned the ecstasy of her body. She could not keep it from him any more.

"There is something between you, I know."

She nodded, rose, and went to the fire. "There is a grave something between us." She spoke with her eyes on the flames; and as she told Karthin of the rape, she saw it as if through Manda's eyes. Her man's face was broad and strong, and it hovered above her, eyes clenched, mouth set in a grimace, bobbing rhythmically with each thrust.

And then the rape—and her tale—was over, and the man's eyes opened to show, briefly, an incongruous trace of fear. The violation, though directed outward, had turned inward and branded an otherwise spotless life with a blazon of impurity.

Womanhood, and now motherhood. Manda's revenge had been working its will on her from the beginning.

Marrget turned around. Karthin had not moved. The thumbs of his big hands were hooked in the soft belt of the Vayllen robe he wore, and his eyes were downcast. "The war was an evil thing," he said softly. "There was grief on both sides."

"I am not speaking of the war, Karthin. I speak of myself and of Manda."

"There was grief on both sides," he said again. He sighed. "I was a farmer for a long time, but the war finally drove me from my plow. There were too many towns burned, too many men and women killed, too many rapes . . ."

"The Corrinians did not rape."

"I will not say that we did. But Manda's tale can be repeated a hundred times over, in a hundred different voices."

Marrget was shocked. "Are you so unfeeling that you can dismiss the rape of a countrywoman with generalities? Have you no loyalty?"

Karthin blinked at her outburst. His eyes showed hurt. "I am loyal to those I love."

"Do you love Manda?"

"I do."

"Then . . . how can you . . ." Marrget bent her head, forced the tears back. Weakness. Everything her body did suddenly seemed weak. Bellies full of children, and spreading her legs to a man's hot presence, and tears . . . "Manda's hate is just, and so is her wish for revenge. And you *deny* it?"

"I deny nothing."

"Then how can you sit there and not wish her assailant dead?" She was speaking against herself, challenging him to hate her.

Karthin sat, pondering the matter before him as a farmer might ponder the imminence of rain: examining the dry fields, the clouds, the bleached and withering crops. "I think that I would indeed wish him dead," he said at last. He rose and went to her, touched her face, ran his fingers back through her long hair. "But as far as I can tell, my beloved, the man who raped Manda is indeed dead. Long dead."

The tears welled up, persistent and weak.

Karthin laid a hand on her belly. "Dead and buried long ago. I never knew him. I know only you. I do not believe that there is a Marrget of Crownhark anymore: I speak to one called Marrha."

Sobbing, she tried to turn away from him, but he caught her and held her, and she did not resist. Her cries racked her body, and her tears soaked the front of his robe as he folded her in a gentle embrace.

"I . . . I want to die . . ." she whispered at last.

"I do not believe you."

"That is well," she said, "for I am a fool."

Karthin stroked her hair. "Come to bed."

"How can I come to bed after what I have done?"

He shushed her. "Come to bed, little girl."

She shuddered as he led her across the room. At the side of the bed, she stripped off her tunic roughly. "Hurt me, Karthin," she said. "Hurt me as once I hurt Manda."

"Never." He shook his head and kissed her. "Never."

Dindrane heard Marrget sobbing as she went down the corridor toward Alouzon's room. The grief was real, she sensed: a combination of fear, guilt, and the unnamed things that could rise up in the middle of the night and reduce even the most taciturn to tears and regrets.

They are not heartless, then. They weep.

Violence had seemed so easy for the people from Gryylth, but now, standing silent in the dim corridor, Dindrane heard the depth of emotion in the captain's cries, heard also the strange juxtaposition of joy and sorrow that manifested as—amid tears and kisses both—Marrget and Karthin made tender love in the darkness of their room.

The priestess was moved. The gentle strength in Karthin's voice and the yielding softness in Marrget's were as pure a manifestation of the Divine as anything that she herself shared with Baares. There was no violence or bestiality here: only an absolute affection, one that knew how to cherish, how to give.

Stepping softly, she went on down the corridor, her thoughts suddenly turning along unfamiliar paths.

And what of Manda and Wykla? They loved as openly and passionately as Marrget and Karthin, and Dindrane had seen the glow on their faces as they had walked, hand in hand, through the gardens of the King's House, their light hair warmed by the colors of the setting sun, their steps guided along the path by bright clusters of early-blooming crocuses.

Their love was wrong, and yet they were happy. Dindrane shook her head, puzzled. Joy and love and happiness were gifts of the Goddess and the God. What did it mean?

The deep thrum of male voices drifted into the corridor from the room occupied by Santhe and his men. ". . . I think, then, that we should avoid drawing steel if at all possible," Santhe was saying. "Their ways are not ours. Fascinated as the children might be, let them be fascinated at a distance. Dindrane is right: there is enough death in this land."

"And if we are attacked?" said a cool, efficient

voice. Dindrane had a vision of light hair and gray eyes. Parl.

"We will do what we can. But we will respect our hosts."

Dindrane went on. So polite. Yet so different.

And Alouzon Dragonmaster would cross the breadth of Vaylle and climb the jagged slopes of the Cordillera. It was a violent action, but Dindrane sensed that Alouzon was motivated by more than a desire for bloodshed. Nonetheless, the thought of an armed party traveling through the soft landscapes of Vaylle made Dindrane contemplate her own responsibilities, and she knocked on Alouzon's door with her mind already made up.

"Come on in."

Alouzon was sitting on the edge of her bed, her elbows on her knees and her chin in her hands, but her weariness seemed not quite that of a soldier or a warrior, or even of a councilor or a diplomat.

She gestured Dindrane to a chair. "I've been expecting you."

"Indeed?"

Alouzon shrugged. "You didn't ask half your questions on the way to the city, so I figured you'd save them up for after dinner. Fire away."

Violent she was, and yet subtle and intuitive. Dindrane perched on the chair, settled her skirts about her, and laid her healer's staff across her knees. " 'Tis to Broceliande you want to go."

Tiredly, Alouzon stared into the fire. Her sheathed sword lay beside her, a cold and unyielding bedmate. "Yeah."

Dindrane eyed the weapon. "Pellam is a wise king. He would not have given you permission to travel in his realm unless he was quite sure of your intentions. I confess I do not share his confidence."

Alouzon nodded. "We're a pretty scruffy bunch." She picked up the sword and rested the tip of the sheath on the ground between her feet. The hilt was in the form of two intertwined dragons, one white, one black, and Alouzon ran her hand along them with an expression that might have been of fear.

Hardly a reassuring weapon, then, even for one who was called *Dragonmaster*.

"What . . ." Dindrane watched Alouzon's smooth brown hands for a moment. Womanflesh, like her own. And yet not. Alouzon had killed, and killed often. "What do you hope to accomplish?"

"Gryylth got hit a couple times," said Alouzon without looking up from the hilt. "I want to find out who did it."

"But you know that now."

"I've got a name. That's all."

"And what will you do when you find out what Broceliande is?"

Alouzon seemed to have no answer. Or maybe her answer was a part of the motivation that lay behind her outward actions: a restless, shadowy horror covered by a thin throw of words and gestures.

Dindrane pressed. "Will you go home then?"

"Probably."

"And then return with armies? And battle the Grayfaces?"

"I—"

"And what of Vaylle?"

Alouzon sighed, tossed the sword behind her, and shook her bronze mane out of her face. She would, Dindrane thought, look at home in neither a man's trews nor a woman's skirts. She was Alouzon: indissolubly wedded to tunic and armor and sword. Where did such a one as this come from?

"Let me tell you a story." Alouzon folded her hands and examined them for a moment as though she read the text of her tale in the twining of her fingers. "Where I come from, there was a country called Vietnam. It was full of people like you and me. All kinds. They lived their lives the way they wanted to. The problem was that no one would leave them alone."

Dindrane started to speak, but Alouzon shook her head. "Hear me out. Other countries wanted things that Vietnam had, and they decided to fight over them. The folks in Vietnam didn't want any part of it, but no one listened, and all of a sudden they had foreign armies on their land, and battles being fought, and people—including their own—getting killed. By the time the war was finished, there wasn't much of the place left.''

"And is it to keep me from sleep that you tell me such nightmares?" Dindrane's voice was thin: Alouzon had uttered her deepest fears.

"No. I just want you to know that I don't intend to let that happen to Vaylle.''

Dindrane's mouth tightened. The arrogance of the woman! "I am glad that you have so ordained.'' Her voice might have etched glass.

But Alouzon looked up, and the priestess was shaken by the tenderness that she saw in her brown eyes. "I care," said Alouzon, and if the Goddess Herself had spoken, She could not have put more sincerity and feeling into the words. "I . . . I love you all. I'm not going to let that happen.''

Kyria's bolt might have slaughtered all the learned men and women of Lachrae, but Alouzon had risked her life to save them. And here again her stated commitment carried an implicit offer of self-sacrifice. Dindrane's mouth went dry. "Who . . . who are you, Alouzon?''

Alouzon laughed wryly. "Sometimes I wish to hell I knew, Dindrane.''

"What is it that you want?''

Alouzon looked at her as a mother might look upon a firstborn child: half in awe, half in fear. "I'll tell you this: there's something in Broceliande besides death, and I'm going to find it. And when I do, it'll mean that you won't have to worry about what happened to Vietnam. I'm not saying that it'll be easy for any of us, but it won't be horrible, either.''

"Shall we learn violence then?'' But though Dindrane tried to find a blossom of righteousness within her, the flowers had withered. Her words fell flat.

Alouzon's motives were a shadow in the darkness behind her. "It might come to that," she said. "Maybe not."

Dindrane rose. She had thought that she had understood Alouzon, that her visit tonight would merely clarify certain points and establish certain boundaries. But it was as though she had peered through the ice of a winter lake to confront the immeasurable and unsettling depths below. "Baares and I will accompany you to Broceliande," she said. "You will need guides, and our people will need protection."

"Afraid we'll scare the horses?"

"Afraid, rather, that you will terrify the people," Dindrane replied tartly as she turned for the door. But her hand had not even found the pull when, plainly audible through the shuttered window, a distant scream cut the night air like a sharp sword.

The White Worm offered itself in terms that were almost sexual, and Helwych, prowling through the darkened corridors of the King's House, saw its indigo eyes and its blue nimbus everywhere: flashing out of sight around a corner, peering at him through an archway, flitting down the length of a hall.

Is this not what you want, my little man? Have you not lusted after me since the day Tireas declared that he had other matters than you to attend to? I am knowledge. I am power. Tell me now: am I not everything you desire?

The Worm was right. He had left his room so as to discover whatever mysteries of magic and knowledge might lie in the King's House and the temple grounds, searching, as always, for something to fill the lack of learning that had dogged him throughout his days of wizardry.

But the corridors had led him nowhere. He was lost now in a maze of passages and windows, of locked doors and forced turns. All the hallways looked the same, and what rooms he entered were empty save for the constant, intrusive presence of the White Worm.

Come. Give me . . . everything. And I will give you everything in return.

"Go away," he mumbled. He turned away and pushed through a side door that led into the gardens. When he turned around, the door had disappeared, but in the middle of the blank wall a face took on form and substance. It was a man's face, and though, like the Worm's, its eyes were the no-color of empty space, they possessed the hypnotic gaze of a specter.

The lips moved soundlessly. *I will be everything to you.*

Helwych shoved himself away from the wall and ran into the gardens. The night sky with its million stars hung like a weight above him, pressing his thoughts to the ground, and the voice pursued him.

All things are possible for me . . .

As he ran through a thicket of thorn bushes, a hand—a man's hand—reached out and tumbled him to the ground. In a moment, Helwych's arms were pinned beside him and the face he had seen was inches away from his own.

"Dindrane! Alouzon! Help!"

"They can't hear you, little man," said the Specter. Though somewhat above middle age, its hair gray, its face lined, Helwych's assailant was unaccountably strong, and nothing the boy could do had any effect on its grip.

"They will hear," Helwych insisted, "for we are in the garden of the King's House. Someone will hear."

The Specter shook its head and laughed dryly. "We're a long way from the garden, sonny. Farther than if you were in bed in Corrin." It spat. "Corrin! Dremord territory, if you ask me!"

"Let me go!" Helwych struggled, but he might have been fettered in iron.

"Let you go?" The Specter laughed again, bent over and fixed Helwych's gaze with its own. "Isn't this what you want? Isn't this what you've always wanted?"

Helwych's vision filled with the blackness of the Specter's eyes. Scraping together what self-confidence

was left to him, he spoke slowly and deliberately, using the formula that was one of the last things that
Tireas had taught him. "You cannot have my soul,"
he said. "I will not yield it."

"Yield it?" said the Specter. "I'm not asking you
to yield anything. How the hell can you yield what you
haven't got?"

"My soul—"

"Has been mine since Kingsbury." The Specter's
gaze sank deeply into Helwych. "Don't worry: you
haven't really been feeling anything since my hound
took you, anyway."

Faintly, with his last shreds of identity, Helwych
heard someone screaming, and then the sharp crack
of a detonation.

The attendants had shown Manda and Wykla to separate rooms, but they slept in the same bed anyway,
for they would not willingly give up what they had
found in one another's touch since they had declared
their love.

In the flickering light of a low-burning fire, Wykla's
skin was the color of pale roses, and when, smiling,
she stretched her arms up to Manda, there was acceptance and love in her eyes, not only for the maid of
Corrin, but for herself as well. It was as if—with each
night, each caress, each passage of pleasure from hand
to body and back again—the girl rooted herself more
firmly and more joyfully into the woman's form that
had once seemed so alien to her that she would rather
have died than endured it.

Manda's maidenhood had been torn from her, and
Wykla's had been forced upon her; but in the union of
body and spirit to which they abandoned themselves
each night, the two women found themselves possessed of that which they had thought they had lost
forever: themselves. And it seemed to both that such
a queenly possession, long desired and long fought
for, could only be truly clasped in the giving of it to
another.

And they gave, unstintingly. Here was a release of sorrow, here a forgetting of the past. In the warmth of their common bed, they had only the present, and joy, and the faithfulness of souls that had grown together.

But what, Manda wondered as the fire flickered into low embers and fluttering ash, did Marrget feel tonight? She, too, had found love, and now she was with child. How distant, really, was the past?

The man who had raped Manda could know nothing of a woman's passion, or of the flutter of life within her belly. His guilt had been his own. Selfish, self-centered, conceited, he had taken his pleasure—and his blood—and had gone away again.

But the woman: there had been fear in her eyes when Dindrane had spoken of her unborn child. And the contemplative bleakness that was now a constant presence on her face was nothing that a man could ever understand.

Was he gone then, Manda's quest for justice all ended? Manda did not know. She curled herself against Wykla's soft, sleeping body and, pondering, tried to find in her lover's steady breathing some reassurance that the past was dead. But just as she was dropping off, she heard a sudden cry, and a sharp detonation, and at the other end of the corridor, a door was flung open with a crash.

Alouzon's voice rang out. "Everybody up! We've got trouble!"

Kyria did not wander the corridors of the King's House to look for magic or secrets. If she had put her desire into words, she would have said that she searched for an end to the persistent sense of entrapment that had shackled her since she had come to Gryylth.

Years ago, she had fought Solomon, and she had vowed that his kind would never possess her again. But she could not fight this utter transformation that had turned her body into that of a young woman and caused her to answer instinctively to a different name.

Her mind was, in fact, so profoundly alien that at times she had difficulty acknowledging it as her own.

But was it, in fact, so alien? Kyria—the real Kyria, the one who smiled softly at her out of her inward darkness—was by no means an intruder. Rather, she was a rebirth of old wants and needs, a revival of an age of innocence, of a time before forced abortion and wrathful divorce had tamped the last spadeful of soil down on the coffin of love and holiness.

Helen Addams looked out through Kyria's eyes now, fighting passionately against the very sense of wholeness that she had once embraced. Day by day she was falling back into the patterns that had once led her into powerlessness, and yet everything that she saw and did told her that she was not at all powerless, that the strengths that lay within her grasp were real. And against her will she was beginning to believe it.

The corridors of the King's House were as straight as the streets of the city, and without difficulty she found her way into the gardens that surrounded the temple precincts. The rose bushes were bare this early in the year, but the crocuses and hyacinths were up, and tulips seemed imminent.

The moon had not yet risen, but the darkness was alleviated by the multitude of stars and by the torches set along the colonnade that skirted the gardens. In the firelight, the flowers sparkled with early dew, and Kyria bent to touch a bloom, surprised that there could be such beauty and gentleness in land created by Solomon Braithwaite.

"Lady Kyria?" An attendant approached her, the golden threads of his livery glinting. "May I be of help?"

She had straightened instinctively at the name, and she cursed silently for her self-treachery. Kyria was not her name. It belonged to that gently smiling face within her. Her name was Helen: why should she answer to Kyria? "I'm just . . . nervous tonight," she said.

He nodded." 'Tis welcome you are to Lachrae, and to

the King's gardens. Please wander as you wish." Soft-spoken, polite, strong and gentle both, he appeared to embody all the desirable qualities of manhood.

And they drop like flies when the Grayfaces come . . .

The attendant bowed and turned to depart. "Wait a minute," Kyria said suddenly, and he stopped. "Are you watching me because you're afraid?"

"Afraid?" He was puzzled.

"I mean, after all, I nearly . . ." Her action outside Daelin had shamed her: she would not speak the words willingly. She shrugged and shook her head.

He understood. "Errors are a part of growth—so the Goddess teaches us. Those who are wise have said that the Goddess herself has made mistakes, though we as men and women cannot ourselves perceive them as such. Nevertheless, She sorrows over them."

"Even Gods have to grow?"

"Indeed. Surely."

She felt like crying. Everything that she had ever wanted was here, but Solomon had created it only to destroy it, bit by bit, before her eyes. And she was too stubborn and too cynical to save it. "Am I allowed to see the temple?" she said abruptly.

"Willing feet are never denied." He offered his hand and, after a moment, she took it. This was Vaylle. She was safe.

Accustomed to places of worship that possessed four walls and a roof, Kyria was at first taken aback when she was led to a ring of roughly dressed monoliths that reared up more than twenty feet from the thick grass. But her senses had been sharpened by sorcery, and she felt the sanctity of the place.

If there was Divinity in the universe, it had taken up residence here in Lachrae, and Kyria had to consciously shield herself from the energy that swirled invisibly about the stones, that reached out to her with gentle but omnipotent presence, threatening to sweep her into ecstasy, or oblivion, or both.

The attendant spoke in a whisper. "The temple. She is here. And so is He."

The Goddess and the God. That afternoon, Pellam had called them Suzanne and Solomon, and Alouzon had nearly fainted on the spot.

Like a miser breaking open a new roll of pennies, Kyria examined her suspicions. The God was Solomon. That was nothing that surprised her. Her ex-husband had obviously set himself up in what he considered to be his rightful place. But Suzanne? Suzanne Helling was as much a victim of Sol's arrogance as Helen Addams.

Or was she?

At the entrance to the ring of monoliths were two smaller stones that rose up to the height of a tall man. At such a distance from the colonnade, the light was faint and uncertain, but Kyria could see that the pair were carved with the life-sized figures of a man and a woman.

She sent the attendant away and, alone, she contemplated the images: Solomon, thin and lined, but with dignity in his face; Suzanne, plump and noble both, a sword in her hands.

Suzanne . . .

Victim? Or just another exploiter?

A scream broke through the holy silence as though a glass had been shattered, and a wave of light suddenly eclipsed the stars. A moment later came an explosion, and, horribly, the sound of a machine gun.

Kyria turned and ran for the colonnade, her staff searing the air with violet intensity. *Sol, you bastard!*

❖ CHAPTER 16 ❖

The King's House and the temple precincts occupied a low hill at the center of the city, and the sounds of explosives and automatic weapons' fire carried clearly to them. So did the screams of the families who lived at the west edge of town.

Alouzon pounded down the corridor, carrying her leathers and sword in one hand, dragging Dindrane after her with the other. "How do we get outside?"

"And is it fighting you want?"

"Hell, yes!"

Dindrane dug in her heels at the first turning and brought Alouzon up short. "Why should I show you, then?"

Alouzon felt like slapping her. "Because your people are getting slaughtered out there, bitch."

The company had quickly assembled behind them. Manda was pulling the straps of Wykla's cuirass tight as the girl tied her hair back. Karthin was struggling into his armor, assisted by Marrget. Santhe and his men appeared never to have disarmed.

Alouzon glanced back. Helwych? Kyria? The sounds of modern warfare that carried across the city told her that a defense without magic would be suicidal.

Dindrane read her thoughts. "Can you do any better than we, Dragonmaster?"

A door opened at the end of the hall, and Helwych staggered out of his room, rubbing sleep from his eyes and gaping.

"Look," said Alouzon, "let us do what we can." Dindrane met her gaze levelly, her eyes showing not a trace of fear. "Come on: move!"

Reluctantly, the priestess led them down the corridor and through several rooms. At last she paused before a door of oak. "This is the western portal of the House," she said. "Straight across the plaza is the West Road. The Grayfaces—"

She stopped. Mixed into the tumult from the edge of the city, clearly audible through the wood and masonry, was the demented howling of a pack of hounds.

Alouzon jerked the door open. The night air spilled in. The howling and shots grew louder. "Are you coming?"

Dindrane shook her head. "I will keep safe those whom I can. And I will find Baares, for there will be healing needed tonight." She looked them over for an instant, and her face turned pained when her eyes rested on Marrget. "Much healing. Go. Go if you must." She turned and, staff in hand, fled back into the House.

"Where is Kyria?" said Marrget.

"Dunno," said Alouzon. She fumbled with the buckles of her leathers. "We'll have to do without her."

Helwych drew himself up. In the torchlight, his dark eyes seemed filled with nothing save the emptiness of the night sky. "She will not be needed."

Alouzon found his inflections disturbing. "I hope you're right, kiddo."

They ran. Their boots clattered on the pavement and echoed off the stone buildings. The moon sent their shadows racing ahead of them like streaks of black oil. The streets were deserted: breached yet again, Lachrae had turned in upon itself—doors barred, windows shuttered—like a wounded animal curling up to sleep . . . or die.

When the flashes of tracers and exploding grenades came into view, Alouzon signaled a halt. Ahead, the screams continued, the hoarse, despairing cries of many voices blending into a hellish counterpoint of pain that was answered by the chatter of the guns and the baying of hounds.

"O, you nameless Gods," said Karthin softly.

Gods. Alouzon supposed that the term included her now. She grimaced.

"I suggest an indirect approach, Alouzon," said Marrget.

She floundered out of her thoughts. "Uh . . . yeah. Good. Helwych: can you . . ." She examined him for a moment. Different. Quite different. And that hound south of Bandon had been *playing* with him. "Can you handle the hounds?"

"I can, indeed." He sounded almost smug.

After a minute's conference, the party broke into three teams. Alouzon, Manda, and Wykla would take a side street and work their way westward. Santhe and his men would circle to the north. Marrget, Karthin, and Helwych would do the same from the south. "I'll warn you all," said Alouzon. "The hounds may be the least of our problems. Remember what happened in Quay? The Grayfaces have weapons like that."

"We remember," said Santhe. He smiled thinly. Battle—and maybe death—lay ahead of him, but his humor flickered through nonetheless. "But we remember the Tree, too, and the Circle."

"Gods bless," said Alouzon. She felt strange uttering the words. Bettering her grip on the Dragonsword, she moved off into a narrow alley that paralleled the main thoroughfare. Manda and Wykla hugged for an instant, then followed.

Although the alley was unpaved, there was no rubbish or squalor: the Vayllens' taste for order and cleanliness extended even to their back streets. Barrels and boxes were stacked tightly together without any strays or leaks, and the three women made their way along the passage silently.

In a lull in the gunfire, Alouzon looked up at a bright window that splashed the alley with candlelight. A man's voice was murmuring:

"Suzanne, be with us . . ."

Alouzon sagged against the marble wall, the Dragonsword heavy in her hand. "I'm just a dumb girl," she whispered. "Don't do this to me."

". . . fold us in Your comforting embrace that, should this be the hour of our death, we may be led to Your lands by the hand of the God . . ."

She could not afford hysteria now. Dragging a breath, she pushed on, fixing her eyes and her thoughts on what lay ahead.

The outlying sections of the city presented an increasingly rural appearance. As Alouzon, Manda, and Wykla continued on, the alley began opening out on one side or the other to reveal gardens and broad, grassy plazas. It finally terminated in a field dotted with trees and stands of high bushes.

Fifty yards away was a cluster of manor houses, their style reminiscent of the Romano-British villas that had once dotted southern England. To the eyes of Suzanne Helling, the student, they were a study in archaeology come to life, fifth-century timber and thatch modified only slightly to embrace marble and slate. To the eyes of the former war protester, they were a horror of anachronistic warfare, with tracer bullets pouring through shuttered windows and ricocheting off stone walls.

But to Alouzon Dragonmaster, they were a problem to be solved, a battle to be fought.

An embankment ringed the manors, its top surmounted by a hedge of crab apple and elder. There the Grayfaces had taken up their position, and the light of the waning moon slanted down on the gas-masked soldiers and on the hound-pack that swirled across the surrounding field in a surging mass of diseased phosphorescence.

A flash of violet burst out suddenly from a cluster of trees at the southern end of the field, sweeping toward the hounds like a searchlight beam. They wheeled away, but one was slow. The violet finger caught it squarely, transfixed it, and melted it into a steaming puddle as its howling turned first to whining and then to a full-throated animal scream of pain.

Detonations. One. Two. Three. Light burst from within the embankment, and a wall of the nearest manor crumbled. Roof slates tumbled to the ground, rooms were left gaping, floors collapsed, and those occupants who were not pitched to the ground were riddled by the spray of bullets from the M-60.

Forgetting the violet energy, hungry for food—or for souls—the hound pack yelped and dived over the embankment.

Crump. Crump.

Alouzon started. Mortars. The sound had come not from the Grayfaces nearest her, but from a part of the embankment farther to the south. How many enemies were they dealing with?

Helwych's lance of energy left the ground and darted skyward. The mortar rounds exploded harmlessly in the air. The young sorcerer was defending admirably, but if he were tied up with mortars, he could do nothing against the dogs.

Kyria, where the hell are you?

Alouzon turned to the other women. "The dogs are busy for now," she said quickly. "It looks like there's enough cover to make it across the clearing to the bunch on this side. Our only hope is to grab one of those guns."

Manda glanced at Wykla, who shrugged. "We do not know the use of them, Dragonmaster," she said.

"I can figure it out." Alouzon started across the field. "I hope."

Trees and bushes provided concealment, but the moonlight was abominably clear and bright. As they dashed from cover to cover, Alouzon kept expecting a sudden burst of fire, tracers streaking like orange sparks, a cry from Wykla or Manda . . .

Another wall of the manor collapsed, and the hounds' baying turned into a frenzied slavering. Above the tumult rose the cry of a woman. "Please . . . please . . ."

Alouzon rushed again, dived for a cluster of bushes, and found herself confronted with a Grayface soldier who had been staring off toward the south, fascinated by the play of Helwych's energy.

"Mercy . . . please . . . *O Goddess, save me!*"

The eyes behind the gas mask narrowed and the M-16 came up, but the Dragonsword was faster. Alouzon opened the man from belly to throat and grabbed his gun as he fell.

She looked up in time to see, to the south, Marrget dashing toward a ditch. Marrget was followed by Karthin, who was, in turn, followed by a line of tracers. At the last moment, Marrget threw herself into the ditch, reached up, and dragged Karthin in after her. The tracers streaked by, whipping the grass and soil into a pulverized cloud.

With Manda and Wykla beside her, Alouzon sheathed the Dragonsword and scrutinized the M-16. She assumed that the safety was off and that she had only to pull the trigger to fire it. She assumed. She had no idea what to do if that were not the case.

Another soldier ran toward them from the embankment, but Manda moved quickly. By the time he realized that conditions within the thicket had changed drastically, he was dead.

But Marrget and Karthin were pinned down in the ditch, and more mortar rounds were hurtling in Helwych's direction.

"Dragonmaster?" Manda was holding the other M-16 as though it were a snake. "This does not please me much."

"Nor me, Manda. Do you want to try that thing?"

"Nay, lady. I am not such a fool."

"OK." Alouzon took it from her and fumbled with the ammunition clip until it slid into her hand. She thrust it into her belt and tossed the extra rifle aside. "We're going in. There are some trees about twenty feet this side of the Grayfaces. We'll work our way across to them. When we go over the rim to hit the machine gun, we'll have to move fast."

Her companions did not hesitate to follow her. Alouzon wished heartily that she was as confident, but

with the Dragonsword guiding her and the greasy, Fi-
berglas stock of the M-16 under her arm, she assumed
that she had bettered their odds at least a little.

The sky lit up as Helwych detonated another mortar
round.

In two rushes, Alouzon and her companions had almost reached the last clump of trees, but then the machine gun roared into action, and the three found the
ground at their feet peppered with 7.62 millimeter bullets. Without breaking stride, Manda pivoted on the
spot and threw herself into Wykla, knocking her free
of the kill zone. Alouzon back-pedaled furiously and
tumbled beside them, behind the lip of a depression.

Manda's head was pressed against Wykla's. "What
kind of monsters are these?"

Alouzon suppressed a sudden wave of nausea. "I . . .
I haven't the faintest idea," she lied.

Manda knew she lied. The glance she gave the
Dragonmaster was level, accepting, but surprised.

The M-60 tracked back across the ground, raking the
edge of the depression. In a lull, Alouzon risked a peek
at the Grayface position, but she saw muzzle flashes the
moment her head cleared the lip. She dropped flat
again. The waning moon glared down, and she cursed
its light, for it made them a perfect target.

But the moonlight cut off suddenly, and Alouzon
looked up to find that a whirling cloud of darkness had
blanketed the sky above the area. Even the stars had
vanished. Kyria's voice, faint but clear, called out:
"Everyone move!"

As one, Alouzon, Manda, and Wykla rolled out of
the depression and, swinging well out to either side,
headed for the Grayfaces.

Mere yards now. Alouzon saw a muffled flash that
was directed upward and guessed that a flare was about
to burst. Off to her left, grenades exploded in the ditch,
and she hoped that Marrget and Karthin had gotten
out in time. To her right, another M-60 opened fire,
doubtless in response to an approach on the part of
Santhe and his men.

The flare burst in a shower of magnesium light just as Alouzon reached the gun emplacement. Bushes, trees, grass: all shone as though graven in silver.

Gas-masked figures turned toward her, but she squeezed the trigger of the M-16, and it bucked lightly in her hands as she emptied the ammunition clip into the men before her. The high-velocity bullets were designed to tumble upon impact: clothing and flesh shredded as one, blood flowed black in the blue white light, bits of bone scattered palely across the gleaming grass.

Manda and Wykla, their swords silver and lethal, fell on those who scrambled away from the volley of death, and the fight was over in seconds.

For a moment they rested, panting, listening to the slavering hounds on the far side of the bank. Alouzon crawled up to the hedge, peered through carefully, and was nearly sick at the sight of the scattered and gnawed limbs and bodies. The woman's cry still rang in her ears: *O Goddess, save me!*

The flare spent itself, and darkness returned. Scattered fire erupted from the north, and grenades pocked the night with scarlet concussions. Kyria's veil was holding, but unless she was willing to risk slipping into her alternate personality, she was as fully occupied with the moonlight as Helwych was with the mortar rounds that continued to arc southward with irritating regularity.

"We're going to have to free up one of the sorcerers," said Alouzon. "If Kyria drops that cloud, we lose our cover. It looks like Helwych's the best bet."

Manda examined as much of the scene as was revealed by the intermittent bursts of light. "I had no idea that Helwych commanded such potencies."

"Neither did I."

The maid swung back to Alouzon. "To my knowledge—to anyone's knowledge—he did not when we left Benardis. Where did he learn these things?"

Alouzon shook her head as she changed ammunition clips, recalling again the playful hound. "You got me.

He's taking care of the mortars, and he can take care of the hounds. For now, that's all I care about.''

"As you will, Dragonmaster.''

"Let's go. South. When we hit the emplacement, keep moving and stay close to them: don't give them a chance to use their guns.''

They crept along the edge of the embankment. The grass cushioned their footfalls, but as they crept to within yards of the Grayface position, Alouzon heard the scrape of an M-60 bipod as the weapon was shifted toward them.

She leaped, kicking the barrel of the machine gun to the side, sending the first spray of bullets into the ground. Swung with the strength of a Dragonmaster, the butt of her M-16 found the gunner's temple, and he rolled to the side, his skull shattered.

Alouzon looked up. In the faint spill of light, ten or twelve Grayfaces confronted her, their features indistinguishable behind the gray plastic and goggle lenses of their gas masks. One was barking orders, his voice flat, muffled, almost detached, and weapons were being trained on her.

She leveled her rifle, but the mechanism had jammed. She threw it at one of the men and dived into another. The bullets intended for her went by harmlessly, but she saw the gleam of bayonets.

Rising, she drew her sword, knocked the first blade aside, and shoved the man back. Wykla was just entering the fight, and her blade dropped him a moment before she drove in on two others. Alouzon was already dealing with several more.

Alouzon let her sword have its way with her, hewing through the flesh and blood about her with broad strokes, pivoting and ducking at the weapon's bidding so as to avoid the thrust of a bayonet or the swing of a rifle butt. But only two of her opponents lay dead on the ground when she looked up and saw that Wykla had fallen.

The girl's head was bleeding, and her sword lay several feet from her limp hand. Manda had been backed away from her lover, and was helpless to do anything about the Grayface that stood over the girl, his bayonet lifted for the thrust.

Alouzon lunged, but she was knocked back. She tripped over the inert M-60 and fell full length on the ground, her head cracking against the canteen of a corpse. The scene blurred for a moment, and when her vision cleared, she saw a Grayface standing above her, pistol in hand. It was a clear shot, at close range, at an unmoving target.

"Eat death, cunt," he said, but his vacant tone was curiously at odds with his words.

But a woman as slender as Wykla had appeared behind the Grayface with the bayonet, and a sword hissed. The Grayface dropped, lifeless, and Marrget threw herself on the soldier who was about to shoot Alouzon as Karthin leaped into the battle to settle the last of those who besieged Manda.

On the far side of the bank, the cries of the hound pack redoubled. Their appetites whetted, the dogs were looking for more flesh, and they were beginning to snuffle and whine.

Manda and Marrget were already tending to Wykla. Alouzon stumbled to the edge of the emplacement and shouted across the field. "Helwych!"

No answer. Cowardice? Mortar round?

The hounds surged about the bases of the manor houses, sniffing and howling. But then, as though their attention had been drawn by the lack of gunfire from the south emplacement, they wheeled as one. In a moment, a wave of glowing beasts was heading straight for Alouzon and her companions.

Alouzon had a sudden memory of Manda's face dissolving beneath a rain of corrosive phosphor: Kyria had never enchanted the weapons of the expedition. "Helwych!"

Still no answer. And Kyria was still busy with the darkness, providing cover for Santhe and his men.

As the hounds approached, Alouzon bent, seized the M-60, hitched the heavy weapon under her arm

and, staggering, climbed the bank, the ammunition belt
trailing behind. Grenades detonated to the north, but
the first wave of the beasts was almost upon her, eyes
flickering lambently, teeth gleaming.

She pressed the trigger. The kick nearly threw her
back down the slope, but Karthin braced her with his
large frame. As she gained control of the weapon, the
line of tracers dropped into the ravening hounds and
tracked back and forth across the pack.

As she had hoped, the impossible beasts were cut
to pieces by the equally impossible machine gun. Several simply disintegrated, puddling the grass with
phosphor and flesh. Others fragmented messily, severed legs spasming beside headless torsos, disembodied jaws snapping even in death, spines twisting and
writhing like worms.

The last of the ammunition belt fed through the
breech. The gun fell silent. The darkness had lifted,
the dogs were gone, and the sounds of battle to the
north had died away; but in the silence that was broken
only by Wykla's pain-racked gasps and the faint cries
of the Vayllens that were still alive within the houses,
Alouzon heard the roar of jet engines.

Airstrike.

Her legs felt as though they must, at any moment,
collapse beneath her, and her arms were numb with
the vibrations of the M-60. She forced herself to turn
around and found her voice. "We've got to get out of
here. How is Wykla?"

Manda looked up. "Alive, Dragonmaster," she
said. "Thanks to Marrget." She nodded to the captain, and a look went between them that came nowhere
near reconciliation, but it was a beginning. "More
than that we cannot say."

Alouzon tossed the gun away. "We'll get Dindrane or
Kyria to fix her up. For now, you'll have to carry her. This
place is going to be an inferno in another minute."

The jets were coming closer. Together, carrying
Wykla between them, Manda and Marrget headed for
the city. Alouzon and Karthin ran for the manor

houses, picking their way through a mucous swamp of phosphor, leaping over the heaped and mutilated bodies of the dogs until they stood at the door of the nearest house.

Vayllen construction was solid. The door had held, and the walls of the structure had fallen only after a prolonged bombardment. Still, although Alouzon and Karthin hammered on the door and shouted, no one responded.

"There's got to be someone alive in there. I heard them."

"Indeed, Dragonmaster," said Karthin. "I saw them at the windows."

Frustrated and angry, Alouzon kicked at the door, yelling up at the blank windows. "Dammit, get your asses out of there! You're going to get blown to bits!"

No answer. The jets roared. Karthin put a hand on Alouzon's shoulder, and she turned to find his face sad and thoughtful. "I think I understand."

"Understand?"

"They cannot distinguish between us and the Grayfaces," he said somberly. "How should they?"

"But we're—" She stopped short. For the Vayllens, violence was violence. She looked up at the windows and the gaping rooms, her throat constricting. "Please," she choked. "Please come out."

The warplanes were already streaking overhead. Karthin pulled Alouzon away from the houses. "Come, Dragonmaster. We can do no more."

"But there are people in there . . ." Alouzon clawed her way free and hammered on the door once again. "I'm not going to hurt you," she called, but with two jets sweeping around and lining up on the houses, Karthin picked her up bodily and ran for cover. He had barely crossed the embankment when the first bombs fell, ripping the manors open like ripe fruit, tearing through the silent Grayface positions, pitching him and his burden headlong across the bloody grass.

The planes swept out and around. "I would Kyria were here," said the big man.

"She was here a while ago," said Alouzon. "Who knows where she is now. Or who . . ."

"Shall we run?"

She shook her head wearily. "We'd just give them an obvious target. Stay down."

The manors were in ruins, their occupants dead. The bodies and weapons of the Grayfaces were mangled beyond recognition or use, and the stench of high explosive and phosphor hung over the ground in a choking cloud. But as the planes banked and began another run, a bolt of violet spat up at them from the edge of the city. The jets were immediately surrounded by a glowing nimbus. A moment later they fireballed and disintegrated, the wreckage spinning through the dark sky.

"Kyria. She came through." But the thought of what the effort might have cost the sorceress drove Alouzon to her feet and sent her stumbling off toward the city.

She found Kyria huddled on the ground at the mouth of an alley, her hands to her face, her staff cast aside. She was whining softly. "I . . . didn't want to do that. I . . . just had to. Those poor kids . . ."

Alouzon waved Karthin on. "Go find Marrget and Manda." She crouched beside Kyria. "Come on, lady," she said, laying a hand on her shoulder. "You'll be all right."

"She's inside my head," said Kyria. "I'm not me. I just want to be me."

Alouzon was bleak. Behind her, smoke from the ruined manors climbed into the sky. "You might just have to let go."

Kyria's head snapped up, and her eyes were venomous. "You'd like that, wouldn't you, bitch?" Her face contorted with the ferocity of her inner struggle. "It's not just Sol, is it? You're in this up to your damned eyeballs, aren't you?"

Alouzon stared. Whether because of Pellam's words in the great hall or some other revelation, Kyria knew. And what would she do now?

"Sol made his part," the sorceress continued, trembling. "And you made yours. You want to tell me why you had to drag me into your personal fairy tale?"

"It wasn't my idea."

"Go on. Next thing you know, you'll be telling me the Dragon planned it all."

The screams of the dying pierced her memory. "I don't know, Kyria."

The sorceress shivered at the name. *"Don't call me that!"* Lunging, she grabbed for her staff. "You want to see what happens to fairy tales? I'll damn well show you—"

Her words were cut short by an explosion that, although it was some distance away, shook the earth and crumbled the buildings around them. Alouzon dragged Kyria out of the way just as rubble showered down and buried the alley several feet deep.

Another detonation, and another. The bombs cut a swath through the city, demolishing buildings, tearing up streets, heaving paving blocks through the air. The air was filled with a continuous concussion that Alouzon thought must surely pummel her body into the ground. "What the . . . ?"

"B-52s," murmured Kyria. Despair was in her voice. "The Grayfaces must have gotten off a radio call for more than the jets."

"Kyria, can you—"

The sorceress was sobbing. "Can I what? Can I bail you out again? What the hell are you doing to this place, Alouzon?"

The roar of thousand-pound bombs was tremendous, sledgehammering at them invisibly, buffeting them as though with fists of steel. "I can't help it!"

"Dammit, what do you mean by that?"

"Stop them!"

"Tell me!"

Alouzon was watching her people die, not by the swords of invading armies, nor even from such comparatively intimate weapons as machine guns and grenades. This death fell from miles above, like the wrathful thunderbolts of a demented immortal. "Kyria, do something. There are kids out there . . ."

How much had Solomon Braithwaite manipulated Helen? How much did Silbakor manipulate Alouzon? She had no idea. But she knew well how passionately Alouzon was willing to pull Kyria's heartstrings to save those she loved.

Kyria knew also. "If I let go now, it'll be a long time before I'm back. Don't do this to me!"

Alouzon grabbed her robe, sat her upright, and put her staff in her hands. "You're so hot on power. Well, use some of it. Save those kids. Give them a chance to know that they've got some of it themselves."

"They're all a bunch of pacifists."

"That's going to change. It has to."

Kyria slapped her, and Alouzon felt a trickle of blood start down her cheek. Funny, she thought: she had braved the Grayfaces without a scratch; it took the slender hand of the sorceress to wound her.

"Don't tell me it'll change," Kyria was snarling. "Nothing ever changes. Sol didn't change."

With a roar, a block of buildings near the center of the city collapsed. Fire leaped up from the rubble, spreading quickly. The bombs continued to fall.

Kyria got to her feet, staff in hand. Her initial blazed out of the wood with stellar brilliance. She pointed at Alouzon. "Just remember this, honey: Kyria can't be around forever. When I get back, I'm going to take you apart. You and Sol both."

With a murmured incantation, she lifted the staff. For a moment, an oppression as of a thousand thunderstorms hung in the air, stretching the fabric of the world as taut as a cry of pain. Then the sky was suddenly filled with the starbursts of flaming bombers.

Kyria had time for one last hate-filled look at Alouzon before she went down, her carefully nurtured anger giving way at last under the onslaught of something that was at once tender and indomitable, gentle and inexorable, meek and well-nigh omnipotent.

❖ CHAPTER 17 ❖

"Murderers."

Dindrane's voice was flat, without a shred of emotion. Even outright anger, Alouzon thought, would have been preferable to the dull resignation that filled the word like a slab of lead.

The morning light in the great hall was pale and colorless, for the stained-glass windows had been shattered by the saturation bombing that had demolished half of Lachrae. Pellam slumped in his throne as though his infirmity had been increased by the wounding of his city, and, beside him, Dindrane and Baares were bowed under the weight of fatigue that had accumulated from three days without sleep or rest. The harper's fingers were raw and bleeding, and his wife's face was drawn.

Alouzon's companions looked no better. They had labored alongside Dindrane and Baares and the citizens of Lachrae, fighting fires, clearing rubble so as to reach those who were trapped, carrying the injured to the nearest healer. In the light of their efforts, the priestess's judgment seemed heartless and unjust, almost cruel, but Dindrane shook her head and repeated the accusation.

"Murderers."

"We did the best we could," said Alouzon quietly, knowing that even their best had not been good enough. She gestured at Santhe, who wore the face of a commander who had seen a good man die, and at

Birk, who looked as broken as if he had lost a lover. "We lost one of our own, too."

"Small comfort that is, Dragonmaster. Have you looked at our city recently?"

"We've seen a lot of your city. It's a miracle that the rest of us didn't get smeared. Dammit, we tried." Alouzon's words sounded hollow even to her own ears, for she was defending actions of which she herself was uncertain. Dindrane called her people murderers: once, Suzanne Helling had flung the same word at the soldiers returning from Vietnam. They had tried, too.

"Enough," said Pellam softly. "What would you do, priestess?"

Dindrane gripped her healer's staff as though to steady herself. "I would send them back to Gryylth. Their boat lies beached near the ruins . . ." She glared at Alouzon accusingly. " . . . the ruins of Daelin. They could be away by nightfall."

"I am not satisfied," said the king, "that Lachrae would have survived unscathed even if the Dragonmaster and her people had not acted. Such knowledge lies within the mind of the Goddess and the God."

Alouzon kept her eyes on the floor.

Helwych spoke. He alone of Alouzon's company seemed little affected by lack of sleep, though he had worked as hard as anyone. At first, Alouzon had put it down to his youth. But no: Manda and Wykla were supporting one another like half-toppled columns while the sorcerer stood straight and fresh-faced.

"I mean no disrespect to the King of Vaylle," he said, his courtesy as unnerving as his endurance. "But I think that it would be better for my people to withdraw."

Helwych, you son of a bitch . . .

He glanced at Alouzon as though reading her mind, but he went on. "We have caused enough trouble here already, and this only confirms my belief that we cannot fight the incursions from Broceliande directly."

Marrget turned on him, seething. "What would you have us do? Wait in our homes for the end of all?"

Helwych examined her ironically, his face betraying his opinion that the best place for Marrget was, indeed, at home. "Lachrae has been decimated, mother."

Marrget went white. Alouzon lashed out. "It wouldn't have been if you'd blasted those planes before they hit." The company murmured agreement. Only Kyria, who stood a little apart from the rest—eyes downcast, white hand upon pale staff— refrained.

"You forget, Dragonmaster." Helwych's eyes were no less ironic when he faced Alouzon, and she wondered whether this smug complacency was supposed to be an improvement over his sullen fits of temper. "I am but an apprentice. I did what I could."

"You slew the hounds," said Manda. "You could not do that before."

"I may improve myself at times, little maid. But you must be aware of my limitations as I am aware . . ." He smiled, glanced at Wykla. ". . . of your infirmities."

The light in Manda's eyes flared. Fatigue had shortened tempers, and only Wykla's gentle hand kept Manda from striding forward and knocking the lad to the ground.

Helwych paid no attention. "We should go home."

Dindrane nodded. " 'Tis glad I am to see sense among you."

Pellam looked uneasy, as though his priestess had decided to walk barefoot across a floor strewn with vipers.

"If it please the king and my company . . ." Although she had worked beside the healers of Lachrae the last three days, Kyria's voice was soft and sweet, and when she lifted her head and shook back her hair, her face was calm, tranquil.

She had come to her senses quickly after her collapse, but the woman who had opened her eyes and reached for her staff had born little resemblance to the one who, raging and cursing, had stopped the destruction of Lachrae. Her alternate personality seemed now firmly entrenched, but though her every word and action bespoke gentleness and nurture, each sight of her was a new pang of guilt for Alouzon, for Kyria had not chosen the persona freely.

When I get back, she had said, *I'm going to take you apart.*

Now Kyria stepped forward softly. "We erred grievously," she said. "There is nothing that we can do that will rebuild Lachrae, or restore the dead to life. But if we can, through our actions, end the ceaseless attacks that have turned Vaylle into a hell, then I might think that adequate recompense."

"There is nothing that can be done," said Helwych.

"There is much." Kyria smiled at him. "But perhaps a mere apprentice should not be expected to know such things."

Alouzon blinked. Sweet though Kyria was, she had teeth.

"And what do you expect to do?" said Baares. His tone was uneasy: half horrified at the potential for violence, half eager for a chance to do his part. Alouzon had seen him at work these last days, bending his mind and music to aid his healer wife, his entire being taut and focused on the work at hand. But he had also, when he thought no one was looking, shaken his fist at the mountains of the Cordillera, his face declaring the earnestness of the gesture.

Kyria regarded him understandingly. "We have business in Broceliande. I trust Alouzon, and I am willing to follow her."

Alouzon found herself wishing that this alternate Kyria could be her companion forever, but felt disloyal for the desire. Who was Kyria? What did she have to do with Helen Addams?

But Marrget was seconding the sorceress, and Karthin and the rest were not far behind. Only Helwych shook his head. "Fools. You have no idea what she wants, and yet you are willing to throw your lives away."

"And is your action any more honorable?" said Karthin.

"Are you calling me a coward, hayseed?"

The big man flushed. "One who was greater than you called me that once, stripling. He was mad, and he died of his madness."

Alouzon stepped forward. "That's enough, both of you. What the hell do you want, Helwych? Are you going home, or are you going to wait in Lachrae?"

He considered, but Alouzon sensed that he had already made up his mind and was only enjoying the attention directed at him. "I will stay here in Lachrae," he said at last. "Should you not return from Broceliande, I will then journey to Kingsbury and make my report."

Manda muttered softly: "And a self-congratulatory report it will be, too."

Helwych pretended not to hear.

"King Pellam," said Alouzon, "will you still let us travel in Vaylle?"

Pellam's wise eyes narrowed in as much of a smile as the circumstances would allow. The Fisher King, crippled and holy, his wounded body an emblem of the land he ruled: Alouzon wondered at her temerity. "And if I revoked my permissions," said Pellam, "would my word bind you?"

Alouzon was silent. She was not following the rules of the Grail legends. But she did not want to, could not afford to, and she hoped that Pellam understood that.

Pellam nodded at last. "So be it. Go your ways to Broceliande. Leave as quickly as you may." He turned to Dindrane and Baares. "Chief Priestess and King's Harper: if you are still willing, I ask that you accompany them as far as the mountains. But I ask also that you consummate a Great Rite tomorrow morning, that the Goddess and the God may look with favor upon our ventures."

Dindrane's lips were tight for a moment. "The temple, my king."

"Most of the stones still stand. And the Goddess will understand our straits, I am sure."

Oh, She understands all right, thought Alouzon. More than She really wants to. "We'll get some sleep and be out of your hair by tomorrow afternoon, then. Thanks."

Pellam nodded to her, rose, and left the room. Dindrane took Baares's hand. "You must forgive our lack of hospitality, Dragonmaster," she said without warmth. "We have more wounded to attend to." She would have departed without another word, but Kyria lifted her voice:

"I will help."

The priestess stood, head bent, mouth working. "We do not need your help," she whispered.

"I think that you do, child." Kyria's tone was kind, unruffled. "I will attend to my own folk, and then I shall be with you."

Was Kyria an illusion, or was she reality? Alouzon did not know. Dejected, she turned for the corridor that led to their rooms, hoping to find some temporary oblivion in sleep. The others, save for Helwych, followed. Manda looked close to tears with exhaustion and anger, and Birk leaned heavily on Santhe's arm. Karthin and Marrget clung to one another like children.

Kyria took Alouzon's arm. "Will you rest, friend?"

"I'm going to do what I can."

The sorceress's eyes were dark and deep. "I can help. Thoughts and cares can be banished . . . for a time."

"I'd like to see Helwych banished."

"Hmmm . . ." Kyria cast a glance over her shoulder. "He has turned strange indeed."

Alouzon had worked at Kyria's side for three days, but she still found this new personality unnerving. How did one address someone who was . . . so different? Even her eyes had changed. "You got any ideas?"

Kyria was thoughtful. "He has become closed to me. I can see no more in him than I can in a mirror."

"It's probably better that he stay behind."

"Maybe . . . But I am not sure that we can speak of *better* or *worse* anymore. We must do what we can." Kyria's eyes turned inquiring.

Alouzon read the question. "You want to know what the fuck I'm looking for in Broceliande, right?"

"If it would help, Alouzon."

Their steps had brought them to Alouzon's door. "You know," said Alouzon, sidestepping the question, "one of these days you're going to wake up as Helen again, and you're really going to cream me."

Kyria's eyebrows lifted. "But I *am* Helen."

Alouzon sighed. "Now I know I'm nuts."

"Helen Addams was—is—many things," said the sorceress. She kept her voice low so that the others, who were bidding each other a good sleep, would not hear. "As are you, Goddess."

Alouzon winced. "You figured it out."

"Aye. It is a terrible weight to bear. But you will, I think, bear it."

"You sound like Mernyl sometimes."

"Indeed?" Kyria smiled. "What an interesting man! I shall have to meet him someday." Her face turned serious. "For now, I wish you rest. I must go and comfort Birk."

Alouzon looked over Kyria's shoulder. Santhe was escorting his warrior into the room they shared. Birk had always appeared impassive. He killed when it was necessary, and kept silent whether it was necessary or not. But, with Parl's death, something had gone out of him. His eyes, empty to begin with, were now void. "He's pretty broken up, isn't he?"

The sorceress shrugged. "He and Parl were lovers, Dragonmaster. Scarred by the devastation of the last battles between Gryylth and Corrin, their hearts had grown together."

Birk shuffled into his room. Farther down the corridor, Manda and Wykla were just shutting their door. Karthin was almost carrying Marrget.

Alouzon wanted to scream. Here she was, facing it

once again. Kyria had healed Wykla—the girl had even been able to help with the rescue operations—but Parl had died instantly in the detonation of a grenade. Healers could not be everywhere, and luck could not last forever. "Am I just going to get everyone killed?"

Kyria, nurturing and gentle, patted her arm. "Death is always a possibility. It is something we must live with."

Alouzon was still thinking about Kyria's words the next morning. Death. She had spent her adult life fleeing from death, but she might as well have fled from the air, or from food, or from the physical nature of her existence. Death was a fact that could not be escaped, that could only be accepted. If there was an answer to death, it was a shrug of the shoulders, an affirmation of one's willingness to persevere in the face of mortality.

But mortality held within it—like the Grail cupping its nurturing waters—a complimentary upwelling of life that had pursued her throughout the years, rolling at her feet like a puppy begging to be picked up. Unwilling though she had been, she had picked it up again and again, choosing always to live, choosing always to go on in spite of the aborted idealism of the 60s, in spite of the shattered bodies of her classmates, in spite of the emotional wreckage that had been left her after abortion, battle, magic, and death had climaxed a decade of hopelessness.

Silbakor had said it. Fittingly, Silbakor had said it the day that she had first sighted Vaylle, when she did not even have a name for the land she had created. *You have both taken life and given it with honor.*

In the company of white-clad attendants, watched by much of what was left of the population of Lachrae, Dindrane and Baares led Alouzon and her company into the temple precincts. Ahead, the toppled stones of the sacred circle bore mute testimony to the efficiency of the B-52's, but they told Alouzon also that even here in what the Vayllens perceived as an inviolable shrine of life, there was—there *had* to be—death.

The path to the stones took them past a fountain that had been undisturbed by the bombs. The water still rose and fell with a sound like crystal, and Dindrane and Baares paused to wash their hands. Deliberately and with ceremony, they purified themselves and passed on, leading the others toward the entrance to the circle of stones.

Alouzon, though, remained at the fountain for a moment. She knelt and washed, her leather armor creaking, her steel wrist cuffs glinting as her brown hands scooped the water. Cupped in her hands, the liquid itself mirrored the unspeakably blue sky and the shining sun; and when she lifted her dripping face, she saw what Kyria had seen several days before: two stones that seemed dwarfed by the monoliths behind them, that bore the likenesses of Suzanne Helling and Solomon Braithwaite.

The Goddess and the God.

The sanctity of the temple was profound, diminished neither by the toppled stones nor by the sight of the ruined buildings of the city. Alouzon might have been looking through a veil of brightness that, falling through the air, wrapped its aura of holiness about temple and worshipers alike, lending an air of grace and goodness even to destruction. And as though her eyes conspired with her thoughts so as to impel her along a path that seemed now so unmistakably marked out before her, she noticed that the figure of Suzanne Helling carried a sword.

She bent her head. "Yeah . . . that's it. I'll be damned if I can understand it, but that's it."

An attendant had stayed with her. "My lady?"

The gilt threads of the girl's livery sparkled in the light, and the insignia of the king of Vaylle shone out of the pale cloth: silver cup, golden knife, red and black thorns. Ecstasy and pain, life and death. Both present. Both essential. Merely two extremes of existence.

"That's just the way it is," said Alouzon. "People are going to live and die whether we love them or not. But it's easier if we love them, isn't it?"

The attendant looked confused. Alouzon rose and followed after the company as though she were stepping once again on the thick grass of Blanket Hill, approaching the pagoda at the side of Taylor Hall to confront the lifted M-1s.

The sun had barely climbed out of morning and into afternoon when the company gathered their horses, checked their provisions, and set off down the West Road that pointed like a bomb-mangled finger straight at the distant, elfin pinnacles of the Cordillera.

Just at the edge of the city were the manors that had been destroyed three nights before. The ruins had stopped smoking, and the dead had been buried, but the charred and cratered remains blackened the landscape like a blight, and the pools of phosphor from the hounds still reeked like so much ammonia and lye.

Dindrane and Baares, who led the way, stopped for a moment, looked, then nudged their horses and continued on. Alouzon waved the company by and stayed a while longer, her lean face growing leaner. Alone save for Kyria, she confronted the uncompromising waste of life.

"It became necessary to destroy the village in order to save it," she said softly. And then she tugged at Jia's reins and went on.

Floating as she was between one world and another—between, in fact, one life and another—Kyria felt strange. Alouzon was quoting the words of a military officer of the Vietnam War. Kyria knew about the war, but the mind and personality in which she now lived grappled with the knowledge only at arm's length. Vietnam was . . . somewhere else. She knew Gryylth, and Vaylle, and magic. And yet a part of her knew Los Angeles, and the lesbian bars on the outskirts of the San Fernando Valley, and the intimacies of Solomon Braithwaite's bed.

Softly, she shook her head and felt her long hair
rustle across the back of her robe. In creating Vaylle,
Alouzon had obviously incorporated a great deal of the
despair and violence that had pocked the late 1960s.
That was both understandable and forgivable. Alouzon
could not control all the intricacies of her own mind.
For that matter, neither could Kyria herself.

When I get back . . .

Yes, Helen was still there: lurking in the corners of
her unconscious, waiting for a chance to return. The
knowledge made Kyria uncomfortable, but she was a
sorceress, and would have to become accustomed to
knowing uncomfortable things.

Beside her, Alouzon rode with shoulders hunched
as though supporting the weight of guilt that Dindrane
had heaped upon her. And, not content with the priestess's accusations, she had added to it herself. Alouzon
was convinced that Vaylle was both her responsibility
and her fault. Totally. Completely.

But the vision of Solomon in his grave, and the direct attack on a house in Bel Air: Alouzon, Kyria
knew, could have had nothing to do with such occurrences. Some other component was obviously in action there, and though for Alouzon there was no
question about ultimate blame or responsibility, Kyria
was beginning to question, and she was doing so as
deeply and as earnestly as had the Dragonmaster when,
alone in a strange world, she had fought with the secret of Gryylth's existence.

When I get back . . .

The half-alien thought traced a thin line of blood
across her mind. Shrugging the pain aside, Kyria patted Grayflank to distract herself. "Good friend," she
said, "I hope that I have not been cruel to you in the
past."

The horse plodded on. Alouzon came out of her
study. "Actually, you've been pretty good to her," she
said.

"It is well." Kyria smiled at Alouzon, the sky, the
flowers. There was terror and hard work ahead, but it

was a beautiful world. The price was, perhaps, appropriate. "Did you sleep?"

Alouzon shrugged. "A little. I have bad dreams sometimes."

"About . . . Vietnam?"

The Dragonmaster looked uneasy, almost distrustful. "Uh . . . yeah. And other things."

Kyria pursed her lips. She had, in the past, alienated Alouzon and the rest of the company again and again. Only dear Santhe had taken pity on the vicious little bitch and had, now and then, brought her a plate of scraps.

"Other things," she said softly. "Like Solomon Braithwaite, for instance?"

Alouzon's eyes narrowed. "Are you still on that?"

"I do not understand."

"You used to go on about how you were going to find him and kill him once and for all."

"Ah . . . yes, I believe I did." She sighed. *Helen, did you have to be quite so nasty about everything?*

But she sensed that Helen was crying in the darkness, and she instantly regretted the harshness of her words. If she wanted to help others, she had to be willing also to help herself.

Alouzon was talking. "Well, you know about Vaylle now. It's my baby. How come you're still on Sol's case about it?"

"Because . . ." Alouzon had likened her to Mernyl. But Mernyl had been sure of his knowledge. ". . . because I sense . . . something . . ."

Alouzon looked tired. "Kyria, if I really thought that there was a way out of this, I'd take it. But there isn't. Don't try to give me hope. I made Vaylle, and I'm destroying it. For that matter, I shoved you into the brain you've got now."

Kyria shook her head. "That you did not. Helen was fighting herself, and she had cut herself off from her sources of strength. She had lost from the beginning."

Alouzon did not look convinced, but she rode on in silence for a time. The horses' hooves made clop-clop

sounds on the stone pavement, and Dindrane and
Baares had reached out and clasped hands as they rode.
Dindrane's head was bowed as though she worried
about the harm that might befall Lachrae in her absence. The harper kept his eyes on the mountains, as
though defying the powers that threatened his land.

"Answer me this, Alouzon," said Kyria. "How do
I fit in?"

The Dragonmaster shrugged. "You got me."

The sorceress fixed her with a look. "Come on . . .
honey." She snorted at the odd feeling of the word on
her tongue. "I do not believe that anything happens
here without a reason. If Silbakor had wanted a wizard, it could have provided you with someone more . . .
ah . . . tractable than Helen. But I . . ."

"You were there. You were available. We were attacked."

Kyria nodded. "Just so. *We* were attacked. Do remember: I was married to Solomon for twenty years."

Alouzon sighed. "How could I forget?"

"Hear me, please. What do you personally have to
do with me? Very little, as I had divorced Solomon
some ten years before you first met him. And yet I
have been brought into this strange place, and given
power, and . . ." She laughed in spite of her gravity.
". . . and a double-barreled personality. Why?"

"I don't know."

"You do not, but perhaps Solomon knows."

Alouzon stared fixedly at the mountains. "This is
nuts. He's dead."

"As you reminded me in Los Angeles," said Kyria
quietly, "we both saw him standing up in his grave."

"But . . ."

"Think about it, I beg you."

"Then what the fuck is in Broceliande?"

Kyria shook her head and smiled slightly. "My
question exactly, Alouzon."

❖ CHAPTER 18 ❖

The afternoon sun danced across the bare pasture-land and silver lakes of Vaylle, and it shone on the green slopes and jagged peaks of the Cordillera, but Dindrane saw nothing of it as she led Alouzon's party down the road. Instead, her sight was turned inward, examining her memories.

Lachrae burning. The frightened, pained eyes of a child who had lost most of his skin. The red, glistening remains of the man and woman who, a few days before, had greeted the morning with a song. The look on Baares's face when he had stood up from a healing, his spirit warring against itself, wanting nothing so much as to kill, to rend the attackers as they had rent his city and his people.

The Gryylthans had brought nothing to Vaylle save death. Alouzon and Marrget could argue that there was already death in the land, but their reasoning was specious. Where before individual houses and steadings were attacked and destroyed, now whole towns and large portions of cities were leveled. Where before the week's dead could be told on the fingers of both hands, now they numbered in the hundreds.

But though she had condemned the Gryylthans, Dindrane wondered privately—the thoughts forcing themselves on her, prying through her defenses—whether it was her own argument that was, in the end, specious. What did it matter whether Vaylle sickened and died house by house or city by city? The dead were dead whether they

257

journeyed to the Far Lands singly or in droves, and peace
lay as bloody and slaughtered by the destruction of one
steading as by many.

At least Alouzon and her companions had tried to
do something about it all. Their methods seemed bar-
barous, their attitudes insane, their affections per-
verse, but still . . .

She gripped her healer's staff. How many would die?
And would they die singly, or in company? She had
no control over the deaths, and now, with Alouzon's
company journeying through the land with King Pellam's permission, she did not even have the power to
decree manner, number, or place and time.

But she realized that, despite her efforts, despite her
ministry, despite the workings of all the healers of
Vaylle, she had never really had that power at all. The
thought reared up and grinned at her: Vaylle was nothing more than a victim.

"My flower?"

She lifted her head. It had been days since Baares
had used that endearment, and it was like a splash of
cool water. She met his smile with her own. "I am
. . . well, husband."

His eyebrows went up. "Oh . . . I see that harpers
are not the only ones who possess glib tongues."

She colored. "What would you have me say?"

"The truth."

She wondered whether he spoke as mortal man or
active spirit, but in neither case could she refuse the
admonition. Softly, so that those behind her could not
hear, she told him of her thoughts.

Baares nodded. "Very different the Gryylthans are.
And yet very like."

"I could ask you to speak the truth, also."

He hung his head for a moment. "I confess, my
priestess: I have harbored thoughts of violence. I can
no longer call them evil, though."

"Nor . . ." She struggled with the words. "Nor, I
am afraid, can I."

He stared, shocked at her admission.

" 'Tis confused I am," she said. "Alouzon was right: they *tried*." She glanced back at the company and noticed with a pang that the Dragonmaster was riding by herself, head down, dejected. "They endangered themselves to save us. Actions . . . worthy of the God. And not the first they are."

"They shame us."

"Husband?"

"Our thoughts of bloodshed stem from anger. Theirs come from righteousness . . . and loyalty. I might even say love." He fell to musing, plucking at the strings of his harp. Dindrane listened nervously for a time, but no: all his strains were consonant.

"We act from loyalty to our Goddess," she said softly.

"I think that we do that thing," said Baares. "But does She expect us to sit and wait for death? The God dies: He sacrifices Himself in the waning of the year and the harvesting of the crops. But He does not wait passively or idly. He struggles against the onset of winter, and the reapers must cut Him with the sharpest of blades in order to fell Him. He dies fighting. And yet He loves."

Dindrane looked at her staff. To turn the energies of healing into a weapon . . . "The Goddess carries a sword," she said softly. "I wonder sometimes whether She does her own reaping, if therefore—"

She fell silent quickly, and a wave of sickness swept over her. She was a healer. She could be nothing else. Leaving Baares to pluck at his harp, she trotted her horse away from the road and huddled in the saddle as she kept abreast of the company. The afternoon sunlight seemed cold, and visions of the dead lay across the land like a film of oil upon a lake.

As they had during the journey from Daelin to Lachrae, Dindrane and Baares stayed away from towns and villages. Alouzon and the others did not question the action. The Dragonmaster even went so far as to order travel for a short time beyond sunset so as to put extra distance between their camp and the last village they had passed.

"I don't want anyone to get hurt," she said in her dark, quiet voice. Dindrane looked puzzled, approving, and reluctantly admiring at the same time.

Dindrane did not understand. Kyria did, though, and she understood also the strain under which Alouzon labored. Staying close by the Dragonmaster's side, she attempted to demonstrate her trustworthiness. Yet, at the same time, Kyria knew that the support she offered was a tenuous thing, for Helen was always waiting for a chance to return.

After the evening meal, Kyria called the warriors to her and spent a few minutes enchanting their swords so as to make them more effective against the hounds. She could not make the blades so potent that they would slay the beasts on the spot, but when she was through they would cut without spraying corrosive phosphor all over the wielder. With the blades so altered, and with her own sorcery to mete out larger powers as they were needed, the expedition had a relatively decent chance of making it to Broceliande and back without great loss.

But even a small loss was a grievous one. Birk—impassive, stoic Birk—whimpered in his sleep that night, and Santhe watched over him like a worried father. Dindrane and Baares seemed not to comprehend at first, but when Alouzon whispered an explanation, they looked understanding, though properly horrified.

The Vayllen mind-set left them, in their own way, as intolerant and ignorant as rigid and uncompromising feminism had left Helen Addams. Kyria recalled her own thoughtless condemnation of Marrget and Wykla. She had wished a hundred times that she could take back her words, but knew that that was impossible. Nor did she have any guarantee that she—as Helen—would not utter them again.

Angry. Spiteful. But she could do something now, and perhaps that was the important thing. Leaving her blankets, she made her way through the dark camp to Santhe. Beside the councilor, Birk struggled with his dreams of loss and loneliness.

"He is not well, then?" she said.

"Not well at all," he said. "The slaughter in the last days of the war was great. All my wartroop was scarred, but these two . . ." He gestured as if Parl still lay at Birk's side. ". . . saw worse than most. But they persevered, and they helped one another." He shot her a glance. "Like the women of the First Wartroop."

Wykla was keeping watch with Manda, and though they stood at opposite ends of the camp, their hearts were as close as if they had been shoulder to shoulder. Marrget was bedded down with Karthin just outside the reach of the firelight, and her soft gasp told Kyria that they were making love.

Man-souled or woman-souled, they were stronger than Kyria herself could ever hope to be. "Even a sorceress can be a fool," she said; and, extending a hand, she let it hover for a moment above Birk's forehead. Birk sighed, turned over, and slept soundly.

"My thanks," said Santhe.

"My pleasure," said Kyria. She started to rise, but thought better of it. "I must thank you also," she said, settling beside him. "You were very kind to me, in spite of my . . ." She bit her lip. A fine sorceress she was, tongue-tied before a handsome man! ". . . my difficulties."

"Lady, I could not do otherwise."

Kyria questioned him with a look.

Santhe shrugged. "After many sorrows, everything ceases to matter. Laughter becomes a kind of a mask, like those worn by children on the eve of Summer's End, and courtesy becomes empty. I saw the Tree slaughter my men and my friends. I saw Marrget stand up and contemplate the terror of a new body. I saw more valor and more horror than I ever wished to see in any number of lives. And I decided then that all was meaningless, that my duty in life was to help as best I could those who were left to me."

Kyria's lip trembled. She bit it again to still it. "You have done well, councilor."

He sighed. "I do what I can, lady." He looked down

at Birk. "I do not think that Birk will be with us much longer," he said softly. "His love draws him to Parl."

"I could heal him."

"Nay, he would not have you do that." Santhe shook his head. "Is there so much love in the world that we can afford to erase even a little of it?"

Kyria was thoughtful. She met Santhe's eyes and, with as much composure as she could muster, she kissed him. "You are wise, sir," she said. "Gryylth has a good councilor."

"And a good sorceress." He smiled.

She heard the emptiness in him and found that she wanted to fill it. But she still had Helen to contend with. "Do not say so," she said, wishing that she did not have to utter the words. "I am as changeable as the moon. I create now, but I could destroy tomorrow."

"True," he admitted, "but . . ."

"But you will bring me scraps nonetheless?" She smiled. Sad. Wistful.

"All the scraps you desire, my dear rabid dog." He smiled again.

She stood up. "I . . ." Much lay behind her: twenty years of marriage to an abusive man, aborted children staring sightlessly at the ceiling of a dank warehouse, the carefully honed vituperation that was the product of a long-festering hate . . .

And yet, in the respite she had been granted, she had, in effect, thrust her head above the stinking water in which she had been wallowing and gulped a lungful of clear air, stared at the blue sky and the yellow sun, breathed a prayer of thanks that such air and such sky and such suns existed in the universe.

There was power, yes, but power did not simply mean the power to wound or to kill. There was power to comfort, to nourish, to strike when necessary and soothe at other times. There was power to choose.

Learn that, Helen. Learn that much and the rest will come.

"I thank you again," she said to Santhe. "Knowing my limitations, will you call me friend?"

He reached up and took her hand. "I will indeed. The Gods bless you, friend Kyria."

"And you, Santhe." She bent, held his hand against her cheek for a moment, then straightened. "Good night. Fear not for Birk: he will sleep soundly."

"I do not fear for him. I . . ." A deeper emptiness entered his eyes. "I fear for you."

She held his hand a moment more. "And I also, friend."

They were under way again at dawn. Alouzon had not slept. The world—*her* world, she reminded herself—looked white and raw to her: the trees too tall for a sky that seemed to weigh down on her head, the grass too frail to force its way up through the cold ground.

Even after a night of wearing her mind bloody with thoughts of Kyria's words about Solomon, she was still not certain how to interpret them. Solomon was dead, and though her feelings about him were mixed, still he was gone. He should, by nature, have no more say in the affairs of Vaylle than Brian O'Hara, the archaeological martinet of UCLA.

The day passed. Vaylle unfurled like a flag, undulating in soft, feminine folds. If Gryylth was a landscape by Turner, then Vaylle was an illustration from a child's picture book. Colors were blue and white and pastels. Rivers wound across the patchwork fields as though drawn with a silver pen.

But the land was pocked with the hulks of burned-out houses and the shredded corpses of cattle that bore the unmistakable marks of the hounds. And what graciousness was left ended at the Cordillera. Rough, uncompromising, forbidding, the mountains lost their elfin quality as, with the party's approach, they rose farther and farther into the sky, their green-clad lower slopes hinting darkly at what they concealed.

Sleepless and shaking, Alouzon looked up at the peaks that raked the sky like granite claws. Guardian or not, God or not, how was she supposed to cross *that*? Or deal with something totally unknown on the other side?

Unconsciously she reached out, groping. Kyria took her hand. "I'm going to need you, Kyria."

"I will be here."

"You sure?"

Kyria understood, and sighed. "As much as I can."

Something flickered between the summits of the Cordillera, and Alouzon instinctively flinched. But no: it was just a cloud.

Cloud? Dark and black and spreading across the range of mountains like an invading army cresting a parapet, it grew swiftly. Soon the peaks were lost in a blackness that reminded Alouzon unpleasantly of what had once gathered about the Tree and, more recently, the ruins of the Circle.

"Dindrane. Baares."

They had already reined in. Alouzon and Kyria came up to flank them. "I see," said Dindrane.

"Have you seen anything like that before?"

"Ah . . ." Dindrane and Baares exchanged looks. "Once."

Alouzon frowned. "About two weeks ago?"

"Indeed."

Something told Alouzon that Dindrane was not saying everything. "Did you see the Dragon and the Worm?" she demanded.

"We . . ." Reluctantly, Dindrane nodded. "We did."

"They headed over the mountains, then."

"Surely."

The wind swept down from the west with an odor as of stagnant pools. Alouzon looked past the shame-faced Vayllens and caught Kyria's eye. The sorceress weighed her staff as though it were a revolver. "I will . . ." She sucked in a breath and squared her shoulders. "I will do whatever I can."

They pressed on, but within a few minutes the wind was boiling dust and chaff into seething clouds of debris. Alouzon looked for shelter, but the land, gently rolling where it was not flat, offered none. "What do you people do in a windstorm?"

"We do not have windstorms," said Baares.

The clouds scudded across the sky, bringing a premature dusk. "Is there a village?" Alouzon persisted. "A stone wall?" Plainly worried about the effect of barbaric foreigners upon their people, Dindrane and Baares hesitated. "Is there a fucking ditch in this godforsaken land?"

Stung by the Dragonmaster's blasphemy, Dindrane thrust her doubts aside. "There is a village. Mullaen. It lies on the shore of Lake Innael."

"Will it hold up in this?"

Dindrane's eyes flashed. "It is built of stone, like all villages in Vaylle. We do not live in huts. And if the Goddess and God declare that it shall not stand, why then my husband and I shall die among our own people."

With that, the priestess swatted her horse and galloped off down the road, Baares at her side. As though summoned, the party's mounts followed.

The clouds surged eastward. The light went from the sky, but the horses sped on; and Alouzon wondered by what powers Dindrane led the animals down the now invisible road, through a landscape enveloped in darkness, across bridges and fords that could only be felt. Regardless of her opinions, Dindrane was a holy woman—a priestess and a healer both—and she apparently had her methods.

Kyria had her own as well. Over the thunder that now cracked across the sky, Alouzon heard the sorceress utter a word of command, and light from her staff suddenly split the darkness.

Lapped about by absolute night, torn at by the shrieking wind, buffeted by the thunder that broke from the clouds, the company raced through a landscape of colorless grass and spectral trees that flickered briefly through Kyria's pool of light.

Just outside the illumination, though, something else flickered. A yellow glow was keeping pace with the company. Alouzon shivered. *Of all the damned luck . . .*

Dindrane led the way still, Baares at her side. Girlish she might have been, and with a deep femininity
that was the product of religion and culture both, but
she did not blench at galloping through a storm that
seemed compounded of equal parts wind, cloud, and
nightmare. As though to demonstrate that Vayllens
possessed their own pride and courage, she forged
ahead, staff lifted, hair streaming.

More flickers. Now to the left.

"Alouzon!" came Marrget's shout. "Hounds!"

"To both flanks," cried Karthin. "And behind.
Santhe! Birk!"

The councilor and his man had already turned to
meet the needle teeth and glowing jaws that were
snapping at their horses. Their freshly enchanted
blades bit deep, and there was no spurt of phosphor,
but more hounds were coming.

Dindrane, riding pell-mell down the road, was unable to stop when one rose up directly before her. Her
horse did not even have time to rear before it smacked
directly into the glowing beast and sent the priestess
sprawling onto the stone pavement. She rolled over
twice and lay still. The hounds closed on her.

Alouzon swerved toward her. "Make a stand!" she
shouted. "Kyria!"

The sorceress reined in, dismounted in a flutter of sable
and silver, and grounded her staff. A sudden starburst drove
the hounds back for a moment, but the concussion made Jia
stumble. Alouzon swung to the ground at what was almost
a full gallop and fought for her footing as Baares, still
mounted, made for his wife. Again, Kyria supplemented
her radiance with a burst of light, but the hounds were too
close for anything more lethal. Nonetheless, their hesitation
allowed the harper to leap down beside Dindrane's still form
and seize her staff.

His face was crimson, and he came up with the staff
just as a hound leaped for him. A dull crunch, and the
beast rolled to the side, twitching.

Baares stared at the staff, at the dead hound . . .

Alouzon ran to help. *Man, that's going to cost you.*

Santhe and Birk had been joined by Wykla and Manda, and the four were covering the party's flanks. Marrget and Karthin were at the rear, and their blades rang together as they severed the head of an attacking hound with simultaneous strokes.

Perhaps a dozen or more of the beasts were milling at the sides of the road, rushing in singly or in small packs. Hacking her way toward Baares, Alouzon called encouragement to Kyria, who was looking increasingly frustrated. Hampered though the sorceress was, her illumination was a priceless gift, for without it the hounds would have had a clear and lethal advantage.

Baares was on his knees beside Dindrane. Another hound lunged for them, but it wound up spitted on the Dragonsword. Alouzon threw the carcass aside with a heave of her shoulders. "Is she alive?"

"Oh, Goddess . . ."

"Come out of it," she snapped. "Are we fighting for a corpse?"

He looked up, his eyes hot. "She lives."

A hound broke through Santhe's defense and made for Kyria, and darkness flooded the road as the sorceress turned her potencies on it. Violet erupted out of the pitch, and when the light returned, a pool of phosphor smoked at her feet.

But the other hounds had used the moment to their advantage. As though sensing Dindrane's wound, they began to congregate around Alouzon and Baares, swamping the Dragonmaster's defense.

"Grab that staff, Baares," Alouzon snapped.

The harper blinked at her, his face now as pale as that of the woman he held in his arms.

"You goddam peacenik freak, grab that staff!"

A shrill whistle sounded as Wykla summoned her horse. In a moment, she was astride. The animal leapt over the clusters of hounds, and, with a bound, cleared the ring of beasts about Alouzon and found its footing beside Baares.

The dogs attacked, and the horse reared and shattered the skull of one while Wykla's quick blade settled another. But while the enchanted sword stanched

the flow of corrosive phosphor as it cut, the hooves of
Wykla's mount were not so protected. The animal's
face was suddenly covered with corrosives. With a
sharp whinny of pain, it fell.

Wykla landed amid the hounds and rolled to her feet as
they turned on her. One reached for her arm, but she killed
it with a thrust between the eyes. Another closed on her
from behind. She spun and nearly decapitated it.

Santhe battled his way toward her. His humor transformed now into ruthlessness, he kicked hounds aside
as though they were puppies, and the muscles of his
shoulders knotted as he swung his sword back and
forth, straight into needle teeth and glowing eyes.
Phosphor flowed, and the road turned slippery with
unnatural viscera.

Motivated at last, Baares seized Dindrane's staff and
tried to repeat his previous success. But whereas before his instincts and rage had guided his body, now
his uncertainty had gained a foothold. Dithering over
a place to strike, he was knocked down by a rushing
hound. For a moment the beast straddled him, staring
down into his eyes, and Alouzon was afraid that she
was going to see the harper's throat ripped out. But
the hound grinned and sprang instead for Dindrane,
who lay unconscious and unguarded.

Alouzon reversed course. Wykla, though, side-
stepped a lunge from one hound, launched herself over
the back of another, and smashed her full weight into
the ribs of the beast that was dipping its massive jaws
toward the unconscious priestess.

The hound toppled sideways, snapping, and its teeth
found Wykla's sword arm and bared the bone from
elbow to shoulder. Dropping to her knees from the
pain, Wykla stared at the wound, horrified, but she
mastered her fear in a moment and calmly shifted her
sword to her left hand as she rose to defend Dindrane.

Wheeling, the hound darted a bite at Wykla and
managed to get past her blade. Wykla instinctively
brought up her knee, slamming the glowing jaws shut

as the hound's momentum carried it into her full-force
and put her on the ground again.

Manda and Santhe had broken through, though they
too were bleeding from bites that smoked and burned
into their flesh. The Corrinian maid severed the spine
of Wykla's assailant with a single blow.

Kyria was calling, her voice faint in the shrieking
wind but loud in the minds of the party. *Drive the
hounds to one side.*

With Dindrane and Wykla both unconscious and
wounded, driving the hounds anywhere was an impos-
sibility. But the pack had thinned to one side, and Alouzon pointed at the fallen women and swept her arm
out toward the gap. Baares nodded and picked up his
wife, and Manda gathered Wykla into her arms. As
Alouzon and Santhe opened a gap in the hounds'
ranks, Baares and Manda carried their lovers through.
In a moment, the beasts milled in an isolated cluster.
Kyria had her opportunity.

The sorceress's frustration found expression in an erup-
tion of magic that knocked Alouzon flat and filled her vision
with a coruscation of violet in all its permutations. The
living light reached out to the hounds, enveloped and incinerated them. The stench of charred flesh and phosphor rose
in a nauseating cloud, but the attack was over.

The wind swept the odor out into the darkness.
Thunder sounded across the land from the upper
reaches of the Cordillera. Staggering to her feet, Alouzon thought she saw lights moving among the distant peaks, but her immediate thoughts dragged her to
Wykla. The girl lay in Manda's lap, soaking them both
in a growing pool of blood.

Kyria's staff punched a hole through the cloud layer
with a sharp crack. The afternoon sun spilled down,
pale and watery, as she ran to help, and Manda looked
up at her approach. "She is too brave, sometimes,"
she said hoarsely. "She would not be thought weak."

"Here, child," said Kyria, though her hands were shaking with strain. "Give her to me." Manda hesitated.

"Please, child. Quickly. Neither of us may have much time."

Reluctantly, Manda relinquished her wounded lover. Kyria sat down in the fading light, cradled Wykla in her arms, bent her head. "Oh, Gods," she murmured. "I am weary of this. Helen, stay your hand, I pray you."

She lifted her staff, and the glow that ran its length told of healing and strength. Manda watched anxiously, but Alouzon had turned to Dindrane and Baares. "Harper? How is she?"

"Unconscious," he said. "I do not know the depth of her wounds."

"Kyria will take care of her when she's done with Wykla. But—" She broke off and stared. "Marrget? Karthin? Birk?"

Tripping over severed limbs that still oozed a slime of phosphor, she stumbled back along the road. At the names, Santhe too had roused himself, and he followed after, his eyes mirroring fear.

The wind was dying, but the clouds were forcing their way back into the hole that Kyria had created. The shadows had closed in once again. "Here, friends." Marrget's voice came to them from the obscurity. Her face, even close up, was no more than a faint blur, but she reached a hand to them, and her grip was strong. Karthin was invisible, but his basso told of his presence.

"Birk." Santhe said the name as though he knew, and he sagged and put his bleeding hands to his face.

"He is with Parl, Santhe." Marrget said no more. Her sword still in her hand, she held the councilor as he sobbed. "Fear not, the Gods will hear his name, and he is at peace."

Santhe choked. "Did he die well, then?"

"Aye," said Marrget. "The dogs had surrounded me. He saved my life."

Santhe shook his head slowly. "He saved both your lives."

"But Karthin—" Marrget understood and caught herself. Santhe was not referring to Karthin. She was silent for a minute. Finally: "If the child is a boy," she said, her voice a whisper, "I shall name him Birk."

More rumblings from the mountains. Lightning flickered from peak to peak. The lights Alouzon had seen were still moving, and they were drawing closer. Quickly.

Silbakor. The White Worm.

The Great Dragon was fleeing the opalescent talons of its foe, pausing in its flight only to turn its own claws on the pallid face behind it. Neither showed any visible wounds, nor did they seem wearied by a battle that had lasted for ten days and nights.

Alouzon leaned on her sword. Physical law did not show injury or fatigue either, no matter how much it was tattered by the workings of magic or despair. There was little difference.

The Dragon's voice thrummed in her head. *Flee, Dragonmaster.*

Flee? Flee where? "Dammit," said Alouzon, "I'm trying to fix this."

The Dragon streaked across the sky, looping back toward the mountains. The White Worm caught sight of the humans on the ground and started to dive, but Silbakor flung itself at the eyes of void and darkness. The Worm screamed and mounted upward.

You cannot fix it. Flee. Return to Gryylth.

"What about the Grail?"

Forget the Grail. Preserve your life. You are Gryylth—and Vaylle also. Your death is the death of all.

Alouzon was shouting. "Forget the Grail? Forget you, you son of a bitch. Whose side are you on, anyway?"

But Silbakor was already turning back toward the blackness that enveloped the Cordillera. The White Worm followed with pale wings and glowing talons.

❖ CHAPTER 19 ❖

They took what horses had been left alive by the hounds and, bearing their wounded and dead, rode for Mullaen under a sky streaked with black tendrils and patched with whorls of darkness. The sun was setting over the mountains in a crimson tide when they spied the town ahead, and by nightfall the horses' hooves were striking sparks on the cobbles of the town square as Baares shouted urgently for help.

Ceinen and Enite, the magistrate and priestess, could not but be startled by the mounted warriors who swept into town in the wake of a preternatural storm; but when they saw the wounds inflicted by the hounds, the unconscious forms of Dindrane and Wykla, and Birk's torn body, they did not concern themselves with questions of barbarity or nocturnal danger. Shouting for the townsfolk to come and help, they set about caring for their guests by the light of hastily kindled torches.

Kyria alone showed no wounds, but she was nonetheless in a bad way. Faced with both inner and outer battles, she had overextended herself even before she had turned her energies to healing. Slumped in the saddle, she watched as the priestess and warrior were carried into the magistrate's house by Baares and several men of the village, and when she slid from Grayflank's back, she staggered and nearly fell.

Santhe dismounted and turned to help her, but she

shoved him away with a snarl. "Get your goddam hands off me, man."

He dropped his arms, unruffled. He had seen this before. "Lady," he said gently, in spite of the wounds that, smoking and bleeding, covered his arms and legs, "I think you need rest."

Kyria shuddered. "I know I do, Santhe," she said, her voice softening. "Forgive me."

"Always." He smiled, took her willing hand, and caught her as her legs suddenly gave way beneath her. "Is there a bed for the lady Kyria?" he said to the Vayllens who had gathered. An elderly couple exchanged nervous glances, then nodded to him. He took her away to their house.

Enite had returned from ministering to Dindrane and Wykla, and she now set to work on the other members of the party. Wielding her healer's staff and her magic with the gruff efficiency of a peasant, she beckoned them to her one by one, closing and stanching their wounds. Under her hands, much of the phosphor melted into clear fluid, and at Alouzon's suggestion, the remainder was neutralized with vinegar.

"Where did you learn of this, Dragonmaster?" asked Ceinen as the dilute acid slowly turned the corrosives into water and assorted salts.

Alouzon shrugged, too worried about the others to care about her answer. Wykla, though healed, was still a mess: it had been necessary to cut the smoking armor from her body. Manda was frantic. Baares was useless for anything. And Marrget, pondering Santhe's words about Birk's motivations, had grown increasingly silent, her eyes those of a wild thing that had suddenly found itself caged.

"High school chemistry," she said simply.

Ceinen blinked and shook his head. "You are wise, Dragonmaster."

She wanted to cry. "If I'm so smart, how come I'm so fucked up?"

Ceinen, as solid and bluff as his wife, ignored the despair in her voice, though his face said that he un-

derstood it well. He rinsed the vinegar from her legs
with fresh water. "Is it sleep you and yours will be
wanting now?"

Though night had fallen like an anthracite wall, Alouzon still felt the presence of the Cordillera . . . and
whatever lay beyond. Sleep, she decided, was a good
idea. It was probably better to die well-rested. "Yeah.
You got a pile of straw somewhere?"

Enite finished working on Santhe. Even though the
night was cold, her brow was damp when she stood
up. "Straw, she says? And is it barbarians you think
we are that we would send you to sleep among the
cattle?"

"Enite, my love," said Ceinen quickly, " 'tis in
jest I am sure she spoke."

"Oh, indeed." Enite was tired, and her temper was
short. She, like her townspeople, appeared to face each
new problem with a fortitude that was, day by day,
growing increasingly brittle.

Santhe smiled thinly, rose, and bowed to her. Since
he had been told of Birk's death, he had cloaked his
emotions in formality. "If we have given offense,
priestess," he said politely, "pray, accept our apologies. It was a hard afternoon, and a worse ride."

Enite eyed him up and down. "A fair face and a
tongue to match," she said. A smile spread over her
matronly face. "We will have beds for you, child, in
spite of your armor and blades."

"I would see to the man I lost," he replied. "He died
well. I will not sleep until I have attended to him."

Enite looked puzzled. " 'Tis the first I have heard
of a good death," she said simply.

"He died saving me and my unborn child," said
Marrget. Her voice was as brittle as a dry twig.
"Surely that means something even to the people of
Vaylle."

Confounded, the priestess shook her head. "Certain
I am that my sister from Lachrae will explain this to
me." The import of Marrget's words suddenly struck

her, and she peered at the captain. "Honor to you, mother."

"Do not call me that, priestess." Marrget turned away suddenly and strode for the door.

If Enite felt horror at the combination of pregnancy and weapons, she concealed it well. "What would you have me call you, then?"

Marrget stood at the door, alone, for Karthin had gone to see to the horses with Manda. "I would . . ." Stripped of her armor, clad only in a linen tunic, she seemed frail and vulnerable, a child bearing a child.

Marrget. Marrha. Mother. Captain. Alouzon saw her weighing the titles as though she had been given a choice of axes for her beheading.

Steps crunched on the straw and cobblestones outside the house. Karthin entered with Manda. "Marrha?" he said when he noticed her expression.

"I . . ." She turned to Manda. "What would you call me, lady?" she whispered. "What name or title would you give me? Marrha? Marrget? Friend? Enemy?"

Manda was tired and in pain—Enite's healings were not as complete as Kyria's—but her sudden pallor did not stem from any physical cause. "I . . . I do not know what to call you."

Karthin touched Manda's shoulder. "Countrywoman—"

She whirled on him. "You do not understand," she said through clenched teeth, and she turned and pushed out through the open door.

Marrget was nodding slowly. "I do," she said. She turned to Enite. "Call me what you wish, priestess. Forgive my discourtesy." Leaning heavily against Karthin, she closed her eyes. "I am weary, O my husband," she said. "Put me to bed."

Dindrane's spirit moved between the Worlds.

The landscape through which she traveled was the image of the spirit of Vaylle, the ghostly projection of material substance upon the half-substantial, half-dreamed swirlings of the spaces between existences.

Rolling plains stretched off into the distance in undulations of blue and gray and lavender. The sky was black, the stars crystal. The Cordillera was a study in angular blocks of jet. And there was something beyond . . .

For as long as she could remember, the realms beyond the Cordillera had been closed to matter and spirit both. Those who had dared the passes that lay above the town of Kent had never returned, and the rash healer who attempted to enter Broceliande in spirit could be sure that she would not awaken with her sanity intact.

Yet tonight the spiritual avenues looked open, and Dindrane had been stung enough by the Gryylthans' valor that she decided to make her own attempt. Surely there were ways to solve the mystery of Broceliande that did not involve bloodshed.

A moment, a flicker of her will, and she had crossed the mountains. She found herself in a region of plains and roads, of poisonously dense jungle and jagged towers, of shadowy movement that writhed at the edges of sight, and of cold stasis. Behind all was a brooding menace compounded seemingly of hate and sorrow both.

She quailed for an instant, but a memory of the Gryylthans rallying about her, defending her as though she were one of their own, steeled her, and, determined, she set foot on a dusty road. As she walked, the landscape changed, blurred, and resolved into green grass and glass buildings. Men who looked like the Grayfaces marched there, the sun glinting on their weapons.

The scene blurred again. Burning villages of thatched huts. Women fleeing, their garments—disturbingly similar to the Vayllen tunic and loose skirts—in flames.

And again. Decayed bodies in a ditch, the odor of rot sweet and ripe with tropical heat.

Dindrane turned away and ran, clutching at her staff, casting about frantically for something that would blunt the stench and decay and death that had suddenly surrounded her with the trappings of madness.

That last day in Lachrae, she had performed the Great Rite with Baares, offering the sacred chalice as he lowered the point of the knife into its gleaming bowl. She was priestess, and she was the land, and now she gathered that image to herself, wrapping it about her as though it were the skirts of the Goddess, willing it to become real, to bring something of wholeness and health to this hellish place.

Knife and Cup. God and Goddess. Man and Woman. Joined. Whole.

But she wondered suddenly: did not that emblem of wholeness and perfection apply to each and all, whether male or female? If Manda and Wykla approached the Goddess and the God, would they be denied their smile and blessing? But who would hold the cup? Who the knife?

Reeling from her thoughts, she saw a wide lawn and a tall white tower that glittered in the sunlight.

Dazzled, she blinked her eyes and felt the utter stillness and peace of this place. Here, in a land of death, was something as holy as the temple of Lachrae, as filled with Presence as the cup and knife, something that, in its own way, modeled the universe, perhaps even contained it.

Afraid, yet emboldened by her fear, she approached the gleaming tower. The marble was flawless, clean-lined, unmarked. Only the door of dark wood showed carving of any kind: runes and figures that she did not understand. At eye level was a single word: *Listinoise*.

She did not recognize the word, but she pushed through the door and found herself in an empty room. Stairs spiraled up around the interior of the tower, white steps on white walls. A golden haze hung in the air.

Forgetting for a moment that, here in the subtler worlds, she could have willed herself to the landing at the top of the flight in an instant, she climbed. The steps terminated at another door, open as though in invitation, and the room beyond might have been suspended between heaven and earth, for the deep blue ceiling was painted with silver stars and the floor was carpeted in the variegated hues of land and sea, tree and field.

Her eyes, though, were drawn to an altar at the center of the room. At first she thought that what she saw upon it was the chalice of the Great Rite, but as she approached, she realized that it was infinitely more, and she dropped to her knees.

Its color that of a hand held up to the sun, its bowl as broad as a child's outstretched arms, the image of a Cup floated above the altar. It shimmered as though with an endless flow of water, and it shone with a visible radiance that was the counterpart of that which she had sensed when, in the ecstasy of the Great Rite, she felt the nearness of the Divine.

Nearness? That was a distant and feeble thing compared with the immediacy of what she instinctively named the Grail. Here, in a form at once terrible and comely, mundane and transcendent, approachable and yet aloof, was Divinity. Here was power. Here was nurture. Here in solitary union was life, joy, victory . . .

Harrowed by the flow of quickening water that invisibly spilled over the sides of the living, beating Mystery, Dindrane's soul knelt before the unalloyed immanence of everything that had been, was, could be. Lost in the rush of divine energy, of spiritual certainty, she could hardly conceive of the slightest question as to reason or origin.

But Broceliande was a land of death. How did the Grail triumph here? And how did this shining magnificence, reified in the receptive form of a Cup, manifest the undiminished energies of both Goddess and God in union?

Shielding her streaming eyes, she gazed into the radiance. "Whom . . . whom do you serve?" she whispered.

Tower, Grail, temple: all vanished in a heartbeat. She found herself kneeling in the dust of a sandy desert, her heart laboring under a weight of sorrow and loss.

Putting her hands to her face, she wept for her foolishness. The Grail could not be questioned. The Grail simply was. Those who approached its mystery could not ask. They had to *know*.

The Specter was almost upon her before she realized it.

Only at the last moment did she hear the crunch of footsteps that echoed hollowly throughout the planes of being. Only when she had but seconds in which to flee did she look up and see a face whose eyes held nothing but the blackness of void. Only by scrambling frantically across the sand did she evade the lean hand that seemed to cover the colorless sky from horizon to horizon.

The withered fingers raked the ground where she had been kneeling, then came at her again. Her pain blunted by danger, conscious only of the revulsion she felt at the proximity of this colossus, she clawed her way out of reach.

The eyes of void and darkness fixed themselves upon her, and a low rumble, as of quiet laughter, shuddered through the worlds. The hand reached, grasping.

"Leave her." The voice of a woman. Though quiet, it was filled with menace and power.

The Specter stayed its hand. The black eyes turned on the speaker. Kyria.

The sorceress stood a short distance away, her face regal. "You shall not harm her," she said to the Specter.

You can't stop me, girl.

"It is not my time to stop you," said Kyria. "It may perhaps not be my place, either. But for now I can command. Or do you wish to see me uncloaked?"

Kyria's face shifted, and Dindrane had a quick glimpse of an old woman, her hair gray, her eyes filled with unspeakable hate. Hands as gnarled and skeletal as the Specter's were suddenly reaching . . .

The Specter pulled back. *We'll meet again, bitch . . . and then—*

Kyria's voice was cold. "When we meet again, we shall see. For now, comfort yourself with your Worm, and with your armies, and with your hounds. Your time—Alouzon's time—is coming.''

The worlds shuddered again, and though the color-less sky weighed down like lead, the Specter with-drew. Kyria turned to Dindrane and extended a hand. ''Come, child. Time to go home.''

''What . . .'' Dindrane slipped helplessly in the sand. ''What was that? 'Tis frightened I am.''

''And I also, child. Come, though. Your husband and your friends are waiting.''

Friends. Did the Gryylthans then consider her a friend? They had saved her life, had fought for her and her people, had stood over her unconscious body and defended her with torn and bleeding limbs. And yet she had seen fit to call them murderers. No wonder it was that the Grail had fled from her! The desert blurred as she wept, and she was still sobbing as Kyria took her hand.

She opened her eyes. She was in a bed in Mullaen. Outside, it was late morning, and birds were singing. Baares was sitting in a chair beside her, holding her hand, fast asleep.

The night passed without incident, and Alouzon awoke to a cold but clear day. The Vayllens believed in fresh air, and the open window showed her the bud-ding branches of an elm tree that swayed gently to and fro in the breeze that came from the east, a promise of spring.

Through half-closed eyes, she watched the sunshine and the elm tree, wanting nothing so much as to be-lieve that she was back in Kent, that the shootings and the blood and the Dragons and the swords were all the evanescent images of a night's bad dreams, that she would rise in a few minutes and cross the campus to the house on Summit Street and find Sandy making breakfast: coffee pot burbling, bagels toasting, apples sliced and ready . . .

It had, in a way, been the morning of an age, and each day had brought new belief, new confidence, new hope. Anything had been possible, and Suzanne Helling had been only one among thousands who had looked out of countless college windows and suburban doorways and had seen that the world lay open—waiting for change, waiting for spring.

Gone. Gone. All was gone. The innocence, the confidence, the hope had tottered and collapsed, and in their place had grown up a despair and a sullen anger that had found its rank fulfillment not only in the puerile and self-destructive machinations of the Weather Underground, but also in the hollow acquisitiveness and empty cynicism that had sunk deep tap roots into the ideological soil of an entire civilization.

Don't trust anybody over thirty, went the saying. But that was only half the story. You could not trust anyone under, either.

And Silbakor? Could she even trust Silbakor?

In a handful of words, the Dragon had destroyed any confidence that had remained to her. Vayllens could die, Gryylth might be laid waste, children could scream their lives away in a torrent of flaming napalm, but Silbakor was concerned only with the preservation of the bare physical substance of land and ocean. *Forget the Grail*, it had said.

Yeah, she thought, and to hell with you, lizard. These people are mine. If they go, I go.

Sighing inwardly at her resolution, she swung her feet off the couch and rubbed her eyes. Across the room, the Vayllen woman who had provided her with a bed was stirring a pot over the fire. "Did you sleep well?" she said, her voice subdued.

Alouzon could not remember her name. "Yeah. Thanks. Thanks very much."

"The Goddess bless you." She was a small, sturdy woman, her blond hair plaited carefully down her back. Alouzon vaguely remembered that her husband had braided it the night before, and the memory pulled her thoughts to Marrget.

But though the captain had slept with Karthin on a nearby couch, she was not there now. The big man

was just then awakening, and he reached for her sleep-
ily, then came fully awake when he realized that she
was gone. ''Marrha?''

''The mother—bless her!—went off at first light,''
said the Vayllen wife. She paused in her stirring with
the air of a woman who was afraid that, at any time,
she would hear screams . . . or shots. ''She told me
that she needed to think.''

Karthin passed a hand over his face. ''She wept in
her sleep, Dragonmaster,'' he whispered. ''I fear . . .''
He shook his head helplessly. ''I do not know what I
fear. She says things to me that I do not understand. I
am a man . . . she is a woman . . .'' He shrugged. ''I
do not know what to do.''

Alouzon shivered in her tunic, but not just from the
cold. ''I don't know either, Karthin.''

''Would you . . . would you talk to her?''

''I don't know how much good it'll do, but I'll try.''

The Vayllen woman folded her arms. ''And how
many will I not be feeding this morning?'' she said
tartly, but with humor.

''We'll be back,'' said Alouzon. ''Sorry about the
delay.''

The wife mustered a smile. ''You saved our chief
priestess last night and brought her to us through great
danger. You need not apologize.'' She took a warm
robe from a chest, handed it to Alouzon, and went
back to stirring the porridge. ''Breakfast will be hot
when you come for it.''

Alouzon pulled on the robe and started to reach for
her sword, but she decided to leave it where it was.
There was no sense in troubling the morning, or the
people, any further. Giving Karthin a pat on the shoulder, she went out into the sun-warmed plaza.

Mullaen was not a small town, since it was a trading
center for the whole region about Lake Innael, but
though Marrget could have been anywhere, Alouzon
sensed that she had not gone far. With a shrug, she
crossed the square, picked a street at random, and
started off, trusting to whatever Higher Powers might

pay attention to the problems of a lowly, confused, incipient Goddess.

The Cordillera reared up as though it were a tidal wave about to fall upon the town, and Mullaen—like Lachrae, like all of Vaylle—showed evidence of its afflictions. The burned ruins of a house stood hard by a shattered wall near the very center of town, and the people in the streets, men, women, and children alike, went about their daily tasks and pleasures with faces that seemed prematurely aged and worn.

Alouzon wandered among them, smiled at the children, patted the dogs affectionately, and even lent a hand to a wine merchant who had gotten his wagon stuck in a low place in the cobbles. Regardless of their daily horror, regardless of the Dragon's sympathies, she would not desert them. If there were belief and innocence left to be scraped up in the world, she would bring them to Vaylle.

As she greeted the people, she asked constantly about Marrget, but she had no news of her until she questioned a woman who, kneeling in her garden, was stoically tending the first spring shoots, pulling weeds and thinning the ranks of early sprouts.

"Did you see a blond lady come this way?" said Alouzon. The woman lifted an eyebrow at her. Nine out of ten Vayllens were blond. "A stranger," she added.

"I saw her," said the woman. "She went off to the temple. She was weeping."

"Yeah . . . I know . . ." Alouzon thanked her and ran.

Mullaen's circle of stones was not so grand as that of Lachrae, but it bespoke holiness and tranquillity nonetheless. As with all the temples of Vaylle, it was open to anyone who might come there for peace and communion with the Gods, and Alouzon found Marrget sitting on the grass at the center of the monument, hood up, face in her hands.

Silently, Alouzon sat down beside her. Marrget lifted her head and pushed back her hood. Her blond hair, unconfined, fell about her shoulders, and she wiped her eyes. ''I am ashamed to be seen acting the part of the silly girl.''

Alouzon shrugged. ''We're all silly sometimes. The guys are no different.''

''Nay, Alouzon, they are very different.''

''Yeah. That too.''

Marrget did not speak for some time. The morning waxed, children played, the dogs barked, traders cried their wares. Life surged like a gray sea about the tranquil island of stones and grass. Marrget, Alouzon knew, was listening to it all—to the children in particular.

''Until yesterday,'' said Marrget at last, her voice soft, ''I thought myself reconciled to my little one. The months would pass, my belly would grow, and come next Summer's End, I would be a mother. But then Birk gave his life for me.'' Beneath the folds of her robe, her hand went to her belly. ''For both of us. And then I promised that the child, if a boy, would be named after him.'' Her gray eyes teared again. ''And it became *real*. And I . . .'' She gasped. ''I . . . do not know what to do.''

Alouzon listened silently, then, when Marrget bent and covered her face, she held her.

Six years before, Alouzon too had been pregnant, but she had chosen to take another path. She could not help but wonder again what her child would have been like. Boy? Girl? Suzanne's straight brown hair? The blond curls of the father?

She lifted her eyes to the stones and the patterns of light and shadow that the sun drew on the grass. One soul she had sent back into the arms of whatever Divinity watched over the planet of her birth. And now, seemingly, it had returned to her: doubled, trebled, multiplied countless times to constitute the population of a world.

And she would not give them up. Not this time.

She did not know what to say. She herself had no one to whom she could turn. Save perhaps the Grail.

OK. You're so big on helping. Here's someone to help. You make such a deal out of nurturing. Nurture this one. You want me to be a God? Gimme some slack, dammit.

Marrget sighed. "I came to speak to the Goddess of this land," she said. "The one the Vayllens name Suzanne. I thought that She, perhaps, might counsel me."

Afraid that her eyes would betray her, Alouzon looked away. "Did She?"

Marrget shrugged. "I heard nothing. But perhaps it takes a priestess to hear the words of a Goddess."

"Maybe. But . . . uh . . ." Alouzon searched desperately for something to say, but found little. "I think that Gods probably work a little different than we do."

"Aye." Gathering her robe about her, Marrget rose. "I shall endure," she said to the silent stones. "I am Marr—" She fell silent, musing. "I am Marrget of Crownhark," she said softly. "I will not dishonor my name, my people, or . . ." She seemed to look within herself. "Or my sex."

Hand in hand, Alouzon and Marrget left the temple and threaded their way through the active streets of Mullaen. Word of the expedition's arrival had spread throughout the town, but though people greeted them and stared curiously and, at times, fearfully, Vayllen courtesy ensured that the two women found nothing intrusive about the attention.

The street took them back to the plaza, and as they crossed the broad lawn, they paused to examine the fountain at its center. It was carved with images of the Goddess and the God, and again Alouzon confronted the faces of Suzanne Helling and Solomon Braithwaite.

Marrget looked for a long time. "Perhaps it is well that She did not answer me," she said. "For I fear that She would tell me that I am flesh only, and that Karthin must be my guiding spirit."

"She's got a sword." Alouzon had noticed the weapon back in Lachrae, but she seized upon it now as a hope and held it out to Marrget.

Marrget examined the carving again. "Aye. I do not understand."

"Neither do I." Alouzon found the sight of her old face, staring nobly and kindly through a wash of foaming water, to be unnerving, and she looked away, feeling ashamed. Solomon Braithwaite had created Gryylth, and had confined women to their homes. She herself had created Vaylle, and had apparently imprisoned her sex within walls of philosophy.

Young, old, middle-aged—all the women of Vaylle were lovely in their own way, but they seemed as incomplete as the hippie women who had, years ago, attempted to find their way back to a simpler life by submerging themselves in stereotyped domesticity.

But answers were never that easy to come by, and living was never so uncomplicated. If the M-1s had not taught her that, Gryylth certainly had.

Her eye fell on two girls who were sitting on a blanket on the lawn, laughing together. One was showing the other how to plait a circlet of dried flowers. Happy they seemed, but—

Alouzon started and stared again. Manda and Wykla. "My God, I don't believe it."

Both young women were clad in the Vayllen tunic and loose skirts, and Wykla's face, though a little wan, was at peace. Fumbling with the unfamiliar technique that Manda was showing her, she laughed merrily at her own clumsiness; and when she saw Marrget and Alouzon, she freed a hand and waved.

"Manda thought that some sun would do me good," she explained when they approached.

Alouzon still stared. "Wykla?"

The girl blinked blue eyes. "Alouzon?"

"I can't believe you're in skirts."

Wykla was unfazed. "My armor is being cleaned and repaired," she said. "Enite lent me these clothes so that I would have something to wear. I . . ." She shrugged, smiling, and set the circlet on her head. The dried blooms were bright against her amber hair. "I find nothing unseemly about them."

Manda had been staring at Marrget uncertainly, but she pulled her eyes away and turned them on her lover. Tenderly, she touched Wykla's face. "Nor should you."

Marrget spoke. "You are not . . ." Words failed her, and she shook her head.

"Yesterday I was a warrior," said Wykla, "and I held a sword and wore armor. Today I am a towns-woman, and I don skirts and plait flowers. Tomorrow I will take up my sword again."

Marrget listened, and a tear found its way down her cheek.

"I . . ." Wykla noticed the tear. She faltered, but her captain shook her head and motioned for her to continue. Bravely, Wykla went on. "I think that a woman's life is one of changes. It is something that I must become used to. Once I was a man. Now I am a woman. I have fought battles, and I have been called a king's daughter. And . . ." She put a new-healed arm about Manda's shoulders. "And I am a lover. I take up each new role as I have need of it."

Marrget contemplated Wykla's words for a minute, then, slowly, she nodded. "The Gods do indeed work in different ways, Alouzon," she said softly. "I have been given my answer." She bowed to Wykla. "And I have also been blessed with a wise lieutenant."

Wykla colored, but Marrget took Alouzon's hand and strolled off across the lawn. "The good wife promised me a hot meal this morning, friend Alouzon," she said, her head up and her tears drying. "And . . . and after breakfast, would you do something for me?"

Alouzon wondered at her. "Anything. Name it."

"Would you . . ." Marrget thought for a moment and smiled softly, almost embarrassed. "Would you braid my hair?"

❖ CHAPTER 20 ❖

As King Pellam examined the slender figure of the boy sorcerer, his white eyebrows drew together as though he were attempting to read beneath the surface of the lad's unexpected request. "Is it inhospitable you have found us?"

Helwych blinked in the glare from the polished floor. The shattered stained-glass windows allowed the full brilliance of the morning sun to flood the hall. Save for his own black robe, there was not a particle of darkness anywhere. "Nay, you have not, my lord," he said smoothly. "I—"

A side door opened, and Pellam's young daughter appeared, her face begrimed with her tomboyish pursuits. She made as if to speak, but Pellam glanced at her and shook his head. For a moment she stared at Helwych with wise eyes, then she nodded and withdrew.

Helwych turned back to Pellam, annoyed that the girl had interrupted, irritated that, in order to be polite to a crippled old man and his ill-behaved child, he had to take no notice of it. "I have decided that it would perhaps be better for me to return to Gryylth and make a preliminary report to King Cvinthil, so that he might be better apprised of the situation in Vaylle."

Pellam nodded his white head. " 'Tis ignorant he is of our difficulties."

"Indeed," said Helwych. "He is still convinced that

288

Vaylle is the source of the attacks. I can assure him that this is not so.''

Pellam debated. ''I might,'' he said at last, ''echo the question of Magistrate Dindrane. Will you then return with armies and weapons so as to make war upon Broceliande?''

Helwych was ready for that question. ''I will have to leave that decision to Cvinthil,'' he said, ''and to Darham of Corrin.''

Corrin. The name was as foreign to him as if he had called it *Dremord Territory*. And perhaps the latter was, after all, a more correct name, for a country that did not honor its sorcerers was deserving of nothing more than pejoratives.

Vaylle, he decided, had given him much more than new sights and sounds and curious nightmares. It had also given him perspective. Darham and Cvinthil were petty little kings of petty little lands, fit for nothing save the mundane affairs of peace and subsistence-level commerce. But extraordinary times demanded extraordinary actions: the events that had overtaken them were beyond their capabilities.

He had come to Vaylle as a frightened and inexperienced child, but he would return as . . . something else. And though there had always been laughter in the looks that had been vouchsafed him in the past, that laughter would stop. Gryylth and Corrin needed a firm hand. Well, they would have it.

And was Pellam also laughing at him now? The glare made the king's form appear to float in the air, his voice, disembodied, echoing through the ruined and wasted hall. ''Darham and Cvinthil. Whom you serve, I understand. Will you have a recommendation for them?''

Silly king. No sword, no shield, no armor. Not even a scepter. Helwych could feel nothing but contempt. ''I will recommend . . . that they wait for news of Alouzon.'' He did not mention the fact that he himself would be the one bringing the news, after which they would not wait at all.

Pellam examined Helwych as though reading his mind. But Helwych reminded himself that that was impossible. A king could never fathom the depths of a sorcerer. That was why Cvinthil and Darham would be so easy to manipulate, why Pellam would find nothing at all unusual in his request to return home.

"Then so be it," said the king. "Depart when you wish. I will instruct one of the fishers of Lachrae to take you where you wish."

He examined Helwych again. Instinctively, the sorcerer shielded himself. Tireas had been fool enough to leave himself open to outside influences, but Helwych had learned from his master's failing. Nothing would affect him. Nothing could.

But as he bowed and went to gather his possessions, he found himself stumbling through half-abandoned thoughts. Vaylle was a pleasant enough place. Why did he want to leave? And Pellam had never laughed at him. He seemed an excellent king.

Laughter. Knowing looks. That dream. And the Specter.

Fighting back tears, Helwych squared his shoulders and marched himself down the corridor. He had a great deal of work to do. But it would be satisfying work. And the fools would pay for their insolence.

Wykla was back in her armor the next day, and as the company saddled up in the early morning, she prepared to depart looking fit and healthy, proud of herself and of her body, secure in her love. She had been saddened to hear that her horse had been among those that had died in the battle, but she patted the nose of a Vayllen mount appreciatively and spoke softly to the beast. The horse seemed puzzled by her armor, but it accepted her, apparently deciding that it had changes of its own to experience.

Kyria also was greatly improved, and there was lightness to her movements as she swung into Grayflank's saddle. With a gracious smile at Santhe, she took her place at Alouzon's side. "Gods bless, Alouzon," she said. "It's a fine morning, is it not?"

"Yeah. Great." Alouzon was looking at Dindrane, who, in contrast, seemed drained. There was color in her cheeks, and she appeared strong enough, but an uneasiness had taken up residence in her eyes and she gazed with uncertainty at Wykla and Manda, then at Marrget and Karthin. With a slight shake of her head and a clutch at her staff, she rode forward with Baares.

"The Goddess bless you," she said softly, her eyes averted.

Baares nodded his greeting. He glanced at Dindrane's staff and looked away, shamefaced, but his wife hardly noticed. "Is the company ready to depart?" he said.

Alouzon half turned in her saddle. "Marrget? Santhe? Ready?"

The captain nodded, her blond braid bobbing in the sunlight. "Ready, Dragonmaster." She patted the head of her mount. "My horse was a little unsure about this Gryylthan wife with whom he has taken up, but he assures me that . . ." She grinned. "That all will be well."

"I hope so." Manda's voice drifted up from the rear.

Marrget's face lost its humor. She bent her head briefly. "Indeed," she said softly. "And so do I."

"Come then," said Dindrane, still abstracted. "We have a full day's ride ahead of us before we reach Kent."

Alouzon stiffened. "Kent?"

Dindrane's unease deepened. " 'Tis so, Dragonmaster. That is the town's name."

Alouzon swallowed her sudden nausea. "OK. Whatever."

The townsfolk saw them off with blessings and good wishes. The people of Mullaen had understood neither the customs nor the motivations of their sudden guests, but their somber assistance had been nonetheless generous and honest. The wounded had been healed, the

weary had found rest, and those who had wished only
to be friends had discovered that, though the Vayllens
lived under a siege of fear and death, many of them
defied both with a quiet dignity that was willing to
embrace even warriors. There were both thanks and
tears at the leave-taking.

The day passed, the road passed, the Cordillera
scraped the sky. Though the rolling land had turned
hilly, there seemed to be no smooth transition from
foothills to mountains. The Cordillera appeared to rise
up from what was a comparative plain in an almost
sheer wall of rock.

Alouzon examined it, wondering again how she was
supposed to travel beyond such an obstacle. Dindrane
came out of her brooding long enough to answer.
"There are passes," she said. "Above Kent."

Alouzon nodded. "OK." What had happened to
Dindrane? Was it fear? "I don't know what your plans
are," she said, trying to be conciliatory, "but we'll
stay out of Kent if you want. And if you can give us
some kind of map of the pass, you certainly don't have
to go into Broceliande with us."

Neither statement seemed to relieve Dindrane.
"Your presence in Kent is the . . . least of my concerns. And as for our accompanying you into Broceliande . . ." She looked to Baares, who was studying
his harp intently, although there was nothing remark-
able about it this morning. "We have made no decision regarding that."

Kyria had trotted up next to Baares. "We do not
know what we may find in Broceliande," she said.
"You told us that no one has ever returned from that
land."

"That is true—" Dindrane caught herself. "I
mean . . ." She trailed off. Her lip trembled.

"Dindrane?"

With an effort, Dindrane composed herself. "May
I ask you some questions, Dragonmaster?"

Alouzon shrugged. "Shoot."

"You seek more in Broceliande than the origin of

the Grayfaces and the hounds and the flying things. May I ask what, precisely, you are looking for?'' Dindrane's eyes were still uncertain, but there was a glint, as of steel, within them that said she would not tolerate further dissembling.

''I . . . uh . . .'' Alouzon looked to Kyria. The sorceress, alone among the company, had heard Silbakor's cautionary words and knew of the Grail.

Dindrane pressed. ''Perhaps a Cup?''

There was an undercurrent of grief in her voice. Alouzon understood instinctively. ''You've seen it.''

''I saw . . . something. 'Twas a holy thing. What do you want with it?''

Alouzon was silent. Could she really explain to Dindrane that all of Vaylle was the tortured creation of someone as human and fallible as the priestess herself? That the Grail—ephemeral, transcendent, immanent—had condescended to make itself available so that the contradictions and flaws of both creation and creator could be amended?

''Tell me,'' said Dindrane. She stared straight ahead, blond and slight, but her shoulders were set with determination. ''What do you want with it? Personal gain? Sovereignty? The—''

Kyria cut her off sharply. ''Do you think that Alouzon is capable of that?''

Dindrane fell silent for a time. Then: ''I do not.''

''All right then.''

''But there was another . . . a man . . .''

Kyria started, and Alouzon felt the nausea rise up again.

Dindrane let go of the reins and put her hands to her face. ''You have brought terrible things to this land, Dragonmaster. I have seen what I wish I had not. I have done things of which I thought myself incapable.'' Baares reached out to comfort her, but she shook her head. ''Not now, husband. I must travel this path alone.''

It was Alouzon's turn to press. ''What did you see?''

''The Grail.''

''No, not that. The man.''

Haltingly, Dindrane described the Specter and her encounter with it, and when she was done, Alouzon looked up at the Cordillera wishing that she could see beyond it. ''Braithwaite.''

Kyria blinked. ''But he is dead.''

Alouzon glared at her. ''That wasn't what you said a couple days ago. Will you please take a stand and stick with it?''

''I am taking a stand,'' said Kyria. She turned to Dindrane. ''Did the Specter look decayed?''

Dindrane's answer surprised them both. ''It was not. But do you not remember, mistress sorceress? You were there.''

''I was?''

''You fought the Specter. And you showed it something that . . .'' Her voice trailed off, and she looked at Kyria almost fearfully. ''I do not wish to speak of it.''

Kyria nodded. ''A vicious old hag, correct?''

''Surely,'' Dindrane replied after a moment.

''This must have happened after Santhe and I—'' Kyria stopped, blushed, and continued. ''When I was asleep. I do not remember anything of it. I suspect I was guided to one who had need of my powers.''

''Guided?'' said Alouzon. ''By who? Who else is dicking around with us now? The Specter wasn't decayed. What the hell does that mean?''

''I have not the slightest idea.'' The sorceress looked worried, then shook herself out of her thoughts with an effort, smiled at Santhe and breathed the air. ''But it is indeed a pleasant day, is it not? A fitting jewel in the crown of the Goddess. Let us be glad of that.''

But the day turned grim. The road grew narrow and rough, and the few isolated steadings and manors that appeared to right and left were deserted. Some had been burned or bombed.

This part of Vaylle had always been a comparative frontier, its towns few and widely scattered, its communications with the coast intermittent and terse. But Dindrane sensed an air of desolation that stretched beyond the ruined cottages and manors and the pitted road. The entire region seemed dead. Even the grass seemed to grow sullenly, unwillingly.

Late in the day, as the cold shadow of the Cordillera was stretching eastward, Wykla called out and pointed to a steading some distance from the road. There was a woman there. Arms wide, she was leaning over the railings of a sheepfold as though to pick up a hungry lamb within.

But when Dindrane and Alouzon rode out to speak to her, they found a corpse whose hands and feet had been staked out wide in a monstrous crucifixion. The desiccated flesh of her thighs was stiff with dried blood, her abdomen had been roughly slit from crotch to ribs, and flies buzzed thickly about her shattered skull. Little remained of her face save a shadow of pain and fear.

To Dindrane, she was more than a countrywoman who lay murdered before her eyes: she was an emblem of what Vaylle had become. Raped, and raped again. When, the priestess wondered, would the final blow be administered . . . and by whom?

Alouzon did not touch the body. "SOP," she said softly. "When they were done playing, they shot her."

Dindrane found her voice. "Is this what happened in . . . Vietnam?"

"In lots of places." Alouzon looked up, glared at the Cordillera. "Happens all the time. This and worse." Turning, she strode back to the horses as though pursued.

Marrget's voice carried faintly from the road. "Did she speak to you?"

"She said a lot," replied Alouzon.

Dindrane stayed for a moment, praying, hoping that the peace the woman would find in the arms of the Mother could make up for what she had experienced in her last moments of life.

But she was still thinking of Vaylle. Had the woman

protested? Or had she allowed herself to be meekly led from her flock and tied down, her eyes wide with pain but her lips closed passively? Against her will, Dindrane was beginning to hope that she had struggled, that she had cursed the Grayfaces and struck at them, that her last words had been a cry for revenge.

The air was still and stagnant and ripe with the odor of fetid water when Kent came into view around a bend. The streets were empty, as was the road. Windows gaped like the empty sockets of a skull. Roofs had fallen in. Whole blocks of buildings and houses had been burned, and the River Shenaen lay at the base of the Cordillera like a broad ribbon the color of a stormy sky.

Dindrane halted the party at the edge of town. Silence. "Enite told me that no word had come from Kent in weeks," she said softly. "Perhaps . . . perhaps this is the reason."

"Maybe they're hiding," Alouzon whispered. "Would they know you?"

"I am chief priestess," said Dindrane, though the title had come to give her no comfort. "All the people know me."

"You want to shout?"

Dindrane thought of the woman at the sheepfold. "Greatly I fear that there would be no reply." But she turned to her husband. "Harper," she said, "harp for us. Sing us a song with some cheer in it, that the people of Kent may know we are friends."

Baares set his harp before him on the saddle. His eyes were downcast.

And Kent lay silent.

"You are wise, priestess," Kyria said softly.

"It is my husband who gives—" Dindrane stopped herself in mid-lie. She felt suddenly distant, as though she had to confront Kent and the horrors beyond it alone. And though she knew unaccountably that she could do just that, the knowledge was a cold stone in her heart.

The Grail: solitary, complete.

"I have . . . seen too much," she said.

Baares had not spoken, but Dindrane knew that he had felt the same way. He had contemplated violence, and he had acted upon his thoughts. He also had seen too much.

But he was still a harper, and he struck a chord that rang out in the still air like a bronze sunbeam. Arpeggios rippled out from his fingers and, in a soft tenor that seemed loud in the hush that covered Kent, he sang:

"The winter is past, the winter is past
The rain upon the hills falls warm.
Rejoice! For in the Goddess' arms
The God awakes and lives once more."

A door creaked open in the distance. "Who comes?" came a man's voice, hoarse and tentative.

Baares lifted his head. "Priestess Dindrane and her consort come from Lachrae," he said. "They bring a company from a far land."

The door creaked open a little more. "Baares?"

" 'Tis I."

An odor like death hung over the town, but there was a soft stirring among the buildings, like a rustle of yellowed satin. Heads peered cautiously out of windows and doorways.

The man who had addressed Baares stepped into view, and his torque of office told Dindrane that this was the magistrate, Rhoddes. Without that clue, though, she would hardly have known him, for his cheeks had grown sunken and pale, his hair sparse and gray. He looked as gaunt as the Specter.

She shuddered at the memory. How much truth had there been in her vision? "Rhoddes. 'Tis I: Dindrane."

He came forward, details of his wasted features crowding toward her. "Dindrane: beyond all hope you have come. Dear Goddess . . ."

Singly, and in twos and threes, the people of Kent

dribbled into the street and gathered about the party. They were all as pale and emaciated as Rhoddes, and the bellies of the ragged children were bloated. Withered hands reached up to Dindrane, and she took them and willed strength into those she touched. Baares dismounted and went among the folk, speaking softly to them, embracing those who seemed on the point of tears with sorrow.

"What has happened, Rhoddes?" said Dindrane. "Have you no food?"

"Food?" he said vaguely. His blue eyes had faded to a milky gray, and he seemed not to comprehend her question. "We have food. We have plenty of food. 'Tis a prosperous town, Kent is."

Alouzon swung to the ground with a creak of leather and a clink of steel. "You're starving, man."

"Starving?" His tone was distant.

Baares looked up. "Starvation of the spirit," he said, "not of the body."

"Indeed," said Dindrane, "I believe that thing."

The peoples' eyes were as empty as the shattered face of the corpse at the sheepfold, and Dindrane felt suddenly ignorant, ineffectual. She suddenly wanted to turn her horse and run away—alone—into the hills. She needed time to think. She needed time to find out what she was—what anyone was—when not simply one half of a divinely ordained pair.

But she stayed where she was, took hands, prayed, embraced the children and their parents. The Grail nurtured. And so would Dindrane of Lachrae.

Rhoddes was staring at the Gryylthans. "You bring weapons?" he said. "Has our devotion been in vain?"

He turned to Dindrane. She felt his eyes on her and tried to meet them, but found that she could not. "Your . . . devotion has not been in vain," she said. "The blessing of the Goddess be upon you."

"And the God's upon you," said Rhoddes tonelessly.

Alouzon had crouched down to comfort a child, but

he flung up his hands and ran away screaming. "She has seen hounds!" he cried.

Dindrane looked after him, shaking with strain. She was understanding Alouzon at last, and the knowledge was a rawness at the ragged edges of her isolation. "Many," she murmured. "More than she ever wanted."

The man's hands were rough with years of battle and callused from the hilt of his sword. They flung Manda to the ground, tearing at her tunic and breeches as she fell. Thirteen years old, blonde and blue-eyed, with a hot temper and a disregard for caution to match, Manda was already fighting him.

Naked save for a bit of rag that had stubbornly clung about her neck, she writhed beneath her assailant and felt herself—unready and still virgin—penetrated with a single cruel thrust that sent a lance of pain through her belly. But though the pain contracted her awareness until it occupied a single point just below her aching womb, still the thought hammered at her, a dull, ponderous, ringing ostinato of purpose and hate:

I am going to kill you, man.

Manda awoke with a gasp. The room was dark and cold. Beside her, curled up like an amber-haired kitten, Wykla slept, her face nuzzling Manda's shoulder.

Carefully, so as not to awaken her lover, Manda swung her feet off the edge of the couch and sat up. About her, lying on couches and cushions, wrapped in furs against the penetrating cold, her companions slept soundly in the abandoned house that had been given over for their use that night. Dindrane slept alone, her face sorrowful, while her husband stood watch outside the door. Across the room, Alouzon tossed and murmured with her own uneasy dreams. Nearby, Kyria lay in Santhe's embrace, and in the dim light of a banked fire the two looked like children who sought security in one another's arms.

And, off in the corner by themselves, stretched out

side by side as was fitting for husband and wife, lay Karthin and Marrget.

What, indeed, was Manda supposed to call her? Rapist? The term seemed absurd now. Marrget could no more rape than could Alouzon or Dindrane. Even her name seemed out of place. Karthin invariably called her Marrha now, and so, at times, did the other members of the company.

Friend? How could she? Enemy?

"Oh you Gods, what shall I do?" she whispered. "She has proved herself my comrade over and over, and yet I cannot find anything but bitterness in my heart. But he . . . he is *dead*."

A few feet away, the woman he had become breathed softly in repose, her hand resting lightly on her husband's chest, and though her hair was braided as was proper for a married woman of her people, a sword lay at her side.

Manda picked up her own weapon, went to the door, and opened it cautiously. "Baares?" she whispered.

He looked up from his harp. "The God bless you, Manda."

The God. The one they called Solomon. Where, she wondered, had He been when a thirteen-year-old girl had been raped? "And you also." She slipped through the opening and closed the door behind her.

"It is not your time yet, Manda," said the harper.

"I could not sleep. This is a bad place, and the river is too close. I think I will scout the shore before I return to take the watch."

"As you wish." Baares scanned the dark street. Nothing moved. Nothing stirred. The well-fed but starving town looked even more dead at night than it had in the daylight.

Eyes vigilant, she stepped carefully down the street. The waning moon shed a faint light on the tumble of houses and buildings. The Cordillera was an invisible mass that eclipsed the stars. The river, fetid and stagnant, gleamed like the blade of a freshly blooded dagger.

She grimaced. Evil town, evil dreams, evil thoughts.

Surely, Kent was a place for nightmares and nocturnal terrors. Having slumped into a numb acceptance of constant violence, its people had seemingly turned into wraiths and ghosts that clung desperately to their bodies as a pauper might defend a meager hovel.

A plash from the river attracted her attention, and she slipped into the deep moonshadow of a wall and examined the blank water. After several minutes, a vague shape detached itself from the dark backdrop of the Cordillera. The light was uncertain, but Manda decided that it had to be a small boat. She made out three, perhaps four figures in it.

Grayfaces.

What was it going to be tonight? Murder? Explosions? Rape? Her formless anger at a man who seemed now forever beyond any kind of revenge seized upon this clear and definite enemy. The Grayfaces would die. If she could do nothing else, she would see to that.

She turned silently back toward the house to rouse her companions, but she had taken only a dozen steps before she was confronted with a pair of glowing eyes and a mouth dripping with phosphor. Instinctively, she readied herself for the hound's spring, but before she had a chance to move or even call out, she was knocked flat from behind.

She skidded across the cobbles, her sword flying from her hand. Stunned, breathless, she was nonetheless already groping for her belt knife, though she knew that the smaller blade would be of little use against a multiple attack. "Baares!" she managed, but her voice was faint.

Jaws snapped at her. She rolled to the side, brought up her knife, and plunged it into the beast's throat. Phosphor gushed over her arm like a stream of liquid fire, and she felt the hilt of the knife turn slick as her skin began to dissolve.

There were two of the beasts, but though she had

wounded one, its companion was untouched, and when she tried to rise and gain her footing, it simply put its muzzle against her back and pushed her to the ground again.

Through the pain that had turned her arm into an open sore, she sensed that the second hound was about to rip her open from the back. Rolling desperately, sliding through the growing pool of phosphor, she managed to get an arm up in time, and the jaws closed on her forearm instead of her head. She heard the crunch of breaking bone, felt the numb prickling of a suddenly missing limb.

Pain and panic freed her voice. *"Goddess!"*

She lashed out with her knife. Grinning, the hound backed, let her strike go wide, then lunged forward, its jaws wide, its phosphorescent throat seething like a pool of magma.

But it did not reach her. With a hollow thud and a ring of bronze strings, Baares's harp smashed into its head and sent it reeling. The big man was suddenly beside her, his feet braced wide apart, his face murderous. "Is it fighting you want? Then by the Goddess and the God, *'tis fighting you will get!"*

A second swing of the stout willow harp broke the skull of the already wounded hound. It rolled over and lay still, but the gush of phosphor struck Baares full in the face, blinding him. "Arms, Gryylthans!" he cried.

Shouts in the distance. Alouzon's voice came faintly to Manda's ears. "Everyone move! Kyria! C'mon, go! Go!"

The second hound had regained its footing and was slowly stalking the blind harper. With a wrench of his dissolving face, Baares composed himself, listened, and put himself between Manda and the beast. "Tell me when it is close enough for me to strike, child," he said softly, "and I will strike."

Manda herself was almost sightless with pain, but she forced herself up on her remaining elbow so as to lift her head out of the stinging miasma of fumes that arose from the hound's blood. "Straight ahead of you," she gasped. "Almost. Not quite. Wait."

The harper was murmuring to himself, but it was not the meaningless ravings of pain. His voice was as controlled as it had been when chanting a song of praise that afternoon.

". . . fold me in Your embrace, that, should this be the hour of my death, I may be led to Your lands by the hand of the God."

"Now!"

The hound leaped. Baares swung. The harp struck the beast directly on the forehead and sent it to the ground once more. The instrument, though, had never been designed as a weapon. With a ripping of bronze strings, it shattered in his hands.

Footsteps approached, pounding on the cobbles. Dindrane shrieked. "Baares!"

Alouzon was barking orders. "Karthin, Marrget: blockade the far side. Santhe, back me up. Kyria, gimme some light."

With a crackle, the street was suddenly illuminated with blue-white incandescence, but the hound was undeterred. Before Manda could warn Baares, it regained its feet and drove in without prelude, catching the harper by the throat and dragging him to the ground.

Alouzon was already on top of it, and Manda caught the look of utter hatred on her face as the Dragonsword went up gleaming. It was a hate that made all others seem puerile by comparison, a deep and deathless anger that was all the more terrible for the fact that it seemed directed not only at the hound, but at Alouzon Dragonmaster herself.

As the Dragonsword fell, Alouzon was screaming. "Damn you! *Damn you!*"

Shock had numbed Manda's pain, but it also made her stare blankly as Wykla dropped to the ground beside her and turned white faced with horror. "Kyria! Manda's arms . . . please . . ."

"I am . . . all right . . ." Manda said tonelessly.

"The Grayfaces . . ." But her memory had turned foggy. What about the Grayfaces?

Dindrane was kneeling beside her husband. Baares was half covered by the inert bulk of the hound that had nearly severed his head. Lifting her staff with a cry, the priestess was suddenly surrounded by a yellow nimbus that rivaled Kyria's blue-white light, and the flow of healing energy was like a breaker that foamed through the street.

But Baares was dead. Manda, though vague with pain, knew that. Nonetheless, Dindrane grasped at all the energies that were hers to command in an effort to restore her husband to life. Sobbing, her hands clenched on her staff, her head bent and her eyes shut tight, Dindrane tried to do the impossible.

Manda's vision was blurring, but she sensed Kyria beside her. "I . . . I . . ."

"Easy." The sorceress's voice was grave. "O Goddess . . ."

"Can you . . . ?" Alouzon's voice.

"Please," said Wykla. "Please."

"Give me room," said Kyria. Manda felt the sorceress kneel. "Child," said Kyria, "you are too badly wounded for me to do this gently. It will hurt. Try not to be afraid."

Manda could not fathom what was happening. "I saw . . . I saw Grayfaces . . ."

A brightness sprang up as Kyria lifted her staff, and Manda felt a flash of fire that grew into a ball of heat and ran through her body like a splash of molten lead. Gritting her teeth, burying her face in Wykla's arms, she tried not to scream, but self-control was beyond her.

As she drew a breath, she heard a burst of gunfire from the river bank, and Karthin was suddenly shouting frantically: "They have taken Marrha!"

❖ CHAPTER 21 ❖

Karthin's story was simple . . . and devastating. He and Marrget had been ambushed by a group of five or six Grayfaces. Karthin, taken by surprise, had been felled by a rifle butt to his head, but in his last moments of consciousness he had seen Marrget struggling with four of the soldiers.

Concussed and bleeding, Karthin had crawled to his feet to discover that Marrget was neither dead nor wounded, that she was, in fact, missing entirely. His desperation had driven him back to his comrades in spite of his disorientation.

Leaving Dindrane sobbing over her husband's body and Kyria struggling to save Manda, Alouzon and Santhe put Wykla in charge of the big man and raced for the river bank. There, the marks of an inflatable boat were plain in the soft sand, and the waffle impressions left by the soles of combat boots were only just beginning to fill with water. Beached nearby were the coracles and wooden boats that belonged to the town. A grenade or two would have destroyed them all, but they had not been touched.

The river lay blank and bare in the moonlight. From far off across it, though, came the plash of oars.

"What do they want with her?" Santhe hissed. "What are they doing?"

Alouzon was staring in the direction of the sounds as though she could will the darkness away. "They want us to follow them."

"By the Gods with names and without, they will get what they want. And they will regret it." Santhe's words carried the weight of a vow, and the moonlight turned his face into a study in silver and black rage.

There was no question in Alouzon's mind about following: she and the others would have swum the river underwater for Marrget. But with Manda badly wounded, Karthin hurt, and Dindrane grieving over Baares, she wondered how she was going to get her company into any kind of condition for traveling.

"C'mon, Santhe," she said, fighting with both her worry for Marrget and her guilt for having sent her and Karthin into a trap, "we've got work to do."

They jogged back to the site of the battle to find Kyria slumped beside Manda. The face of the sorceress was thin, and she looked as though she had been without sleep for days. "I did all I could," she managed. There was a trace of shame in her voice. "She will live. Her arm, though . . ." She shook her head.

Struggling against Wykla's protests, Manda sat up. Her wounds had been healed, the phosphor neutralized, but although her right arm was as good as ever, her left terminated just above the elbow. White-faced, she touched the stump and passed a hand over her face.

Dindrane was covered with Baares's blood. It had pooled in her skirts and smeared her white arms almost to her shoulders, but she hardly noticed. Shoulders shaking, she was bent over him, her face pressed against his. "Follow the light, husband. Take the hand of the God, and He will lead you—" But she choked and fell silent.

The street was filled with the reek of phosphor, but aside from the remaining members of the expedition, it was deserted. The people of Kent had become inured to suffering. They were no longer even curious. "Yeah," said Alouzon. "I should have known this would happen." She shook Kyria by the shoulder. "Can you take care of Karthin? He's pretty bad."

The big man was staring blankly as though he would have been unconscious but for his alarm. Kyria hardly looked as though she could take care of herself, but she nodded absently and crawled to his side, her robes smoking with spatters of phosphor and her long hair trailing on the ground.

Manda, gripping Wykla's arm, got to her feet. "Marrha . . . is she . . . ?"

Alouzon nodded. "They've got her."

Manda looked ragged. The strength that Kyria had given her was merely a surface gloss that did nothing to eradicate the near-bottomless exhaustion left by her wounds. "We must follow."

Alouzon examined her dubiously. "You're in no shape to do anything, Manda."

The maid's face was set. "I am well enough."

"Manda—"

Manda bent and retrieved her sword. "Would you desert your friend, Dragonmaster?"

"No. Never."

Manda nodded. "Well then . . ."

Nearby, Kyria was healing Karthin. When she was through, though, she was nearly stupefied. She sat on the cobbles, her staff lying across her lap as though she no longer knew its purpose.

Alouzon turned back to Manda. "It's going to be hard travel."

"I will live."

"You're not even Marrget's friend!"

Manda sheathed her sword. "I will live. And so will she."

Alouzon could not guess her meaning. "OK," she said. "If you can stay on your feet, you and Wykla go find us a couple boats down on the shore and get them ready. We'll have to move fast, before the trail gets cold, so we'll strip the packs down to only what we need. The horses . . ." She paused, undecided. The horses would never be able to deal with the steep slopes of the pass, and in any case, the Vayllen mounts would panic at the first sign of battle.

Kyria spoke, her voice a blurred mumble. "I can instruct them," she said. "I can spell them to return to Lachrae."

"What about you?"

A flash of hard black eyes, and the words exploded out of the sorceress. "What the hell do you care, honey? I'm just here to patch everyone up when you get them shellacked." She put her hands to her face and sobbed. "I'm so tired. I want to go home."

Santhe knelt beside her. "My lady, we have duties . . . and friends . . ."

With a wrench that contorted her face, Kyria shoved Helen back into the shadows. "I know, Santhe," she said. "Duties and friends. We will attend to both."

Which left Dindrane. The priestess was cradling what phosphor and fangs had left of her husband, heedless of the fact that her own garments were beginning to smoke and dissolve with the powerful corrosives. Earlier that day, she had said that she had not made a decision whether she would enter Broceliande; now it seemed utterly absurd to suppose that she would follow the expedition into further danger.

And time—Marrget's time—was passing like a swift stream. There was no time for rest, there was no time for grief, there was no time for mourning. There was hardly time for preparation.

"We'll leave Dindrane with the people here," said Alouzon. "She at least knows the magistrate, and—"

But she broke off. Dindrane had lifted her head, and there was a seething emotion in her eyes. "I will come."

"But . . . Baares . . ."

"He . . ." Dindrane spoke with an effort. "He is gone. Forever. I will meet him again in the Far Lands, not before."

"But—"

Tenderly, Dindrane laid Baares on the cobbles. A smear of phosphor clung to her cheek. It was smoking, burning into her flesh, but she paid no attention to it. "I do not desire your approval, Dragonmaster," she said, standing up. "I am chief priestess of Vaylle and magistrate of Lachrae: I am informing you of my intentions."

She turned to the blank, silent houses behind her. "Rhoddes! People of Kent! Come forth!"

Slowly, a few shutters creaked open, spilling lamplight into the street. "Dindrane?" came Rhoddes's voice.

"Come down and attend to the body of my husband," said the priestess. " 'Tis buried and spoken for I want him within the hour."

Rhoddes's voice was tremulous. "Will the Goddess accept him? He died with—"

Dindrane cut him off. *"A good deal more he did than you, maggot!"*

There was a stirring within the houses, a collective gasp like a flutter of graveclothes. "I . . . I will see to it, priestess," said Rhoddes, his voice hardly more than a whisper.

Bending, Dindrane took the knife from the harper's belt. "I will keep this," she murmured, "so that it will not be defiled."

Wykla and Manda were returning from the boats. "We have two coracles, Dragonmaster," said Manda. Her hand covered her stump half-protectively, half in unbelief. "They—" She caught sight of Dindrane and fell silent.

"Child," said the priestess, still holding the knife. "Will you go to my bundle and fetch my chalice and the wine skin? I would perform a Great Rite for my husband before I leave."

A flare of torches was spilling into the street. Rhoddes approached. "You will need a priest, Dindrane."

Dindrane wiped at her cheek and winced as the outer layers of skin peeled off. "I will be my priest," she said. "And priestess, too. And the knowledge . . ." Her voice was hoarse, her eyes fixed on her dead husband. "The knowledge was dearly bought."

* * *

The two coracles moved across the still waters of
the River Shenaen like autumn leaves skimming the
surface of a pond. Karthin and Santhe propelled them
with strong, skilled oar strokes, leaving no more of a
ripple then a leaping fish.

Alouzon and Wykla crouched in the rear of the
boats, steering, and the rest of the company kept low
so as to provide less of a mark for a round from an
M-16. Kyria alone kept her head up, watching for
tracers or muzzle flashes, her glowing staff lapped in
a fold of her cloak but ready for instant use.

Dindrane was plainly still in shock, her sight and
thoughts turned inward. Clad now in a tunic and a pair
of trews that Wykla had lent her, her staff and torque
the only indications that she was of Vaylle, she murmured softly to herself in a quiet, repeating cadence.
From the stray words that now and then carried the
length of the boat, Alouzon guessed that the priestess
was chanting a litany for the dead.

They made the crossing without incident, and the
moonlight guided them in to a sandy shore set about
with a tumble of black boulders. When they landed,
Karthin again found the marks of the Grayfaces' boat,
and, some distance from the water, a low, wet stretch
of sand showed footprints with a distinctive waffle pattern.

Six men. Two, it seemed, were walking in a line,
their footprints deeper, as though they were . . .

"Carrying her," said Alouzon, straightening.

"Aye." Karthin tipped his head back. A few feet
away, the rocks rose up sheer—the feet of the Cordillera—and the peaks were lost in the heights. Moonlight glimmered on the cliff face and sparkled on the
dense vegetation that appeared far above.

Alouzon followed his eyes. "I'm not even going to
wonder whether we should wait for daylight," she said.

Karthin said nothing, only nodded; but his manner
indicated that even if Alouzon had called a rest for the
night, he would have gone ahead by himself.

In her Gryylthan tunic and trews, Dindrane looked

boyish and lean. Owl-eyed, she nodded when Alouzon asked her about the passes. "You wish to go on?"

"Do we have a choice, Dindrane?"

She shook her head. "We do not. Come."

Dindrane led them southward around boulders and across sand bars that sucked at their boots like living things. The river was stagnant and still, the air unmoving and filled with the odor of rot.

Karthin and Manda scanned the ground as they went, periodically finding evidence of the passage of the Grayfaces. "How much time do they have on us?" Alouzon asked.

Karthin squinted at the footprints that he had just found. Kyria knelt beside him and called up a light from her staff. The big man nodded his thanks and raked his fingers through the sand. "Perhaps an hour," he said. "Perhaps a little less."

They continued. The sheer wall of rock to their right became a little less vertical, and cracks and fissures appeared in it, widening gradually into ravines and small valleys. Soon, Dindrane was leading them up a canyon, its walls steep and rocky and difficult to climb. Streams trickled down from above, but here, in contrast to the thick vegetation on the slopes above, nothing seemed to grow, not even moss, and the stream bed itself was as featureless as if it had been scribed with a burin.

The trail brought them back to the outer face of the mountains. Far below was the river, and Kent was a deeper patch of darkness in the silver and sable of the moonlit landscape. The slope gentled, and trees and shrubs now appeared and grew thicker and more numerous as, paradoxically, the air turned warm and humid. Soon they found themselves forcing their way through thick jungle growth, and the path beneath their boots was soft, muddy, and dank with decay.

"Does this remind you of anything?" said Kyria as they paused to catch their breath.

Alouzon had to gasp for a moment before she replied. Simply moving this hot, moist air in and out of her lungs was an effort. "Yeah. And I don't like it."

"Nor do I."

An hour's lead. Alouzon tried not to think of what condition Marrget might be in. And she tried even harder not to consider what the Grayfaces planned to do to her.

Manda caught up with them. "Come," she said. But she staggered and would have fallen had not Wykla caught her.

"She is not well," said Wykla. "I fear we will have to rest."

Kyria called for the others to stop and, with Wykla helping, lowered Manda to the soft ground. The maid's eyes were glassy with exhaustion and shock.

Karthin came tramping back. "We must continue."

Alouzon pointed ahead. The trail grew steeper, hedged about thickly with elephant grass and thorn and bamboo that shut out the moonlight and dictated that any further traveling would be slow and in single file. "You want to tell me how?"

Karthin, strained and frightened, had little judgment left to him, but he knew it. Alouzon watched conflicting desires battle across his face, their fight made more violent by the harsh shadows cast by the moon.

Kyria was working with Manda. "I am heartily sorry about your arm, child," she murmured. "If I were not so afraid, I—"

From above came a roar of jets. Alouzon's head snapped up. Aqua light was pouring across the jagged peaks, reflecting on the underside of white wings. "Oh, for chrissakes . . ."

The sorceress rose. "Whom do they seek?"

"Can't tell. I think choppers would be better if they were coming after us, though."

Three Skyhawks descended in a tight spiral to the east of the mountains, their cockpit canopies flashing in the moonlight and their exhausts burning blue.

Keeping in tight formation, toylike with distance, they lined up on the town.

Dindrane stood, shaking. "Baares." Her voice was faint.

"He is gone, priestess," said Santhe gently.

" 'Tis well I know that," she said. "All is gone."

The scene below might well have been from a newsreel of the late 1960s. The Skyhawks approached and swept across the town. Their napalm pods tumbled like fat seeds during their short fall to the ground, then bloomed in great billows of red and orange. In moments, Kent was burning, its streets turned to rivers of fire, its houses to crucibles of flame.

But save for the whine of turbines, the bursts of the napalm pods, and the dull mutter of the greedy flames, the town died in silence. No screams, no cries, no frantic attempts to escape. No one even left the houses.

"Do they not care?" said Santhe. Like the others, he was watching with horror and fascination both.

Alouzon shook her head. "They didn't care in 1970 either. No one cared." But here in Vaylle, Kent State seemed far away. The battles and blood, the magic and mystery, the hope and despair—all had gradually thrust her tragic college days farther and farther into the past, providing her with a dubious perspective. She no longer knew who to blame. She hardly knew what the sides had been.

Kyria and Wykla had carried Manda to a patch of dry ground. The maid was sleeping, whimpering as she unconsciously felt for her missing forearm. The sorceress was worn, but she stood up and answered Alouzon. "Some of us cared."

Alouzon watched the town burn. Then, as now, there had been many ways of caring. And Helen Addams had stated her political ideology in definite and uncompromising terms. "How much did you hand over to the Weathermen?" she asked bitterly.

Kyria hung her head. "I made a mistake."

"We all did. Theirs was thinking that you could

build something up by hating it into existence. Mine was giving up because of their idiocy. I . . .''

She glanced about her. Manda was unconscious. Dindrane appeared to be on the verge of silent hysteria. Santhe and Karthin were staying on their feet through sheer effort of will.

Alouzon sighed, discouraged. ''I'm still making them.''

''There is no harm in that.''

''There's lots of harm, Kyria. I just wish that it didn't take a fucking God to tell the difference between good and bad.''

Kyria's eyes were appraising.

Alouzon heard her thoughts. Somewhere, the Grail was waiting for her to lift it, to bathe herself in its waters, to drink of its knowledge. And afterward, she would no longer be Suzanne Helling or Alouzon Dragonmaster, but something else entirely, something that might well be able to know the difference between good and bad, that could appreciate the intricate ramifications of every thought, word, or deed, no matter how trivial, that could bring sanity to a world made insane by its very creation.

The Grail . . .

She turned away from the burning town, willing to give up even the memory of the Grail in exchange for Marrget's safety. ''The Grayfaces are going to have to rest, too,'' she said. ''We'll take two hours. I'll watch.''

Kyria had cast a gentle spell of sound sleep over the company, but Manda tossed in uneasy dreams at Wykla's side. Over and over, she felt the hound's needle teeth close on her left arm, felt the jerk, the ragged release of rending flesh, the sudden feeling of emptiness. In a moment she had been transformed from whole to maimed.

Shocky though she was, Manda had seen the grim sorrow in Wykla's eyes and had felt its presence in her own, for the pain of her wound was a shared thing, a mutual loss that went far beyond the physical absence of a limb. Since they had declared their love for one another, their hands had spoken their affections as eloquently as their voices, reaching out to touch, to caress, to bring comfort or pleasure or joy . . .

The hound might as well have ripped out her tongue.

Existing wraithlike in her memory, Manda's missing arm burned with the fire of outraged and bewildered nerves as she opened her eyes to the jungle and the nocturnal heat that seemed a suffocating blanket wrapped about the camp. Wykla's arm was draped over her protectively, as it always was when they slept together, but aside from that one association, Manda felt that she had been estranged from all the familiarity of her former life as effectively as if she had been killed and resurrected.

Manda the one-armed. Manda the maimed. For the rest of her life, her infirmity would dictate her gestures, the way she walked or ate, the manner in which she made love . . .

Bravely, she thrust her tears away. She was a warrior. She had taken a warrior's risks, and matters had come out against her. She had no cause for complaint.

But as Kyria's spell closed her eyes again, she thought of Marrget. Profoundly as Manda's life had been changed, that alteration was as nothing compared with the depth of the transformation inflicted upon the captain. Maimed though Manda might be, she was still a woman. She had known her body from birth. Marrha, though . . .

Marrha. Manda herself had called her that. And if the loss of a forearm could change her life and make her think in terms of death and rebirth, how much more so the sudden acquisition of a new body?

Kyria's spell rained sleep on her eyes, but Manda murmured softly: "He is dead. He is *dead*."

Dawn came up gray and misty, carrying with it the promise of brutal midday heat. The company, though, had already been traveling for several hours through the faint pre-dawn light that was even fainter after it had fought its way through the dense jungle that pressed itself against the narrow trail.

Through gaps in the leaves, they watched Kent dwindle into a tiny, charred patch, and as they climbed still higher, their lungs aching with the altitude, they could see the blue curve of the ocean, and a gray haze that obscured the distant horizon.

Somewhere in that haze, Alouzon knew, was Gryylth, the land that had first roused her affections from their dormancy and then laid tenacious hold upon them. She had become, in fact, more of Gryylth than of Earth, for Los Angeles now seemed as far away as Kent State, and her meaningless, cryptozoic existence at the edge of UCLA was here overwhelmed by purpose, devotion, and loyalty.

"What a bitch that I have to go back," she muttered to herself as Karthin helped her up the side of a ravine that cut across the trail like a gash from an axe. She, in turn, reached back, took hold of Manda's hand, and, with Karthin acting as an anchor, pulled the maid up through a tangle of creepers and the slime of river mud.

They climbed, trudging up the dank trail, at times scrambling through muck and decay. As though in defiance of the altitude, the jungle grew thicker. Vines, creepers, ferns—every imaginable shape of leaf and stem in every possible shade of green pressed close about them. In the afternoon, the air turned suffocating, sweat pooled beneath leather armor, and the temptation to drain the water skins was almost irresistible.

After a meager ration of water and a bite standing, Alouzon and Kyria took over the point. The trail was unmistakable—a narrow slot of hot, damp air hedged in by overhanging walls of vegetation. When it forked, Dindrane would consider for a moment and then indicate the right direction with a silent nod of her head.

At first, Alouzon wondered how the priestess knew the way so instinctively, for Dindrane had, by her own admission, never attempted these passes before. But the Dragonmaster reminded herself that, like all the people of this world, the priestess was a recent creation, brought into being with all her knowledge, skills, biases, and preferences in full bloom. If it was necessary that Dindrane know the way to Broceliande, then she knew it.

But who—or what—had determined such necessity or granted such knowledge? How could a finite and limited mortal determine and meet the manifold needs of an entire world? It was, quite simply, impossible, and Alouzon, befogged with heat, cast about in her mind for a more competent agency.

She stumbled and caught herself on her hands and knees, murmuring: "You're really pushing me, aren't you? You really want me for the job."

But as Kyria bent to help her up, the words clung to Alouzon's lips, for, inches from her hands, a thin filament stretched across the path, a silvery quivering in the damp air and muted sunlight. Fine as a hair, taut as a wire, it waited for something—or someone—to brush against it.

She found her voice. "Everyone freeze. Don't move."

Her tone was enough to halt them in place. Cautiously, she backed away from the thread and stood up. "Do you see it?" she asked Kyria.

"I do," said the sorceress.

"Boobytrap."

"Yes. This is probably the reason the Grayfaces wanted us to follow them."

Alouzon was shaking. She did not know for sure what the wire was connected to, but she knew some possibilities. Had she not fallen, the entire company might well have been reduced to blood, pulverized flesh, and splinters of bone. "It's just damned lucky that I took that tumble."

Lucky? Or planned?

Mouth dry, Alouzon looked up, around, down. Where did one turn in order to address a Sacred Cup that embodied the universe? "Uh . . . thanks," she said.

"Alouzon?" Kyria blinked at her.

"Nothing." Alouzon wiped her face with the back of her arm. "Damn this heat. I'd do anything for a t-shirt and a cold can of pop."

The wire remained in place: quivering, waiting. "What do you want to do with this?" said the sorceress. "Magic?"

"No." Alouzon considered. "No, someone might pick up on that. And I don't want to try to disarm it, either. I've got an idea. If this is why they wanted us to follow them, let's give them just what they want."

She led the company back down the path. When they were some distance from the trip wire, Alouzon explained its use and probable effects. "Can anyone here throw a knife or a rock real good?"

"I was skilled with a knife," said Manda. "But now . . ." She glanced at her stump. "I cannot vouch for my balance."

Alouzon patted her shoulder. "The balance will come back, Manda. Give yourself some time."

Manda stared ahead. "Marrha does not have time."

"We're going to do something about that. Karthin? Santhe? Wykla?"

Dindrane lifted her head as though to object to being left out. She opened her mouth to speak, but she reconsidered and remained silent.

Santhe smiled in spite of the situation. "Wykla has proved herself in the art of throwing stones," he said. "As some of the less tolerant youths of Kingsbury can attest."

"Wykla?"

"It is true, Alouzon." Wykla looked sad, as though she were considering aspects of her home that she had been able to ignore for a time. "Taunted by the young men, and unable to meet them sword to sword, I . . ." She seemed almost ashamed. "I took up an occasional cobble."

Alouzon almost laughed. "That explains that poor

schlep back at the Hall. Good for you. Do you think you can hit that wire from here?''

Wykla squinted. At this distance, the wire was more a presentiment than a presence. "I can."

"Can you turn around the second you let go and dive for cover around the curve of the trail?"

"Aye."

Karthin folded his arms. "She will find herself dragged if she does not," he said.

"Then let's do it," said Alouzon. "Karthin's right about grabbing you. It's going to get nasty. Don't hesitate. We'll catch you."

They took cover around the bend. Alone, a smooth stone in her hand, Wykla confronted the wire at a distance of twenty yards. The girl hefted the stone, her body loose and relaxed, and then her left foot slid forward and her right arm swung out. It was a woman's throw, awkward and graceful both, but skilled, powerful, and accurate. The stone flew toward the wire.

In one flowing movement, as though it were nothing more than a curious follow-through, Wykla spun, flexed, and threw herself into Karthin's arms just as the trail ahead erupted in a shattering detonation that sent foliage, earth, and stone high into the air. Buckshot the size of pebbles shredded the grass and leaves, and the air was acrid with the smell of explosive.

Wykla had prepared herself for danger, but her face was white as she looked out from Karthin's protective embrace. "Alouzon . . ."

"You did good, Wykla."

"But what kind of person would make such a thing?"

Alouzon shook her head. To a certain extent, the answer to Wykla's question was unknown even to her, for although she had accepted responsibility for Broceliande and its attacks on Vaylle, she could not reconcile the absolute cruelty exhibited by the Grayfaces and the hounds with any part of her conscious will.

The party moved out, and within the hour the jungle

thinned, dwindled to low scrub, and faded into the gray rocks. Steep, precarious, and slippery, the trail switched back and forth up the sheer wall of the upper slopes.

"This is a pass?" wondered Alouzon. But Dindrane, dogged and obsessed, the phosphor scar a white blotch on her fair face, only nodded and forced herself forward.

Just at sunset, they topped the crest of the pass and looked out over a high plateau that stretched off toward the horizon in arid, remote, featureless desolation. It was a gray land in which color, shape, and outline were blunted, a place of uncertain existence and shadowy fear that clung parasitically to the borders of the real.

Alouzon had seen its like before, for Dythragor had once entered a region like this, and his confidence had been shaken, even destroyed. And now she had come to Broceliande. And now she understood.

"The Heath," she said. "It's the Heath again." She sat down on a stone, staring. Dythragor's Heath had been small: merely a mile or two on a side. Hers went on seemingly forever, stretching its dull and ravening presence out to the edges of the world.

"Oh Gods," she said, "it's worse than I thought."

❖ CHAPTER 22 ❖

Night descended like a curtain. Here there was no lingering dusk, but rather an absolute dichotomy of light and dark, as though the simplistic opposites of political expediency had manifested themselves in the workings of a world. The sun set, the sky turned black, and the stars appeared in dispassionate glory.

Strangely enough, Kyria suddenly felt full and powerful, as replete with a sense of her abilities as she had when, once, she had stood on the shore of the Atlantic and watched the gray breakers roll in under a morning sky. But in New England, she had been a girl facing the sea and wondering about herself and her future. Here, she was grown into womanhood, her memories rife with twenty years of abuse, her unconscious the dwelling place of something that was both alien and consubstantial. But she was still wondering.

Wykla stood with her sword drawn as though contemplating the dangers ahead. Flashes of aqua light flitted through what was now a sea of jet. "The Heath, Alouzon," she said. "Aye, I recognize it."

"You worried?" said Alouzon.

"I braved the Heath in your company once," said the young woman. "And though I hardly knew you, you gave me confidence. Now I know you." She smiled quietly, proudly, and reached out and took Manda's hand. "And I am not afraid."

Alouzon laughed, but to Kyria it sounded more like

a sob. "All right," she said. "Let's take a break. Two hours, as usual. I'll watch."

Alouzon had taken the single watch at every rest. Kyria did some quick mental calculations and decided that the Dragonmaster had not slept in two days. Even in the faint light that flickered from Broceliande, her face looked haggard, and her eyes were sunken with exhaustion and worry.

The others threw themselves down where they were and were almost immediately asleep. Karthin cried out once, and then was silent. Kyria planted herself next to Alouzon. "You also need rest," she said.

"I'll rest after we find Marrget."

"We are not going to be able to find her if we must be carrying you."

Alouzon hung her head. "I can't sleep anyway," she said. "I keep worrying, even more than Karthin. You didn't see that body near Kent. I did. I keep thinking that she looked a lot like Marrget."

A flash from Broceliande, and, incongruously, the whine of turbines. Phase-shifting with interfering harmonics, the sound grew into a roar: the distinctive sound of a jet engine.

Another, and then another. Runway markers coalesced out of the darkness below, and Kyria and Alouzon watched three sets of wing lights streak along the ground and then mount into the air.

Alouzon tensed, but Kyria shook her head. "Call it intuition if you want," said the sorceress, "but I think they are going to strike Mullaen."

Alouzon put her face in her hands and sobbed. "They were good to us there. Ceinen and Enite . . ."

"They were indeed. But for now my hands are tied." Manda's stump was a constant reminder to Kyria of her unwillingness to risk a change in persona. With effort, she could have given the maid a new arm, but that would have meant . . .

She winced. Helen was screaming again. Another reminder. "Striking at the planes magically would only attract the attention of whatever agency is active in Broceliande," she managed.

"Solomon?"

"Something . . ." *Helen, please, I beg you. These people need both of us.* "Something like him."

The jets gained altitude rapidly, then swept across the mountains and off to the east. Alouzon watched them. "What do you think?"

Helen's screams subsided to an angry mutter. "I think I need more information," said Kyria. "You and Wykla referred to something called the Heath. What did you mean?"

Alouzon lifted her water skin but only moistened her lips. The streams they had passed had all been fouled with decay. Thirst was rapidly becoming as much of an enemy as fatigue.

She wiped her mouth with the back of a grimy hand. "When Sol made Gryylth, there were things that he wouldn't cop to, things that he didn't want running around in his world. They all got balled up and thrown into something the Gryylthans called the Blasted Heath."

Kyria lifted an eyebrow.

Alouzon read the question. "Yeah, you were in there, and that was bad enough for him. But there was also something called the Tree of Creation. It represented change . . . the change he couldn't handle."

"And it killed him?" There was no satisfaction in her voice or in her heart. She felt only a quiet sadness, and although Helen screamed, she almost pitied the man.

"Kinda. Karthin's people were getting wasted by the war, and their sorcerer finally got hold of the Tree and started to use it as a weapon."

"That explains the First Wartroop."

"That was one thing he did, right. Then he slaughtered most of the Gryylthan army, and then he wanted more. Mernyl defended with the Circle, but it was a deadlock, and the battle was going to unmake the

world. Sol ended the fighting by bringing part of the
Circle down on the Tree. He died doing it.''

"And you got stuck with this." Kyria swept an arm
out.

"Yeah." Alouzon moistened her lips again and
laughed with a dry parody of humor. "The war ended
cleaner than it did in Vietnam, but the peace didn't
last any longer. Vaylle showed up. And Broceliande.
They're my babies.''

Kyria dropped her eyes. She thought of her own
children, dead, thought also of the comparative children who lay sleeping on the ground nearby. Adults
though they were, they had lived only just past their
first decade. And the lives of Dindrane and her people
could be measured in months.

The fullness in her heart returned, and she flushed
with determination. They were going to live. All of
them. They were going to be happy. She—whether she
was Kyria or Helen, alive or dead—was going to see
to that.

"And Sol—"

"It's not Sol out there," said Alouzon. "It's my
fantasies about him: all my hate, all my anger. As a
grad student, I put up with his goddam pettiness for
months, even though what I really wanted to do was
kick his teeth down his throat. And then when we got
to Gryylth, I was close to killing him a bunch of times.
He was a sadist, an obnoxious kid let loose with
swords, spears and armies, someone without any kind
of conscience at all . . .''

Alouzon's words raised an answering cry from
Helen. Yes, she screamed. Solomon was all of that.
And he was worse, too. My babies . . .

Kyria bent her head, tears starting from her eyes. *I
can adopt. I can adopt now. Please let me adopt.*

". . . someone who actually *liked* to kill," Alouzon
was saying. "He was the Establishment during Vietnam. He was the soldiers at My Lai and the Chicago
police in '68. He was the National Guard when they
shot my classmates at Kent."

Kyria looked up. Kent State. Alouzon's motivations and reactions were suddenly becoming comprehensible.

"And when I finally understood that there were a few good things about him, it was too late. I'd already made Vaylle, and I'd made it a victim. And I made Broceliande, and a Specter of Solomon Braithwaite to go with it." She laughed nervously, almost a little hysterically. "And you know, dammit, I probably made him omnipotent."

Kyria shook her head. "He is your fantasy. He is not a God."

"You better talk to the Vayllens about that. You saw the statues as well as I did."

Kyria shook her head again. Alouzon was wrong. The Specter was one thing, but that corpse rising up out if its grave was something else. And the Grail . . .

Yes, there was a Specter at the dark heart of Broceliande, but there was something else, too: a Cup that could strengthen, that could counter the horrors with the hopes, that could make Alouzon into something that she did not want to be, but that she nonetheless had to be. And, dimly, with Helen clawing at the soft walls of her psyche and shrieking in her mind's ear, Kyria was beginning to wonder if all the destruction, all the trials, all the deaths—everything, in fact, that had happened since Alouzon had come to Gryylth— were not, after all, necessary. The Grail could not be approached casually, nor could it be gained save by those who had passed through the refining fire.

It would be difficult, and the outcome was still in doubt. Silently, Kyria gripped her staff and summoned power to herself. It was not much of a spell, and even Helen could understand what was needed.

The Dragonmaster was still staring out at the roiling darkness. The runway lights had vanished. Pustules of aqua luminescence pocked the velvet sea, burst, and then subsided. Far away, something cried out, but it did not sound as though it were either human or animal.

"And Marrget's down there," said Alouzon. "We have to save her before . . ."

Kyria readied the magic. "You have been pushing yourself too hard, Alouzon."

"I can't sleep—"

But Kyria invoked the power she had summoned, and, in a moment, Alouzon was enveloped in the spell. She was already asleep when her legs gave way beneath her. Kyria caught her and lowered her gently to the ground.

It was cold at the top of the pass. The sorceress covered yet another of her adopted children with her own cloak, and then she stood watch over them all, wondering at herself.

Broceliande was, by day, a high, arid plateau, its colors dominated by a pall of formlessness that overspread everything. Within its borders, shapes, topography, climate, and scenery were all uncertain; and as Alouzon led her people down the slope and across the border that separated the mundane world of substance from the potentials that lurked in the gray lands, she felt the unclean wraiths of her unconscious rising about her as though she were stepping into a stagnant tide pool.

At first nothing happened, but Alouzon did not find that at all reassuring, for such had been the case when she had entered the Blasted Heath with Dythragor. Broceliande was taking its time: feeling out the weaknesses of those who entered, searching for exactly the right apparitions with which to confront them.

The sky, blue and clear in the mountains, turned milky and disturbed. White mist swirled a dozen feet above their heads, and Alouzon, like Dythragor, kept her eyes fixed on the horizon, unwilling to confront the suggestive and half-formed shapes that were presented to her.

The plain stretched off into the distance, and they trekked slowly across the featureless sand. There was no sign that the Grayfaces had passed this way, but

Alouzon recalled the words that Marrget had spoken in the Blasted Heath: *I have heard it said that the Heath changes, that two men entering separately will find a different terrain. They might not find each other.*

If that was true, then Marrget might be gone forever. Or she might well be within the reach of an arm, and those who sought to rescue her would never know it.

Alouzon shook her head. No. It could not be. If being Guardian counted for anything, if Dragonmaster was more than a mocking, empty title, it was not going to be that way.

She turned to Kyria and noticed that the sand beyond the sorceress was strewn with contorted rock formations. Wary of such sudden changes, she glanced around and found that the rock formations were everywhere. "You're a sorceress," she said with dry lips. "Can you pick up anything?"

Kyria grounded her staff and closed her eyes. A minute later, she opened them. "What do we call it, Alouzon? Bad shit?"

"Yeah."

"Nothing more, I am afraid."

"No sign of Marrget?"

"None."

Alouzon examined the rocks that lay straight ahead. "I'm hoping that they don't know we're after them."

Kyria shrugged. "That could well be."

"But that's a problem in itself," said Alouzon. "If they think we're dead, then Marrget isn't useful to them anymore."

Kyria's eyes hardened. "Then let us continue. And quickly." She turned around to address the other members of the party, but she simply stared and said nothing. Alouzon, puzzled, turned to look.

Broceliande was operating as expected. The others were gone.

Alouzon let out a lungful of air in a long, tired sigh. In the distance, from amid a cluster of rocks, something cried out as though in reply. Gelatinous and gritty both, the voice hung in the air like a bad smell, and Alouzon and Kyria cringed instinctively.

The sorceress came to herself quickly, though, brought up her staff, and spoke a word of command. But the wood remained no more than wood, and the initial just above her hand flickered uneasily. Kyria's brow furrowed. She spoke again, and she thumped the staff once on the ground. This time, a violet sheen sprang up about it.

She examined it doubtfully, as though it were an otherwise dependable automobile that had inexplicably turned balky. "I was never schooled," she murmured. "I do not know what to make of this." She faced Alouzon. "What do you wish? Marrget is gone, and now so are the others. And—"

The cry again.

The Dragonsword was in Alouzon's hand. "Looking for them would just cost us time that we don't have," she said. It was a brutal, almost heartless decision, but with Marrget still missing, it was the only one possible. "They've got about as much of an idea where they're going as I do, and we'll just have to hope that the Grail will protect them." She hefted her sword. "But I'll tell you, Kyria: if I were my unconscious, I wouldn't want to mess with any of those people."

The import of her words suddenly struck her. As the Tree and the Circle had been for Dythragor, so the Specter was for her: an archetypal creation of deepest drives and impulses. If it were killed . . .

And who would be Guardian then? What would become of Vaylle and Gryylth?

The cries continued. Hands shaking, Alouzon took a sip of water and handed the skin to Kyria. There did not seem to be any way out save through a death that would unmake the world, or through the waters of the Grail. And the latter was as much an unknown as the entity that lay hidden among the rocks, screaming.

Kyria passed the skin back and gestured in the direction of the screams. "I have no wish to have that pursuing us through this waste."

"Me neither," said Alouzon. "Want to tackle it before we move on?"

Kyria glanced uneasily at her staff once again, then nodded. "So be it."

"You go right, I'll go left." Kyria bowed and turned to go, but Alouzon detained her for a moment. "And . . . uh . . . thanks for the nap."

Kyria smiled. " 'Twas my pleasure."

Alouzon was careful to keep the sorceress in sight as they separated and circled out so as to approach the rock cluster from opposite directions. She had the Dragonsword and Kyria had her staff. She assumed that they were armed about as well as was possible.

The air was clear at ground level, and Kyria's robes were a dark shadow against the misty whiteness of the horizon and the dull gray of the sand and rocks. Boots crunching, sword bright, Alouzon slipped from boulder to boulder, straining her ears for any sounds that might indicate movement ahead. What screamed amid the rocks might be dangerous, or it might be a chance concatenation of stray anxieties. There was no way to know save by looking.

Above her head, the mist swirled, and her thoughts tried to follow suit, threatening at any moment to collapse into a melange of panic. Grimly, she held to her mind as she held to her sword, but faces were peering down at her from the sky, familiar faces, loved faces . . .

. . . dead faces.

Sandy was there. And Jeff. And Allison. And though she had not known Bill at all, he was there too. Impassive and dead, their eyes misted over with the staring whiteness of incipient decay, they gazed down on her.

Those who entered Broceliande, whether they found a trackless forest in Brittany or a gray netherworld on the far side of a galaxy, entered to be tested, to be tried; and when Alouzon approached the stand of contorted rocks and peered through the narrow passage between two boulders, she saw the four inert bodies lying tumbled together in the middle of an asphalt parking lot, their blood mingling in a crimson river that, bright red against the gray waste, streamed across the painted lines and the oil stains and dripped into the storm drain with thick, viscous sounds.

But they were dead. They did not cry out. Something else. Something that moved among them, that took her back to another death, one that she had freely chosen to inflict upon another who, at the time, had not even a voice with which to protest its fate.

She drew back. "No . . . please . . . ."

How long had she been pregnant when she had had the abortion? Eight weeks? Twelve? The doctor had not told her, but the fetus that lay among the bodies of her classmates was a mangled heap of bird bones and throbbing tissue, and it opened its fragile mouth and uttered a scream that sent Alouzon reeling away from the rocks, her sword arm clutched across her belly, her free hand pressed to her eyes as though it could shut out both vision and memory.

And the screams continued, pursuing her, resolving into words of accusation that decried her sanctimonious pacifism and the cultivated neurasthenia to which she had clung throughout the years following the Kent shootings.

Was she horrified by violence? Here was violence by her own hand, an echo of the blood-stained parking lot, a harbinger of all the swordplay and the slaughter that was to come. Kent had begun it all, but she, hypocrite that she was, had continued it.

She sank to her knees, eyes clenched. The voices of the dead dinned at her: *Why didn't you die? How come someone else had to take the bullet? Why did you kill me?*

Something touched her arm, and she flinched away with a cry, rolling over and over in the sand to escape from the blank, staring fish-eyes of the fetus that had wormed its way toward her through the sand. It came on, mindlessly tracking her, leaving a trail of slime and blood that glistened in the shadowless light.

Terrified, Alouzon scrambled to her feet, raised the Dragonsword, and prepared to strike. Surely the preternatural blade could kill something as soft and helpless as this unborn thing.

But it was not simply the stagnant guilt of the abortion that was writhing its way toward her. It was more. It was her life. Lanced and mutilated on a May morning in Ohio, it was as stillborn as the child she had denied in a clinic in Dallas, and her actions since then had been the predictable manifestations of a spiritual decay as incontrovertible as any physical putrefaction.

She lowered the sword. Solomon Braithwaite had denied everything. But if she ever hoped to win the Grail, to attain its peace and wholeness—not for herself, but for her people— then she could deny nothing.

Shaking with strain and fatigue, half mad with unexpiated guilt, she looked up at the sky and confronted the swirling faces. "I won't say I won't kill again," she said. "But I'm gonna learn the difference between doing something right and doing it wrong. Even if it . . ." She stared the faces down. Her classmates were dead; but if ever a fitting memorial could be built for them, it would be constructed not of marble or granite, but of the lives and actions of those who remembered them. "Even if it kills me," she finished.

Flopping and whimpering, the fetus had reached her feet. Stooping quickly, so as to act before her courage failed her, she scooped the tiny helpless thing into her arms, met its eyes, and laid her cheek against its face. "You were mine," she whispered. "I'm sorry for what happened." Blood was running down her arms, the blood of the unborn, the blood of the preterit. She sobbed, felt her tears mingle with the slime of thwarted birthwaters. "But I've got to tell you this: if I had it to do over, I'd probably do it again. And I'd still be sorry."

The fetus writhed in her arms. The tiny lips parted. "Mother," it said.

And then it was gone.

* * *

She was not sure where she was. She was no longer sure even of her own identity. Her name itself seemed distant, alien, unconnected with this stripped and bleeding woman who had been dragged and force-marched across rocks and through malodorous jungle, who seemed to have no appellation other than *cunt* or *bitch*.

Her head still throbbed from the blow it had received when she had first been captured, her arms had been pulled behind her and the forearms lashed together from wrist to elbow, and her shoulders burned with the white-hot pain of imminent dislocation. What few moments of real consciousness she had were bounded by a haze of injury and pain that turned her surroundings to an indistinct blur into which only snatches of sight, sound, and sensation—a masked face, a barked order, a shove of a rifle butt—penetrated.

Dumbly, she stumbled forward, no longer aware of what lay before her: perhaps trees, perhaps rocks, perhaps sand. It did not matter. Her mouth parched, her bare feet raw and blistered, her gravid belly bruised and battered, she made her way blindly in accordance with kicks and curses.

She had no idea where she was being so driven, but a faint cognizance of what was planned for her was beginning to force itself on her unwilling mind, and she had little of either strength or will to protest. In an oblique way, she could even see the justice of it all.

Manda . . . your wish has been granted.

Would it do any good, she wondered, to struggle? To protest? It had done Manda no good at all.

Perhaps, she thought, she would no longer be conscious when the time came. Perhaps she would already be dead. That was a good thought. To be dead. The Grayfaces could not hurt her any more if she were dead.

But her native pride intervened, and she dashed off the haze of pain as she might have, had she the strength, ripped the strands of wire that bound her arms and hobbled her feet. She was a warrior. She was Mar—

The pride faltered. Marrget was a man. And she, as the Grayfaces constantly reminded her, was a woman.

But I am a warrior.

"Move it, cunt," came the voice behind her. "We're almost home." The butt of an M-16 slammed into the small of her back, and she stumbled forward.

Manda . . .

As Kyria rounded the boulders, the screaming stopped as though cut off by an axe, and she was confronted not by gray rocks and pale sand, but with a lush, green lawn and a tall marble tower set in the middle of it. White, glittering, its walls unfigured and yet graceful, the tower pointed skyward like the slender hand of a virgin.

She glanced behind her. She saw mist to be sure, but it was moist, billowing, redolent of the sea; and the slope of a hill led down to tidal flats. Beyond was forest. There was no sign of Alouzon, only the white tower and the mist and the trees, and, far off, the sound of waves.

Broceliande again.

But this was a peaceful place, seemingly unconnected with the nascent horror of the land beyond the Cordillera. There was even a sense of the holy about it, a sense that increased as Kyria approached the single door of the tower. She laid her hand against the carved wood, her eyes puzzling out the runes and figures incised upon it, seeing in them her own history, the sins that she could faintly justify but could not deny.

Here was a woman lying in bed as her womb, newly flensed of its offspring, cramped and writhed like a fish in a desert. Here, she crouched in darkness, considering the instructions of her lawyer. Here she was weeping. Here plotting. Here waiting.

And at eye level was the single word: *Listinoise.*

She leaned against the smooth marble wall, her eyes

misting. Transformed though she might be in body and, partly, in mind, her being was still indissolubly linked with that of Helen Addams. The screaming was too loud, the claws too sharp, the anger too unblunted: no, she could not enter. The very sanctity of this place would have told her that even had she not seen the antic carvings.

Strange: as Helen Addams, she had occupied herself obsessively with questions of power. She had made a name for herself through her seminars about its accumulation and its use. And here she had not even the potency to open a single, carved door.

Footsteps were crunching up the path from the shore, and she pulled herself out of her sorrow and memories and slipped behind the tower. Peering cautiously around the edge, she saw an old man approaching. He was dressed in leather armor, like that which Alouzon wore, and his head was bent.

Solomon.

At the top of the trail he stopped and tipped his head back so that he could look at the tower. He was old. Very old. His hair was gray and lank, and his face was deeply furrowed. His withered hands hardly looked capable of drawing the sword at his hip.

He is tired.

And although he was her ex-husband, and although he had hurt her, and although a part of her still harbored for him the most unmitigated and undying hatred, that realization struck her as though a sword had pierced her heart. He was tired.

She could not but pity him for his age and his exhaustion, for the confusion and the pain that etched his face as deeply as his years; and she found within herself an echo of all his afflictions. Though her body was young, she was old, and she was tired, and the burden of life and the mere demands of physical existence seemed suddenly more than she could bear.

And yet she could bear them.

Drawing back, she examined her white hands, touched her smooth, young face, stared in wonder at the staff she held. If indeed the Grail was operating behind the scenes—manipulating, shifting, motivating—then it had bestowed its favors upon her and had brought her to this place and time for . . .

For what? Here was Solomon: exhausted, frightened. And here was Kyria, who found herself suddenly possessed by both unutterable hate and unconditional love.

She heard his steps scuff across the grass, heard him approach the door. A moment of silence.

What did he see in the carvings? His own life? Or was he looking at the machinations of his ex-wife, examining her treachery, understanding her passions?

With a rattle, the door swung wide, and she knew that he had entered the tower. Panicked at the thought of the holy place being so rudely forced, she ran around to the door, found it gaping open, saw the tracks of muddy boots leading across the white floor within.

She hesitated. Profane though he was, Solomon had entered, and she had no idea what he might do within. But her own sense of guilt still barred her from following him, for if she added her own footprints to those that streaked this temple with blood and dirt, she would merely pile one desecration upon another.

And yet now, from the sounds that echoed from within the tower, he was climbing stairs.

She touched the white wall. "Please," she whispered. "Please grant me this favor. I ask not for myself, but for you."

No reply. She had not really expected one. Feeling the depth and recklessness of her temerity, she set foot on the floor of the room within, inching out across the marble as though it might suddenly open and pitch her headlong into an eternal abyss.

She continued toward the base of the stairs that spiraled up around the inner wall, her steps lengthening. She might have been a mother rushing to keep her child from harming another . . . or himself; but as she climbed the steps, her apprehension grew.

An open door at the top of the stairs led into a carpeted room, but she did not enter. Rather, she stood silently on the landing, contemplating the man who stood before a low altar with a shapeless mass of black silk in his hands.

She almost called his name.

But then his shoulders tensed as they always did when he became angry, and though his words were but a whisper, she recoiled as though he were screaming in her face. "You damned bitch," he said. "Where are you?"

He made as if to turn, and Kyria, confronted by his rage and his temper, wilted into the role she had played for twenty years, when she had renounced strength for devotion, courage for tenderness, self-respect for loyalty. Frightened of his words, of his hands, of his power, she slammed the door, barred it, and fled down the stairs, her footsteps clattering on the stone, her black hair flying wildly.

She passed through the outer door, but still she ran, pursued by her past, by her fears, and now, faintly, by Solomon's voice: "Helen!"

For an instant, she glanced back, but the tower loomed over her, ominous and erect. She was not Helen, and yet she was, and as she fled into the encircling mist, she half fancied that she could hear, behind her, the sound of breaking glass and splintering wood.

❖ CHAPTER 23 ❖

Here beneath the jungle canopy, the air was stifling. Tree trunks—moss-covered, lichen-spotted, vine-clad—rose up in massive austerity, but their branches, as though caught in an incestuous bond with the layers of rot and mildew that covered the earth, twisted down again to add their weight to the roof of vegetation that lay over the path like the lid of a tomb.

After what seemed to be several hours of fruitless search, Santhe called a halt. "I fear we are lost."

"It is the way of the Heath, my lord," said Wykla. "I saw this when I was with Dythragor. He vanished from our sight when he was not an arm's length from Alouzon."

Dindrane sat down on the path, drew up her knees, and pressed the side of her face against them. Tired though she was physically, her mental fatigue had slowly shut down all of her extraneous thoughts, and she now considered only whether she had to move or not.

Santhe was stroking his stubbly chin. "Well, regardless, they have vanished. Or perhaps we have vanished. It is a hard thing to say." He laughed quietly, and Dindrane wondered what sort of man could find amusement in such a place as this.

Karthin and Manda scouted the trail ahead, but when they returned they had nothing to offer. "We can find no trace of the Grayfaces or Marrget," said Karthin. "This path seems to have been unused for days."

Wykla shook her head. "I do not believe that it has existed for more than a few hours."

Karthin frowned. "I do not understand."

"This place changes," said Wykla. "It presents a different face from moment to moment. We ourselves find trees and moss. Alouzon and Kyria might well be facing an ocean, or a desert."

Karthin had been containing his emotions admirably, but Wykla's words all but broke his control. "Then . . . then Marrha—"

"Peace," said Santhe. "We will find her."

"How?"

"We will find her." Santhe scratched at his stubble again. "And, the Gods be willing, we will find Kyria . . . and Alouzon."

Manda's eyes flicked from tree to vine to some inward vision that creased her brow. "It is my fault . . ."

Wykla touched her gently. "Beloved, you cannot—"

Manda shook her head violently. "Back in Quay, I cursed her with just this wish."

Santhe looked grave. Wykla stared at Manda as though the maid had struck her. "You . . . cursed my captain?"

Karthin stepped forward and put his arm about Manda's shoulders. "Peace, countrywoman. Your words may have brought us to an evil pass, but they cannot be unsaid." His voice shook as he spoke. "Let us mend what has been broken."

Santhe spoke carefully. "Marrget is my friend and comrade. I would know more of this."

Manda shoved Karthin's arm away and ran up the path, her hand pressed to her face.

Dindrane lifted her head. She felt like a dog that had been beaten for no good reason. "She cursed a woman?" The outrage was gone from her voice and her heart. There was, instead, a kind of numb acceptance. Vaylle was a victim, Baares was dead, her beliefs lay in tatters. Nothing mattered anymore.

"Aye," said Karthin slowly. "But before Marrha was a woman, she was a man. And the man who was once, but who is no longer, raped Manda years ago. The maid has not forgotten it, nor has she . . .'' He pressed his lips together, fighting the urge that made him want to plunge blindly into the jungle, calling for his wife. ''Nor has she been able to forgive it, either.''

Dindrane blenched at the mention of the rape, but the disclosure of Marrget's former manhood was nothing: the revelations of the last days had inured her to change and novelty, and even to most common forms of horror. She was beginning to understand the spiritual dullness that Orlen of Armaeg had exhibited before King Pellam; and the inner death of the people of Kent now made perfect sense.

She suppressed a shudder and got to her feet. ''Let us follow after Manda,'' she said without emotion. '' 'Tis unwise to allow her to travel alone.''

Santhe pulled himself out of grim thoughts and nodded. ''We cannot afford to separate any further.''

Wykla had already started up the path. ''Manda!''

The trail twisted and turned. Manda was already out of sight. Wykla, running now, had almost reached the first bend when from around it came a shattering explosion. Shredded leaves and bark peppered her face, and the concussion put her on the ground. But the girl had only caught the faint edge of the detonation. The brunt of the trap had fallen on the trail beyond the turning, where the killing zone of the claymore mines had filled the air with shock waves and buckshot.

The realization hit Wykla within moments, and she was suddenly scrambling to her feet, screaming Manda's name. She rounded the bend, followed closely by her companions, but she found no trace of her lover, or, in fact, of the explosion. A lake—still, placid, unmarked by violence—stretched off into the distance, terminating abruptly in a range of low hills silhouetted against a westering sun.

Santhe sighed, rubbed at his eyes, and looked again. ''Evil, and more evil. First Marrget is taken from us, and then Alouzon and Kyria. And now Manda.''

Wykla's face, cut and bleeding, was streaked with tears. "What if . . ."

Santhe shook his head. "I do not believe that she is dead, Wykla. If she were, Broceliande would be happy to show us her body." He took Wykla's hand, drew her to him, laid his head against hers for a moment. "We will find her. We will find all of them." He straightened. "This water looks shallow: let us cross it. Regardless of what we see, we will maintain this direction unless reason gives us cause to turn aside."

Karthin put a hand on his arm. "And when you find Manda, what judgment will you exact upon her for her curse?"

Santhe stood, frowning, staring out at the slimy water.

"Do you blame her?" the Corrinian pressed.

"Manda is a comrade," said Santhe. "I will defend her."

Karthin's blue eyes were like ice. Marrget was his wife. Manda was his countrywoman. He was loyal to both. "And . . . ?"

Santhe looked him in the eye. "My best friend became a woman," he said. "And, therefore, a small part of me became a woman, too. I understand Marrget's plight. Perhaps I understand Manda's also."

So saying, he unbuckled his sword and, holding the weapon across his shoulders, led the way into the scummy water.

Manda rounded the turn in the trail and stepped onto a road. Torn though she was by emotion, she turned back to call to her companions; but a plain full of stagnant rice paddies and low hills now surrounded her. The road stretched across it like a taut rope. In the distance, the jungle was a dark green sea.

Panic welled up, but she had panicked once before—when she was a girl and Marrget was a man—and it had done neither of them any good. Therefore, she caught hold of her spinning emotions, grappled with the sudden sick nausea that filled her belly, and forced herself to think.

Despite the danger of being separated from her companions, there was a certain small advantage to it. Broceliande was huge and changeable—she had no difficulty believing Wykla's description of it—and a search for Marrget would be better performed by several independent groups than by a single body.

The thoughts of a warrior. She held to them as she held to her sword, and gradually she regained control of herself. She scanned the horizon for signs of life, checked the sky, and, though she knew the action to be futile, dropped to one knee and examined the dusty road.

She saw nothing. This landscape might well have been created an hour ago, which, she reflected, was probably the case.

The hot sun that had suddenly appeared along with a blue sky shimmered on the dry land and rippled on the water. For a moment, she bent her head. *O Goddess of Vaylle: if you can hear a supplicant in this terrible place, guide me to Marrha.*

But for what purpose did she want to find the captain? To save her? Or to watch the unfolding of the words that she had spoken in Quay, the final utterance of a wish that had been engendered within her on the day of the rape and carefully nurtured throughout the years? Which was it?

She did not know. It bothered her that she did not know.

Moving cautiously, she set off down the road, scanning the dirt for any sign of a footprint or for a disturbance that might indicate a trap. Unschooled in the technological crudities of modern guerrilla warfare, she hardly knew what she was looking for; but her sharp, peasant eyes knew the natural from the unnatural, and so she picked her way around pebbles and stones that did not look or feel right.

The sky remained clear, the sun hot. Toward evening, she approached the jungle that stretched across the far edge of the plain like a green wall, but heat, thirst, and fatigue had so addled her brain that at first she did not realize that she was hearing voices, and when she did, she was unsure whether she was surprised, frightened, or elated.

Fading in and out on the dry wind that swept across the plain, the voices were faint and intermittent. She caught snatches of words, fragments of emotion.

"Come on, cunt. We've got something special planned for you."

A sound like that of an ox being clubbed. Manda winced. But then there was silence again.

Did the sounds come from the jungle, from the plain, or from a piece of Broceliande that was neither, that perhaps overlaid both invisibly—another landscape that, had she the wit to put her arm out in the right direction, she could reach . . . and enter?

Voices again: strange, toneless, flat. "Pick her up."

"The dink don't have a lot of gumption."

"Just pick her up."

Fading again. But just as the sounds had reached the threshold of inaudibility, Manda heard a moan. She recognized the voice, and her thoughts turned suddenly clear, focusing with laser-like intensity on one name, one woman, one objective.

Marrha . . .

Trembling, licking cracked lips with a parched tongue, Manda approached the jungle. Damp odors of decay reached out to envelop her as she skirted the edge of the paddies, and she slipped in the soft mud until she found a trail that led into the dark growth.

But the voices had faded, and the sun was setting. Even if she had been certain of her destination, to travel at night in such a place as this was the action of a fool.

She crouched at the edge of the water. The paddies stretched off across a plain that almost seemed to undulate in the fast-falling darkness, taking on new shapes and new features as though the strain of holding its form had become too great a burden. As Manda watched, the paddies flickered, ebbed and flowed, assumed the vague outlines of a river . . .

She blinked. Though the darkness was almost complete, she was sure that she was looking at the Long River. The sensation of home was uncanny, complete. She might have been a girl again, squatting with Kasi beside a basket of laundry, talking and laughing about commonplaces—

The flare of light dazzled her. Blue sky. Green land. It was the Long River. And it was Corrin. And there *was* a basket . . .

. . . and a hand seizing her from behind.

She was spun around. Gripping her firmly, as she remembered him, was Marrget of Crownhark: manly, square-jawed, his eyes holding a curious blend of lust, contempt, and a streak of guilt.

The guilt held her eye for the moment that they stood, unmoving, face to face. Here she was once again at the morning of her womanhood, her blond hair bright with ribbons; and here he was, a man who desired only to vent his sex and his anger on a Dremord body. But he himself was unsure of his deed, for up until this hour his honor had been spotless, his valor and pride a legend in both Gryylth and Corrin.

A moment. She had only a moment to ask as she felt his breath on her face. "Did you . . . did you really want this?"

He did not answer, but the guilt was still in his eyes as he tore at her tunic. The seam at the shoulders gave way, and he threw her to the ground.

But though Broceliande had conspired to return her to girlhood and violation, years of training had given her strength, and endless nights of brooding had fueled her anger. Her response, one-armed though she was, was sure and quick. Without a word, she lashed out and caught him on the chin with a solid blow. Marrget fell back, and Manda had time to regain her feet.

She kicked the man in the head as he tried to rise, and she drew the sword that she knew, despite illusion, was at her side. She leveled the blade. "Did you want this?" she demanded.

He only stared at her, his guilty eyes pleading for quick atonement.

"Answer me!"

"You know better than I," he said softly. "Kill me."

A low rumble from the river, the plash of a moving boat. "Starboard shore," came the cry. "Dinks. Man the 60s."

Manda held the blade a hand's breadth from Marrget's throat, but she knew that what she faced was not the captain, but rather another creation of Broceliande. And though the sight of his face had maddened her, she could not but sense that this apparition from the past was in some way a test that would determine whether or not she would ever find the real Marrget. "Answer me, man!"

"Answer yourself. Kill me."

She heard the boat draw closer. A quick thrust would let the life out of him. For an instant, she imagined him bleeding and gasping amid the sand and the river reeds, but then she jerked the sword away. "I will not."

A burst of machine-gun fire from the river scored the shore, the water, and the jungle. Manda threw herself behind a low bank just before the deadly hail reached her. Rolling over in the razor grass and bamboo, her bare flesh torn and cut by the sharp blades and stiff shoots, she listened as the gun tracked back across the face of the jungle.

Voices again. Faint. Drifting.

"Gimme her wrists. See, asshole, you do it this way."

A sound, as of wire straining over wood, a long, sustained creak that shivered the air. And still Manda sat, unmoving. She had not killed him. He had asked for death, but she had not given it to him. What, she wondered, was the deeper punishment? And for whom?

Suddenly, the light went away, and there was silence. The plash and rattle of the boat was gone, as was the lap of river water, the rustle of trees and

leaves, and the sigh of reeds. Utter stillness. She was
not even certain that she could hear her own breathing.

Only the voices remained. "C'mon, honey, relax."

"Hey, she's got a nice ass."

"I'm gonna kick yours in another minute, man."

And then the voice became low and confidential, as
though the speaker were whispering secrets into the
ear of the listener. "You and yours, cunt, been kicking
up some kind of fuss out there in the country. We
wasted them, but we liked your face. So we thought
we'd keep you around."

Marrget was gone. Dead. Dead long ago. Dead the
moment Manda had picked herself up from the sand
and had stumbled to help Kasi wash the blood from
her thighs. Dead the second he had climaxed. Dead
the instant he had penetrated her.

Dead. And now . . .

"You wanna play with us, sweetie? You wanna
fucking *play?*"

Marrha. Floating in a dark world of silence, she
extricated the name from the morass of memories that
bubbled stagnantly in her mind, fought to replace the
face of the man with that of the woman, set the present
against the past.

Marrha was herself. She had waged a war against
her very being and had won. If freedom and honor
were to be had in the world, she was worthy of both.
She was . . .

"C'mon, man, knock it off."

Dry laughter. "I'll knock it off. Reckon I'll knock
off a good one. You hear, sweetie?"

The jungle came back, dense, hot, matted with vines
and studded with fungus. Trees she could not name
stretched up into darkness, their trunks deeply fis-
sured, their branches dripping with moss. Insects rustled in the undergrowth. Night creatures prowled
through the branches and the ferns.

And the voices were close. Very close. As were the
harsh, sucking gasps of a woman she knew, a woman

who would not allow herself to cry out, even though pain and fear and guilt had overwhelmed her.

Ahead, faint in the darkness, was a glow of light, and from within it came the voices and the gasps. Manda gripped her sword and stood up. Armed and in armor, the maid eased forward through the tall trunks and the meshes of intertwined creepers as though she herself had become a denizen of this dark place, as though, hungry for something other than the flat staleness of revenge, she now stalked a more elusive prey. Her steps silent, her eyes and ears straining, she crept toward the goal she realized she had been pursuing since the day she had been violated.

"C'mon, cunt. Let's see what you can do."

They tied a wire to the bindings on Marrget's wrists, and then they threw it over a tree branch and hoisted her arms up behind her. With a gasp of pain she tipped forward, a river of fire flowing up her spine and pooling between her shoulders. The splinters of the rough wooden crate ground into her breasts, and her cheek scraped itself raw on a ragged corner.

These were final moments, the clear-cut, hard-edged instants that trickled out just before the termination of a soul. She tried to recall something of her past that might give her strength—some memory of Karthin, perhaps, touching her tenderly among the furs of her bed; or of Alouzon, risking her life to save others—something that would shield her from the absolute, uncompromising starkness of what was going to happen to her; but another pull of the wire, another stab of white pain from her shoulders brought her back to the jungle, to the night, to the harsh voices of the soldiers.

She did not even know their faces. The few times that the curtain of pain had lifted enough for her to see, she had been confronted only by the gray plastic and goggle lenses of the masks they wore. Their words had been nasal, hollow, muffled: distant echoes of the words that she herself had heard from the soldiers of Gryylth in the last years of the war, when rape and brutality had been ranked alongside feats of arms and valor.

There was a little Dremord girl there, and I . . .

There had been a little Dremord girl for Marrget too, one with hair the color of buttercups, who, with wide, fearful eyes, had nonetheless fought until overpowered. Penetrated . . .

(And Marrget heard a Grayface step up behind her, heard him remove his mask and take a deep breath of the dank jungle air. With a mutter, he kicked her legs farther apart and fumbled with the fastenings of his trousers.)

. . . held in enforced passivity, she had nonetheless stared her rapist directly in the eye, filling her memory with his face and the emblems on his armor. She would remember. She would have revenge. The curse had begun from that very instant.

(And the soldier touched her lightly on the rump as though to steady her, then stroked his penis against her shaking thigh until it was erect, firm.)

Marrget laid her head down on the wood, closed her eyes, waiting, helpless, trying to recall some image of past valor or courage. But a woman's life was one of change, and the days of valor now seemed forever fled. And all she could remember of the past was the frightened, determined face of the little Dremord girl.

There was a sudden rush of movement behind her, and then a sound that was halfway between an impact and a wet slither. The soldier's hands fell away, and her back turned warm and wet. Blood was sheeting down her thighs. But it was not her own: it was that of the Grayface.

A scuffle, a stray shot, the sound of a sword pommel smashing a skull. A woman's voice:

"In the name of the Goddess, you shall not have her!"

Manda.

There were six of them, standing casually in the circle of illumination provided by glowing globes of

light, their weapons far from their hands, their
thoughts centered on the naked woman bent over a
wooden box, her arms bound, her legs wide.

They had thought that Marrget's companions had
been killed by the trap in the Cordillera, and so they
were taken utterly by surprise when Manda leaped into
the light, her sword quick and her one-armed awk-
wardness offset by a warrior's controlled wrath.

The Grayface who stood behind Marrget went down
with a single stroke, the pulsing arteries of his severed
neck spraying crimson through the air. Trailing blood,
the head spun across the clearing and hit the ground
at the feet of another soldier, also unmasked, who
stared in shock. He alone had his weapon at hand, but
his moment's hesitation gave Manda an opening. The
slug from the M-16 whined by her head harmlessly,
and the pommel of her sword broke his skull.

Pivoting, screaming her challenge, Manda evaluated
her targets quickly. Had she friends to back her up,
this would be a much less doubtful fight. As it was,
she had only surprise on her side, and as moments
passed, that advantage was evaporating.

She kicked herself away from the body, evading a
burst from an automatic rifle that shredded the corpse
into bone splinters and raw flesh. Frantic, the Grayface who was firing attempted to track her and wound
up cutting down one of his own men.

Three left. Weapons were being leveled. Manda
crashed into one soldier and sent him sprawling. Cursing, he grappled with her while the others held their
fire for fear of hitting him. He grabbed for her left
wrist and came up with nothing. Manda jammed the
stump of her arm into his eye.

He shrieked, and his hands lost their strength. But
as Manda scrambled for cover, she saw the end of the
wire with which Marrget's arms had been pulled nearly
vertical. It was tied to a tree at about eye level.

She had no time to think, only to hope. With a lunge,
she sliced through the wire with her sword, pulled the

blade free of the trunk, and cut deeply into the man
who had come forward to seize her.

Marrget collapsed on the box with a harsh groan,
and Manda dived behind a row of barrels just as the
remaining Grayface opened fire. The bullets ripped
the containers open from top to bottom with a ragged
tearing of tortured metal, but the oil in them stopped
the slugs before they reached her.

Within seconds, though, the oil had flooded out
through the gaping rents, covering the floor of the
clearing with thick, viscous liquid. The ragged, empty
barrels provided no cover. The first soldier paused to
reload while the man with the wounded eye kept his
rifle leveled, forcing Manda to stay where she was.
They could kill her at leisure.

But the second soldier suddenly cried out as Marrget
staggered up from the box and, with a scream, threw
herself into him. His rifle flew from his hands, and he
stumbled toward the jagged remains of the barrels.
Though he saved himself from being impaled on the
razor-sharp edges, Manda kicked a barrel out of the
way, and her sword severed his spine as he fell.

Marrget had fallen at the feet of the last Grayface.
Gasping, too weak to rise, she lay with closed eyes.
She had obviously bitten her own cheek to stay her
pain and fear, and a dribble of blood flowed from her
lips and pooled on the thick layer of oil.

The soldier aimed his rifle at Marrget's head and
looked up at Manda. Here in Broceliande, stripped of
his mask, he was no longer an ominous, omnipotent
presence. He was, rather, a pale, undistinguished man,
his skin as gray as his uniform, his eyes young and
curiously unfocused. He could have been anyone. Or
no one. "Put down that sword, dink."

Manda stood, debating. If she moved, Marrget
would die. If she did not move, Marrget would die.

"Put it down or blondie here gets it."

She took a step forward. "That would be a more
honorable death than what you planned for her a minute ago."

"Drop the sword."

Debating, Manda gazed at the half-conscious woman on the ground. Perhaps, if she moved quickly enough, she could slay the man before she died, thus saving Marrget. But Marrget was wounded, helpless, exhausted: unless she found help, she would die anyway. And what chance of help was there in Broceliande?

Behind the Grayface, something stirred in the jungle: something pale, something that gleamed in the light of the radiant globes that hung above the clearing.

"I will not surrender," said Manda.

"Give it up, girl." The muzzle of the rifle rested, cold and blue, against Marrget's head.

Karthin's face hung in the air behind the Grayface. Moving noiselessly, his feet feeling out the silence of each step before they took his weight, the big man glided toward the soldier. He was smeared thickly with a layer of slime and mud, and his bare arms and legs were covered with black leeches the size of his thumbs. His eyes, though, shone as luminous as stars, and he closed the distance between himself and the man who threatened his wife and his countrywoman with a sense of terrible purpose.

Manda held the eye of the soldier. Not a flinch, not a quiver of her lip betrayed Karthin's presence. "I will not surrender," she repeated.

The soldier was becoming impatient. The bodies of his companions were bleeding about him, and his sole opponent had only a sword. Manda could see the reasoning in his dull eyes. It would be an easy thing to—

Karthin struck. The rifle clattered away and the soldier's arm snapped like a twig. The Grayface cried out, but Karthin lifted him into the air as though he were a child. Holding the soldier above his head, the big warrior slowly bent him backward.

The soldier's eyes widened. His mouth opened to scream, but Karthin's right hand was clamped about his throat, and the sound was no more than a pinched gurgle.

Farther back, and farther. Manda heard the grinding of bones, but not a word came from the huge Corri-

nian. His jaw was clenched, determined; and his face
was a pale mask of fury, a fury that stemmed from
days and nights of sleepless, frantic travel, a fury that
was now being vented upon the body of the Grayface.

The soldier struggled for an instant, and a frantic whining came from his constricted throat. Then, with a dull
crunch, his spine fractured, and Karthin flexed him in two
as though he were an eel, bending his head back to meet
his knees before flinging him into the jungle.

Karthin's mouth worked, but, shaking with hatred,
he could not move, could not even find the presence
of mind to kneel beside the woman who, bound and
bleeding, was weeping on the ground at his feet.
"Marrha," he said softly. "I am here."

Marrget wept. Manda threw her sword aside, sloshed
forward through the oil, then knelt beside the captain
and pried the bindings off her forearms. "Is Dindrane
near?" said the maid. Her words were faint and
hoarse.

Karthin's breathing came and went in gasps as harsh
as Marrget's. "I . . ."

Manda did not wait. Forcing her throat to open to
the storm of emotion that filled her, she screamed.
"Dindrane!"

Tears blurred her vision, turning the lamps in the
clearing to misty moons. She jerked the last of the
bindings free and pulled Marrget up and into her arms.
The captain stared at her with bleak, frightened eyes.
Manda kissed her on the cheek.

A soft step told of the priestess's approach.

"Dindrane," Manda choked, "please heal my
friend."

❖ CHAPTER 24 ❖

The Specter came as a cold mist that wrapped itself about Alouzon. Moisture beaded on her face, liquefied the dried blood and mucus on her arms, turned her bronze mane to lank tendrils.

She saw nothing but whiteness, but beyond the deadly chill, she sensed and recognized a malign presence that did not blench at the slaughter of infants, that calmly allowed others to die while it mouthed platitudes about patriotism and valor. Solomon Braithwaite had been the perfect vehicle for it, and now his Specter was here with her: birthed from her own fears and hates, empowered with the strength of a lifetime of despair, distilled and refined into the very essence of uncaring and gratuitous destruction.

A face seemed to stretch across the sky, its blue-black eyes a window into utter void. Graying and elderly, the Specter of Solomon Braithwaite nonetheless held in its hands the counterpart of the Dragonsword that Alouzon carried.

"You can't take me, girl," it said. "You never could."

She tightened her grip on her sword, felt the slickness of her aborted child on her hands. "I know what you are."

The empty eyes crinkled in amusement. "I'm Doctor Solomon Braithwaite."

"No." She tried to see it only as a man, but it existed here in Broceliande as an omnipresent phantom: she might have turned in any direction and found herself still eye to eye with it. "No. Sol Braithwaite died for his people."

"And you kill your people, girl."

Solomon's voice sounded within her skull, torturing her with the old guilt. For an instant, her belief wavered.

The Specter pressed, coalescing into a man-sized figure before her. "You've been killing your people since you set foot in Gryylth. What excuse do you have for all those Dremords who never went back to their families because of that sword in your hand? What about the Vayllens who were bombed into jelly back in Lachrae? What about—?"

The words were like razors in her mind. She rebelled. "You were the one who started the war," she screamed. "You sent the bombers."

"Make up your mind. Am I you? Or am I Sol Braithwaite?" It clucked knowingly, secure and confident in a gray suit and conservative tie. "You can't play both ends against the middle."

She wanted to spring at it while it was still of human proportions, but she held herself back. If the Specter was indeed a part of her, then in attacking it she would only be attacking herself.

"Selfish little bitch," it said, turning away casually. "You went through those poor boys in Bandon like crap through a goose. And all because you wanted to save your little ass. Just like you saved it at Kent." It started to vanish into the mist. "Who took your bullet? Sandy? Allison?"

Goaded beyond endurance, she leaped, but it was ready. Its gnarled fist struck her in the face and sent her sprawling onto the damp, worn floor of the temple.

Temple? She lifted her head, fought with blurry vision. About her, yellow stone billowed in cyclopean proportions; and overhead, a shallow dome of aqua porcelain stared down at the immense, circular room like the blind eye of a leper.

And the carvings that adorned the stone depicted the

wreckage of her life. Here was Joe Epstein, and a dozen other men whose beds she had shared but whose names she had forgotten. Here was her daily schedule of cold breakfasts and rushed cups of coffee, a headlong, thoughtless plunge through an existence that became more meaningless with each passing hour. Over here, in meticulous detail, was her abortion, the pleading eyes of the dead child filling one entire wall with reduplicated horror. And the sprawled corpses at Kent State. And at Bandon. The Circle. Lachrae.

The Specter was before her, squatting on a square block of stone like a gargoyle. "You're just like all the rest of your fair-weather idealists. A bunch of spoiled brats. And the Weather Underground showed your true colors. You wanted peace? Bullshit. You made bombs just like the very military you protested. And you used them with even less justification."

But Alouzon stood her ground. "I take responsibility for my own actions." She pointed at the Specter. "Maybe I made mistakes. Maybe I'll make more. But I'm trying to do better, and that's a damn sight more than you'll *ever* do."

The Specter's eyes narrowed. It rose up from its crouch, the Dragonsword gleaming.

Alouzon took a guard stance. "Come on. I fought you in the 1960s. I'm still fighting. We had a good idea. It went bad, but it started good." She readied her sword. The heady exhilaration of the idealist was upon her again, and as she had once faced police nightsticks and tear gas, so she now confronted thirty-three inches of cold steel, finding in herself a readiness for sacrifice that she had not known since she had watched the Guardsmen level their M-1's.

A wind suddenly stirred outside, whining through the vine-choked cracks in the walls, rising within moments to a roar. She heard the beating of immense wings and the thrum of a voice:

Alouzon!

With a harsh cry, the Specter threw itself on her.

* * *

Kyria had fallen to her knees, attempting to find in the sea mist that enveloped her a memory of a time when she had not been afraid, when her body and mind had not been the property of either man or deific abstraction, when the world had lain open to her, beckoning her forth onto fields of praise.

Solomon had cursed, and she had wilted. Although she carried the staff of a wizard, still she held within herself the green girl who, in immaturity and naivete, had taken the hand of the uniformed hero freshly returned from Korea, surrendering her power and autonomy to one who had valued neither. And standing between the two, shrieking with rage, was Helen Addams.

Bent as though with nausea, she opened her eyes to find that she was kneeling on the floor of a dark warehouse. A few feet away stood a metal table, the nylon restraints hanging limply, the stirrups only recently swung back. Blood trickled slowly from its level surface, splattering, drop by drop, on the floor.

Inches from her face, heaped on the worn linoleum, were the remains of a child. It might have been hers, might have been anyone's, but its expression was peaceful, and its dusty eyes regarded Kyria with an understanding that went beyond matters of mother and child, or even of life and death. It was a look that reached out beyond the boundaries of forgiveness, an absolution that carried with it a call to duty.

For me, life is done. But you have others now. You have a world.

The words might have been shouted into her ear. They put her back on her feet and clasped her fingers about her staff.

You have friends.

She blinked at the shabbiness about her, knowing full well that this was but another face of Broceliande.

You have other children.

She had failed before. She had failed many times. She would not fail again. Alouzon's time—Kyria's time, Helen's time—was approaching.

Go.

"Alouzon!"

The child faded, and Kyria's voice echoed off the bare walls.

"Alouzon!"

A wind arose.

She flinched instinctively. But this wind was a beating as of great wings. And though she recalled that such a beating had presaged her summons to Gryylth, still she sensed with all the subtle perceptions of a sorceress that these wings were different, that, having previously ushered her into a dimension of unreality, they were now stripping illusion away.

The wings pounded, tumbling the table across the floor, scattering dust, drying up the blood. The warehouse room shifted and blurred as though it were a water-color running in a spring rain, and its place was taken by a clearing in a jungle. Ahead, a temple of yellow stone rose up, jagged buttresses and eaves jutting out from above massive walls. Windows gaped like hungry mouths, and a flight of steps—vine-choked, worn as though from a thousand years of feet and rain—led up to a dark archway.

But above Kyria's head was the Great Dragon, its eyes clenched and its iron-colored head thrown back as, with huge wingbeats, it drove one of many layers of phantasm from a small part of Broceliande. The essence of balance and existence, Silbakor slashed at the shifting morass of fantasy as a man might scythe down a field of weeds.

The temple solidified. The jungle became real. Silbakor stilled its wings and opened its eyes. "My lady Kyria," it said, and the name struck the sorceress in the face like a splash of cold water, clearing her thoughts, firming her resolve. She knew what she had to do, knew also that she could do it. "My lady, Alouzon is in need."

From within the temple came the sound of sword against sword. A scream as from a throat lined with thorns echoed against the yellow stone.

It was answered by another. The White Worm was diving at Silbakor.

The Great Dragon turned and struck black talons into the pale throat. The Worm jerked away, leaving Silbakor clutching scales and flesh. Wounded, but living, it darted for the temple. Silbakor pursued.

"What about you, Dragon?" Kyria shouted.

"Forget me. Save Alouzon. Without her, Gryylth is no more."

Silbakor caught up with the Worm and pulled it back. Clawing, biting, hissing, they fought just above the tree tops, their massive wings flailing, leveling trunks, scoring the jungle floor.

Lifting her skirts, Kyria ran for the steps of the temple as the sound of combat and screams rose in volume. Now she could hear Alouzon crying out.

"You can't have them, dammit! They're mine!"

But the only response to Alouzon's shout was a mocking howl of glee and a yelp of satisfaction.

The ground suddenly gave way beneath Kyria's feet, and amid a shower of moss and a choking cloud of dust she plunged downward toward a thicket of sharpened bamboo spikes. In a moment she would be impaled, and she barely had enough time to swing her staff over her head.

The ends caught on the sides of the pit, and she dangled, her feet inches from the flame-hardened points beneath her. A few feet away, a centipede swarmed up the crumbling wall of earth; and something slithered under the blanket of moss that had fallen among the spikes.

"Punji stakes," she murmured, squinting against the cloud of dust.

Above, the Dragon and the Worm were still locked in combat, and Alouzon's sword was ringing against cold steel. "It's not that easy," the Dragonmaster was shouting.

The thorn-throated scream stopped, and another voice answered. "You used your friends like Kleenex."

"Fuck you, asshole. You sent our boys off to be cannon fodder just so the corporations would be in the black at the end of the year."

Metal struck metal. The Worm screamed. Silbakor was terribly silent.

Kyria hung her head and choked out a sob. She recognized Solomon's voice. Helen did also: the angry ex-wife threw herself against the walls that hemmed her in, and the sorceress's consciousness reverberated like an iron grating struck with a club.

"They're dead, girl," said the Specter. "They're all dead. You deserted them, and now they're dead. But I'll let you live if you stop interfering with me."

Alouzon's voice went cold. "And what the hell are you going to do?"

"I'm going to get things back to normal, girl."

Kyria forced her eyes open. The walls were too far away to reach, too crumbly to climb. Magic was a possibility, but Helen was staring her in the face.

It is not time yet. Not for that.

"Please," she murmured, closing her eyes, "someone . . ."

And when she looked up again, she stared into a sweet but dirty face framed by amber hair and set with two very blue eyes. The face blinked at her, then vanished. Above the tumult of battling Dragons and clashing Dragonswords, Kyria heard Wykla's voice calling urgently. "Santhe! Karthin! I found Kyria!"

In a moment, strong hands had seized the ends of her staff and lifted her out of the pit. Soft arms encircled her waist and supported her as she was set gently down on the ground. She felt the touch of warm healing.

"Is she badly hurt, Dindrane?" came a familiar voice that she had not heard in days.

"She is not."

Kyria recognized Marrget suddenly. Beneath armor that had obviously been donned in haste, her clothing was in rags; and her blond hair was matted with blood and dirt. But though her eyes were haunted with recent horror, there was a reservoir of peace in them that even Dindrane must have envied.

"Marrget," said Kyria. "You are alive."

"Aye," she said. She bent her head and sighed. "I am. So are we all."

Kyria shook herself back to sense. She saw Wykla, and Karthin and Santhe. Manda had her good arm about Marrget's shoulders, and Dindrane stood nearby. All save Marrget were covered with mud and river slime, and trickles of blood ran down from leech bites.

The Dragon and the Worm battled. Alouzon fought her nemesis. But in a lull in both conflicts, Kyria heard the familiar but incongruous sound of a rifle bolt being slammed home, and a warning exploded from her lips. "Grayfaces!"

They dropped flat on the ground as tracers ripped across the clearing, swung wide, and ricocheted off the temple facade. Keeping low, Kyria gestured at the building. "Alouzon—"

"Is alone," said Santhe. "But that shall not be the case for long, Grayfaces or no." His voice was flat, his humor was gone. He had seen his men cut down with magic and with swords, had seen his closest friend subjected to abominations; and all he had left was a single-minded determination to preserve the lives of those he loved. "Marrget?"

"Dindrane is skilled," came the reply. "I can fight."

Santhe's emotion drove him close to tears. "I do not even know what we may be called upon to face, dear friend. I would spare you further battle."

Karthin looked as worried as Santhe, but he was silent: Marrget would make her own decisions.

The tracers sang by, inches above their heads. As Kyria tried to press herself deeper into the earth, she heard Marrget's voice. "A woman's life is one of changes," she was saying calmly. "And one of strength. I know both now. I will fight."

"Are you sure, Marrget?" said Santhe.

The captain's mouth twisted into a wan smile. "Call

me Marrha, friend. I believe I have earned that
honor.''

Alouzon fought on, feeling each blow she landed on the
Specter as a dagger of pain in her mind. She knew that all
the skill that the potencies of the Dragonsword could give
her could do nothing against an enemy that was, in essence, herself. She could not win. She would die before
she ever won. But to give up was unthinkable.

The Specter's sword flicked out and scored her
throat. An inch deeper and she would have died. Alouzon rolled back, came up on her knees, and hewed
the Specter's legs from under it, screaming with the
pain that she inflicted upon herself.

She was not surprised to find that, when she opened
her eyes, the Specter was as whole as ever. From moment to moment, her hates renewed themselves. She
would only banish the Specter when there was no longer any room for hate in her being.

But the Specter, though whole, halted its attacks.
Shimmering, convoluting in a thousand different ways,
it climbed back up on its block of stone, eyes fixed on
the doorway that led outside.

Alouzon risked a look. Marrget was there. And
Kyria. And the others. They were not dead. In fact,
despite indications of long fights and hard struggles,
they looked stronger and more determined than ever.

Trembling, she got to her feet. ''You got any more
lies for me today, dude?''

The Specter glared. From above came the sound of a
crash. The porcelain dome cracked in a tracery of black
lines. Another crash. Stones fell. *Dragonmaster!*

The Specter pointed at Marrget and Wykla. ''Hav-
en't you learned your place yet?'' But the words rang
hollow. The Specter had unleashed the inner terrors of
the party, confident that they would never be able to
withstand such a confrontation. But it had been wrong,
and, having failed, it was reduced for the time to puerile catcalls and innuendoes.

Wykla spoke. ''Indeed, I know my place well. I am

a woman. And a warrior. And a king's daughter. But you . . ." She pointed her sword at the Specter, her eyes flashing dangerously. "You know nothing of me."

Marrget examined the Specter with the determined expression of a warrior sizing up an opponent. "I know not what you are," she said, readying her sword, "but I would show you what a woman can do."

"Where is your husband, girl?"

Again the catcalls. But the Specter's mockery changed to bewilderment when Marrget laughed suddenly, brightly, and touched Karthin's arm. "Here," she said. "This is my husband."

Alouzon felt a fullness in her heart, a glow of pride. These were her friends. These were her people. Confronted with the unendurable, they had, nonetheless, endured. Indeed, they had apparently flourished.

Another blow from above sent porcelain showering into the room. Daylight poured down through a rent that was quickly widened by black talons. Yellow eyes appeared at the opening. *Dragonm*—But a white wing wrapped itself around Silbakor's head and jerked it out of sight. Wingbeats sounded, inhuman cries lanced the air and echoed within the temple.

"Give up," Alouzon said to the Specter. It was not a question, it was a command.

Again, the eyes of void and darkness widened and expanded, the image of Solomon Braithwaite blurring, growing, filling the room. Alouzon's company had readied themselves for a physical attack, but as she watched, a mist covered them, and they stiffened and stared.

For a moment, Alouzon wondered what the Specter could have in mind, since the innate strength of her people had already foiled its best attempts to drive them to despair. What else was there with which to confront them?

Kyria was fighting her way through the illusion, struggling to make herself heard. "Alouzon, it's going to tell them about Gryylth."

Alouzon was confused. "What about it?"

"Its creation."

"Damn!"

The Specter spoke in Alouzon's mind. *I can do anything to them.*

Alouzon gripped her sword with both hands, and her voice, though a whisper, cut through the room like the edge of a razor. "Leave them alone."

I can make them despair. Or I can strike them dead right now. But I'll spare them if you worship me.

Alouzon advanced toward the block of stone. The Specter was diffused, but if it had a heart, it existed in the sluggish pulsation that hovered just above the perversion of an altar that occupied the center of the room. "You can't have them," she said. "They're too strong. And they're mine."

You're nothing.

"I'm everything." She stalked the heart of the Specter as, once, she had stalked her own emotional death. "I'm the Guardian here."

You're nothing.

Alouzon sprang, her sword cleaving the turgid air above the stone. "Dammit, I'm a fucking *God.*"

The impact knocked her almost senseless, and she fell to the ground at the base of the block, her mind a white hot maelstrom of pain. The Dragonsword dropped from her numb fingers, and her mouth was full of the acrid bile of dry retching.

The Specter's words were thick with derision. *Some God.*

She tried to will her hands around her sword, but they refused to move. It was no illusion of the Specter: it was mortal weakness. She choked. Some God.

But the veils that had shrouded her friends had been torn away, and they shook off their paralysis. Marrget was the first to come to herself. She leaped forward, sword flashing. She had no idea what it was that had dropped Alouzon to her knees, that swirled above her in nebulous and half-formed existence, but she was not willing to allow it to continue to exist unscathed.

But the Specter struck again, diffusing toward her in an icy cloud. Deprived of even a doubtful target,

Marrget halted, puzzled, but Dindrane, eyes wide with sudden realization, jerked her back as the deadly mist licked out at her.

The cloud surged forward, lethal, eager. Acting quickly, Dindrane stepped forward and interposed herself. Priestess and magistrate both, she at last confronted the being responsible for the deaths of her people, the murder of her husband, the horrors inflicted upon her friends.

"Leave us," she said. Careworn, her garments muddy and torn, her torque of office caked with river slime, she stood nonetheless as though in the temple at Lachrae. Planting herself before the other members of the party, she lifted her staff: a challenge and a threat.

They've profaned your land and your temples. They've killed your people.

Dindrane held her ground. "As I am the land, as I am the Goddess, I know them. They are my friends, and they carry my protection and that of the King."

You're nothing without your man. And he's dead.

Dindrane's mouth tightened. "He is dead because you killed him. But I have seen the Grail, and I know what I am. You shall not touch them."

Worship me.

"That I shall not. What power is mine to protect and to cherish, I will use against you." The Specter seeped toward her like a killing frost. Dindrane closed her eyes, grounded her staff, and threw into the battle the only weapon she possessed. "Great Lady," she whispered. "Goddess, Suzanne: descend, I pray you, into the body of your priestess, that your children may be protected."

Alouzon reeled for an instant, for she was suddenly seeing the room from two points of view. Her own . . .

. . . and Dindrane's.

A flood of energy washed through her, and she seized the Dragonsword and stood up. Dindrane was staring at her, startled, frightened, faced suddenly with the mystery of the Divinity she worshipped.

Alouzon could see the conflicting emotions crawl

across Dindrane's face, and she felt them in her own heart. Alouzon? A Goddess?

The Specter was still infiltrating the room, and Dindrane pulled herself out of her wonder. With a nod to Alouzon and a sweep of an arm, she called up a warm, yellow glow. "These are my children," she said, wrapping it about the company, and Alouzon felt herself uttering the same words and knew them to be true.

They killed your people.

Dindrane frowned. "Killed?" she said. "Or saved? Tell me, creature: what are *your* plans for us?" The glow intensified. "These are my loved ones. These are as my own flesh. And . . ." She smiled defiantly. "And as my own spirit."

The Specter made an ineffectual movement toward the party, but Dindrane's glow flared into a solar brilliance that seared the mist like a hot iron. Screaming with the pain of an encounter with pure healing and unconditional love, the Specter recoiled and plunged back onto Alouzon. In a moment, it had solidified before her and was driving in, sword raised.

But a flash of violet suddenly illuminated the room. The Specter sprawled on the floor. Kyria, her staff glowing dangerously, advanced.

Since her warning to Alouzon, she had been standing silently and by herself, her hood up and her head bowed as if gathering strength. Now the hood was thrown back, and she confronted the obscenity before her. "It is time."

"Go home, woman," said the Specter, rising. "Go home to your children."

Kyria stood calmly. "My children were killed before they could take their first breath. But I have found others, and I will not let you harm them."

"You can't stop me."

Kyria nodded. "Perhaps. But there is one who can." She struck her staff on the stone floor, and its radiance turned blinding. Her voice rang out. "You are not what you call yourself, Specter. True: you are hate, and anger, and spite, and all the despair of a decade of misunderstanding and war. But your arrogance has caused you to believe that your being is supreme among its kind in this land.''

The Specter tried to diffuse again, but Kyria's eyes turned hot, and with another thump of her staff, she chained it to its form.

"But there is another hate," she said, dropping her voice to a whisper. "There is a hate that eclipses your being, because it grows and broods with all the passion that twenty years of stifled anger and terrified hopelessness can bring. It belongs to me, and yet it is embodied in another.''

Santhe started forward. "Kyria," he said. "Please—"

She shook her head. "I have come to love you, Santhe, but I cannot do other than this.'' With a soft step, she went to Manda. "Child," she said, "I wronged you. I could have remade your arm, but I was afraid.''

The Specter stared.

Manda shrugged, bewildered. "You could not help that.''

"Maybe.'' Kyria glanced back at the Specter. "But maybe I am afraid no longer. If you would allow me to heal you, I would consider it an honor.''

"But—'' Manda gestured at the Specter.

"Please.'' Kyria reached for Manda's stump.

Alouzon understood suddenly. "Kyria, are you sure?''

The sorceress forced a laugh. "Friend Alouzon, I am more sure of this than I have been of anything in my very short career. If I do not survive, I beg you: remember me as a woman and a healer.'' She thought for a moment. "And as a feminist, too. I will not have that forgotten.''

Manda had no chance to question or to protest. The energies that Kyria summoned enveloped her shoulder, spread down her stump, and continued in seething incandescence to etch out the form and appearance of a woman's arm. Elbow, wrist, fingers, knuckles, nails—all were blazoned forth in a flow of living light.

Kyria's eyes were clenched with the strain of pure

creation. Calling forth the elements of the universe, she channeled them into Manda, reformed the missing limb, breathed life into it. When the light faded, Manda held up her hands, staring. "My lady . . ."

But Kyria was gone. In her place was a lean, gray-haired harpy whose eyes blazed with unspeakable emotion. Her bony hands terminated in black claws, and the robes of a sorceress hung upon her like the tatters of a scarecrow. It was not Helen Addams who stood thus before the image of Solomon. It was but a piece of her, a reification of all her hates, as much a specter as the creature she faced.

She lifted her staff. The Specter was suddenly growing, filling the room, its head reaching to the top of the porcelain dome and its massive feet rooted to the ground on either side of the altar. It lifted a Dragon-sword that dripped with venom.

But the hate that had been given form and substance by Kyria's sacrifice did not wait. Before the Specter had a chance to move, she had leaped for it, her staff lengthening and reforming in her hands until its tip gleamed with adamantine sharpness and brilliance. In a moment, she had reached the colossus, and her spear struck home, driving deep into the fold of its thigh.

Blood was suddenly everywhere. Alouzon collapsed as a shaft of pain rived her skull.

Screaming, the Specter flailed out blindly, caught its antagonist with the back of a hand as large as her body, and flung her across the room. She struck against the carved stone midway up the wall with a crack as of a hundred bones, then slid to the floor in a heap of blood and ragged cloth. With a cry, Dindrane and Santhe ran to her.

But the lance, impelled by the pent-up emotion of a score of years, had succeeded where even the Dragonsword had failed. The Specter shambled about the room, staggering, dwindling, fumbling at it. Darkness flowed from its thigh, spreading across the floor in a growing pool.

The light from the hole in the dome dimmed as a

pale face with eyes as void as the Specter's peered in. Wings were suddenly buffeting the temple, claws were ripping the dome away in chunks, and Alouzon and her company scrambled to dodge the falling stone as the White Worm descended into the temple and took the wounded Specter on its back. Still wearing its incongruous, elderly form, the Specter turned to Alouzon, the lance stiff and erect in its wounded thigh. "I'll be back," it said.

If Alouzon had been able to cross the sea of rubble that the Worm had left, she would have attacked. But the blocks of stone were too heaped, the pain in her head too searing. "You and what army?" she managed.

The Specter smiled in spite of its wound. Deliberately, it took Kyria's staff in its hands and pulled it free. A fresh river of blood ran out to feed the growing pool. "You'll find out. My boy Helwych does his work well."

The pain was a crowbar through Alouzon's mind. "Helwych? What does he have to do with it?"

The Specter snorted, its face twisting with fierce agony. "You'll find out."

Casting the lance aside, it gave a shout, and the Worm spread its wings and rose into the air.

❖ CHAPTER 25 ❖

The wingbeats of the Worm had not yet faded into silence when a rocket slammed into the left side of the wide doorway, spattering the interior of the temple with stone fragments and glowing metal. The size of the room and the heaps of rubble saved most of the company, but Santhe, who had leaped to shield Dindrane and Kyria, cried out as a piece of shrapnel slipped beneath his armor and buried itself in his back. A moment later, a machine gun opened fire, and the room came alive with the whine of ricocheting bullets.

Alouzon felt hopeless. The company was trapped. Kyria might well be dead. Dindrane would not kill. Arrayed outside were an unknown number of Grayfaces with everything from M-16s to 3.5-inch rockets. Without the advantage of surprise and darkness, armor and swords were useless against such weapons.

The temple shook as a mortar round landed near the door, and from the distance came the sound of approaching Skyhawks. It was only a matter of time: whether the temple caved in under the blasts of mortars and rockets or disintegrated beneath napalm and air-to-ground missiles, the end would be the same. And even if, somehow, the world continued to exist after her death, the Specter and the Worm would rove free and unopposed.

Alouzon seized upon the thought. The Specter was loose with the White Worm. And Silbakor . . .

Another mortar round demolished an outlying wing of the temple. Dust filled the air, and the concussion knocked the wind out of Alouzon even as she was trying to shout.

Silbakor. The Worm was gone. That meant . . .

She found her voice. "Get your ass in here, Silbakor!"

It was there in a moment. Wings black as iron beat the air, and as adamantine talons reached for the tumble of rubble lying on the floor, Alouzon was already scrambling forward. "Do I have to tell you everything?" she screamed. "Can't you take any fucking initiative at all?"

The yellow eyes glared at her, and the great wings unfurled for a moment, lifted up and out like vast canopies, and caught a falling mortar round in mid-air. The concussion was a burst of light and sound, but did not even mark Silbakor's skin.

But other rounds would be on their way, and the Skyhawks were approaching quickly. Alouzon scrambled onto the Dragon's back. "Stay down until this is over," she called to the others. Dindrane, bent over Kyria's body, did not look up. Santhe lay still, blood seeping from beneath his armor. The rest, pinned down by fire, could hardly acknowledge her words by anything more than briefly lifted hands and terse nods.

With an uneasy glance at Dindrane, who now knew what fragile Hand had created Vaylle, Alouzon prodded Silbakor. "Let's go."

The Dragon hesitated. Machine-gun fire raked the doorway, spattered off its hide.

"Look, Silbakor," said Alouzon, "if you're going to give me the same shit you gave Dythragor about the Tree, I'm going to tell you you're fucked."

It blinked. "I shall not. But—"

"C'mon. *Move.*"

The Dragon was airborne instantly. Flashes erupted from the encircling jungle: mortar rounds. Without a word from Alouzon, Silbakor swept in and smacked the shells aside, detonating some, sending others back

to fall among the Grayface troops. Explosions ripped
through the trees. Alouzon heard screams.

She had no sympathy. "Take 'em out, Silbakor."

"Dragonmaster, I would not endanger you."

"Dammit, I'm safer here than anywhere else except
my living room in L.A. Get 'em. Now!"

The Dragon dived at the mortar emplacements.
Tracers streaked toward it, but the gunners might as
well have been firing at a cliff of basalt.

Clawed wings ripped through the ranks of panicking
men, knocking some senseless, crushing others, flinging bodies through the air. A rocket exploded above
Silbakor's left eye, but the armor-piercing warhead was
designed for earthly materials, not for a substance that
defied both physical law and the decrees of biology.
Wings beating, claws flashing, eyes glowing in pas-
sionless fury, the Dragon methodically rooted out the
last of the Grayfaces.

It did not take long. In a minute, the only sounds
were the steady beat of Silbakor's wings and the rush
of the airstream.

Alouzon searched the skies for the jet fighters and
spotted two faint dots in the distance. Confronted with
the fury of the Great Dragon, they had turned and fled,
but Alouzon was not willing to allow them to run loose
either in Broceliande or in Vaylle. She ordered Silbakor to pursue them.

Again, the Dragon seemed filled with doubts. "They
are far away, Dragonmaster."

"Are you saying you can't do it?"

"No."

"Then go after them, dammit."

In seconds, the Dragon had increased its speed to a
furious drive. The daylight flickered, and Alouzon had
a brief glimpse of stars and nebulae swirling about her.
When the sky came back, Silbakor was high above the
jagged peaks of the Cordillera, stooping on one of the
Skyhawks.

The pilot had hardly enough time to scream before
the Great Dragon's claws smashed through the plastic

canopy, tore through aluminum and steel, and left the fighter a truncated corpse of an aircraft that tumbled down toward the green plains of Vaylle.

But the second plane banked sharply, lined up on Silbakor, and squeezed off a Sidewinder missile.

Silbakor pulled up and spread its wings. "Hold, Dragonmaster."

Alouzon understood: the Dragon intended to present its own choice of target to the missile. If this suddenly daft Dragonmaster was going to insist on attacking the culmination of centuries of destructive technology, then it was Silbakor's job to protect her.

Grappling for a hold on an iron hide that, vertical, seemed as slick as a mirror, Alouzon bent her head against the Dragon's neck and clenched her eyes shut.

The Sidewinder smacked into the Dragon's belly at over twice the speed of sound. The explosion loosened Alouzon's grip, and she was suddenly staring down through ten thousand feet of clear air. Far below, the rolling fields and pastures of Vaylle were rioting in a verdancy that only summer could bring.

Summer? But spring had hardly begun when the expedition had set off from Kingsbury. The journey to Broceliande had taken a little over two weeks. How then had summer come so quickly upon the land?

The Specter's words came back to her: *You'll find out.*

The two-mile drop stared her in the face. Green, green, green. Everything was green. Crops were ripening, cattle were browsing in rich pastures, sheep were grazing. And, in Gryylth, men were picking up swords and donning armor, and Helwych was . . .

How long had they been in Broceliande? Months, it appeared. And that meant that Helwych—*my boy, Helwych,* the Specter had called him—had already returned to Gryylth.

Silbakor banked, slid beneath Alouzon, and caught her. Alouzon's head was still reeling from the altitude, but she struggled with words as she pounded on the Dragon's back to attract its attention.

"Dragonmaster," it said, "If you die, everything of substance is no more. I beg you: give up this madness."

"That's just fine with me, Silbakor," she shouted above the rush of wind. "Take me to Gryylth. Quick."

Though the rocket blast and the concussions from the mortar rounds buffeted her like great hands, Dindrane hardly noticed. Her attention was elsewhere: reaching out onto subtler planes of being, probing the psyche of the woman she had known as Kyria.

It would not be an easy healing. Kyria was bleeding within and without, her skull had been crushed, and her heart, faced with such damage, was faltering. But there was something else, too; something that was grappling with the spirit of the sorceress, hanging like a weight about it, dragging it down toward death.

Faintly, Dindrane heard a rush of wings, heard Alouzon cursing the Dragon; and then all sound faded as she willed herself into the injured woman. At first she mended bones, closed interior wounds, healed skull fractures; but then she set off into the darker regions that lay beyond the physical body, where Kyria's soul struggled to return to life.

Dindrane stepped softly along the floors of vast, empty caverns, the only light that of her staff. Her feet made hollow sounds on the ebony floor, and ahead there was a sense of dread and an oppression.

I do no harm. I tread these paths to bring healing and strength; and whether I bear this soul back to life, or yield it to the gracious Goddess, I do so with courage and love.

The words of the healer's prayer helped her on her way, but it also left a nagging doubt. The Goddess . . .

The Goddess was Alouzon.

Though Dindrane fought with the knowledge, she could not deny it. It was true. She knew it was true. All the violence, all the sorrow, all the conflicts that Dindrane had seen in the Dragonmaster were not flaws or vices or failings. They were, rather, inescapable aspects of the very Deity who was worshipped from a thousand stone circles scattered across the length and breadth of Vaylle. It had been Alouzon's hand that had made her, her land, her people.

And yet Alouzon was as mortal as Dindrane herself, and had, in fact, required healing after she had saved Pellam's emissaries from Kyria's blast. Dindrane knew herself to be a witness to the playing out of a great and terrible mystery; but, priestess though she was, she could not comprehend it. She was not sure that she wanted to.

She pushed the thoughts away. She had reached the mouth of the cavern. There was another healing to be done.

Forcing herself through the narrow opening, she found herself walking on a close-cropped lawn. Before her, heaped among sheltering trees and bushes, were the ruins of a house: shattered plaster, broken wood, twisted metal. Fires were sputtering into life, and smoke was drifting up.

And Kyria was in there.

Dindrane glanced about uneasily. The night sky was washed out as though by a blaze of light that, though hidden by the surrounding trees and hills, must have stretched off for many leagues in all directions. Beyond the ruins, glowing globes hung from poles, and moment by moment a sound like a whistling shriek, rising and falling, was drawing closer.

Shoving aside boards, pushing through chunks of plaster, stepping carefully around heaps of broken glass, Dindrane entered the wreckage. The house had been flattened as though by a great weight, and soon she had to drop to her knees and crawl, her back scraping against timbers and the sharp points of nails.

The shrieking was quite close now, and the fires were taking hold. Dindrane found herself forced onto her belly. Staff in hand, she squeezed through a passage. The fumes from the spreading fires choked her, and she could see nothing. But as she wriggled forward, her outstretched hand encountered flesh and cloth, and she brought up the light of her staff and found herself face to face with the ancient hag who had thrown herself at the Specter.

"Dindrane."

" 'Tis I.''

"Glad . . ." The hag shuddered. She was obviously in pain. Beyond her was the sorceress. Kyria lay still, her eyes closed, her breathing shallow. The hag gestured. "Help her?"

"I . . ." Kyria seemed essentially unhurt. Though pale, she might have been sleeping. "I have done all I can." She met the old woman's eyes. "I think I have come here for you."

"Not much you can do. Gone." The hag coughed. A trickle of blood appeared at the corner of her mouth, and she wiped at it with the back of a clawed hand. " 'Bout time."

"That is not—"

"Shut up." The gray eyes turned hot. "Did my job."

"You . . . ?"

The hag laughed: a dry, metallic sound from a throat that had previously known only screams. "Just learned how to talk," she said, "and I'm gone. But I got Sol."

"Sol?" Dindrane felt cold. Was she now going to be told that Solomon, the God, was that . . . that *thing?*

The hag shook her head. "Not yours. Mine."

"Who are you?"

"Part of Kyria."

The fumes from the fires were gathering, darkening the air. "What do you want?"

The hag nodded at the the sorceress. "Save her."

"And you?"

"Kill me."

Every particle of the healer's being rebelled at the demand. "How dare you—"

The hag grabbed the front of Dindrane's tunic and dragged her forward. "Can do it," she hissed. "You can. I'm gone. You want to keep Kyria, you kill me."

"I . . . I cannot do that."

The hag cuffed her. "Little cunt. Just like all the rest." She struck Dindrane again, harder, then turned and scrambled toward Kyria, claws lifted. Dindrane gasped, lunged after her, and hauled her back by one skeletal leg.

What followed was a battle of hands against claws, of reflexes against snapping teeth. Rolling back and forth among the splinters and glass, jabbing at the hate-filled face with her healer's staff, drawing up her legs to knee the hag in the belly, Dindrane fought desperately as the fires spread and the smoke thickened.

"I kill her," screamed the hag.

"That you shall not," said Dindrane. "I fought the Specter, and I will fight you. I declare this woman my friend and my comrade, flesh of my flesh and spirit of my spirit."

"Words."

"They are more than words."

The hag looked for an opening, but as Dindrane caught what breath she could in the growing smoke, she found that she had managed to work her way around to the other side of her opponent. Kyria was only a foot or so behind her.

But the sorceress had not moved. She seemed suspended in a strange state between life and death, a precarious balance in which the slightest jolt could tip her in either direction.

The hag was suddenly upon her, reaching, clawing. Dindrane struck with her staff, struck again, thrust the glowing wood between the gnashing teeth. She found herself screaming curses, found also that she was no longer trying to push the hag away physically, but was actually shoving her spirit toward oblivion. The healer's staff lent her potency and strength, and the hag's efforts grew more feeble as death overwhelmed her.

A lurch, a shudder, and the clawed hands fell limply to the glass and plaster that covered the ground. The gray head dropped between the arms. Behind Dindrane, Kyria stirred.

At the sound, the hag opened her eyes. "Gotcha," she said. "I told you: kill me. You . . . did." She shuddered, and her eyes glazed. "Thanks."

The Dragon turned its blunt nose eastward and gained altitude. The sky shifted toward dark blue, then black, then into the nothingness that characterized the spaces between worlds.

Alouzon was already planning her next moves. At the speeds and dimensions that the Dragon commanded, she could reach Gryylth within minutes, warn Cvinthil not to attack Vaylle, and just as quickly return to Broceliande and lead her friends to safety. And then . . .

And then she had to deal with the Specter.

She stared out over the Dragon's head, wondering what she could do against an opponent that was, after all, only a part of herself. Kill it? But by doing so she would only kill herself, and then Gryylth and Vaylle would be no more. But to allow the Specter its freedom condemned everything she held precious to slow attrition and death.

There was one hope. As the Grail could bring such integration to her as would end the conflicts within her psyche and the lands that represented it, so it would in all probability lay the Specter to rest. But that meant that she had to find it . . . and the Cup seemed farther away now than when she had first come to Gryylth.

Hanging her head, she sighed. She had been over these same thoughts before, and they had grown stale.

"I'll take care of my friends first," she said. "That's the important thing."

When she looked up, the sky was still black. The Dragon was still forging through void. Odd: she would have thought that Silbakor would have reached Gryylth by now.

"Hey, Silbakor, what's going on?"

No answer.

"Silbakor?" She pounded on its head. "Answer me, dammit."

The reply came slowly, reluctantly. "You are Gryylth."

"Yeah, it's come to my attention."

"If you die, the world is unmade."

She fought down an urge to swear. "You're not telling me anything I don't know."

Again a pause. Then: "I am returning you to Los Angeles. Your work is done here."

"Done?" she cried. "It's hardly started. I've got—"

The Dragon was intransigent. "The Specter flies loose, and you are in danger. I am sworn to ensure the safety of the land. Therefore, I am taking you home."

Home? Home was Gryylth. Home was Vaylle. She no more belonged in Los Angeles than did Wykla or Manda. Frustrated, she beat on the back of Silbakor's head, but succeeded only in bruising her hands. "Dammit, I can't leave my people like this."

The Dragon flew on. Alouzon felt a cold anger.

"I'm gonna give you one more chance to turn around, lizard."

Silence.

Alouzon drew her sword. "By your oath, Silbakor, I command you to take me to Gryylth."

"I am fulfilling my oath."

She had no idea whether even the Dragonsword's preternatural steel could harm the impossible beast upon which she rode, but she was desperate. Tensing her thighs about the Dragon's neck, she lifted the sword above her head and prepared to strike. "One last time, Silbakor. You gonna turn around?"

Silbakor had no chance to respond, for there was a sudden flurry of white wings about Alouzon, and she looked up into blue-black eyes and gleaming teeth. Without thinking, she turned her stroke on the Worm, but it dodged away and clubbed her on the side of the head with a huge talon.

Alouzon spun to the side, nearly losing her grip on Silbakor. "Asshole," she screamed. "I'm not safe anywhere. No one's safe."

But though Silbakor banked and dodged, the Worm closed on Alouzon. Shrieking in a voice that the Dragonmaster heard more in her mind than with her ears, it plunged down on her, claws extended. On its back was the empty-eyed visage of Solomon Braithwaite.

She swung, but she had no leverage, and Silbakor's sudden evasive maneuver pitched her off into the void.

Alouzon felt herself falling, the sounds of draconic combat fading into unimaginable distances. Slowly, singly, in twos and threes, lights materialized below her: diamond points that glowed with the color and beauty of jewels. She thought for a moment that they were stars, but though her long fall through void drove her to the edge of panic, a part of her that remained inexplicably calm—a fragment that glowed golden at the edge of thought—knew that they were not stars.

Lights. Stretching off into the distance. Gleaming in a thousand different colors. Approaching with ever-increasing rapidity.

She struck the ground hard, and her breath went out of her like a ball of hot fire. But just as she lost consciousness, she heard the incongruous chirp of crickets.

Dindrane awoke to a sunlit temple. After her time in the dark wreckage of the unknown house, the light dazzled her, and it was some seconds before she realized that Kyria's black eyes were open, clear, almost luminous.

"Kyria?" Dindrane was almost afraid that the hag would come back. But she remembered that the hag herself had chosen death. Nobility and violence both? Unwillingly, she had begun to understand the combination.

The sorceress blinked, stared at the temple and the tumbled blocks of stone about her as though seeing them for the first time. Her face was pale but fair, and if it showed any pain, it was only for an instant.

She sighed. "Yes," she said. Though a trace of sadness lurked in the depths of her eyes, she smiled at the woman who healed her, touched her cheek. "Thank you," she said. "You are very brave."

"I am a healer." Dindrane felt the lie in her words. Moments before, without remorse, she had killed an old woman.

Kyria's smile held understanding. "She wanted it that way," she said. "There are all kinds of healing. That was one of them." But she noticed Santhe, who was still bleeding and in pain from the shrapnel wound, and her smile vanished. "Oh, dear." She looked up at the others. "Help me get his armor off."

Marrget and Karthin came to help. "Keep watch, please," the captain said to Wykla and Manda. "There may still be Grayfaces about." Her face was set, but when she noticed Karthin's anxious look, her expression softened.

The gunfire had ceased. Its place had been taken by utter silence. Wykla crawled carefully to the doorway and peered out. "Marrha—I mean—my captain . . ."

Marrget was unlacing Santhe's armor. "Lieutenant?"

"My captain, there are no Grayfaces. In fact . . ." Wykla stood up in an archway that was now blazing with golden light. "There is no jungle anymore."

Manda was beside her in an instant. "It is true, Marrha," she called back. "I can see the mountains."

"And Alouzon?"

Manda shook her head.

Marrget looked worried, but gently, with the careful hand of a woman, she eased Santhe's armor away from his back as her husband supported the councilor. Santhe stifled a cry as Kyria's pale fingers probed into the glistening wound just above his right kidney. The sorceress's brow furrowed for a moment, and she pulled out a six-inch sliver of steel. "You are lucky, Santhe," she said. "This did not hit anything critical."

Santhe's face showed pain, but he laughed. "That surprises me little: small wounds hurt the most."

Drained, incapable of further healing, Dindrane

handed Kyria her staff, but the sorceress shook her head. "I do not think I am going to be using a staff anymore, Dindrane." Her voice was calm, gentle, without regret. She touched the priestess on the shoulder: the gesture of a friend. "I have understood a few things, too."

Her soft hands worked at Santhe's flesh for a moment, and then the wound was gone. "Be cleansed," she said softly. "Be changed. Be healed."

Karthin reached out a big hand, and Santhe allowed himself to be helped to his feet. "Be cleansed?"

Kyria shrugged. "Healing is a cleansing. But I was thinking of your heart."

His eyes turned sad. "You know me better than most, Kyria."

She smiled. "I cannot take any credit for that. You told me more than you told most."

He was examining her face as though afraid of something. "I . . . I found healing in your arms."

She drew him to her, laid her head against his chest wearily. "There is more to be had there, if you want it."

"But . . ."

Kyria shook her head slowly. "She is gone, Santhe. I am but Kyria now." Her eyes were hopeful and tragic both. "Now this world is the only home I have." Santhe folded his arms about her, but Kyria seemed to be looking beyond the temple. Perhaps she was seeing a ruined house in a strange land. Perhaps she examined a ruined life. "But it is a good land," she said. "And it is ours." Her eyes flicked to Dindrane. The priestess understood: Kyria knew. About everything. "And Alouzon is ours, too."

Dindrane hung her head, shamed once again by the strength of those she had once branded as murderers. She felt empty, drained, the casually accepted realities of her existence shown to be the tattered backdrop of another's dream. But Kyria called her by name, and when Dindrane looked up, the sorceress was smiling

at her fondly, a friend, a co-conspirator in the secret
of the world.

"It is a good land," she said again, and Dindrane
nodded slowly. She had changed; everything had
changed. But it *was* a good land, and Alouzon was a
good woman. There was hope.

For a time, they waited in the temple for Alouzon
to return, wearied disciples of a Goddess who had as-
cended into the heavens on the wings of a Dragon. But
hours passed, and the Dragonmaster did not return.

Santhe's face was grave. "Marrha? Have you advice?"

The captain shrugged. "Like Dythragor, Alouzon
has her ways. She is doubtless confident that we have
ours."

"Do you think that . . ." Santhe was unwilling to
continue, but even Dindrane guessed his meaning.

Kyria spoke suddenly. "No. That is not possible.
We would know without doubt if she were dead." Hers
was no hope-filled wish: she spoke with the air of one
who knew with certainty.

And so, Dindrane supposed, she did. More than any
other member of the party. More, even, than the once-
arrogant Dindrane of Lachrae who had been humbled,
not by being informed that she had overstepped the
bounds of her womanhood, but rather by being shown
that those bounds were far larger than she had ever
dreamed.

Her hand was on Baares's dagger. He had known,
in his last moments, what she knew now. She would
not forget. For his sake, for the sake of the Goddess
she knew and the God about whom she was afraid to
ask, she would not forget.

Santhe was examining the bare, flat land that now
surrounded the temple, conferring as he did so with
Marrget and Karthin. "Let us wait no longer, then,"
he said. "The jungle is gone, the mountains are in
sight. Let us return to Vaylle. Without some further
indication as to Alouzon's wishes, we have no further

business here, and I am loath to spend another night in this land.''

They set out, striking directly for the mountains. There was no jungle, no mist or tower. The land was, in fact, almost featureless now, as though the real topography of Broceliande was but a blank canvas which required a thick coating of illusion in order to come to life.

But there were no illusions now, and the mountains were very close. By sunset, they were climbing the slopes that rose only a few hundred feet above the plateau, and they pushed on well into the darkness. They were tired, hungry and sore, worn in both body and mind, but even the jagged passes of the Cordillera were preferable to the hospitality of Broceliande.

It was Dindrane who first noticed the strangeness in the weather. The east wind that whistled through the mountain peaks did not seem particularly cold to her. In fact, it was quite warm, unseasonably warm, and scented with the odor of vegetation.

Not until dawn did she understand. Though her sleep had been fitful, broken often by nightmares and memories, she awoke at first light. The warmth was still in the air, and as the sun rose above the rim of the world, she looked out across a greening land.

The warmth was not unseasonable. Not at all. But the season itself . . .

'' 'Tis impossible,'' she cried.

Her companions, awakened by her voice, got to their feet and examined the country, murmuring softly to one another. Dindrane understood their confusion, for she shared it, but she could not comprehend the fear and alarm that she sensed in their reactions.

''We must make haste,'' said Santhe at last.

''Agreed,'' said Marrget. ''Cvinthil may well have set sail already.''

Dindrane blinked. ''Your king is coming to Vaylle?''

Marrget dropped her eyes. ''Our king,'' she said. ''And an army.''

Thunder rumbled from far away, shuddering through

the air, seemingly rolling through the very substance of the world. For an instant, the Cordillera wavered as though made of jelly.

Puzzling over Marrget's words, wondering at the thunder, Dindrane looked beyond Vaylle. The sea stretched out and away, and on the horizon lay a faint haze of green that she knew to be Gryylth. But as she watched, the thunder rumbled again, urgent and immanent, and a scud of darkness suddenly veiled the distant land, roiling up out of nowhere, solidifying into an impenetrable curtain of shadow.

ABOUT THE AUTHOR

Gael Baudino grew up in Los Angeles and managed to escape with her life. She now lives in Denver . . . and likes it a lot.

She is a minister of Dianic Wicca; and in her alter ego of harper, she performs, teaches, and records in the Denver area.

Her previous books include STRANDS OF STAR-LIGHT, GOSSAMER AXE, and DRAGONSWORD.

Gael Baudino lives with her lover, Mirya.